THE SON OF
MR. SULEMAN

ALSO BY ERIC JEROME DICKEY

The Business of Lovers

Before We Were Wicked
(Ken Swift)

Harlem
(eBook)

Bad Men and Wicked Women
(Ken Swift)

Finding Gideon
(Gideon Series)

The Blackbirds

Naughtier Than Nice

One Night

A Wanted Woman

Decadence

An Accidental Affair

Tempted by Trouble

Resurrecting Midnight
(Gideon Series)

Dying for Revenge
(Gideon Series)

Pleasure

Waking with Enemies
(Gideon Series)

Sleeping with Strangers
(Gideon Series)

Chasing Destiny

Genevieve

Drive Me Crazy

Naughty or Nice

The Other Woman

Thieves' Paradise

Between Lovers

Liar's Game

Cheaters

Milk in My Coffee

Friends and Lovers

Sister, Sister

ANTHOLOGIES

Voices from the Other Side: Dark Dreams II

Gumbo: A Celebration of African American Writing

Mothers & Sons

Got to Be Real

River Crossings: Voices of the Diaspora

Griots Beneath the Baobab: Tales from Los Angeles

Black Silk: A Collection of African American Erotica

ERIC JEROME DICKEY

The SON of MR. SULEMAN

DUTTON

DUTTON

An imprint of Penguin Random House LLC
penguinrandomhouse.com

LIBRARY OF CONGRESS CATALOGING-IN-PUBLICATION DATA
has been applied for.

ISBN 9781524745233 (hardcover)
ISBN 9781524745257 (ebook)

Printed in the United States of America
1st Printing

For 38109
38152, much love too

I am only responsible for my own heart, you offered yours up for the smashing my darling. Only a fool would give out such a vital organ.

—Anaïs Nin

Two damaged people, thrown together in a hostile world, doing their best. What else was there to life, in the end?

—Stephen Baxter, *Proxima*

I was too trusting, too naive. I felt like it was all my fault. It would take me years to accept what now seems obvious: rape is not a punishment for poor judgment.

—Chessy Prout, *I Have the Right To: A High School Survivor's Story of Sexual Assault, Justice, and Hope*

So long as you remain blindly obedient to your own culture, other cultures would always remain as "other" cultures.

—Abhijit Naskar, *Build Bridges Not Walls: In the Name of Americana*

THE **SON** OF **MR. SULEMAN**

Inside each story lives a thousand more tales waiting to be told.

—Eric Jerome Dickey

SUMMER 2019

THE SECRET LIFE
OF PI

CHAPTER 1

WHEN GODS BECAME bored in heaven they walked among mortals.

The stranger to my green eyes was dressed in a skirt with stunning embellishments and intricate tailoring that rode her curves like a Chevy cruising Riverside Drive at sunrise on a Sunday morning. Her sleeveless blouse was on the same level. Voluptuous woman, thick hips, rounded backside, small waist—an impeccable figure to die for, an hourglass. About five nine without the five-inch heels, she was akin to a movie star in a room of extras. Under her gravitational pull, a victim to the weight of her presence, I watched her as I engaged in conversation with my colleagues.

She stared at this BMFM, this Black man from Memphis, with the same curiosity.

I was thirty-one, five eleven, 180 on the scales fully clothed. Hair short on the sides, six inches of trendy pillow-soft kink from forehead to neck, a radical Black man's Mohawk. Skin a light ebony brown, the complexion that said sometime after the mass kidnapping in Africa, my ancestry, the bloodline of the first mathematicians, philosophers, kings, and Moors, had been integrated either voluntarily or by force.

We were at an annual repeat of a Cybill Shepherd movie called *Being Rose* that popped off on Main Street at the state-of-the-art Halloran Centre, an astonishing thirty-nine-thousand-square-foot space big enough for almost four hundred people and open to the public. It had an amazing theater and the night was sponsored by the University Along the Nile. UAN was my alma mater, and where I worked as an adjunct. By someone determined to take control of both my career and my life, I'd been mandated to socialize.

When the open event moved to the ultraprivate reception at the Pink Palace Museum and Planetarium, we peeped at each other across the room. The UAN after-party was a high-priced classy affair with plenty of alcohol and finger food, where they played Marc Cohn's hit song "Walking in Memphis" on repeat. I took in her amber skin and cute smile. She had dimples, those beautiful indentations, plus freckles and a pronounced chin cleft that gave her face symmetry. Wide eyes paired perfectly with pillow-soft lips, soup coolers painted dark with mystery. Simply. Gorgeous. Beautiful enough to make it impossible to ignore. Her eyebrows were on point, but her lashes were an omen, two black butterflies confronting me each time I spied her way.

I went to her, but not too fast, not with thirst, introduced myself. "Professor Pi Suleman, UAN."

"I'm Gemma Buckingham, from Brixton."

She walked slowly, an invitation, and I moved with her at a snail's pace.

Without preface she said, "Meghan really is beautiful, innit?"

"Thee Stallion?"

"Meghan Markle."

"Everyone is beautiful to someone."

"Even a stallion."

British humor touched American hip-hop humor and we laughed.

I asked, "Big fan of the duchess?"

She beamed. "I'm in America. Her America. I get to see how she lived. I get to see her world."

There were murals and displays on Native American pottery, which spoke to us as we strolled with the crowd. She nodded in approval at pre-Columbian relics, the same with Clyde Parke's Miniature Circus, then became interested in the fossils and dinosaurs, mounted animals. She took in our past in silence. For thirty minutes she became a student. She wasn't interested in the displays on World War I and II, had no idea who the significant Black Memphians were, but she read the identifiers for the history exhibitions that focused on the roles of song and cotton in my city on the Nile, tuned in on the exhibit regarding the changing roles of women.

We paused in a living room with adornments from the 1920s.

I continued talking as if we'd never paused the conversation, said, "Brixton?"

"London, where American Meghan Markle moved, only to be ridiculed and treated harshly."

"Ridiculed?"

"For being mixed race. As if that means *subhuman*. They've attacked her mother as well."

I nodded. "For being gifted with melanin."

"*Incessantly.* By the tabloids. Battered on Twitter by racists. Waves of abuse and harassment."

"Racism that bad over there?"

"Not as blatant as here, but yeah. The West End is hostile. My sisters get charged twice as much to enter a bloody club. Some have had to change names to get jobs. I swear to you, it's unending. A cesspool of racism. Worse for Meghan than anyone. Being American has exacerbated the issue."

"I bet she regrets that choice, same as Princess Di did."

"What should be a fairy tale has become a nightmare. I feel her pain and depression."

"Had no idea." I stroked my soft beard. "The nasty Thames is your muddy Mississippi."

The transition was awkward, but her body language told me it was appreciated.

"Pretty much. You're landlocked here. You have the river, but that's not like having a real beach. Only a fool would get in those nasty waters. So sad you have to drive six hours to Dauphin Beach."

We stopped moving and I smiled a little more, fascinated. "You grew up on a beach?"

"No, but I could get a train from London Victoria to Brighton Beach in an hour."

"Still, we both grew up in port cities."

"Mine has over thirty bridges connecting East and West End; yours has only has two."

"Yeah. The Memphis-Arkansas Bridge and the New Bridge, the Hernando de Soto Bridge."

"So, tell me about the University Along the Nile."

Wearing my best smile, I told her what made the UAN Pharaohs stand out was the main building, which cost three hundred million dollars and was a duplicate of the defunct glass pyramid that sat on the Mississippi. We had fifteen- to thirty-foot-high statues of Egypt's pharaohs across the yard.

"How large is UAN? Sounds massive."

"UAN has about twenty-two thousand people, seventy countries represented, three hundred areas of study, one hundred seventy buildings. There are sixty statues of pharaohs, mini-pyramids, and Egyptian hieroglyphics placed over a thousand acres, which makes the campus a museum from end to end. It takes twenty minutes to walk the yard."

She said, "Wasn't there a terrifying incident at UAN a few days ago?"

"Almost. We had word some racist was on the way. He'd posted his intentions on social media. He made it on campus. The active-shooter alarm sounded, and UAN was put on lockdown for a few hours. Our security had the racist cornered by the Little Pyramid until he surrendered."

"So you're famous."

"We were mentioned on CNN."

Gemma Buckingham said, "Everyone I passed seemed to be in little groups, whispering like it's a bloody secret. They talk so loudly, then whisper concerning certain topics, but they are bloody whispering louder than their regular speaking voices. Almost everyone in here uses their outside voices."

"UAN is a proud uni, so of course we talk about the attack by a lone-wolf, southern-fried terrorist in whispers, the way southerners do all of their families' dirty laundry."

She said, "Also overheard campus police here are like the military in Israel."

"With all the campus shootings in the USA, and with a couple threats directed at UAN for some unknown reason, the university thought it was a good idea to let the security company they had contracted go and hire the Aggressive Six to protect the students. They're a team made up of steroid-chomping men built like Arnold Schwarzenegger, John Cena, the Rock, Rambo, Lou Ferrigno as Hercules, and Popeye the Sailor. They are some mean motherfuckers, no doubt paid to be that way."

She laughed at my descriptions, then mocked me, "*Motherfuckers.*"

"Pardon my French."

"In French *motherfucker* would be *enculés* or *enculées*, perhaps *connard*, *couillon*, or *conasse*."

"Lots of ways to call someone a motherfucker in France."

"Because there are a lot of motherfuckers in Paris."

We laughed together.

Her scent was erotic, the kind that made a mortal fall in love with a deity.

She grinned. "By the way, love your Memphis accent."

"I thought you had the Brixton accent. My bad."

"Southern, wise, deep, intellectual. You're an African American Matthew McConaughey."

"He wishes he had my swag."

"If only you were the rule and not the exception."

"Something happen?"

She chuckled. "I took an Uber to Graceland, had the ultimate VIP tour to see your royalty. Not exactly Kensington Palace or Windsor Castle. Interesting décor, to say the least. I paid two hundred US and saw Elvis's collection of over-the-top jumpsuits, his famous pink Cadillac, the gold records, jets."

"That whole strip, Elvis Presley Boulevard, is dedicated to the King from end to end."

"Noticed that. I realized I was in what is called Whitehaven, saw a mall nearby, thought it would be akin to Knightsbridge."

"Oh boy."

"I thought the circus was in town. One fellow talked so loudly, bragged about how much he spent for his *forty-six-inch rims*. Must one have rims so ginormous it makes your car look like a bloody clown car?"

We laughed at her snark.

She asked, "What's your name again?"

"Professor Pi Suleman."

"Professor."

"Pi. Call me Pi."

"Pie? My weakness, especially a meat pie, a good posh pie. What's yours?"

"Not the food, the number 3.14."

"The mathematical constant."

"Been called worse by my own skinfolk."

"Curious. Why did your mother name you Pi, Pi?"

I paused. "Because I was born on March fourteenth."

"You were born on Pi Day. This is truly odd. Talk about odd birthdays."

"Yours?"

"April twentieth."

I laughed. "For real? You're a four-twenty baby?"

"It seems to be a big deal here in this part of America, not so much where I'm from."

"You were born on Colorado's get-high day. A day to celebrate marijuana."

"If I'd been an American, I would've been called Marijuana and teased all my bloody life."

I said, "You're a Taurus."

"And you?"

"Pisces."

"I used to be all into Zodiac signs when I was a teenager."

I asked, "What you remember?"

"Taurus needs a physical connection; Pisces are emotional. But are supposed to have *amaze-balls* sex."

"Gemma."

"Gemma Buckingham, if that is not too much to ask. Hate to bother, but I'm particular."

As we stood to the side, Blacks chatting among whites who occasionally spied our way with suspicious eyes, as if we needed to integrate for their comfort, I asked, "What's your IG?"

"Instagram? Oh, my love, I don't do social media."

"So, Black woman from London, you're not keeping up with Black Twitter?"

She turned her body away, suddenly annoyed, then tendered a UK smile that made clear being pushed irritated her. She had left the conversation, her way of telling me the gotdamn answer she gave was her final answer and to not ask her the same fucking question over and over in different ways.

The room of socialites rumbled and began to applaud.

Judge Zachary Beauregard Calhoun and Dr. Helen Stone-Calhoun came in like potentates. A squad of twelve followed like disciples.

Gemma Buckingham whispered, "I take it these are important people here."

"In the tristate area."

"Tristate?"

"Tennessee, Arkansas, and Mississippi."

"One would think King George and Queen Elizabeth had arrived on a magic carpet."

"Yeah. One would think."

CHAPTER 2

THE OVERSIZE JUDGE was the UAN man *The Commercial Appeal* dubbed Memphis's "Judge of all Judges." He was six six, taller than President Lincoln. He was a fat fucker, bigger than the largest man the USA ever had elected. President Taft had clocked in at 380. Judge Calhoun weighed more than 400 pounds.

The giant among men rocked his standard seersucker suit and worn oxfords.

The judge came from a legacy of southerners who took their sheets from their beds and wore them on their heads for the delight of terrifying Black folks in the thick of the night. If a Black man walked into that judge's courtroom accused of stealing half a honeybun to feed his starved child as his first offense, he could end up gone for two decades plus ten.

Judge had married a beauty queen from Brownsville, Tennessee, where once upon a time the denizens fought tooth and nail against the freedom of African Americans and were willing to die trying to kill the battle-weary wishes of Blacks being freed on paper by President Abraham Lincoln.

Dr. Stone-Calhoun saw me, gave me an authoritative stare; then it looked like a powerful feeling of joy rocked her, but only for as long as it took to blink twice. She saw me with a beautiful Black woman and her eyes turned greener than mine, that lasting three blinks. My jaw tightened.

She had given me the invite and told me that it was mandatory that I attend this social event or there might be a problem with my coins somewhere down the line. She had me in a trick bag, demanding I kowtow to her every demand, and it was worsening. Not for meeting Gemma Buckingham, an act of rebellion, I'd be gone, would be at Love Club, partying with the Fastest Swimmers, on my second scotch, getting turnt.

I scowled at that Bitch from Brownsville and thought of the ending of *Of Mice and Men*.

Dr. Stone-Calhoun was probably the most beautiful woman of a certain age on campus, her beauty accentuated by wealth and boosted by power. The power-hungry woman who lorded over me and stole my joy always wore upscale swag from Lori James boutique and was rarely seen in the same outfit twice in the same season. She was known for having her precious, luxurious blond hair movie-star fresh every day. Rumor was she was up in her personal wing in her southern-fried former slave mansion getting her locks done in her beauty salon by a professional each sunrise while the rooster crowed.

They moved on.

Ass-kissers and bootlickers followed them, trying to become a part of that powerful clique.

In the same breath, one of my students entered the room.

Had to do a triple take.

She usually rocked dark braids and ripped jeans.

Tonight she was a diva. Lavender hair with glam waves cascaded down her back.

She saw me with Gemma Buckingham, slowed her stroll, sipped her drink, did a hair toss, and resumed her march, hips on fire, lips pursed, looking ready to tell me ten things she hated about me.

When the devil was bored, she put on her fuck-me pumps and went to destroy mortals.

CHAPTER 3

THE DIVA IGNORED Gemma Buckingham, squared off with me. "Professor Suleman. Good evening."

"Jennifer."

"Komorebi DaShiarra Regina Devin Jackson. I'm in one of your intro classes."

"How may I help you, Miss Komorebi Jackson?"

"Professor Four Ds said you'd be here. May I speak with you regarding my paper?"

"This is beyond my office hours."

"Your office hours conflict with my schedule. I have eighteen units and two jobs."

"Use the established portal. E-mail me."

"I bought both of your books from the discount rack at a Goodwill by Mall of Memphis."

"Thanks so much."

"I bought one of your father's books too."

"My father?"

"I assume he's your father. Same eyes and last name. Only he's the *world-famous* writer and no one knows who you are. Same complexion. Same face. He's older, but you look like his younger photos."

That almost triggered me, damn near shut me down. "E-mail me, Miss Jackson."

"I need you to sit down and meet with me so we can see why you refuse to up me at least one letter grade when I know my work is the ish. White people writing all vanilla, writing ten janky stale pages about a tree on the side of a road. Getting As for writing what impacts me like Sominex. My writing is fire, about some real shit. I deserve two As but won't be too mad if you make it a B. I need you to do your job and go over my work page by page with me so I can prove my point before you submit my grade and it becomes permanent on my record."

"Last time. E-mail me via the port—"

Komorebi shot me an ugly smile. "Those who can't write, teach."

"Those who can't do that barely pull a C."

"You know who I am, then."

"Once you said your name. Hardly recognized you dressed up with your new hairstyle."

"You know *we* have to come here looking a certain kind of way. Now, about upping my grade."

"You attend every other lecture, if that, which, being Black, I find insulting."

"Regardless if I miss a lecture or two, I always do the assignments. Need you to know my work is A-level work. I'm going to be the new Toni Morrison. One question. How do I get published?"

"How do you get published? Everyone wants to get published but no one wants to take the time to actually learn how to write. Learn to write. Chase skills, not fame. When you have skills, fame will find you. Train for the marathon before you jump in thinking you're ready to run twenty-six miles."

"How's that working out for you?"

"Well, I'm not inviting myself into other people's conversations and asking you for advice."

"It's not like you're as brilliant as Ethiopian writer Maaza Mengiste."

Jaw tight, anger held by invisible reins, I simply said, "Burn."

"Your work, unlike your father's, is a complete waste of time. Trees line up and sacrifice themselves to be one page in your father's books. Trees would be appalled at being in one of yours. It's a shame when what could've been good two-ply toilet paper or wipes are sentenced to become pages in horrible novels."

"Miss Jackson. I'll excuse your behavior because I can smell the liquid courage on your breath."

"How will helping a sister out by bumping up her grade hurt you in the long run? This time next year you won't remember, but it will have an impact on the trajectory of my career. It will change my life, not yours. You can help me succeed or watch me fail. You know white people do the same all day every day and most of the time they don't even have to ask. That's why they fail upward all the time."

"Do the work."

"What?"

"Do the work."

"I *do* do the work."

"Over on our rival's yard, when the legendary Memphis State Eight set foot on the campus of Memphis State University in fall of 1959, when they integrated that joint, they didn't come to a professor and try to go out for drinks. White students wouldn't even sit at the same table with them. They had separate classes, so they were isolated. You know what they did? They did the work. You have all the advantages they wished they had back in '59. Do the work. Do the gotdamn work. Work harder, get smarter. I grew up eating potted meat, okra, and hoecakes. I did the work to get here. U of M turned me down and I still landed on my feet. I busted my ass and not once did I ask for a grade I didn't deserve. By my calculations I've done over sixty thousand hours, and I'm still hustling and working my ass off. Never missed a class as an undergrad. Never missed a day of work at any job I'd ever had since I was fifteen. Never asked for more than I deserved. Get out of my face and do the damn work like the rest of us did in order to set an example, Komorebi."

She did a hair toss. "Can't you—"

"No means no."

"Blacks who don't know they're Black keep siding with the crackers who will eventually remind them of their place. Eventually. If not sooner."

"Wow. You just called me an Uncle Tom. I think we're done here."

She tried a new angle. "I heard from Professor Four Ds that the DJ at Love Club is your sister."

"Tell me something I don't know."

"She's famous, has billboards all over."

"Five or six along I-240 and one in midtown. Hyperbole not necessary."

"Her photo shoots are the bomb. Controversial. I want to be a crop-top shawty like her on IG with that many followers. Stanning hard. Can you get me on her list tonight so I can meet her?"

"Not appropriate."

"Your sister ain't no regular, schmegular like you. I want to meet her so I can tell her my situation and see if she can talk some sense in your head."

"I'll e-mail you through the portal within forty-eight hours, using UAN guidelines, regarding revisiting your most recent assignment."

"All that winning in your family. You must be a disappointment. You are to me, my brother. Lot of talent in your family. Too bad you weren't able to make it the day they passed it out."

"Likewise."

She was about to take her petulance away but paused. "Where did you go to high school?"

"Why?"

"Was hoping you went to Manassas so you'd relate to me better."

"I left high school behind me years ago."

"We hood people."

I nodded. "I'm a Cobra. Carver High until the day I die."

"I'm sorry what I said about your stanky little books. I mean, wipipo published them, so they must be good, at least by wipipo standards, right? Dunno. Maybe I should've read it backward."

She turned and ticktocked away, anger in her hips, putting the kiss-my-ass in Manassas.

Gemma Buckingham hummed. "Interesting. Immature and persistent, if nothing else."

I rubbed my beard, took a breath. "She's a piece of work. Known for her antics."

"You've written two novels."

I snapped out of a trance, grinned. "Yeah."

"Book titles, if it's not too much a bother, please?"

"*The Terrorists Within* was my first."

"Second?"

"*Laugh to Keep from Dying.*"

"Interesting."

I chuckled. "You use that word a lot."

She winked. "It's my mot juste."

"Mot juste?"

"French. Means the right thing and at times only thing needed to say."

"Mot juste."

"And this is your complete oeuvre?"

"Yeah. Just two novels. Working on a third."

I was upset Komorebi had invoked the motherfucker I despised, my father, a man my family said was my doppelganger, that randomness a sign, an omen, that the clock was about to strike thirteen.

I asked, "How do you like Memphis?"

"I was in the ladies' room and a woman who had to be at least seventy-hundred years old took a little pink gun out of her Burberry purse so she could get to her lipstick. I guess I lost the plot. She laughed and told me not to worry, that like almost everyone else in Memphis and Mississippi, she had a license to carry, and she only shot ugly men."

"No guns in London?"

"We prefer to stab each other."

"Old-school."

"Since Jack the Ripper."

"Good to know."

"Over here every woman with a gun thinks she has a twelve-inch wanker."

"And a wanker with a gun thinks he's Wyatt Earp and will double pop and drop somebody down on Main Street over a parking space. Or wants to police what kind of music Black people play in their cars. He thinks he's the overseer on some imaginary slave labor camp run by radical evangelistic slave masters."

She said, "What is a slave labor camp?"

"That's what the plantations were. There were over forty-six thousand slave labor camps."

"From what I read in *The Commercial Appeal*, plantations are the preferred place for weddings. I find it *interesting* that some Black Americans would voluntarily return to sites of trauma to marry."

"There are no Jewish weddings or a single bat mitzvah at Dachau, Belsen, or Auschwitz."

Her phone rang, and she answered, her Brixton accent thickening.

She told whoever was on the other end, "My guesstimate is around two hundred million dollars to leave the board of directors and give up his voting shares. In Memphis. The one in America, not Africa. Will try. By my calculations that's 5.9 billion dollars to reconstruct the destroyed anglophone regions. Okay. Later."

I was intimidated and impressed. More the latter than the former.

She hung up, sighed as if that billion-dollar call was no big deal. "Now, where were we?"

CHAPTER 4

BEFORE WE COULD continue our conversation, we were interrupted again, this time by my colleague Professor Quarry and his wife, Sammie-Lynn, the King and Queen of Gossip.

Professor Quarry smiled at Gemma Buckingham, then asked me, "How's your mom, Pi?"

"She's fine. We did lunch today. Sushi at Sekisui Midtown."

He turned to Gemma Buckingham. "He tell you his mom looks all of twenty? She's an educator over at LeMoyne-Owen and a very sexy body-builder. She looks like a goddess carved from stone. We call her Momma Nike, after the goddess of speed, strength, and victory, not the shoe."

"She sounds impressive."

"He didn't brag that Momma Nike won her division up in Nashville? Remarkably fit. Very impressive woman, and her students love her. Rarely have I seen a woman so beautiful. She had Pi when she was young, and if you see them side by side they look more like siblings than momma and son."

Gemma Buckingham said, "Professor Suleman and I only met a moment ago."

I introduced everyone.

Sammie-Lynn took Gemma's hands, looked her over. "You are a

stunning creature. And *British*. Pi, you better get down on one knee, then take this one to Brazil. She's a keeper."

She said, "A woman usually has to get on both knees before a man gets down on one."

They laughed, Professor Quarry the loudest, almost cackling.

Professor Quarry looked at her left hand, saw a vacant ring finger, and jumped into Gemma Buckingham's personal business. "And why is a woman as lovely as you not married?"

With controlled anger, the Brit replied, "I've yet to meet anyone in my generation who is married and truly living their best life. Well, I've yet to meet a gathering of women who are truly independent and empowered and somehow elevated by having an accoutrement such as a husband. Marriage for them eventually is a burden. Why must one always ask if a woman is married? It's as if we are considered defective unless tethered to testosterone."

Gemma Buckingham's smile was pure irritation.

With southern snark, Professor Quarry said, "Well, don't you sound sophisticated, well-read, and aware of the world."

Gemma Buckingham reciprocated the snark. "Since I've been to every country on the African continent, and since my studies have been intense, I concur, and will take that remark as a compliment."

The Afro, the body language, the undeniable strength. Her white side had been muted.

She shut the conversation down. Her tone said she'd had it dealing with white men, Black men, racism, misogyny, and maybe even white women. I smiled. This was Gemma Buckingham.

"I didn't mean to insult you."

"And your name is Pikey?"

"No, Quarry. Professor Quarry."

"I'd swear you were a Pikey or a Wazzock."

Gemma Buckingham smiled, nodded. Every smile a woman wore wasn't a smile of happiness; every nod didn't mean agreement. Some smiles were trained responses, tools used to de-escalate an uncomfortable moment, a grin manufactured to short-circuit an unwanted situation. A smile and a nod didn't mean shit was cool and there had been a meeting of the minds. Sometimes it was mask worn over irritation, the hider of disgust, a pleasant look waiting for you to shut the fuck up and go away.

Others around me regarded her with confusion, were unable to figure her out, but I had a feeling that to know her all a man had to do was watch and listen. Her phone rang; she excused herself without bothering to say good-bye. As she sashayed away, hips moving with a snarkified British accent, the gossipers moved in closer.

Professor Quarry whispered, "Another UAN lawsuit. An ingénue from Nutbush. Something happened in the booth, in the back, in the corner, in the dark, because a million is being paid and a new policy is being enforced, effective immediately."

He was speaking about white girls being assaulted, as if there could be no other victims.

Sammie-Lynn shook her head. "They come here from where they could leave their front doors open all night, from towns half the size of the UAN campus, and quickly learn about the real world."

A few more words were said; then the tipsy lovebirds became all touchy-feely.

Professor Quarry said, "Since I'm out of juicy gossip, it's time for us to head toward Cordova."

Sammie-Lynn nodded. "I have to show three houses tomorrow. Starting at ten."

As I told the newlyweds good night, a member of the Aggressive Six stopped me from leaving. It was the Schwarzenegger, their leader, mean mugging me like I had slapped his momma with a cast-iron skillet. He pointed. Just beyond a group of Alpha Kappa Alphas, Delta Sigma Thetas, Zeta Phi Betas, and Sigma Gamma Rhos chatting it up, Dr. Stone-Calhoun snapped her fingers at me like I was a pet, summoned me.

The Greeks all noticed; some clutched their pearls. So did the Kappa, Que, and Alphas who were scattered around the room.

As I approached, the Judge of all Judges loud-talked me and asked, "How on God's green Earth do you get your hair to grow like that?"

Dr. Stone-Calhoun held his hand in solidarity as she chuckled. "Looks like a field of cotton that needs to be picked."

THE SON OF MR. SULEMAN   23

Par for the course. The chronically ignorant ridiculed that which they could not comprehend.

Unamused, I asked Dr. Stone-Calhoun, "You called me over for a reason? I was just leaving."

"You must socialize until the end. I will have it no other way. This shindig cost UAN a lot."

The obese judge proclaimed as if he were on his bench, "We were having a discussion and suddenly we have arrived at a point that requires the expert opinion of a UAN man such as yourself."

Dr. Stone-Calhoun expounded, "Black unemployment is at its lowest levels in history. Some people have never learned how to say thank you when someone ordained by God helps them. The percentage of Blacks on welfare and food stamps has fallen to its lowest levels in history. My president did this for you."

"I'll send him a toilet-paper-made thank-you card first thing in the morning. If he hasn't been impeached."

The Judge of all Judges rendered his verdict. "My president has done nothing illegal."

"I guess you missed where 45 has people locked up in cages and dying at the border."

Dr. Stone-Calhoun snapped, "Illegals. Professor Pi Maurice Suleman, why would we want unemployed immigrants from Mexico and the Bahamas when we have homelessness and unemployment in the tristate area that we have failed to get under control? We need to build walls, close the borders, and clean our own houses and let them fix their own countries. Heck, it's not like they are Puerto Rico. We were very nice to those people."

The Judge of all Judges reached up to comfort her by massaging her neck to calm her the fuck down. The moment the judge touched the perfect hair on her neck, she popped his hand and seethed.

The cold exchange let me know the house they lived in wasn't the Disneyland of Bluff City.

They nodded at each other, then held hands, came back at me as if their fight had never happened. The judge's jaw tightened, telling me to re-know my place, but I resumed talking. They asked me a motherfuckin question, so they were about to get an answer.

It was as frustrating as hell was hot to keep having the same repetitive conversation about racism with people who pretended to have no basic understanding of the fundamentals. They had a willful ignorance deeper than the Mariana Trench. Made me want to slap the taste out of their mouths. Discussing racism, diversity, inclusion, and justice with the oppressors, the ones who upheld the blueprint for the Black woman's woes and the Black man's agony, it was a waste of good breathing. Calling me over was a setup; neither of them had any real interest in my POV or the gotdamn major aspects of my professional and personal life. They didn't give a fuck about a BMFM.

I stood my ground like an iroko tree deeply rooted under an African sun. "Y'all judging something y'all don't understand. Y'all opinions are based on your position in this culture and life. You commoditize people, same as the founders of this wonderful country once did, and the people in charge still do. I know Christians like you. You claim to praise the Lord, have Jesus on your walls, wear crosses, yet you think that things like Puerto Rico and the Bahamas are OPP, other people's problems."

"Are you saying we do nothing to help?"

"You write checks and help from afar. You don't get your hands dirty. You send some of your hard-earned tax-deductible money. Get your vaccination shots and go there, meet the people, sweat, help them rebuild. I would if UAN was paying me over six figures a year like it does y'all."

Dr. Stone-Calhoun did some calculation, stepped my way, unhappy. "I hear you live in a small house in *South* Memphis. How many unemployed refugees are you willing to take into your home before you feel the strain of no good deed going unpunished? At what point does your home feel so crowded with others that it's no longer your home? Can you imagine taking in two hundred who have no jobs? Why should my America do that on a grander scale? Why should my tax dollars pay for my own demise?"

"Jesus led by example and fed five thousand with five loaves of bread and two fish."

"You're not Jesus."

"But I try to walk like 'im, even when Kanye's song isn't helping me lead the charge."

"And I bet all five thousand left with their stomachs grumbling all the way back to and beyond the Sea of Galilee. Get yourself five loaves of bread and two fish, go to the border, see how that works out. I'll order the bread for you from Muddy's. I'll buy you the fish—snapper, not tilapia—from Hollywood Fish Market myself. Roll up your sleeves, put on your Kanye music, go feed 'em."

"Like a good Christian, I would."

"Are you in doubt that I am a good Christian? My people were the original ones."

"There are no white people in the Bible, far as I know. Not in the two testaments I read. Hashtag on usher board. Hashtag in church most Sundays. Hashtag somebody lying to themselves big-time."

"Must we go there? We all have the same god."

"Looking at my history, how your people treated mine, and more or less still do on a systematic level, all due respect, that's debatable. We prayed to your god and were lynched for sport. Something ain't too Christian in one of our camps. Lynching Black folks. Slavery. Jim Crow. Ain't none of that real Jesus-like. Once again, just going by the Bible I read. One of us is worshipping the fallen guy and might not know it."

"Insults my president and my god."

"Truth should never be an insult. Your president lies on his lies. His lies are deeper than Russian nesting dolls, only with his lies the deeper you go, the bigger they get. You'd think gaslighting would be extinguished by facts, but that rule has never applied to cults."

"Is that another attack on religion?"

"If it is, it's on yours, not mine. Mine produced no strange fruit."

Looking like he was barefoot standing on broken glass, Judge dug into his back pocket, violently yanked out a pint of Jack, guzzled it until it was empty, then shot me the ugliest smile, the kind that told me he was imagining men in white hoods standing before a flaming cross, with me on that cross. Used to be by rope, but now they shot that which they couldn't own or control. Weren't content until there was fear in your eyes, something that left them feeling less impotent and more empowered.

I think some of Gemma Buckingham's energy had infected my attitude, and I embraced it. Maybe I was tired of the bullshit.

He said, "Have you forgotten who I am?"

"The damage you've done to Black folks in Memphis is legendary. We know you. You suffer from the rewards of being white, male, and two rungs below mediocre. Not one thing original about you, not even your racism. It's so 1950s. Update the hate before it's too late."

"I know the president of the USA. One call and I can ruin your life in ways J. Edgar Hoover wished he'd ruined that philandering enemy of the state named Martin Luther King."

"A fake and a fraud had a baby and called it Donald. He's a backstabbing Twitter-addicted racist and New York grifter who did just like you, used his KKK-loving daddy's money and white privilege to rise to the top."

"Careful how you talk about my president. Be real careful, boy."

"God bless the Electoral College, the only university in the universe with members dumber than a graduate from Trump University."

They looked at me like I was suicidal.

Tonight, maybe I was.

I threw gas on the fire. "So glad you called me over. We were having a discussion, me and a few African American professors, and suddenly we arrived at a point that requires the expert opinion of a UAN man such as yourself, Judge Calhoun. Both you and your wife. I watch Fox News. Opposition research. Black people would love to know, can white folks tell when other white folks are lying to them? Asking for my friends."

He said, "Real smart at the mouth, like Barack *Hussein* Obama."

"That's his name and we love it. We call him Barack *Hussein* Obama with no shame because that is a name that can't be traced back to a white plantation. His name is as non-slave as a Black man's name can get."

"What's he hiding? Why did he call himself Barry?"

"He used Barry to make certain white folks feel comfortable and not shake up bigotry and ignorance. Face it, you can't trace his name back to a planation, only Kenya, so we had an African president in America."

Eyes dark, Judge clacked his dental implants a few times, scowled, then chuckled without moving the rest of his face. "Let me go to the buffet, find a big sharp knife, and cut me a big chunk of pie."

He dug into a second pocket, pulled up another bottle of Jack, and left guzzling a second pint of liquid fire made in Tennessee, its recipe stolen from a Black man and credited to a white slave owner.

Bit by bit Dr. Stone-Calhoun's Russian Red orifice eased into a Kremlin smile that said she wanted to see me lying in state in the Little Pyramid. "Make sure you socialize until the event concludes, as required. We will chat regarding this matter again. Do enjoy your evening. May God bless your soul."

I wasn't tenured, didn't have guaranteed, permanent employment, not like the arrogant ones.

A brother like me, a professor who wasn't tenured, could be fired at any time, let go for pretty much any reason. People with power could yank your chain for kicks, could kick you to hear you holler, or make your job so fucking miserable you wanted to flip over a table and quit. But I couldn't afford to do that; no dignity came with being fired, but an unemployment check didn't come with quitting.

The racism and aggressions continued, as they had done since before the 1600s. Some habits were too hard for some folks to break, even when detrimental to their health.

I searched for the lady from London but instead ran into my homie, DaReus Danian D'Angelo Darellson—literally bumped into him. Towering over me, Professor Four Ds gave me a powerful Wakanda salute, and I did the same.

He asked, "Mane, how you gonna run over a BMFM when he six feet seven inches tall?"

I said, "Mane, and darker than midnight on a moonless night."

"Mane, this night ain't got no moon and you should've seen my Blackness in this whiteness."

"Was blinded by the bling from all this old money."

"We ain't nigger rich, but these rich white folks got rich off enslaving African kings and queens and turning them into cotton-picking niggers."

"Right, mane, right."

"We ain't nigger rich but they got rich off niggers."

"They made a nigger factory."

"Just add Africans."

"Owners gone but the factory still in bid'ness."

"Watch your six, Cobra."

"What you see, Cobra?"

"Mane, the way Dr. Stone-Calhoun looking at yuh right now ain't nothing nice."

"Racists have never been known for critical thinking. That's for sho. Mane, she keeps giving me trouble on a good day."

"Mane, mane, mane. You in trouble with ya boss and her mane, mane? Yuh might as well be on bad terms with MPD, the sheriff's department, and the folks running the 901 court system."

"Mane, she snapped her motherfuckin fingers at me like she was calling a gotdamn mutt to its feeding bowl."

We hunted for a place to loiter. We code-switched and talked proper when we were too close to our other colleagues, had curt convos. Most were political, no better than what the Calhouns had had to offer.

We smiled, added nothing, told folks to enjoy the night, moved the fuck on.

Four Ds griped, "White politicians and pundits get three sheets to the wind and debate opposing white politicians and pundits over who will be kinder to the neglected Negro in order to secure the Black vote long enough to win the next big election, then leave the melanin in the dark, again bamboozled. They love the Black vote and hate Black folks."

"Why the fuck didn't we go to an HBCU like MLK and Spike Lee?"

"Out-of-state tuition. Carfare. Last summer with Cobra girls."

"Too scared to go too far from the nest."

When I was with Four Ds he took me back to when life didn't seem as complicated. Whenever we were in the same room, we became twelve-year-old Negroes from South Memphis. He had grown up in a small red house with trained pet roaches. Now he had a real nice home in Mary Lou Heights. I could do my yard work in an hour, but it took him half a Saturday to cut his grass. He rode a mower while his wife and ten-year-old twins cleaned five bedrooms and as many bathrooms. I was jealous of him and not ashamed to admit it. Melissa was a good woman, Jabari and Swain good kids. Didn't matter if Four Ds was working hard to take care of three people and having money problems from time to time due to the strain; he had the life I wanted for myself one day. The house where I'd love to test out a riding mower.

In this damn-near melanin-free environment, Four Ds was as happy to see me as I was him. But when Black men were happy and minding their own business, someone had to spit in the Kool-Aid.

Professor Thor, an older German professor, saw us off to the side and changed his direction, walking into our personal space smiling. He raised his drink toward us. "Well, if it ain't Nelson Obama and Barack Mandela, dressed up and socializing with top-notch colleagues at last. Here for tapas and reparations?"

We stared at him, hard stares, the kind that ran fools from South Side back across Third Street.

His brand of privilege knew no fear, had roots deeper than white oak, hickory, black gum, sassafras, sweet gum, Japanese pagoda, butternut, and pines. In the South it ran deeper than the wild fig tree at Echo Caves in South Africa. His brand of privilege had been tested by time, proven unstoppable.

He laughed, then whistled the hook from the Popeyes chicken commercial. He sang his own lyrics to the fast-food spot theme song, "*Negroes killing each other for Popeyes.* Killing each other over a chicken sammich? I guess that's the new crack for Blacks. *Negroes killing each other for Popeyes.* The violent way your folks are carrying on over some bird, must be lacing their chicken with menthol."

Bigger than me, but smaller than Four Ds, Professor Thor left cackling on racism hard enough to choke. He'd done shit like that to me at least fifty times by my count, each time feeling like a cultural assault. Powerful white men claimed to be the most persecuted, oppressed people in society, yet dealt out bigotry in a way that was hard to prove, by trying to be a third-rate comic at my expense. Professor Thor was what you'd get if Don Rickles and the Joker had a baby underneath a burning cross.

I was out of fucks and was rapidly running out of Black forgiveness coupons.

But we grew up under this umbrella. Saw no reason to scream or shout. We moved on.

Four Ds stared across the room. "Mane, you see Komorebi in that dress? She done changed up her hair and everything. She brand-new."

"Mane, don't board the *Titanic*. Sinking ship if I ever done seen one."

"Mane, that dirty Diana singin' in the rain and looking like she wanna have a good time."

"Mane, you better cross your legs and turn around. Bunny hop away from them thoughts."

"Mane, she brand-new tonight."

I said, "Mane, let's hit Love Club wit' Sis the DJ tonight. Drinks on me."

"Mane, my wife bedtime is my bedtime and its almost her bedtime and I'm 'bout to be on her testing our new mattress from Sleepy ZZZ's." Four Ds gave me dap. "Mane, I spent my last supporting this stale event, so loan a married BMFM with two kids at home two of the bills they reneged putting Harriet Tubman's face on 'fore I go put in some work. Melissa got a bro on a PB&J budget right now."

I didn't have it to spare, but I gave him forty. Then spoke to him acting our age.

"You've been married ten years. What's your secret?"

"Jealous?"

"You've been married for a decade, and compared to you all I've ever done was dated, broke up, dated, broke up, dated, broke up, bought my red Nova, dated, broke up, dated, broke up, dated, broke up, graduated from UAN, dated, broke up, dated, broke up, got my first real job at UAN, dated, broke up, dated, broke up, dated, broke up, bought my first house, and still been dating and breaking up ever since."

"Pi, all I know is a woman will tell you what she wants or leave you to go get what she needs. I make sure Melissa gets what she both wants and needs. I'm lucky I got me one who loves to do the same for me. Ten years have flown by and I ain't never needed to touch or kiss another woman. Don't get me wrong, tell the truth and shame the devil, I get anxious and I go car shopping every now and again, browse a few lots from the curb, but I don't step on a lot trying to get a test drive. My car running fine. I might give a few church hugs and brotherly kisses on the cheek, but I ain't trying to make no baby."

A final complicated handshake and that BMFM was gone, checking out Komorebi's blessing as he strolled, admiring a woman well made, then shaking his head like he was vowing never to try for a test drive. She saw a damn near seven-foot-tall raisin leaving this bowl of white rice, grinned, then hurried, made her heels click like a pony doing a trot. She caught up with her calculus professor's long-legged pace. She bit her bottom lip as she grinned at him, her flirt game strong. I hoped his wedding ring was stronger and was made of thot repellant. Komorebi was desperate. Angry, desperate, and from the hood of all hoods. If Four Ds forgot he was born on Farrington eating Spam from the can, he would get a new lesson to learn, the kind that would have his paycheck going one way while he was sent off in the other.

I moved on, hunted, and found Gemma Buckingham on the other side of the Pink Palace.

CHAPTER 5

GEMMA BUCKINGHAM HAD been pulled into a never-ending conversation, and her expression begged me to put on my cape and save her. I took her hand, and we skedaddled outside together.

It was close to midnight and Memphis was hot like four in the afternoon.

She growled and slapped her arm, killed a mosquito with a vengeance.

She said, "Thank you very much. Some people never take the batteries out."

"What were you talking about?"

"Barely understood a single word. Think I witnessed a dead language being resurrected. Even worse, when I speak they look at me funny, like I'm using words with no vowels."

"They are from the smallest of small towns in the tristate."

"Never in my life have I heard such gibberish."

"Their country grammar is strong. I understood them."

"May I never end up there needing directions back to civilization as I know it."

"You're frustrated."

"American words and phrases leave me dumfounded."

"For example?"

"Ballpark. Sneakers. Soccer. First floor. Zip codes. Freshmen. Sophomores. Juniors. Seniors. John Hancock. Flake. Democrats. Republicans. Rain check. Jumped the shark. Riding shotgun. I get lost and it becomes gibberish. And the way you mispronounce words like *vitamin, aluminium, privacy, schedule, garage, water, mobile, advertisement,* and *herb* is abominable, southern accent withstanding."

"Vitamin, aluminum, privacy, schedule, garage, water, mobile, advertisement, and herb." I laughed and pronounced them all the red, white, and blue way.

"And other words like *street, shrimp, strawberry, straight, specific, computer, Buick, library, February,* and *ambulance.* Can no one here speak those bloody words correctly? Sorry. Pet peeves."

"Street, shrimp, strawberry, straight, specific, computer, Buick, library, February, and ambulance. And I can say *vitamin, aluminium, privacy, schedule, garage, water, mobile, advertisement,* and *herb.*"

She smiled. "Impressive. That did something to me. Let's not get into your misspellings."

"You're as perplexed with Americanisms as I am with Londonspeak and British pronunciations after watching an episode of *Doctor Who.*"

She grinned, surprised. "You're a Whovian? Do Americans even know the show exists?"

"Big-time. But I don't know your history as well, so the show loses me along the way."

"*Doctor Who* has some of the most gorgeous mixed-race women on its show."

"Never noticed. Will pay close attention next time."

"*Downton Abbey* fan as well?"

"Don't push it."

She laughed. "Lots of Brits are here putting on American accents and working in film and television. Freema Agyeman. Thandie Newton. Gugu Mbatha-Raw. Sophie Okonedo. When my hair is straight, a lot of people have said I look like Maisie Richardson-Sellers, which is a compliment."

"Yeah?"

"I have to get used to your television programs. Nothing I'm familiar with exists here. It's as if I've entered a bizarre dimension where Harry

Enfield, *I'm Sorry I Haven't a Clue*, *Just a Minute*, *Morecambe and Wise*, Peter Kay, Reeves and Mortimer, Stewart Lee, and Victoria Wood never existed."

She picked up her phone, went to the Uber app. "Mind keeping me company until my ride arrives?"

If she left now, I'd never see her again. It had taken thirty-one years to meet her.

"Gemma Buckingham of Brixton, how can Pi of Memphis get in contact with you?"

"Give me your phone."

I did as commanded.

She tapped her number in. I took my phone back, looked at what she'd entered.

"Wait. You typed in 901-803-30."

"Problem?"

"Hold up, pretty momma. 901-803-30. Area code, exchange, then you left out two numbers."

"Want to chat again? Figure out the correct permutation."

"Serious?"

"I gave you eighty percent of the information. Now solve the next twenty percent."

"Two numbers. Nine choices on each. That's possibly one hundred numbers I'd have to try."

"Only one rings me."

"Can I at least get the next digit?"

"It was nice meeting you. If I never hear from you, thanks for saving me. All the best."

"I'll figure it out." I raised my cell. "Look for a call from 901-9—"

"That's all I need to know."

"What if you don't answer?"

"My voice is on my answering machine. It sounds like London; Brixton to be specific."

"No problem. I can send out one hundred texts, and when I hit you, hit me back."

"Sorry, love. No texts. Something gets lost in translation."

"Not if you send back a smiley face."

"Especially if I send a smiley face and I'm not smiling because you reached me. Texting is for cowards. They will send the message they won't dare say to your face. Followed by an emoticon to soften the insult. A sentence with ten words, each word emphasized with each reading, can yield ten different interpretations. Face-to-face, or on the phone where voices are heard, no room for ambiguity."

"Night's still young. My sister is a DJ. Let me take you to her club for a drink."

"Not tonight, love. Had flights from Memphis to New York to Sydney and back to here."

"Here to New York is a couple of hours."

"Closer to three."

"How long is that flight from New York to Australia?"

"If you're a Harry Potter fan, you can watch all eight movies in nineteen hours and thirty-nine minutes."

I looked at her digits. "When should we start trying to figure out your number?"

"I already know it by heart, so any time convenient for you, love."

"One question."

"If you must."

"Of all the places in the world, why Memphis?"

"Does it matter?"

"You don't have to say."

"After a massive breakup I felt lost in the doldrums for weeks. Months, actually. One day after a barrel of shots and a bucket of tears, I picked up an old map of America. Threw a dart. It landed on Memphis. Knew nothing of the place. I surrendered all I knew, friends, and family to alleviate a broken heart. I moved here, gave up the best African and West Indian food. Yams. Plantain. West Indian hard dough bread. Jerk chicken. Rice. African jollof rice. Came to where all the people drink cold beer, call football *soccer*, have no idea who Arsenal is, and live to barbecue in the parks on Saturdays. I came here to get away from a toxic relationship and all things venomous in London."

"You okay?"

The way I said those two words did something to her that all the jaw jacking before had failed to accomplish. She looked vulnerable, ten years younger, like a wall was being set aside.

"No one has ever asked me that before."

"We can go somewhere, to Denny's, and talk. No strings. I'll listen, or we can sit in silence."

"Professor Suleman, each offer you have made has been tempting. Full disclosure, something I rarely do, and never with a stranger. I ordered myself a bit of dinner before I came to the first UAN event, intending to pop in for two seconds, then saw your green eyes, became mesmerized, was curious, and ended up here for hours, to chat you up. My food will be on my porch waiting for me cold when I return home. Saw them leave it when Ring was activated. Not to complain, but I am exhausted, and I haven't eaten a crumb worth mentioning since before noon; at this point I might literally pass out before I arrive at my new dwelling. Being almost thirty and suddenly single, a bit quirky and alone since I arrived in America, eating my meals alone at home or in a restaurant with strangers, is not the big fun."

"I feel you. Even as a man, being single isn't always fun."

"I bet it is on a Friday night."

"Especially not on a Friday night."

"Two drinks and we reveal our true selves."

"That we do."

"Your green eyes."

"Your lips."

"My mother had a thing for green-eyed men."

"What about you?"

"I'm a sapiosexual as well as a demisexual."

"You keep it sexual."

"Professor Pi Suleman. Mr. 3.14, Pisces from Memphis, this Taurus from Brixton admires your voice, each word a chill down my spine. Your wit, intelligence, and personality appeal to both maladies. Your green eyes. When I first saw you, it felt as if I'd seen you before but had never met you."

She touched my wooly mane, felt my history, an indicator of how my life had been.

I touched her soft, wavy hair, assumed her life had been just as easy, without many kinks.

The faculties of sight, smell, hearing, and touch had been satisfied. I wanted to taste her.

I whispered, "What perfume are you wearing?"

She grinned, matched my tone. "My perfume is called Fucking Fabulous by Tom Ford."

"And that you are. Fucking fabulous."

Her nostrils flared with each heated exhale; she, too, was beyond turned on. We maintained eye contact as she bit the corner of her pillow-soft British lips. I licked mine. She shuddered.

I leaned, but not too much, and Gemma Buckingham did the same. I was aroused. Her breathing quickened; her cheeks flushed; a moan escaped her lips. I wanted to taste her more than anything in the world.

Gemma Buckingham pulled it together. "Interesting how you look at me in that way."

"And how is that?"

"Like you want to fill the blank spaces."

"Which means?"

"As Maxwell sings, you want to know 'how does it feel.'"

"D'Angelo sings that."

"My bad. They sound the same to my British ears."

"How do you look at me?"

She whispered, "I'm one second from my wild thoughts turning into a reckless action and dancing with a stranger until the sun comes up and goes down and comes up again. One second away."

I whispered, "One thousand one."

I leaned in closer, needed to kiss her now more than I needed to breathe. Gemma Buckingham shivered, slowly placed the palm of her right hand on my rapidly beating heart, but with horny eyes she reluctantly shook her head; anything more would put us on black ice.

I nodded and backed away.

She pulled me back to her.

I inhaled her scent, set afire as I nibbled her lobe.

She squirmed and moaned, danced and dug her nails into my arms. She held my head and I sucked her ear as her delicate moans rose, until her knees tried to give way, until her hand moved between my legs, rubbed what was calling her name.

"Well, if it ain't Malcolm Waters and Auntie Maxine X out here looking totally inappropriate."

We jumped like we'd been caught by MPD in the bushes after hours at Riverside Park.

Professor Thor came our way, old-man whistling as he headed to his ride. With a David Duke smile he slowed down as he closed in, whistled louder to be noticed. When he had eye contact, he sang, "Flirting and feeling each other up. Maybe I should've called y'all Kamala Brown and Willie Harris."

He put a bullet in the heart of a sensuous moment, then skedaddled away, amused with himself to the point of multiple mental orgasms.

I explained what had just happened so she'd be aware of CNN smiles over Fox News hearts.

Gemma Buckingham was offended. "Was he taking the piss?"

"What?"

"Am I supposed to take the Mickey?"

"What?"

"Is this an unwarranted insult that I am the butt end of?"

"Yeah."

"Why? Have I done something offensive?"

"You're in the South. Here you're supposed to take the insult disguised as a joke because when white men like him see Black people, even when we're educated and exist on this level, they see niggers."

"Niggas."

"No, niggers. The classic pejorative ending in *e* and *r*, not *a*."

"Does my *hed din.*"

"Huh?"

"People like him piss me off."

"Gets my goat too."

"Pardon?"

"Pisses me off too."

"Seems like I'm encountering unwarranted insult after insult."

"Apologies for my people."

Wrestling with anger, she shook her head the way we Black folks did with practically every insult rained down on us for four hundred years.

In a poetic British accent Gemma Buckingham said, "I'm mixed race. Not undeniably Black like you. Look white from a distance. In some instances, when my hair is straight, it's not until someone is close to me they can tell how to judge me. I've seen smiles lessen or disappear as people came closer. I've seen fear and disappointment. I know racism, UK style. When in London, I live in three worlds. If I'm out on a high street with my white English mum, I get a certain treatment. If I am in public with my dark-skinned African father, it's a different narrative. And if we are all together, yet another experience. Only one of the three scenarios is occasionally favorable. And I do mean occasionally."

"Three levels of racism."

"I'll never forget one Boxing Day. We were on the Tube and a man asked loudly, 'What do you get when you cross a saltine cracker with a chocolate biscuit?' He motioned at us. Then he said it's too bad my parents weren't like a horse and a donkey who'd made a mule. A mule can't reproduce. People laughed. As he left the Tube at Hammersmith, he laughed the hardest and shook his head. I'll never forget how my father pulled me closer. I was a child then. Seven and forever scarred."

"Racism has no bottom and no respect for gender or age."

"When I'm with my mum, I wish I had her nose and hair. When I'm with my dad, I wish I had his skin tone. Just to keep people from staring. To keep people from whispering. A white American just insulted me because I exist. I can only imagine what Meghan Markle endured here in America. Your racism is so bloody harsh. And deadly. Very deadly."

She sounded unnerved, afraid of this country's reputation.

Gemma Buckingham, mixed race, from London, born in Brixton, mother British, father African, accent like Thandie Newton or Helen Mirren or the Black girl who was on *Doctor Who*, with a militant Afro, rang as being familiar, yet very different; she was a woman undiscovered until she stood before my eyes, an exoplanet. Something that existed outside of the Memphis, solar system, and universe this BMFM knew. Still our histories were both connected to colonialism and the slave trade. But her complexion, in a world of racism and colorism, had probably given her options my mother and sisters never had.

I explained the Popeyes insult to her. Black people and fried-chicken jokes, some served with watermelon on the side, were older than Jim Crow.

This bullshit was bigger than a fucking Popeyes joke. I couldn't care less about Popeyes. Every racist microaggression was a shank move to the soul of Black folks. It was like a smiling man calling a woman a cunt, doing it each time he passed, going out of his way to find and verbally assault her, and when she lost it, him saying it was just some words, no sticks and no stones, no one was hurt, so she's tripping, better watch her, she's a problem, she's crazy, always overreacting.

An Uber pulled up. Gemma verified the plates, compared the face of the female driver to the picture of the Asian woman on the app, then gradually headed for the back passenger-side door.

I asked, "Sure you don't want to skip eating a cold dinner and go dance?"

"I've seen the way your people here in Memphis dance. Not sure I can dance that way. It's pretty unique and intimidating to say the least. Memphis jookin' looks harder than doing ballet."

I confessed, "I want to see you again."

"Find me. If you can. Do the work."

I repeated a phrase that took me back over a decade, "Do the work."

I opened the rear passenger door for her, inhaled her sensual scent as she passed me. Her seat sighed with happiness as it molded to and held the shape of her sweet ass.

I spoke a simple, soft, and easy southern "Good night."

"Again, all the best."

Her Uber disappeared. Two black butterflies passed by, an omen dancing for my attention.

When gods were bored on Earth, they returned to sleep among better deities.

My phone buzzed with a group text from Momma wanting to make sure the Fastest Swimmers were okay. Momma was superstitious. The message said, *Wasn't going to say anything but three days ago I heard a black cat in my backyard meowing at midnight. Next day I opened the back door and a bird flew in and out of my house. Yesterday I dropped a glass and it broke. All those are signs that there will be a death soon. Everybody text and let Momma know everybody okay, and right now.*

I texted I was okay, then went back to inhaling the scent Gemma Buckingham had left behind.

Professor Thor eased by driving his Cadillac ATS. Least expensive of the brand. He tooted his horn, laughed, then yelled for me to stay away from Popeyes and eat with the Christians at Chick-fil-A to stay alive.

He could go dress in new white sheets and fuck himself with a flaming cross.

He had acted so cool, so liberal, when I was first hired, congratulated me with a firm handshake and eye contact. He had shown me his CNN smile and hidden his hypocritical Fox News heart. Lot of Justin Trudeaus were out there. Acted like they were in your corner when they were at your right side, then snuck off to smear leftover black shoe polish on their pale faces. I called them cross-racers.

Four Ds drove by in his ten-year-old Chevy Malibu. I thought he'd left a long time ago. Then I saw why he hadn't gone home to his wife. He'd been distracted. Soon as he passed by, Komorebi sped by driving a white and gray two-seater Benz Smart car with drive-out tags. She was on his bumper, rocked a hoopty hipper than Four Ds'. It was nicer than mine, but it would never be worth as much to her as mine was to me.

I whispered, "Do the work."

They both turned in the same direction.

I hoped they weren't leaving here together.

Friday night. Everybody was lit and looking for something, even if they had it at home.

"Mane, c'mon nigh. Don't need both of us caught up in no bullshit."

I knew a lot of sisters like Komorebi. Poverty bred them and the government fed them. She didn't swing from a pole, not as far as I knew, but she mos def had what we called on my side of the tracks the stripper's mentality. My side of town had PhDs in that survival skill before we hit puberty. How to hustle was all she knew; winning was all that mattered. Otherwise we'd all starve to death. I was born into a hustling culture that wore hand-me-downs, and we knew how to make rags look like swag made for fashion week in NYC. At each turn she had tried a different technique. Hood recognized hood; that's why she came at me hard. A woman like her was always a ride or die as an ally and made you expendable when you weren't on her team. She scared me. Stacked women like her would ruin your life for kicks, then move on to the next while eating curly fries and sipping on a grape coke. Right or wrong, that was my opinion, my interpretation of Komorebi. And I hoped Four Ds saw her the same way.

I repeated, "Mane, c'mon nigh. Get your ass home to your own mattress."

I drove away, not knowing a backbiter bringing next-level trouble was following.

My Nova was getting parched, coughed to get my attention, and I saw the gas hand lingered between an eighth of a tank and running on fumes. I stopped at a University of Memphis–branded gas station, colorful larger-than-life sculptures of U of M Tigers all over the place, reminding all who ran the city. Gas was at 2.19 a gallon here, cost a grip closer to the highway, high-test as much as 2.69 for four quarts. If I'd had the time to swing by a twenty-four-hour Kroger I could've saved thirty pennies off each gallon. I filled halfway, washed down my front windows, and hit the road again.

Trouble closed in with the stealth of a rattlesnake. Not for the gas stop, I would've escaped another fiend, at least for now. That three-hundred-second layover would be the hold that changed everything.

I ran through a stale yellow light, made it across before it turned high-ass ticket, but right away irate headlights from an arrogant MPD SUV appeared behind me flashing from high to low furiously.

The cops had been lying in wait.

M the P to the goddamn D was about to be all over me.

CHAPTER 6

I KILLED THE ignition, silenced my rumbling Nova. Rolled down my driver's-side window. Music off. Put my hands on the steering wheel at ten and two. Prepared to be guilty of breathing while Black. Whispered to myself to chill, stay calm, be polite no matter how fucked the cops acted, don't give them an excuse to send Momma shopping for a tombstone. For the skinfolk on my side of the tracks, survival was rote, had become mechanical because it had been drilled into us from the moment we left Daddy's sacs in search of Momma's egg. Momma had sent me a message warning of an impending death. Black butterflies had danced in my face, an omen. A roll call of hashtags scrolled by in my mind. I had a Pavlovian response, multitasked while on autopilot. I took short breaths as if each might be my last. Until this was resolved, this was more about survival than being right. The goal was to outlive a traffic stop, to see another Sunday dinner with Momma and the Fastest Swimmers. I was no longer in control of my freedom or my life. For my skinfolk, the end of the road came on any sidewalk of the oppressor's choosing.

The count toward another BMFM's pearly white coffin resting at N.J. Ford and Sons began.

One second passed. I was still alive.

Two seconds passed. I hadn't been double-popped.

Three seconds. I wasn't hashtag bound.

Four seconds passed. I was still able to breathe.

Five seconds. Didn't run away, so no shots in the back, reload, repeat.

Six seconds. They were plotting how to hang me in a county jail cell and bill me the blame.

Ten seconds went by. I wasn't being wrapped up in plastic.

Something was wrong.

Cars passed, most of them speeding, half of them boldly running the same light.

Not the behavior of drivers when they were coming up on MPD.

My eyes adjusted enough to see it wasn't Johnny Law on my ass. What had run me off the road was a brand-new Cadillac Escalade, platinum edition. The driver opened their door to that hundred-thousand-dollar SUV fast and angry, like I had cut them off a few miles back and they had caught up to bring their road rage.

Someone jumped out; their silhouette moved like a paratrooper heading to start a war on D-day. She reached in my open window, dark and apocalyptic, gave me a soft slap, then, without warning, cracked a wicked smile. She ran her tongue across her Russian Red lipstick, sighed, struggled with herself, then gently touched my thick black cotton, casually played in my field as if it were hers to till.

"Hurrying off to a new midnight lover?"

Heart thumping, I asked, "What can I do for you? This is past my office hours."

She sang, "Time for some quid pro quo."

Dread covered me, pulled me underwater. I shook my head. "No."

"You know that at this point you don't have a choice. This horse has been let out of the barn. Quid pro quo, I spent money to get you a ticket so I could see you, and now I'm entitled quid pro for my efforts. Think of all I have done for you; the lunches, the presents. Let's be reasonable."

The moment became a blur. Words were said, lost in memory; we had a back-and-forth.

MPD hit the siren once, eased up on us, lights flashing. They saw Dr. Stone-Calhoun, saw her wave and smile like all was fine, like they could run off and mind their business until further notified.

She said, "Nothing to see here. Have a good night. Please make it home safely."

The law knew who she was; the slave catchers resumed their hunt.

I said, "Don't get me in trouble. I get caught with you like this and Johnny Law will find some old miscegenation law still on the books and give me life in prison."

"Over there."

Dr. Stone-Calhoun headed back to her SUV, ass moving with anxious anticipation.

I pulled to the side of the road. She whipped and stopped in front of me.

She hurried inside my car, undid my pants, and went down on me.

I tensed.

Same as last time, I remembered the order to keep my grubby little paws on the steering wheel and not mess up hair that always looked freshly done at a beauty salon first thing in the morning, every morning, as the rooster crowed. I held the steering wheel like it was prison bars, eyes ahead, as lights from traffic whizzed by.

Dr. Stone-Calhoun was in fetish mode, worked me. "Relax."

I put my mind in another place, made this fade away, went somewhere else.

She was determined to make the *Titanic* rise 12,500 feet from its depths.

Resistance became futile. I wanted to get this over with, my mind anywhere but here.

On London. Her fucking fabulous voice. Her fucking fabulous aroma.

Vehicles whizzed by, brake lights and headlights as I held the steering wheel at ten and two like a man tumbling and trying to not fall too deep into the Sunken Place. She finished her Big Gulp but didn't quench her thirst, because she had gagged, and most of my natators had dripped from her mouth. When she saw her reflection, she looked quizzical, then grinned, laughed like a child with melted vanilla Häagen-Dazs splattered on her face and Russian Red lips. Brownsville had robbed me again, had ripped me off of something valuable. She'd taken part of my soul. In my frustration I tried to figure out how I ever got myself into this no-way-out situation.

She had invited me to a working lunch. We ate at Pho 64 a few times in Bartlett, and it was innocent, always shop talk, tips to get ahead, until she let her interest be known. She wanted to go down on me. She made that clear. No sex. Last thing she'd want to have to explain to the Judge of all Judges was a brown baby popping out of that antiabortion antebellum coochie. I told her what she was asking was way out of line. The beauty queen from Brownsville couldn't believe my fantasy wasn't to have a woman of her stature slob on my knob to boost my ego. With a look of hard-core consternation, she let me know she took my hard pass as both an insult and a challenge. She loved a good challenge. She asked me if I wanted to keep my job. I had been blindsided. All I knew at that moment was the threat was real, and my rapid heart beat out in Morse code that I had to keep my job, I had no other options, and she could block me from walking over to U of M and getting suited up in blue and gray like Tom the Tiger. Losing my position would be a loss of prestige around here. I had fought my way down a hard road, had put up with too much and wrestled with too many ign'ant people who either didn't look like me or looked like me but didn't care for their hardworking skinfolks on my side of town. I had come too far to get turned back at the bridge because a Bitch from Brownsville wanted to blow me for two minutes. People in my area looked up to me, saw me as the brother who made it simply because he had his own house and a nice yard, and white people smiled and referred to him as a professor whenever they saw him on the street. I had earned respect.

I reached up to touch the hair in the kitchen of her delicate neck. She smacked my right hand away, slapped it hard. Her breathing thickened and her dark, tight-jawed look cursed me.

Of Mice and Men; Of Mice and motherfuckin *Men.*

A church bell rang inside my head, sent a loud ringing of bells throughout my brain. I wanted to grab her delicate throat, become Lennie, let her have the same fate as Curley's wife, only the police would be George the executioner ten times over. Minutes ago, the freedom takers had seen her tipsy ass standing next to my red Nova. A car the shade of a dead woman's blood on a glove found at OJ's crib.

If this was reversed, if I was a white woman, everything would be different.

A ton of my truth would never weigh as much as an ounce of her lies.

The interior lights of her SUV came on.

I came out of the last of my haze, the surrealness fading, reality coming back in a rush.

A giant as tall and large as any president stirred, began getting out.

Judge Calhoun struggled toward my Nova, wobbled on a slant, and fell down.

Again words were exchanged in a moment of panic, my panic.

Brownsville wiped her face, redid her Russian Red lips, then eased out of my car, marched down the side of my Nova toward her husband. Judge was so fucked-up he had to hold the SUV door to stay steady on his feet.

Dr. Stone-Calhoun tussled, struggled with his bulk, a small woman carrying the deadweight and ego of Goliath. She grunted and groaned and helped the judge stuff himself back in their ride.

She came back to my driver's window. More words, more demands were made.

She straightened out her hair, checked out the Russian Red, and took her time going back to her ride. She left me trapped like a prisoner celled up down at 201 praying for someone to post my bail.

Judge did something that set Brownsville off. Dr. Stone-Calhoun raised her hand and smacked the judge twice, then drove away yelling like she was more powerful than his maker.

He had dared to touch the hair on the nape of her neck, seeking affection from his wife.

I turned on my signal and joined late-night traffic fast as I could, made a screeching U-turn so fast and hard my new iPhone flew off the mount and smacked me upside the head so hard I yelled like I'd been shot. Almost had an accident bad enough to flip over ten times.

I didn't slow my retreat. Soon I was clocking ninety in a forty-five, screaming at the top of my lungs, going nowhere fast. The iPhone danced around with the turbulence from my muscle car and ended up upside down in the lap of the passenger seat. Even my phone had pissed me off by not standing its ground when the ride was rough. Or maybe that mount was its prison and it wanted to break free from anything holding it in place. Now it rode shotgun. Misery loved company.

I had no idea that was her ride rolling up on me in loco mode because she drove a hundred-thousand-dollar Lexus LX 570 to UAN. She'd bitched that she had wanted the two-hundred-thousand-dollar Porsche Cayenne Turbo S, but she and the Judge of all Judges had had a little spat right before Jesus's born day and he'd ordered Santa to leave that lesser-value luxury Lexus wrapped in a bow in their driveway as a render of punishment.

His verdict was the ultimate word.

Unless it was about her luxurious Nordic mane, hair done with the crowing of the rooster.

CHAPTER 7

IN LOVE MEMPHIS was a top-shelf lounge and bar, a hot spot out east on Winchester Road. We just called it the Love Club. Or Club Love. Swank with roped-off VIP areas. Private tables. Selective admission. Grown folks. Everybody at my favorite watering hole was at least twenty-three. Three bars of thirsty women dressed like IG models. Plenty of seating. Delicious food. Sis was DJing and making the building rock as the booties popped. The drinking and dancing were nonstop until last call, right before three in the morning. After I parked in my sister's VIP spot at Love Club, I changed from my white shirt to a dressier black shirt. Songs by Yo Gotti, 8Ball, and MJG went by before they started playing my motherfuckin old-school hip-hop jam. The hip-hop Holy Ghost took over my soul. Just like that I had the energy to shake off the negative and head toward the positive vibes I needed tonight. I stepped out of a loveless world and went up in there dancing my Black ass off, Cali Swag's "Teach Me How to Dougie" loud and strong, and I didn't miss rapping a lyric. I showed up and showed out, went up in there acting a fool.

I wasn't going to let anybody in the building out-Dougie this BMFM. You would've thought I was rocking a million-dollar grill with the top row made of Kanye diamonds and the bottom of A-Phi-A gold. This Black man from Memphis let the volcano inside him erupt and showed out like he'd never showed out before. I left my stress at the door and stepped into a spot made to be in the heart of South Beach, only with a whole lot of brothas, a whole lot of sistas, and a couple of white folks. This was a one-eighty from the event put on by UAN, and my emotions felt the same turn.

A white girl was showing out, had her arms bent at elbows, hands moving like some sort of incensed sign language, and she knew how to sway those hips in a grinding way, did all of that while she made stank faces like it felt good and hurt at the same time. I stood in front of her face-to-face dancing my Dougie while she gave it her best shot to beat me down with the sweetest Milly Rock ever danced.

The sisters weren't mad at her; they howled, and everybody gave her some love.

A horn blasted and Sis showed why she pulled two g every time she went to her side gig.

She took to the mic and showed her vocal and lyrical skills. Sis pushed up the fader, busted the meter, shook the tweeter, played her shit sky-high, then switched from Badu mode and put on Dr. Dre's nineties jam "The Watcher." She led the charge and the room was a choir rapping from the heart, because as far as we were concerned, that should be our national anthem.

Sis was styling in a wide-legged soft-pink jumpsuit. She gave shout-outs to people from the Raleigh-Egypt Pharaohs and Sheffield Knights, who were having their ten-year class reunion tonight.

I posted up by the bar in front of a larger-than-life artistic painting depicting a pale-skinned woman, her face ghostly white, full soup coolers that matched her flaming-red fingernails, her mouth open like she was waiting on some unseen lover's happy ending to start. I felt angst, moved away.

Sis was excited, pointed at an empty table in VIP. We met, hugged, then copped a squat. She showed me a new video on Black Twitter. A new racial attack video was posted not long ago.

"Sweet Meat, mane, look. Supremacist called a sista a nigga in a convenience store, in front of the sista's children. A *real* brotha saw that ish and knocked the prick *dah fuq out*. Look at this shit? Damn. I mean *skraight* up knocked that racist ass out with a Tyson to the chin. On behalf of our Black peoples across America I accept all victories no matter how small or Pyrrhic."

Me and my overeducated U of M sister did a fist bump followed by an explosion.

She hurried, paired music with the video, and broadcast the assault on the big screen. "Momma Said Knock You Out" rocked the room as people cheered the Tyson blow. Blackness celebrated that small victory. She came back pumping her fist and dancing in celebration.

When Sis caught her breath, she told me she was glad I had finally left the white folks.

Sis bitched, "Never should have bought that dang Toyota. I was staying at my girl's place Wednesday night. Started the car Thursday at six thirty A.M. It made a loud noise. Got it towed and the auto shop told me the catalytic converter had been stolen from my car. Replacement cost three mf-ing g."

"Three thousand? That's a new used car."

"That was my New York money so I could surprise Momma and take her to see *Hamilton*."

"Never heard of that crime."

"State Farm said that this ish is one of the fastest-growing crimes in Memphis. Mofos can come, hoist your car, and remove your catalytic converter in ninety seconds. Why had I never even heard of this ish of all ish? Got to get a new converter plus purchase a catalytic converter lock from Amazon."

"Will that stop those so-and-sos?"

"Nothing can stop a roughish *summer*-bitch; nothing stops 'em cause they gonna steal whatever they wanna steal; slows 'em down because they have to cut through a lot to get to the converter."

"Welp."

Sis checked the time. "Looked at houses with Momma. We found three more foreclosures."

"Tell me later. Came to party."

"Sho ya right."

I asked, "Where er'body at?"

"Behind that preposition."

"Smartass."

"Only kind of asses U of M makes."

"Where the rest of Momma's Fastest Swimmers at?"

"Like I said, behind that—"

"Quit playing. Where er'body?"

Sis told me that our siblings had carpooled to the casinos in Tunica.

Sis said, "They were up in here acting a fool the last four Fridays and decided to mix it up."

"And nobody told a big brother there was a tailgate party?"

"On the group text you said you were busy. You said you had been forced to attend another white-people movie for work and kick it with pale folks you didn't care to be around at UAN."

"Et tu? Still could've invited me."

"Momma got everybody committed to meeting us on the biz tip too darn early in the morning, hungover or not, so take it out on them when you see 'em."

I smelled that Bitch from Brownsville rising from my pores. She had overwhelmed me, and I could no longer smell Gemma Buckingham, that Fucking Fabulous aroma robbed from me as well.

I went to take a leak and when I came out of the john I ran into Komorebi.

Drink in hand, she talked over the music. "Stanky leg with me and chat about my grade?"

"You're not old enough to get in. It's twenty-five and over tonight."

"I have fake ID from Blue Light Studio and can walk in heels like I'm thirty."

"Stop being a flea in my gotdamn ear."

"I want to meet your sister. Haters all over her because she did a nude photo shoot, well, booty nekkid except for the sexy top she had on that read LYNCHINGS WERE ENTERTAINMENT. TOO BAD WE DIDN'T DIE LAUGHING. I need to meet her. Unlike you she has mad skills and slays at all she does."

"You just crossed a motherfuckin line. Don't come near my sister or my family."

"I can't meet your sister?"

"No."

"I need to be her friend. We don't have to be drop-in friends. Can let her mentor me over Twitter. I'm her fan. Stan hard. Sister went to U of M and graduated with honors. Self-employed. Not waiting on the white man to get a paycheck. The main reason I know we can be BFFs is the music she posts speaks to me. She creates remixes to Jhené Aiko, Nicki Minaj, and Mahmood. *We. Like. The. Same. Music.*"

"I'm going to tell security you used a fake ID to get in."

"Wait. Hold on. Snap. Then Miss Infinity is your mother too. Get outta Dodge. They had a picture of Miss Infinity and N'Jadaka-Marie on Facebook, IG, and Twitter asking to guess who was mom and who was daughter, and everybody across social got it wrong, including me."

"Get the fuck away from me."

I marched away and Komorebi caught me, boobs twerking like a stripper's booty.

"Professor, just talk to a sister for two minutes."

Exasperated, I asked, "Why are you here?"

"Professor Suleman, I heard from Professor Four Ds that the DJ at Love Club is your sister."

"No, why are you here?"

"I am a Black woman willing to do whatever it takes not to fail."

I took a hard breath, didn't need to cause a scene, and followed her outside.

"So, what do I have to do to get bumped up to a B or an A?"

"Do the work."

"While other folks help each other fail upward to the White House, instead of helping me over the wall, you're kicking away the ladder. If you're not part of the solution, you're part of the problem."

"Do the work."

"I went to a public school."

"So did I."

"Worked at Dairy Queen from after school until it closed and studied half the night."

"Piggly Wiggly until sunrise doing stock, then to school with sleep boogers in my eyes."

"My solid Bs and almost As at Manassas were basically low-end Ds in the white system."

"Had the same Bs and a few As that huddled with an occasional C at Carver."

"I didn't go to Houston High or Collierville High or White Station or a private school."

"Neither did I."

"Barely had bus fare."

"Stood in the heat, rain, cold, while others got cars soon as they were sixteen."

"Our test scores for English, chemistry, biology, and history didn't compare to white schools."

"Was the same issue at Carver. Our standardized test scores . . . I don't need to explain it to you."

She was emotional. "I did my best, I swear, and I still need help catching up on certain things. I've never failed a class, not until UAN. Came in blazing, took eighteen credits while everybody else did twelve. Had to drop one right away. I thought I was prepared, but kids from certain schools had already taken the same level subjects in high school and were repeating classes they knew they could get easy As in. I was just starting calculus, struggling with the concepts, and they had taken differential calculus in high school, then took basic courses for an easy A. I don't want to fail. I can't. I don't have parents like theirs."

"We all have the same story."

"You know why I take your class?"

"Because I'm Black."

"And I hoped you'd be able to relate. I had a white teacher and I swear to god I spent so much time explaining Blackness. If he didn't get it, it had to be incorrect or deleted. Explaining your Blackness to them with every assignment, *exhausting*. Wanted a Black woman teacher, you were all they offered. Can't do another Anglo teacher, not if it can be avoided. They Eurify my work up. You can't grade what you don't understand, and I bet they keep Black hands and Black critics' eyes off their work. My last instructor didn't have the perspective required and wanted me to rewrite and make my homemade barbecue sound like his generic mayo.

My high school English teacher told me to never let anyone sterilize and castrate my brilliance until it's powerless and impotent. Miss Hollenbeck understood where I was coming from. She told me my writing was seasoned with some Slap Yo Momma mixed with homemade Kick Yo Daddy, not table salt and regular old pepper, and they can't take the flavor. My last creative writing teacher was from Utah and his 'I don't get it so therefore delete it' attitude killed me."

Impatient and irritated, I took a slow breath. "Anything else?"

"My book gonna be one of the greatest novels ever written. Just don't fix my English because it ain't broken. We be talking just fine. I don't be needing no fixing. You don't get it, go kick rocks."

"Be serious."

"Look, Professor, Black skin to Black skin, I don't have access to another Black teacher in your department. This is why I need you and your help. I need someone who gets me, and I know you do. Review my work again, give me what I know I deserve. Up my grade. Help me over the wall."

"Are we done here?"

"Professor, I know with my swag and having fun breaking standard English like a bull in a china shop, all you see is Manassas High."

"Komorebi, all that to say?"

"I know my *ikigai*."

"Your what?"

"My *ikigai*. That's a Japanese word meaning 'one's personal reason for living.' I know mine. Do you—with all your hubris and chastisement and hypocrisy—do you know yours?"

"Again, so I'm not rude, are we done here?"

She saw I was exhausted with her, but she pressed on. "Maybe we should meet somewhere else."

"What does that mean?"

"Maybe we should meet at the Peabody."

"For what purpose?"

"I checked out your social, Professor. You don't have a woman. At least you're not claiming nobody online, which means you ain't got nothing serious going on."

"Why are you stalking my social?"

"To know who I'm dealing with."

"I don't post my life on social. Where are you going with this?"

"Was thinking that maybe we can get away from everybody, get away from UAN, meet downtown, hook up and watch the famous Peabody Duck March."

"You're offering to meet me at a hotel."

"At the bar. I love it when the adorable ducks swag it from the roof to the elevator and come out to a standing ovation in the lobby, then wobble along the red carpet to the big fountain and take a dip in the waters. We could get a cocktail right there at the bar, chill with the rich folks, watch that cute little duck show, then find a more private spot to conduct our business. We could get our heads right and I could read my work to you so you can hear what I'm saying. I'm not trying to write for white folks. I'm writing for them as much as they are writing for me. And that's the problem, Professor. See, I think you grade me by trite and played out jabberwocky and bullshit like *Jane Eyre, Sense and Sensibility, Little Women, Catcher in the Rye, The Great Gatsby, The Scarlet Letter, Lord of the Flies, Macbeth, Animal Farm, Unwind, Fahrenheit 451, The Outsiders.*"

I added, "*Of Mice and Men.*"

"White folks' literature standards we were forced to read as we assimilated. We get bombarded by their culture and points of view and it's maddening. I don't connect because I'm Morrison, Angelou, Hurston, Achebe, Hughes, Haley, Walker, Baldwin, Chimamanda, Armah, Sanchez. In my blood live African sense and sensibilities. My soul craves the works by Blacks and Africans, works and knowledge and experiences whites will never add to their biased and bland curriculums. I need to learn what's been stolen from me, allowed to feast on meaningful works by other Africans, Forna, Mabanckou, and Dangarembga, not revictimized through the educational process. I am all that set on fire and burning bright blue-white with thermite and rigged with nuclear explosions, and with a little help I'm destined to be a trailblazer for the next generation. I'm serious. We meet. Have drinks. My treat. Watch the ducks. Maybe get a room to have some privacy, review my work. See what happens."

"We're done here."

She made that career-ending offer and I stormed away, marched back toward the Love Club.

She exploded, "Do you know what my damn book is about? Do you even fucking care? It's called *My Existence* and is the Black version of *The Handmaid's Tale*. It's a reflection of Black women put into a dystopian setting of my own imagination, one not far from the truth. We have lived in an American dystopia since the 1600s and I am reclaiming our narrative, not letting it be taken away from us."

I didn't slow down. I was two seconds away from a parking lot fistfight—I sensed it.

"*Fuck you, nigga. Fuck you. Fucking mediocre ass. Fucking fuck you, you fucking sellout.*"

Her Android had been in her hand, a phone with every feature better than what I had on my brand-new iPhone. She had held it turned down awhile, then angled it so the camera blessed my face. She had me at a club, tipsy, alone with her. Her Manassas-going ass had no doubt recorded my every word since she Megan Thee Stallioned her way until she could stand two feet from my face. That former Manassas Tiger was trying to bait a former Carver Cobra, maneuver a setup, get that unearned A any way she could. That was why she wouldn't take a no and bounce. She knew I wasn't riding dirty, because my reputation was as good as the tags on my car.

I danced my frustration through the crowd, sat back down in VIP, scowled, gulped my drink.

Sis stopped checking social and asked, "Why you upset, Sweet Meat? Burning when you pee?"

"Just tired. Dealing with Black folks and white folks is taxing. They find a way to steal everything."

I put my phone down on the table.

Sis said, "Hold up. You got the new iPhone?"

"Hater."

"You like the new iPhone?"

"Yeah. Hadn't had a new phone for at least five models."

"Thousand for a phone."

"Twelve hundred. Apple got me good."

"You got a new laptop and iPad too."

"And now iBroke."

"Don't let Momma find out. She raised you better than that."

I had lied to my sister. It bothered me. This situation had me lying to keep it under control. One day at work doing lunch with Four Ds in the Pyramid I told bruh that I had dropped my iPhone and the screen was cracked corner to corner like a spider's web. Camera was busted, speaker was crackly. I couldn't afford a new one because I was saving to get a newer MacBook Pro. Mine was eight years old. In the high-tech world that made it a jalopy.

The next day when I was driving home from UAN, I got a call from the Apple Store at Saddle Creek to come pick up a few things that had been purchased for me the night before right at closing.

They had all my information. I thought it was a mistake and rolled out that way to help straighten it out. I group messaged the Fastest Swimmers and asked if somebody left something in my name at the Apple Store to be picked up. I joked and said somebody owed me gas money for going out there. They had no idea what I was talking about. Same for Momma.

All of a sudden, I was standing in nerd center looking like it was Xmas. Someone had gone on a shopping spree, then left my name and address on a mountain of merchandise that had been paid for in cash. They reassured me it was all mine. Thought it was a mistake at best, a joke at worst. Or a setup to get me sent downtown to 201. They loaded my car. MPD didn't come after me.

Dr. Stone-Calhoun came by my office the next morning, Starbucks in hand, new dress, blond hair fresh, red lips in a huge smile, winking like we had a secret between us.

She told me she had been my secret Santa. She had been in the Pyramid seated next to me when I was telling Four Ds I needed new Apple swag. She'd ear hustled our conversation and gone shopping.

I told her I'd pay her back. I'd pay her back every dime in installments. MacBook Pro. iPad. iPad mini. Brand-new iPhone.

She told me, "Professor Suleman, now, you know better than to look a gift horse in the mouth."

"Didn't mean to seem ungrateful."

She told me she wanted to contribute to my literary efforts and ensure I was capable of communicating with my UAN students through the portal. Was hard to turn down those gadgets. Dr. Stone-Calhoun told me she liked the new iPhone so much she bought one for herself. No way a woman could shop for someone else and not get a little something to give her that shopper's high. I told her that I'd stayed up half the night like a kid on Christmas playing with his new toys. She had done the same with her new phone, played with it until the rooster crowed.

We laughed a good laugh. Had a kumbaya moment.

Her CNN smile woke up my MLK grin.

I told her she was the second angel I'd met in my lifetime.

She told me we all needed to pay it forward.

Then invited me to go eat Pho.

WHILE I SAT in that memory and hated myself for keeping secrets and telling lies to folks I loved, Sis's phone rang; she put a finger up to her ear and took a call that lasted two minutes.

She spoke up over the music. "Car problem solved."

"Our mechanic hooking you up or nah?"

"Same blessed folks who all but called me a whore in *The Commercial Appeal* because I did a risqué shoot and posted it on IG, they saw how many likes and reposts I have. Haters want to do a nude shoot with a beautiful brown-skinned girl from Memphis. Oh yeah, they gonna pay to get my car fixed."

I nodded. "Once again, I'm in the wrong business. I need some income coming in like that."

"When you're this pretty you'd be a fool not to cash in on it before things go south. I make money by any means necessary as long as it's legal and comes with a binding contract."

"She so vain."

Sis said, "Don't go home without me, Sweet Meat. Need a ride back to 38109."

"I don't accept bus passes."

"Momma dropped me off and refuses to come back to get me. Left me stranded."

"You know she ain't burning up no more gas in her VW than she has to."

"Couple honeys in here want to show me where they live, but I'm not in the mood."

"What happened with the pretty Mexican girl?"

"I was doing shots and told her about my Puerto Rican. Wish I never said a damn thing about that junt. Had me so mad we started going at it and I was about to roundhouse reset her brain."

"You can't keep Kang Rhee–ing everybody who pisses you off upside the head."

"Was about to Ronda Rousey her ass. Like I had to do the crazy Boricua."

"Why did you do that?"

"She was talking about all her lovers, then jumped mad when I talked about one of mine."

"You made that suspicious mind." I laughed. "You're juggling, what, forty-eleven relationships?"

"I want to have fun and play the field after getting out of an abusive relationship."

"You need Jesus."

Sis sang, "Maybe I'm just like your momma; she's never satisfied."

"You ain't never lied."

"That no-count Morris Chestnut–looking . . . I married a *Morris Chestnut*, then left him and got with a *Boris Kodjoe* for a while, his fine ass, but I was too broken and bitter to make a real relationship work."

"Should've listened to me when I gave you my report after they came to Sunday dinner."

"With your whack relationship skills? How dumb is that?"

"Pot calling the kettle black."

"Smarter than you. I went to the U of M. You went to UAN with the haters and copycats. Worst football team ever. Y'all can't beat a FedEx corporate team in nothing involving a ball or a bat."

We laughed to hide our individual pains. A couple of people stopped by, flirted, left.

I told her, "They all over you tonight."

"I enjoy having these fools and heifers eat out of the palm of my hand, trying their best to see me again. It's not too difficult to juggle everything. I have it figured out. I see them on different days."

"You not messing with any of our neighbors, are you? Wouldn't be cool."

"Sweet Meat, I don't want anybody who can pop in without burning up a tank of gas. My traps are way out in Moscow, Atoka, Mason, Oakland, Brunswick, La Grange, Grand Junction, Eads, Dancyville."

A ginger made his way by all the brothers and came up to the table and introduced himself. He came on strong yet respectful, had swag like comedian Gary Owen, and was trying to get my sis.

Sis huffed. "I've been known to date a few odd men in the past, never had a particular type, but a white guy with dreadlocks ain't it; hard pass on that shit. Won't be a Sunday dinner for him."

The room was on the floor, dancing the sprinkler, white boy throwing it down.

I said, "Gingerbread Man said he ready to marry you and spend the rest of his life dancing."

"Not funny, Sweet Meat. Don't hate because I awaken the thirst of all in my view."

"I'll check back tomorrow to see if we need an extra place setting on Sunday. One that requires extra mayonnaise in the potato salad. You're mean to the people you really like."

"Hate you, Sweet Meat. Can't stand you because you know me too damn well."

Sis took to the floor dancing, showed everybody how it should be done.

Sis was one of the most talented people in the state: singer, songwriter, rapper, record producer, dancer, actor, painter, video producer, artist, drummer, graffiti artist, basketball player, stuntwoman, fashion designer, and content creator. Jill-of-all-trades. And like Komorebi had said, had billboards across M-Town. I was an adjunct by day. For the paycheck. Then half of most nights I went into my fortress of solitude, became a struggling novelist with an idea for a comic book no one gave a shit about.

Kanye came on and I jumped to my feet and joined in, looked to the sky and led the booty-shaking walk with Jesus, white girl rocking booty-length box braids at my side, my ally and loyal disciple.

Women were all over the place begging to get a taste of me, and London wanted to get chased. The way women outnumbered men and would be ready like Freddie in a teddy in the beddy in two heartbeats, only a fool would play games and waste time figuring out a math problem when he had no idea if the half a phone number she put in my phone was straight-up bullshit. Only a fool would play games with a woman wearing Fucking Fabulous just because she looked like she'd be a fabulous fuck.

Thoughts of Gemma Buckingham were demolished when I raised my head and realized the enemy was watching me. She'd watched me since I arrived. No matter where I moved, she taunted.

Bitch stared at me, was high over my head like an overseer on his horse.

The arresting artistic painting of the ghostly white woman with Russian Red lips followed me, stalked me everywhere I went, her mouth open and ready to rob a stronger man without using a gun.

CHAPTER 8

WE LOADED UP my Nova with Sis's DJ equipment: monitor, speakers, mixer, turntables, headphones, vinyl records, a laptop computer, and software.

Soon as she got in, she turned her nose up. "Why does your car smell like a Becky Sue?"

"What?"

"Smells like white woman perfume. Smells like Riverside Park in the bushes on a Friday night."

"Let the windows down."

"You been in here smashing a white girl? Is that what you did when you vanished for a while? You run off with that white girl who was on you like butter on toast? Don't have me sitting in your mess."

I shrugged it off. "Gave a coworker a ride to her car at UAN."

"Your clothes smell like that ride too. White woman perfume. Must've been a doggie-style ride."

"Hugged a lot of people tonight at the event, so I might have a bit of perfume on me."

"This one fresh and strong. I better not be sitting in no DNA or mess she left behind."

"I'm a cocoa-butter man. Some patchouli every now and then. Never been into the quiche."

Sis picked up a strand of blond hair left behind by my personal doctor Svengali, the Bitch from Brownsville. "Hair all over the dash. Bitch shedding like a Saint Bernard."

"She combed her hair while I was dropping her off."

"Last girl I saw used to do that. Pissed me off how she left weave all over the place."

The evidence no doubt had come loose when Dr. Stone-Cockhound had hand combed her precious mane, and it had floated and landed on the dashboard. That meant her hair was all over my car.

The Bitch from Brownsville was as inescapable as air.

Anger rose.

I almost told Sis, wanted to, needed to tell somebody, but I reeled it back in. I was a strong Black man. I could fix this shit. One way or the other, I'd fix this shit. Then we were humming toward South Memphis, windows down, stank of perfume thinning. Going down Winchester Road I cruised by one of Sis's billboards. Another one held sentry over on Lamar Avenue. She was definitely Memphis famous.

I smiled at Sis, teased her, gave her a fist bump with an explosion. She was outdoing all of Momma's Fastest Swimmers.

Love Club was forty-eleven southern subcultures and sixteen miles from Blair Hunt Drive, about twenty country minutes from the 38125 to my driveway in the 38109. There was no traffic and most of the route was across I-240. At three in the morning, two hours or so before sunrise, it was a soothing ride. The predawn breeze on a warm summer night between the old night and a new day was melatonin to the soul. Con-FunkShun's "Love's Train" played; we sang that mood, but my mind remained elsewhere. In my mind I saw a league of white men in pickup trucks coming after me, trying to box me in a corner, guns and ropes in hand.

I said, "I need to go to Southaven tomorrow, after the house hunting."

"Where?"

"Gun shop."

"I love Double Barrel Gun Store. What you looking for? I want a new Glock."

"I need a new shotgun to go with the one I have. Might look at hand-guns too."

"You can get a shotgun same day, got both mine there, but a handgun has a waiting period."

"I know. Not sure what to get. Something that makes thunder sound like a whisper."

She grinned, excited. "Get a Benelli Montefeltro. So far as a handgun, stick to a nine."

"Need both. Be like you and Momma. White folks acting up at mov-ies, concerts, and in the house of the Lord, so we gotta give the NRA-loving folks some business and get ready for the revolution."

"I can sell you one of my nines, then use that skrilla to buy my Glock."

"Nah. You stay woke and stay ready. I'll get my own."

"Something going on I need to know about?"

"Racism. Always hunting season."

Sis yawned. "We should hit Bullzeye Shooting Range tomorrow."

I caught her yawn, then changed the subject, said, "The foreclosures. What y'all see?"

"Three spots. We scoped out a three-bed, one-bath on Bradley."

"How old?"

"Built in the forties."

"How bad?"

"It needs a lot of work."

"How much?"

"Bids started at one thousand dollars."

Not knowing if I'd have a job much longer, I sighed. "What else?"

"Looked at a crib that was in a little better shape on Frisco."

"How much?"

"Worth thirty thou and the opening bid is at twenty."

"Too much."

"Looked at the last house on Alford Street, and they want the bid to start at thirty thou."

"Cancel that one too."

"Just telling what we looked at."

"You and Momma get together and sign a contract on the spot because you think it's a good deal. We do as we planned, stick to properties that we can Section 8 so we get a guaranteed part of the rent from the government. Next thing I know you and Momma will scheme and have us trying to buy Clark Tower and the Raymond James building downtown. I told you, we have to be conservative with—"

"But if we don't take any risks, we can't make—"

"Section 8 stuff so we are guaranteed a monthly check from the government."

"Don't yell at me. It sets off my trigger. Don't ever yell at me."

"I get tired of repeating myself and wanted to be clear."

"You know when men yell at me the way my ex—"

"I hate repeating myself."

"—like my ex always did . . . it messes me up, Pi."

"I'm sorry. Look, you know I'm not making wipipo Germantown money, so I have to make sure I don't overdo what I can do, that's all." I took a breath, that deeper fear still hidden, masked as I pretended my anger was about real estate. I patted her hand, knew her history. "We good?"

"Momma wanted to go look at a foreclosure that could be used as an office, or a beauty and barber shop, or rented out to be a daycare or something."

"See? Clark Tower."

"I'll need your two g, your part of the investment, depending on what we do this time."

"Okay. My joke of a royalty check gets here next week, so I can't do anything until then, unless you float me. Either way, I need to see the properties before I dehydrate my malnourished piggy bank."

"Don't yell."

"Not yelling."

"Don't make me get upset, black out—"

"Didn't I say I'm not yelling? This is not yelling."

"You get overexcited, get upset and get loud, and you get this look that is scary, and it looks like you 'bout to have a hissy fit and one of those personalities inside of you, the one from so deep in the hood Tupac would've been scared to go there and Biggie would've kept away, it makes me defensive. I look at you and I swear your way of thinking, the words inside your head change, like the way *Flowers for Algernon* was written and the main character can't remember his name, evolved and then devolved in the way he represented himself in writing based on his mental state. Too tired to analyze you. Don't call it code-switching, because when you hit Blair Hunt a brand-new you there too."

She covered her mouth, yawned, leaned against the window, closed her eyes.

"Shit."

"What?"

"No wonder I'm cranky. It's almost time to leave an impressionistic painting under the blanket."

"Long as it's not in my car."

"I hate you."

"Go to sleep."

Sis shifted around until she was breathing easy. Seconds later she was gently calling hogs. I low-rapped some of the fun song Momma loved, "Life Is a Rock," to stay occupied, was having fun by myself until my phone rang. It was Dr. Stone-Calhoun yanking my goddamn motherfuckin chain again.

I hung up. She called back. We did that dance five times back to back. I didn't want to wake Sis.

The blond Bitch from Brownsville was the soft-legged monster in my ever-shrinking closet, a constant bugaboo that kept this BMFM as restless as a terrified child, the beauty queen who made it impossible for me to catch forty winks and sleep properly, because I, too, was an early bird and I, too, woke with the crowing of the roosters. With her in my life, the cry of a rooster heralded the evil of the day to come. She kept calling, yanked my chain until I clicked the flashing green. I almost answered cursing her out but didn't say a gotdamn word. My nasty mood was in my breathing, undisguised. Just like hers.

CHAPTER 9

IN THE TONE of an innocent southern belle reminiscent of Scarlett O'Hara in *Gone with the Wind*, she asked, "Professor, hear what happened tonight? It will be all over social media by morning."

Jaw tight, I responded. "Okay. I'll play along, Doctor. As a parting gift, I'll play along."

"The Judge and I were on the way home after an event honoring Memphis's own former Miss Tennessee Cybill Shepherd put on by the almighty Pharaohs. On the way home we stopped because the judge we all know, respect, and love, my Good Samaritan husband, saw one of the UAN's adjunct's vehicles on the side of the road. He thought we had come across someone in their time of need. We stopped like any good Christian in Memphis would do. The judge had a bad headache, so I volunteered to go see if my coworker needed any assistance. So stupid of me. Professor Pi Suleman asked me inside his vehicle to show me the problem. He had been looking at me oddly all evening at both the movie and its after-party, now that I think back on it. His eyes were on my bosom when he came to conversate with my husband and several other colleagues. They noticed too. Five witnesses. Once I was foolishly inside of his red Nova, he asked me to do him a sexual favor, a disgusting sexual favor, and when I refused, he demanded said favor, and when I said no, he became violent and assaulted me while my husband, our Judge of all

Judges, was ten feet away. He threatened to do bodily harm to the judge if I yelled. He was going to harm the man I love second only to God. Professor Pi Maurice Suleman and his South Memphis ways assaulted my mouth repeatedly. Sodomy. It was disgusting, but I was saving the life of my husband by sacrificing my reputation and capitulating to being sodomized. I cried for my Lord and savior to save me from that animal while being manhandled. I am a fragile woman and had no other choice in the matter. He did that humiliation practically in front of my husband. And since he tried to force me to ingest his disgusting behavior, and I'd never do such a thing, and he came like a racehorse, I spat to keep from being choked to death, and I have at least half a gallon of the come stains soaking into my brand-new silk designer blouse to prove it."

Silence from me, heart rate elevated, as my sister snored.

I'd bring a generation of shame on Momma and the Fastest Swimmers.

A new ton was added to my lazy man's load.

Point made, her tone became a hurricane. "Do we have a problem, Professor?"

"Doctor, if you don't think we have a problem, that means there is no problem."

She took a breath and dialed it back. "To be clear, we can find ways to be comfortable and make this work out in both of our favors. I have always been the smartest one in this survival of the smartest. I came from Brownsville, and look at me now, dining with kings and queens. Down here every smart southern woman secretly brags about how she has outsmarted a rich man and made him a husband. You don't have to worry about me being a tattletale if you obey me without an attitude, because nobody brags about snagging a poor man. Know your value, know your worth, adjust that attitude accordingly."

"We done?"

"Head filled with cotton needs to be picked has the nerve to be insolent with me. Ever since you've let your hair grow wild like the rest of the heathens, you've become quite belligerent. Don't think I forgot about how you embarrassed me tonight in front of my friends. You had quite the prepared speech. Quite the speech. Head filled with unruly cotton,

I'd advise you get that entire field picked clean before I see you again. Do it yourself or have your mammy grasp your black cotton balls at the root and twist every cucabud out of the boll and drop it into a filthy rucksack as she sings gospel. Harvest all of that black cotton from the field at the same time. Or pick a bushel a day. I leave that up to you. Or I will bring new Walmart clippers and help get rid of that nappy so-called black cotton myself. I can garden that batch of black cotton that looks like a dumb Afro on your pretty face. Now, let me go do my vodka routine on my skin and get forty winks of beauty sleep so I can be alert this afternoon. We're doing brunch at the Peabody with my senator and I want to look well rested as we sit and confer regarding arranging me and Judge and my private beautician to an overnight trip to the White House so we can sleep in the Lincoln Bedroom before having breakfast with the president of the United States."

CHAPTER 10

SIS'S THREE-THOUSAND-DOLLAR PROBLEM was chilling out in front of Kansas Street Automotive. Three thousand dollars. If only my problems could be solved by dropping my issues off at my local mechanic. My Nova waved at Sis's ride as we cruised by. Our local mechanic has been keeping my Nova in shape since I bought it from a neighbor who'd lost her husband when I was a junior at UAN. Miss Virginia had seen me breaking my neck to get to the 31 Crosstown Kansas either morning, noon, or night for two years. One day in December, I'd missed the 31 and was standing out in the snow, each exhale making fog, fingers cold because I had to run out without my gloves, trying to figure what I was going to do. Miss Virginia came out on her porch wearing her worn duster and waved me over so I could get my hands warm. She was sitting in the window, saw me running, and saw the bus refuse to stop another ten seconds to let me get on. Told her I was trying to get to UAN, and now I was going to miss my final. She told me I better get my narrow butt a car and stop depending on buses and other people. I told her that was my goal. She asked me if I wanted to buy her car. Pointed at the Nova, a car I couldn't afford because I barely had bus fare. I had enough coins to get to UAN and back, no extra change for snacks in between. Told her that I was flat broke, and that was no joke.

Miss Virginia laughed, shook her head, said, "Lawd have mercy."

She went into her kitchen, opened a drawer, rustled around.

Her house was comfortable, warm. I took in her world. Pictures were up of her during the civil rights movement. That history paused me.

Miss Virginia came back jingling keys and saw me looking at Black history. She told me that she and her husband had marched in dozens of protests. Had just as many arrests. She told me that she and Herman were beaten and bloodied one Sunday in Alabama for trying to cross a bridge named after a racist. They were with MLK and others. They were taught to take the beating, turn the other cheek, not respond to violence with violence, have a peaceful spirit despite the broken bones and head injuries they suffered. She made it possible for us to attend UAN and MSU. She'd stood with Herman and done the work.

She said, "It's your turn to get across town and do the work we've made possible for you to do. We fought to get our people into UAN."

She handed me the keys to the Nova. Told me she couldn't drive a lick, didn't plan on learning when she was this close to meeting Jesus. All that red car was doing was getting dirtier by the day and dry rotting. She said that she swore to God that red car called my name every time I stood across the street waiting on the 31 Crosstown Kansas. The Nova had been so dirty it had looked gray to me. Miss Virginia told me to get to my college and take that final exam. Said she was selling me her deceased husband's car, that would make Herman smile, and I had no other choice because it made her heart sing when she knew her Herman was smiling down on her from heaven. So far as money, I could pay her whatever it was worth to me whenever I could afford to pay it. If I didn't pay one thin dime, she would be fine with that too. It was near Christmas and she would call it a Christmas present and not look back. When you give something to somebody, you should mean for them to have it. All she needed me to do was take that final across town at UAN, and toot my horn every time I passed by her house on Kansas Street, so she'd know everything was all right. Tooting the horn would make her Herman smile too. I would've thought it was a joke, but she signed over the pink slip on the spot and designated the Nova as a gift. She did that to keep title transfer and registration fees at a minimum. I wasn't going to take her car and not pay her what it was worth; I wasn't raised that way.

She said, "College boy, just pay me what you can when you can."

"I promise, I'll pay you what's worth plus—"

"Just what you think it's worth is fine."

I broke down crying, hugged her like she was my madear, and she had to shove me out the door. Her friend Miss Callie was coming to run her to the grocery store at Southgate, and she had to get ready.

Miss Virginia told me, "Do the work. Do the work and make all us proud. We had a gal killed at those apartments on Vaal the other week, and the paper came over here and what they wrote about us made it sound like we were animals living in a jungle. I see you doing something positive, and God told me to help you. For me and Herman, do the work, don't cheat, show them who we really are on Kansas Street, and if they let you, get your picture in the paper holding that degree in their faces."

I drove away a poor country boy with tears in my eyes vowing never to let my people down. One problem was solved, and another came to life. A Black man got a secondhand car from an angel, upgraded his life, moved from chasing the 31 Crosstown Kansas every day to learning the price of freedom. I became a target. Once a young brother had a hoopty the police fucked with him every time his tires hit the rich side of Parkway. I had a car and all the rocks that came with the farm.

I paid Miss Virginia back bit by bit, gave her seven hundred for a five-hundred-dollar car, never missed a class at UAN, and did the work.

Every time I passed her house, I blew the horn.

CHAPTER 11

"BABY DOLL. BABY Doll. Baby Doll. Yo. Yo. Yo. Wake up, wipe the slobber from your face."

"Only Momma get away with calling me that, Sweet Meat, not you. I'm not your Baby Doll."

I laughed and playfully whipped into her paved driveway hard enough to toss her like a runaway iPhone. She had a two-bedroom, one-bathroom home that was about a thousand square feet.

I said, "Your grass needs cutting."

"You kill me with that grass shit." She stretched. "Help me get unloaded."

As soon as I killed my rumbling engine, the living room lights in a two-level brick house next door came on. Pretty redbrick house with white trimmings and red awnings. Big shade tree in the front yard, property lined with hedges three feet tall. Yard immaculate, rooter to tooter. A red-and-white twenty-inch sign greeted whoever stepped in her front yard.

NO SOLICITING

FOR ANY REASON

NO EXCEPTIONS

BUH-BYE

STILL HERE!

I POLITELY INVITED
YOU TO LEAVE
NOW YOU'RE
TRESPASSING
TURN AROUND
NOW
KEEP IT MOVING
GO
FASTER
FASTER
BUH-BYE

While we were getting out and sharing yawns, Sis's next-door buga-boo shoved open her front door so hard and fast it scared us both.

"Y'all done lost your minds screeching in the driveway like you doing a drive-by."

A beautiful woman dressed in red-and-white Nike gear marched out. Her natural hair was long top, short sides, sassy, curly, and überchic, a tapered natural Afro with subtle color designs on the sides. She was in incredible shape, like Ernestine Shepherd and Elisabeth Akinwale wrapped into one.

I stretched. "Hey, Momma."

Momma snapped, "Fastest Swimmers, don't pull up with all that racket at four in the morning."

Momma called all of us the Fastest Swimmers because in the mara-thon of millions we were the winning sperm to swim to the egg, to fer-tilize her egg. The Fastest Swimmers. Her children. My siblings.

Sis said, "*Wayament*. Thought you were going to the gym when you dropped me off."

"You thought like lit."

Momma's weighed-down gym bag was at her side.

I said, "You're carrying a lazy man's load to your punch buggy?"

"Momma hate making two and three trips. Sweet Meat, you know that. Don't talk stupid." Then Momma called behind her, "Momma Nike ready to go to the gym. Finish in the bathroom so I can roll."

Her front door opened behind her. A melanized-as-a-Moor, dark-as-a-blue-Weimaraner, well-built brother who was definitely a gym rat came out of my mother's immaculate home. He was wearing shorts and a FedEx T-shirt. He stood next to her. Nervous. He was about five seven. A clean-cut brother.

Momma said, "Black Kevin, these my hardheaded children. Two of 'em, anyway."

She went back inside to turn her lights off. She did that to leave us alone with the dude.

Sis became confrontational. "What you do, Black Kevin?"

"Work at FedEx. Handler. Hold up. Ain't you . . . ?"

"I used to be one. College gig."

"You're on the billboards. A celebrity. Talking to me. I need to get a selfie."

"I don't do selfies with randoms at four in the morning. Black Kevin your real name?"

"Kevin Black my government name, but they flip it for fun."

I asked, "Where you meet my momma?"

"Game at the Liberty Bowl."

Sis asked, "You took her on a date?"

"We went to Civil Axe Throwing. She's good at throwing axes. Took her to Insomnia Café a few times. To the movies three or four times. Horseback riding at Shelby Forest. She really y'all momma?"

Momma came back out. Black Kevin told her good night and headed to a Chevrolet that was parked on the street. He took a hard U-turn, went south toward New Horn Lake Road and I-55.

I said, "Lover boy banged a hard and cold U-ey like a pro."

"That's not all he banged." Sis stood with her arms folded across her breasts, fiery eyes chastising Momma as if Momma were the child. "Your ephemeral romances. You need an intervention."

I announced, "Let the clapbacks begin."

"My ephemeral romances are nunya business, hater."

"You get 'em out the door before the 31 Crosstown Kansas start running."

"What's that to you, Baby Doll?"

"Momma, get a man your age."

"A man my age wants a little girl your age because she too easy to impress."

"It's embarrassing. My neighbors can see your business and pass judgment on me."

Momma asked me, "Sweet Meat, gas in your car?"

"Ma. Really? What's wrong with your punch buggy?"

"Don't make Momma stop on Parkway and get gas in the darkest of the dark. You know two people got shot at a filling station on Elvis Presley Boulevard and South Parkway at one this morning. Cops anxious to put Black folk in handcuffs so let me get to the gym before MPD wake up hashtagging."

I handed the queen my keys. "Make sure I have half a tank when you bring it back."

"If I bring it back on *E*, you bet' not say a word, as much money I've spent on feeding you."

"Well, drop me off at home."

"Boy, walk. I'm going the other way. Gas prices too high and you got two good legs."

"You always bring it back on *E*. Out of gas and dirty."

"Wash it, fill it up, problem solved. Now, give me some sugar." Momma tiptoed and kissed my cheek before she hurried and hugged Sis, kissed her too. "Hong Kong Phooey, you're getting fat."

"Hong Kong Phooey? Could you be a bit more racist?"

Momma's playful tone took a sabbatical. "Racist? How is that racist?"

"Asian I dated said that show was filled with stereotypes. Racist."

"Heifer, please."

"You don't have to call me out my name."

"Black women been at the bottom of the barrel since we were stolen from Africa and forced to be here having white men's children and forced to wet-nurse white women's babies, and that funny you don't like because it's about you makes me racist?"

"Momma—"

"You just jumped the shark and took this morning in the wrong direction. I sent your volatile ass to Kang Rhee when you were in middle school until you got your second-degree black belt. You do that karate mess. It was a damn karate reference. And I get dragged into left field and called racist before breakfast? Momma made a very funny reference to a cartoon kung fu dog that had a very funny name, a reference relative to my generation, did a joke referencing a cartoon from the seventies whose voice-over was a famous Black actor named Scatman what's his face, and again the cartoon dog used the voice of a Black man, so the dog was a goddamn Black man, and the dog was given the secret identity of a lowly stereotypical jive-talking janitor. And I'm racist? That's what America fed us Black folks on Saturday mornings. If anybody should be offended, and offended on at least two levels, it's a nation of hardworking Black people. But guess what? We watched it from our redlined districts and laughed, then when *Soul Train* came on we all danced to another Black man singing he was kung fu fighting, and the lyrics had more stereotypes than an Archie Bunker diatribe. We all danced together and still laugh and dance the bump when the song come on. That make me and other Black folks racist too?"

Sis tried to shut her down. "Okay, Momma. Okay."

"Learn your history and respect mine and stop trying to be so faux politically correct when it suits your needs. Y'all overdoing it. I lived that era, revisionist history not needed. Every show or movie white people made in the seventies was racist. Almost every Black woman on television was a prostitute and every Black man was a damn Huggy Bear stereotype in pimp shoes. We lived past civil rights and swam in racism to get a paycheck. Bugs Bunny had racist episodes on repeat and to this day they still show Judy Garland in blackface on the white folks' movie channel, and Agatha Christie had a book called *Ten Little Niggers.* So sit your ass-wanna-be-woke tail down with that momma-you-racist racist noise."

"Momma, neighbors are in the window."

"What funny to Momma gonna be funny to Momma until it ain't funny to Momma. Are we policing all cartoons and shows from days gone by? Let Momma know so I can submit my list."

"Momma, can you leave and go to the gym?"

"Momma not done. Finally, you grew up under my roof and you know this is my humor, the way I tell my jokes, my South Memphis world unobstructed by any opinions be it Black or white or Asian, and this is what I laugh at on my side of the railroad tracks, appropriate or not to outsiders and others, and I do it unapologetically. Be careful who you let influence you. If the others come to my world, they better adjust themselves accordingly, just like I do when I go into theirs. Called me racist. Over a good joke. That would've gotten a big laugh in any Black comedy club. My own daughter has forgotten her people's history. My oldest daughter. Stop poking your lip out. Get dog-walked. Yes, I'm offended. Momma humor is gold. As other cultures have their own humor that only insiders appreciate, you know we have our own, so adjust your attitude before I revoke your Black card. Understand me, little girl?"

"Yes, ma'am."

"That's more like it, Baby Doll. Hit me with a low blow and Momma won't hesitate to cut you off at the knees. Be glad I only hobbled you this time. Now, firstborn daughter, what's your problem?"

"I'm just tired and irritated and hungry."

"Get in line. I've been up all night."

"We noticed."

"I think it's time for you to come home and start dating Black folks again. Enough is enough."

"And that's not racist?"

"Little girl, don't try me."

"Okay, Momma."

"Momma done."

I said, "Sis, you know trying to win an argument with Momma is like trying to out-sing Patti LaBelle while you're ten feet underwater."

She snapped, "Oh, go to hell, Sweet Meat. Go directly to hell."

They always got like that. Generational differences. Different experiences. One moment like sisters, and the next like mother and child. Momma served hard truths based on her experiences as a Black woman from Memphis. Whenever she went at it with one of the Fastest Swimmers, I stayed out of it. Momma had endured a lot as a Black woman, as a Black woman of the less-favored hue, and had been triggered by one word, by one accusation, and had picked up her weighty history, the unseen things all Black women carried, and gone into a mix of momma and professor mode, but she cooled down. The way I argued, the way I lectured, the way I got triggered, I got that passion from her blood. At times my voice was the echo of her pain. Sis backed off, deferred to the queen. The queen took a breath, then gave a smile that said she loved us no matter what, but be careful what you said. She was a fun momma, but still Momma. Sis went to Momma, leaned against her, acted like she was all of five years old.

Sis asked, "Ma, argument over?"

Momma said, "Moving on."

"Please do. You gave my cramps a headache."

"And you gave me a heartache."

"Called me fat."

"Called me racist."

"Don't hate the curves, She-Ra. Real men like a woman with some softness around the edges."

"See my IG? I jumped fifty inches vertically from a seated position."

"I'm a size six, Memphis-skinny, our size zero minus two."

"Sweet Meat, I caught Baby Doll eating a KFC chicken sandwich doughnut burger monstrosity."

"I took one bite to see what the hype was all about."

"Stop wasting your money on these high-cholesterol fried chicken trends. Eat with me when I eat. I had two cups of white sushi rice, cinnamon, vanilla, unsweetened almond milk, and Truvia."

"And a protein shot."

"Baby Doll, last time, don't get dog-walked."

"Momma, because you look twelve doesn't mean you have to act it."

"I follow you on IG. How much more naked you plan on getting?"

"I'm in workout gear, getting the likes you wish you were getting."

"Thirsty as thirsty can be."

"Look who's talking. The thirstiest of the thirstiest."

"Momma feels parched ever' now and then and takes a quick drink, but Momma never thirsty. Momma don't need no man; man need Momma. That's why they always up in my face and at my door begging to take a sip. Momma a woman. Catch me on a good day or bad night, treat me right, he might—"

"*Momma*. Please. TMI. I am your daughter, not your sister. Act accordingly."

"Baby Doll, 'member who you talking to and learn to do the same. I see your business too. Over there in your glass house throwing stones but can't handle Momma throwing back bricks."

Sis and Momma argued while I unloaded the DJ equipment. After I grabbed my companion, a hunter-leather rucksack overloaded with my laptop and everything I needed to grade papers, or work on a novel or my Vathlo comic idea, at any coffee shop or library, Momma kissed us good-bye.

Momma said, "Momma gone. Bye."

Momma revved the recently rebuilt 350 engine of my Nova hard and loud enough to piss off every neighbor between Joubert and Modder, then burned rubber, made the V-8 block yield some respect to its wannabe NASCAR driver. She took off, seventies pop music blasting on the radio.

Sis said, "If I didn't think she'd move in with me, I'd burn her house down."

"You know she'd move in with me. You have six cats and Momma has allergies."

"Your momma is so immature, crude, childish, infantile, uncouth . . . and I hope Momma don't end up pregnant again. I'm too old to be a sister again. I don't need her to be Eve with no Adam."

"She's too old for that, I think."

"Momma still paints roses in the bed."

"Okay."

"Elizabeth's husband, Zechariah, refused to believe when an angel said his old-ass wife would become pregnant, yet she did, so the same could happen to Momma. Just like Abraham's old-ass wife, Sarah. With my luck she'll have a baby, die in childbirth, and I'll have to raise the rug rat because I know you and none of our lazy and no-'count siblings would lift a finger to help. I'll run away and eat locusts and preach in the wilderness if she does. Or put that baby in a basket and send it down the Mississippi."

"You really don't plan on having kids, do you?"

"You go first. You should have two kids like Four Ds by now."

"Money."

"Money ain't never stopped nobody from having a baby. Besides, you got all of us to help."

"Four Ds has been struggling month to month ever since he jumped the broom. He married a woman who don't work and won't work and uses those twins as a reason to stay home in bed all day."

"Four Ds our play brother; you're our real brother, and we ain't letting nobody struggle."

"He's happily married. Don't hate."

"Nobody with two kids working the same job and eating the same pussy or sucking the same dick for ten years is happy. No one is happy when all they do is work, do laundry, cook, and look after kids. Seems like all we do as women is fight to be free from misogyny and the bullshit put on us in a patriarchal society, then find some way to make ourselves slaves again. Just the idea of having to schedule a date night like it's a business meeting, having to schedule a fuck night, takes away all the spontaneity. No one is happy. He's pretending and she's lying to herself. That's the way it goes."

My mind went back to the way Four Ds had stared at Komorebi's new style tonight. Was too hard for him to ignore a beautiful Black woman with a body and who walked in heels like she was thirty.

I yawned. "Get some sleep. Eat some chocolate and pop a few Midol too."

"Burn some sage in your car when you get it back. Get rid of the negative energy left behind."

We kissed cheeks.

I adjusted my heavy backpack, pulled it on proper. Sis went inside, made the porch light flash three times to signal she was safe. Cicadas were singing. They loved to mate in the fig, peach, and apple trees a few neighbors had along the block. When I was yawning toward Blair Hunt Drive, a dog began savagely scratching on the sidewalk. *Savagely.* Another sign that there would be a death in the family soon.

CHAPTER 12

WHEN I GOT to my house and moved past the tulip poplar tree whose roots were buckling my driveway, I saw the tip of a cigarette light up on my next-door neighbor's porch. Wasn't surprised to see a six-foot-five, thin silhouette sitting on a metal chair in his underwear, bony legs crossed.

I called out, "Mo Fo, Mr. Moses Ford, that you out here in the middle of the night?"

The sole white man living at my end of the block called back. "Enjoying the quiet. Had a Yoo-hoo, now sipping on a beer, smoking a joint, and hiding from everybody I love who live inside my house."

His wife called out, "I heard that."

We laughed.

I said, "Good night, Pokey."

Her name was Pocahontas Rebecca Ford. We called her Pokey. Pokey was a nurse three or four days a week and on her days off she was the neighborhood Cake Lady. She baked cakes so good they made you want to slap your momma and drop-kick your daddy. Pokey was parsimonious to the nth degree and made all of their family's clothing. Socks, drawers, everything. Her well-behaved kids always looked good. Like Kardashians. Pokey sat at her old sewing machine and made the best knockoffs between midtown Memphis and Times Square.

She came to the screen door. "Fatima was looking real sexy today."

Pokey was four foot eleven with a middle-brown complexion. She had on jeans ripped at the knees and a plain white T-shirt. Her long hair went down her back in nine braids dyed in deep reds and golds. When it was down, her hair looked like sunrise or sunset over Maui.

I said, "Widow Fatima looks good every day. Always drippin'."

"She only ran six miles at four this morning."

"I was up. Saw her leave."

"She came over for front-porch gossip a little while ago."

"How was our princess looking?"

"Like a movie star. Had on a cute little black dress and shoes that left me jelly. She bought some hot stilettos with a slender ankle strap. They look good on her little feet. Oh, and she changed her hair again. After she ran, she spent all day at the beauty salon giving them lessons." Pokey laughed. "Yes indeed, Little Miss Audrey Hepburn was straight up looking like a beautiful Black Barbie doll this evening."

"Audrey Hepburn. Last time you said the Nubian Barbie doll looked like Jackie Kennedy."

"Well, now she looks like a Black Audrey Hepburn to me. Cute little nose and those perky little lips."

"Rocking stilettos. She must've had a hot date."

"She had a work event today. The doctor from TSU was supposed to escort her, but she says he stood her up and she went by herself. She had flown out to Las Vegas and done a turnaround trip and gotten her hair done at some fancy place she saw online called Red Carpet. Second time this month he's left her hanging. She was hot under the collar."

"What happened to the good doctor?"

"She said he was stuck over in Smackover and left it at that."

"You met him? Anybody met him?"

"Not yet. He's never over in the daytime. Just at bedtime. He pulls all the way up in her driveway and goes in her back door, so we never speak. He drives a real nice Mercedes. I like her car better, though."

Widow Fatima's seven-year-old Nissan 370Z was in her driveway. Silver with black interior. She kept it clean. The frames on her back plates said she was both a graduate of Auburn and an educator at an HBCU. The tag on the front announced her allegiance to her sorority. A bumper sticker said she loved to run half marathons. A flag from the islands hung from her rearview mirror. The two-door coupe screamed she was a SBWNC—single Black woman with no kids. Her Japanese sports car could allow only one passenger in her life at a time. Her car told you who she was. Educated. Employed. Pro-Black. West Indian. Sorority girl.

That was a message for all men who looked at her to think twice.

If anyone wanted to ride in her world, to be close enough to inhale the same air and share energy, they had to be invited, maybe had to wait until her mood was right for their particular company, until space in her heart for a wingman was available.

The sign in the widow's front yard told part of what she believed.

WE BELIEVE

BLACK LIVES MATTER

NO HUMAN IS ILLEGAL

LOVE IS LOVE

SCIENCE IS SCIENCE

WATER IS LIFE

WOMEN'S RIGHTS ARE HUMAN RIGHTS

INJUSTICE ANYWHERE IS A THREAT TO JUSTICE EVERYWHERE

There was no *we* that I knew of, unless it was the doctor from TSU. The sign predated his midnight appearances and before-sunrise vanishings. Nobody knew what that relationship was like. What looked like bimonthly booty calls could turn into a broom jumping down by Big Muddy at the Renasant Convention Center. More than a few neighbors had similar political signs, most posted to keep the unwanted roaches away. More than a few neighbors still advertised for former president Obama.

Pokey hummed. "She still up. She plays soca half the night."

I nodded. "I see her in her front room dancing when she's cleaning."

"Like a peacock showing off for somebody she too scared to say she likes. She calls you Idris Denzel. Says you look like Denzel Washington and Idris Elba had a fine baby and gave him green eyes."

I laughed. "I don't want to imagine my boys Idris and Denzel procreating like that."

"I bet she imagines you like that."

Mo Fo playfully snapped, "Pokey."

"Love of my life, father of my chirren, this a conversation between A and B, so C your way out."

"Stop meddling and trying to be a matchmaker, honeybun."

"You meddle too, my forever boo."

"The widow might not want him knowing all that."

"If she didn't want me to tell him, she know she never should have told me."

Pokey laughed along with Mo Fo. She sang a love song to God by Yolanda Adams as she went back inside their two-bedroom house, a crib that housed five of the best kids I'd ever met in my lifetime. Five kids. After they had twins, they decided to go for one more and had triplets, ended up one shy of being a Brady Bunch. A sewing machine kicked on.

Adjusting my backpack again, I asked Mo Fo, "Everything okay over here?"

"We blessed. Not as blessed as you but blessed enough to look foolish complaining."

Mo Fo was forty, a disabled vet, had two small businesses on the side, a tire shop out east on Jackson and a liquor store up by Carver High School, where he was part owner. He was always in pain and smoked weed to be able to get from one day to the next without killing somebody.

I took a deep breath. It smelled like three or four cakes were baking at the same time, but I couldn't appreciate the aroma. My secrets had created a mental burden heavier than a sky-high lazy man's load on a Tractomas semitruck, and those semis carried 150,000 pounds in one go.

Mo Fo said, "Somebody we never seen before came knocking on your door today."

"Who?"

"White man in an expensive suit."

"What kind of white man?"

"Richer than me by a long shot. Fat man."

"Fat Man he is."

"I saw him once, but Pokey said he came by twice. I saw him the first time. Looked me in the eyes and didn't speak. Didn't bother to wave, but

I waved at him anyway. Fancy car. Fancier suit. Don't mean to get in your business, and tell me when I ask too much, but I saw him, and he looked anxious and I was worried for you. I sits out here half the night cause in the day this house so loud I can't hear myself think, and I've noticed you been up like me all through the night a few months. Not snooping, but you have all your lights on and when it's dark I can see you in there pacing the floors. You're troubled. You don't have to tell me nothing, but if there is anything, anything, I can do to help you, let me know."

"Insomnia from overthinking a few things at work. No problems here that melatonin can't fix."

"What kinna problem you got on the job?"

I had said too much and had to follow up, so I chose the lesser of the two evils.

I waved it off. "SSDD."

He nodded. "Same shit, different day."

"Some people don't listen to your grievances."

"Which one of 'em?"

"Feels like all of 'em came at me tonight. But it's just a coupla white folk and a student."

"Something bad done happened?"

"Let's say if you see a problem and tell them you have a problem with said problem, if they don't think there is a problem, then this isn't a problem, and for speaking up, you become a problem."

"That was me every day in the damn military. Government decided what was a problem. And our job was to agree their problem was our problem. Iraq, Afghanistan, Vietnam."

"Nothing I can't handle. Rocks come with the farm."

He nodded. "Had to ask. Now I know, I can sleep a little better, when I can hear myself think."

"You okay over there? How you been?"

"Between PTSD, a nagging wife, these damn mosquitoes, barking dogs, two roaches, three ticks, dealing with the VA, and five ungrateful children I love like I love no one else 'cept they momma—"

"Love you too," Pokey yelled from the back, sewing machine humming. "You my forever boo."

Mo Fo went on, "I'm all right. Long as I got my weed. Yes, sir. Want some?"

"I'm good. Catch you on the rebound. I got to get up in a couple hours and cut my grass."

"Tell your momma 'nem Mo Fo and his family said hello when you see 'em again."

"Will do first thing tomorrow."

"You making some of that good coffee you make?"

"I got you."

His face illuminated when he held up his phone. "Siri, play me some music by Big K.R.I.T."

Pokey yelled kindly to her forever boo, "Keep the volume down. Chirren trying to sleep."

As I headed across the grass to my crib, my phone rang, number unavailable. I answered.

He slurred, "This number was on my wife's phone. She just called you. Who is this?"

"Who is your wife?"

"Dr. Stone-Calhoun. You are speaking with the honorable Judge Calhoun."

"This is Professor Pi Suleman."

"Why is Dr. Stone-Calhoun calling an adjunct from UAN at this time of the morning?"

To the man who insulted me by dialing my fucking number I replied, "Ask your wife."

There was hard breathing, like Archduke Franz Ferdinand had just been assassinated and this was the start of World War I; then his drunk ass ended the call of the cuckold. His wife's stench permeated me, the stench of scorched earth after a wildfire. Now he'd violated me. That phone call had me ready to grab my shotgun and act like a whole fool.

CHAPTER 13

I WAS SO fucking angry about that call that if Momma didn't have my car, I would've taken a road trip. I threw my overloaded backpack on the unorganized dining room table, then looked at the number the Judge of all Judges had called from. I was tempted to call that motherfucker back and tell him all about his wife.

I was a Black man from Memphis assaulted by a rich white woman who was treated like she was the First Lady of the Volunteer State. My zip code couldn't touch hers. My zip wasn't respected. I was an adjunct. She was coveted. The optics. I didn't have a fuckin chance. I didn't have a fuckin choice. Even if our status at UAN and finances were reversed, she'd come out on top and I'd end up writing letters from a Tennessee jail.

My shame would stain my family and community.

What to do wasn't always clear.

It was torture, but torture was nothing new. It felt like we lived in a state of torture every day. Living in the shadows of Jim Crow, with the PTSD from slavery passed down through our DNA, with the knee of this country still on our necks, Black folks were the kings and queens of grinning and bearing it. I'd grin and bear it. It was a survival skill.

I rocked back and forth like I was on a hobbyhorse. Leaning against the wall by my dining table was my Seagull S6 acoustic guitar. A harmonica kept it company. Momma made sure we all could play a musical instrument. Hadn't played in a while, not even at church. Hadn't been happy enough to sing. I'd maintained a smile in public, with my friends and family, but I hadn't felt musical on the inside.

I picked up my worn and bumped-around guitar, tried to get my Babyface on, but was unable to strum anything that made sense. Tried to sing a song to distract myself, couldn't. I'd been robbed of that too.

What Dr. Stone-Calhoun had done to me felt surreal. Every woman knew another woman who had been raped, if she hadn't been raped herself. But no men confessed to knowing another man who had a rapist.

A blow job. It was just a fuckin blow job. And she was attractive. She wasn't what the stereotype of desperation and depravity looked like.

She looked like a good Christian, the white people's version.

Black women would scoff, laugh, and show the middle finger to my plight. To them, on the road they traveled, I was no victim. I had nothing to be stressed the fuck out about. It was a white woman. Not like I'd been abused by a Scout leader or a priest. That was what I felt, and it hurt like nothing else. They would tell me welcome to their daily pain, to the secret hidden behind their darkest secrets. They would tell me to man up and move on. I nodded, understood, would keep this ish to myself.

Maybe it would dry up and go away.

Maybe she'd sober up.

In the meantime, I kept trying to see how I was to blame for this.

I never touched women inappropriately. Momma taught me early that a man never knew what a woman had been through, how she'd been treated or traumatized in this world. Even if a woman always smiled and laughed at jokes, you never knew what a woman had been through.

I never came on to Dr. Stone-Calhoun. I never put my hand in the small of her back. I never touched her on her knee. Never winked at her. Never leered. Never complimented her. I was work friendly, smiled softly and briefly when needed, always turned off my 38109 swag and used my East Memphis work voice on that side of town, always dressed professionally, code-switched, and sounded like a professional BMFM at UAN. I always stood at least five or six feet away from Dr. Stone-Calhoun.

The unexpected gifts.

Never should have accepted them.

The invitation to eat pho.

Never should have gone.

The grooming, then the assault.

I swallowed, rocked, and chanted to myself, "This isn't my fault. Not my fuckin fault. Keep it moving. Just keep it moving. This will pass."

Had to keep it moving.

Women were assaulted and went to work the next day. They took their kids to school. They went to church and sang in the choir. They prayed and shouted, and no one knew why they were really breaking down and giving in to the Holy Spirit. They compartmentalized, segregated their trauma from other parts of life.

They went on until the lazy man's load was too much to bear.

I went in the bathroom, slammed the door, put my hands over my face, and released a muffled scream, tried to scream the Bitch from Brownsville and the Judge of all Judges out of my gotdamn system.

When I was done I threw water on my face, dried it with a towel, put in eye drops, then called out, "Alexa, play R and B. Level four."

A bumping song kicked on and I scowled.

Alexa was about to get damned and cussed out ten times over.

"Alexa, *never* play R. Kelly music."

"Sorry, I haven't learned to do that."

I laughed at myself, at my rage, at how I was coming unglued, saw my face in the mirror, then joked, "This is why Siri is my side chick."

"Hmm. I don't know that one."

"Alexa, play the Bar-Kays. Momma's playlist. Can you manage that?"

"Shuffling music by the Bar-Kays. Momma's playlist."

My eyes went to all of my neighbors' homes and I wondered who else was up in the darkness of their windows binge-watching mine. At least six families could've seen me looking like a man ready to cut off an ear. The widow would've had a better view than anybody except for Mo Fo. Had to be the reason she barely spoke to me, never came to my side of the road to sit on my porch and gossip, and never looked me in the eyes. She'd see me and look away as fast as she could. She thought I was crazy. She had seen me stress pacing around half-naked, in nothing but my boxers, scratching my balls off and on. They could see me when I moved to certain parts of the dining area. Felt watched by everyone under the moon. Had to act the same Poplar and Dunlap way I'd been acting to seem like everything under my roof was in excellent order.

My home was small, under eight hundred square feet, two bedrooms, one bath, dining room, small kitchen, like pretty much every other house on Blair Hunt and Kansas. I could clean it top to bottom in an hour. Could do a deep cleaning in four. All the walls were white, but in each room, there was an accent wall, a pleasing shade of either red, gold, or green. My queen bed took up most of the bedroom and had bedding the colors of Africa with ankh symbols, same as the rug in my living room. A sixty-inch LG television was mounted facing the bed, took up the whole wall along with my three-hundred-watt sound bar and wireless subwoofer. Another idiot box ten inches larger with a much better sound-bar setup was in the small living room. Books were in every room, but mainly on an IKEA bookcase filled with novels, graphic novels, and comics. A worn NIV Bible was on the front room table. The graphic novel I was working on, and other literary ideas, cluttered the dining room table, a six-foot farmhouse tabletop I made myself but that looked like it came from Pottery Barn. I'd been working on Vathlo Island for a while. I wouldn't always be an adjunct. I'd surpass my father's accomplishments if I did nothing else in life. I'd get my own section at bookstores. Be on CNN. Be asked to travel the world to talk to people about my accomplishments. I'd do it to make my momma proud.

My eyeballs were floating so I hurried into the bathroom, rushed to ease my bladder.

Took a deep breath as water broke water, the relief orgasmic.

I showered, went to the closet, moved my Remington Model 870 Express tactical pump-action shotgun from where I had left it leaning against the wall and put it back on the shelf.

I called my shotgun Lightning. Lightning always came before thunder.

Then I pulled on a pair of golden workout shorts. I cleaned up my dining room. The seventy-five-by-forty-six-inch dining room table I'd made had six chairs, room for the family to have Sunday here when it was my turn to let my castle be our kingdom's playground. I was going to sit at the table, get a few more pages on my Vathlo project done to occupy my mind, work until it was a decent hour to crank up my lawn mower, but first I needed to do something physical, not mental. I took my phone, went to my backyard. As soon as I opened the back door, the sensors lit up. I made sure my yard had no puddles of water to attract mosquitoes. The landscape was immaculately manicured, filled with herbs: lavender, lemongrass, lemon thyme, mint, rosemary, marigolds, common lantanas, everything I needed to create a mosquito-free zone. I had citronella and eucalyptus oils, plus thyme leaves inside to run away the virus carrying bloodsuckers.

A big stack of one-dollar cinder blocks and two dozen redwood slats were in a pile, still pretty fresh from Home Depot. I had used Mo Fo's truck to pick everything up two weeks ago. Had planned on doing this little patio furniture project, then got busy with Momma 'nem. I stacked and arranged two dozen blocks and planks so I could create a rustic flat table. I made a rectangle table base, used more blocks and planks to make four benches. Gorilla tape was wrapped around each end to keep the planks in place.

I heard a noise and jumped, was about to go grab Lightning.

Next door the bedroom windows were down. Their window fan was on high, magnifying sounds inside their home. Reverend Jacob and his six-months-pregnant wife, Leah, were making their bedsprings rock while the headboard attacked the wall. They were having their own little war.

Still restless, I picked up my phone, dialed the next number in the 803 sequence.

Gemma Buckingham answered, her voice smooth, even, wide awake. "Pi, Pi, Pi, Pi, Pi."

"Gemma Buckingham?"

"Pi, your writing. I started reading your first novel when I was in the Uber. Downloaded it from Amazon. It's pulled me in. You don't hide from the grit and reality of the world as you see it. It takes place in Memphis, but it takes me back to Nigeria, back to Africa, takes me to the home my father and grandparents know, to a place in my mind only a few Black Americans relate to."

"Wow, thanks."

"It leans toward the obscene, like Henry Miller. Mostly it highlights materialistic success and moral decline like John Roderigo Dos Passos. But this one particular chapter, the one I now have read a handful of times, it becomes pornography and poetry making love on Grace Bay in Turks and Caicos."

"Porn and poetry making love. If only the reviewers had been so kind."

Her voice thickened a bit. "I've read you, learned part of you, feel as if I now know you in a very personal way, as if I have been allowed to tour inside your mind, and now I see you in a different light."

"What does that mean?"

"Your pen is as strong as a good lover's tongue."

"It's the only instrument I've mastered."

"The pen or the tongue?"

"Flip a coin."

"We have personal and intellectual affinity. It stirs my sapiosexual nature. I find intelligence sexually attractive and arousing."

"I'm a sapiosexual as well."

"Professor, I think I like you. You are different. Foreign. Your accent arouses. Handsome. Stylish. You're exotic to my British eyes. Not just another Mr. Adonic Fandangle. Something about you makes me want to let go of my inhibitions and find a way to disport myself with you in very naughty ways."

"Likewise."

"And you found me."

"I did."

"I will be honest. I told you what I've gone through. Right now, I need a rebound guy."

"An accessory."

"An accoutrement. I need nothing serious. Just someone to help with my Friday night blues."

"Well, I could use a Friday night girl."

"But no drama. Is that too much to ask?"

"Where are you located?"

"Why do you ask?"

"Asking because some people live way out in the boondocks. How far from where I met you?"

"Crump Boulevard and South Fourth Street."

"Whoa, you live in the area that was once upon a time voted the worst in the country?"

"I was advised that there is a fair amount of crime here. I don't know the landscape, which areas to sidestep. Back home I know when to avoid Southwark, Haringey, and Hackney. But I hear it's worse here. Again, your guns against our knives. I use my UK-born common sense and do things in the day."

"You make it sound like you're in a prison."

"I'll be fine, and I am pretty comfortable, which is why I stay in my abode most of the time."

"You live alone?"

"We wouldn't be having this conversation at such an hour if I lived otherwise."

"Where did you land in the 901? General vicinity so I can plan the evening."

"My phone says my latitude is 35.1 degrees north and longitude is 90 degrees west. That helpful?"

"Not at all, but okay. I get the point. Do you dance?"

"I do. But not where your sister works. I'm not trying to meet your family, only to know you."

"Okay. No Memphis jookin' at Love Club. I'll find a spot to burn off the dinner."

"I'm looking forward to having fun in Memphis with one of its acclaimed novelists."

I wanted to talk until sunrise, but Gemma Buckingham ended the call without saying good-bye.

I guess that was how they did things in London.

CHAPTER 14

EARLY MORNINGS BEFORE sunrise, before the Memphis streets were reheated by the waking of the blazing sun, before the heavy dank air was repoisoned by the rudeness and dull taste of fresh carbon monoxide, those cockcrow moments were God's little gift to the South. By midday we were squirming in the basement of hell, drowning in our own sweat. That was why I skipped sleeping and got my chores done early. If I started too late in the morning, I'd catch a heatstroke. I was unable to imagine our kidnapped and enslaved ancestors being tortured and terrorized in the slave master's cotton fields from dawn to dark under an overseer's bloodied whip in the devil's heat. But before darkness broke, each new day was forgiving and invigorating, a promise of a glory yet to come, and each deep breath delivered my skinfolk, friends, and kinfolk to the door leading to the main vestibule in heaven.

An hour before the rooster crowed to shake awake a new sunrise, that was when my widowed across-the-street neighbor came outside. She was twenty-seven, could pass for twenty-one or act like she was thirty-five, depending on her mood. Been a widow a decade. A blood clot shot up her husband's leg and blocked his lungs; a pulmonary embolism took him away. She'd only been married three months.

She yawned as she stepped into the warm and humid air in her form-fitting and ergonomic running gear—rose colored and viridescent against midnight skin. Seeing her made my insides rumble with extreme hunger, grumble like a famished man on day thirty-nine of a forty-day hunger strike. From my window seat across the street, when she returned an hour later, she was dripping melanin as she caught her breath walking her cooldown with her fists on her narrow hips.

I bet the widow's morning post-workout sweat was sweeter than West African thaumatin. I bet each droplet was as dark and pure as it was nutritious, better than premium unadulterated black seed oil from Turkey or Israel, its purity amalgamated with next-level thymoquinone, then mixed with all the omegas a man needed to make her highness his secret fountain of youth.

Just love daily, nightly, and all hours in between.

She was made from the good nutrients, highly educated and sophisticated, but was born on the lesser-valued side of town. Like me. She could revert to being unfiltered, crank up the unrefined when needed. Like me. She was made of sugar and spice and I came from nothing nice. She was capable of being as cold-blooded as she could be kind. Like me.

She was a virgin to my most wicked carnal desires, each hidden behind an innocuous good-morning smile and conversations about slow-changing Memphis politics or the fickleness of the Big Muddy's 901 weather when we were face-to-face with our other neighbors.

We were both professionals at local universities, professors who'd risen above our put-on circumstances.

We were always polite to each other, no matter the season. We waved to each other from our front porches during the winter. We spoke in passing when we ran across each other in midtown during the spring or at a fall game at the FedEx Forum. We chatted in the streets during the summer with a neighborhood crowd. We acknowledged each other as human beings but never had engaged in a conversation one-on-one over the last five years.

We were friendly but not friends.

We were neighbors.

Across-the-street neighbors.

We were connected by living on the same end of Blair Hunt Drive, by being mortgage-paying neighbors. We watched out for each other and kept away from each other at the same time.

Widow Fatima stretched her arms as she went up her driveway. She stopped in front of her one-car garage and did squats for about two minutes, flexed her hamstrings, did twenty push-ups, and from that position gradually went into a gymnastic handstand. She raised herself up until her arms were straight, then raised her legs until she was straight up and down like six o'clock. From there she went into an upside-down Chinese split before slowly bringing her legs down between her arms. She never let her bottom touch the ground. Her control was impressive. She raised herself until she was straight up and down like six o'clock again, repeated that routine six times in a row. She was feminine and graceful with crazy upper-body strength.

I've been out front on a devil-hot morning cutting my bluegrass, no shirt on, and looked across the street and caught her standing in her front window, furtively watching me sweat and labor. Mutual admiration.

TWO HOURS AFTER that I was sleep deprived, pulling stubborn weeds from my bluegrass and mowing my lawn in the Bluff City's morning heat. A new Escalade stopped in front of my house. It parked in the shade that my big tree cast on the street. It was abnormal enough to make neighbors look out of their front windows or step in their doorways. An average-height chubby white man in his early fifties stumbled out just as two black butterflies danced in my face. The heralds of death passed by, but they failed to steal my attention.

Fat Man was back, rocking a gray business suit early on a blistering Saturday morning. Heat was so strong I could throw three eggs on the pavement, add shrimp, and make a two-minute seafood omelet.

The way Fat Man quickly evaluated my blue-collar neighborhood was offensive; he looked like a man behind enemy lines. If this was East Memphis, where there were homes with eight fireplaces, Fat Man with the perfect suntan would fit in, and nobody for two miles would look at him twice. But this wasn't East Memphis. A white, well-dressed man had always been suspicious to my neighborhood.

THE SON OF MR. SULEMAN   99

Fat Man adjusted his suit, smiled like a politico, called out, "Mr. Pi Suleman?"

Right off, his dull and overarticulate accent told me he wasn't from any part of the South. It was a West Coast accent, that neutral pronunciation you heard on television, which, down south, for the white people who waved Confederate flags, was worse than being a Yankee.

Sweat draining down my back, I turned my mower off. "Who wants to know?"

He introduced himself, said his name was attorney Carlton Jones.

Still Fat Man to me.

Fat Man extended his hand for a shaking, but I shook my head, wasn't happening.

I said, "Before I press flesh with a strange man in a suit, I need to know who he is and why he's in my front yard calling out my name like we went to school together or we're Sunday friends at church."

"It's pretty hot out here. And humid. May we go inside your home to discuss this matter?"

"No." I said that like I was a man who never befriended anyone in this world. "Last time my trusting people invited a stranger like you in, he shot up a church. I don't want to talk about the first time my tribe befriended yours on the shores of Africa. Whatever you're selling, I ain't buying."

He swallowed, repeated he was an attorney and had come all the way from his home in Beverly Hills to meet me. Fat Man told me my father was ill, said something had gotten him and taken root, said the man who had statutorily raped Momma was going down slow like a Bobby Blue Bland song. He wanted to meet me, wanted to fly me out to Cali as soon as possible, wanted his illegitimate outside child to go to some meeting with all of his other legitimate inside children, and also wanted me to sign some paperwork in case whatever malady had him leaving on the next train going south got the best of him before I could arrive and stand by his side and for the first time look in his emerald eyes.

"He wasn't interested in seeing me live, so I'm not interested in watching him die."

"He was impressed with your literary accomplishments."

"Why would the man who assaulted my mother send you to my front porch?"

"He's been trying to contact you for a few months, since the initial diagnosis. Mr. Suleman wanted this matter resolved with his estate and holdings before he became confused and incoherent."

"My phone ain't never rang with his number. Why now?"

"He contacted your mother. At her address on Kansas Street."

"My mom was under eighteen. He was a grown-ass married man."

"I flew on a red-eye from Los Angeles to deliver the message and talk face-to-face."

"Since you're the appointed messenger, tell him I said God bless and rhymes with *duck him* too. I'm glad he's made it through the seven stages of grief, same as I have when it comes to knowing he exists. Whatever has him on that train, I'm glad he's traveled through shock, denial, anger, bargaining, depression, testing, and acceptance and arrived at the pre-active or active phase of dying."

"Mr. Suleman, pardon me but it's amazing how much you look like the elder Suleman."

A duplicate of the no-soliciting sign Momma had was in my front yard. I pointed at it, made sure Fat Man read and understood every word.

NO SOLICITING

FOR ANY REASON

NO EXCEPTIONS

BUH-BYE

STILL HERE?

I POLITELY INVITED

YOU TO LEAVE

NOW YOU'RE

TRESPASSING

TURN AROUND

NOW

KEEP IT MOVING

GO

FASTER

FASTER

BUH-BYE

"Now, get off my property before I test the law and have you arrested for trespassing."

Fat Man said something else as he took measured steps in retreat, but I didn't hear him because I had restarted my weary lawn mower and went back to cutting my front lawn.

Neighbors were in their windows and on their porches watching, concerned and nosy.

Fat Man headed back to his vehicle, dabbing sweat on his forehead, then sat in the coolness of his chariot, off my property and on streets owned by the city, on his phone, talking to somebody.

By the time I finished with my backyard and came back to the front, Fat Man was gone.

Mo Fo was out on his front porch, looking like Abe Lincoln in his slim jeans and Barack Obama tank top. "Er'thang a'ight?"

"Some buster from California trying to sell me a bill of goods."

Across the street Widow Fatima Martinez-Bowman came out.

She wore a fitted Auburn Tigers T from her alma mater and a long, colorful salmon-pink and apple-green skirt.

In unison me and Mo Fo said, "Morning."

"As-salam alaikum. Mo Fo. Professor. Morning, gentlemen."

The widow adjusted her pretty skirt, then kicked a small rock with her Roman sandals. She studied her yard, maybe compared it to mine.

Her hair had been pressed and was silver with white highlights. I'd rarely seen her with straight hair. She looked like the perfect Storm.

I called to her, "Didn't see you too much last weekend."

"Was over in Alabama with my sorority and alumni from Auburn protesting and trying to tear down a few more Confederate statues."

I raised a fist and said, "Hello. Tired of living with the ghosts of Jim Crow putting a shadow wherever we stand. Put that racist ish in a riverboat museum so we can set it on fire during a riot and eat ribs from the Rendezvous while we watch it sink like the *Titanic*."

The widow exhaled hard, frustrated. "The things we've had to march for sound ridiculous. To be able to drink from a water fountain. To sit in the front of a bus. To be able to sit at a lunch counter and get a sandwich. To not be killed."

I nodded. "We need more than a statue of MLK here and there."

She mirrored my expression. "We need statues dedicated to abolitionists put up down south. Ain't nothing more American than that. Our history is American history ignored and muted."

Again I nodded. "All day, every day."

"We live on dang streets in neighborhoods named after racist white people, but I've never seen white neighborhoods down south named after Black heroes. I doubt I'll ever meet a family of happy rednecks who live in a trailer park on Malcolm X Boulevard."

"This is too much."

In a West Indies tone that rang of profound dignity and integrity, the twentysomething professor at our HBCU said, "Racism is a delusional act backed by legislation and guns."

In the same tone I asked, "I concur. How do we end it?"

"Black people can march, we can protest, but we can't end racism. We don't have the power. We can't penalize racists for being racists."

"Your argument is flawless."

"We don't have a military. We don't have a bomb. We don't get respect. We're not feared. We didn't free ourselves. If we started a war and we won the battle, if we were granted a state and given sovereignty, we'd still have to trade with other countries, would need to be invited to the world stage, and we see where that got Haiti in the long run."

"Again, how does it end?"

"Racist people started it and they have to want to end it."

"In the meantime?"

"We wave Black Lives Matter banners and march."

"Until when?"

"Until we have the same freedom."

"Why keep protesting?"

"You can't stop water from being wet, but enough heat makes it evaporate. We just have to keep the heat going. We keep the fire going; water can be still, but we don't get to be still. We don't rest."

"You ain't never lied. Our parents, now us. Same issues."

"You know? Fighting for equality from the womb to the tomb is too much. We spend our whole lives fighting instead of living. I wish we could collectively quit America and create a new country."

I said, "Call it New America."

She shook her head. "Not America."

"Nueva Africa."

"Not Africa."

"What, then?"

"Africa's original name. Her erased, forgotten name."

"Enlighten me."

"Alkebulan. The mother of mankind. Our new Garden of Eden."

"Even Africa was renamed."

"If you worked at an HBCU, you'd know your history a lot better."

"Don't start."

"We're Africans. Watered down, but we're Africans. It's irrefutable. Our DNA doesn't lie. America ain't our home. Here it feels like we are trapped in foster care, only it's a system we can never age out of."

"I agree, but we need realistic, ground-up solutions."

"UAN, you have the floor."

"Laws say we're equal. Laws by Uncle Sam. They have to follow and enforce their own laws. Protect us. That's the first step. And they have to back the eff off, allow us to live as free as the freest white men, and protect us the way they do pretty white women."

"They rape their drunken women behind dumpsters."

That triggered me, sent a jolt up my spine.

She said, "He should've been thrown under the jail. He was caught on the downstroke. Caught in the act of rape but he got a free pass."

I nodded, shook off my pain.

She said, "He came from money. He was valued as a white boy and said they didn't want to ruin his future, *his future*. Her trauma was ignored. Her trauma meant nothing to the man who judged that case."

"Good point."

"The evidence shows that the powerful don't think much of their own women. Not in the big picture. They had to beg to vote. Won't give them equal pay. Controlling their uterus like they're doing ours. Men have no business legislating a woman's health."

"I agree."

"But white women, relative to Black women, from where I'm standing, they still have governmental power. The police don't drag teenage white girls wearing bikinis out of pool parties, and there is no white-woman equivalent to Sandra Bland. Not to my knowledge."

"HBCU, no lies detected."

"The problem isn't the law, but how it's administered and who administers it. We don't get the same treatment or the same time for the same serious or frivolous crimes. Our treatment is always draconian."

"So we march. Until the water evaporates."

"We need a moratorium on white folks leading. Particularly white men. Their time is up. So much incomprehensible incompetence."

"Anything else need rectifying?"

"Karen."

"Karen?"

"The white Karen and not Karen White. White Karen calls cops on Black people based on the 'what if' playing inside her head. Not facts. She thinks she's blessed with the powers of the Precogs in the movie *Minority Report*. When the police show up, white Karen lies. White Karen is delusional. Dragging white Karens on social ain't good enough. They are mental, calling cops, hoping we're incarcerated, beaten, or murdered. And they are never penalized for the frivolous calls and eating up my tax dollars. They're using our tax money to harass and hashtag us. Ain't right. We need an anti-Karen law. This goes for all of those Barbecue Beckys too. These incidents are unpunished hate crimes. We don't bother them, but they keep harassing us on the daily."

"Seems that way."

"Because it is that way. I have the receipts stored on YouTube."

We laughed.

I said, "You're in a mood this morning. What triggered you?"

"Guess I am. I saw the French film *Black Girl* and it set me off. Finished watching it this morning. The racism in the first ten minutes had me screaming. Made me wonder, do racists even know they're racists?"

"Do they even care?"

"Did I ever tell you I interviewed at UAN years ago?"

"No, you never mentioned that, Miss HBCU."

"When I interviewed at UAN, the provost, a white man, told me I was well-spoken. Now, you know, I could've done without that."

"Damn. You get that too?"

"I have two degrees. He knew my credentials and . . . well-spoken. Your provost was surprised this Black girl could form coherent sentences and possessed a modicum of a vocabulary. What did he expect?"

"Ebonics and gang signs."

"Was I supposed to walk in eating chicken and watermelon?"

"He didn't offer you some?"

"I was born in the South, have lived in the Bible Belt, up north in two other states, on two of the islands, and I choose to speak with a cute and sassy southern swag at home. I talk Black erudite at work. I know when I'm breaking their language rules. Around them our playful *slippin* becomes *slipping*. *Sammich* becomes *sandwich*. *Skraight* becomes *straight*. And *your momma* becomes *your mother*."

"Well-spoken."

"When the mood hits me I can sound straight Caribbean, or like the perfect Dominican or Cuban, or speak the Queen's English so well Miss Elizabeth would sound illiterate."

"You and me both."

"I've been a bilingual avid reader since I was four. I play piano and viola, did that in orchestra. I listen to everything from NWA to the Eagles, and don't get me started on island and country and blues and African music. Latin music too. I am beyond being well-rounded. Way more than they are. When I was twelve, I studied medical terminology for fun. I road-race cars, read sheet music, go to both Beyoncé and Yanni concerts, have two degrees and ready to obtain at least two more, unique and not fungible, and still have to prove myself to certain effin people while those certain ones always seem to get the benefit of the doubt."

"Exhausting."

"I'm judged by skin color and hair in person and zip code on paper."

"Same here. All day every day."

"I speak what they view as speaking intelligently, better than they do, and they act like I must've come from the darkie side of the moon."

"Intelligence is *never* their default setting for us."

"Stupid is never theirs."

"Never."

"Bet he'd never say that to one of those white girls from Odenville, Alabama. If that's how they greet you, they don't need to meet you."

"Mr. Charlie got your goat that day. Prob got mine the next."

"He said it so darn casually. Saw nothing wrong or offensive with what he'd said. Well-spoken. He told me my skin color was unique, then asked me where my people were born. I told him we were American, like him, and he looked at me like I'd lost my mind. Then he offered me the job and I smiled and turned it down. I walked out of there and drove my well-spoken butt over to LeMoyne-Owen and took a job with my well-spoken people."

"You never told me that."

"Don't get me started on how he looked at my natural hair. *He touched it*. He freakin' touched my hair. Like I was his puppy."

"Some folks will never get it. Hey, let me consult you regarding one of the Black female students I have. A girl named Komorebi Jackson. Get your perspective."

I gave her Komorebi's argument.

"The sister has a point. Why would I let the offspring and DNA of white peeps who didn't allow Black women like me to put a pinky toe in the same swimming pool, drink from the same water fountain, the DNA of terrorists who hit Black women with fists, metal pipes, clubs, chains, and brass knuckles for sitting at lunch counters, to judge and edit and control my narrative?"

"Thanks. I'll take that into consideration."

"Tell her to stay strong."

"She went to Manassas."

"Do high school rivalries ever end?"

"Yes."

"And when?"

"Same day sorority rivalry ends."

"She needs to be at our HBCU."

"When they go low."

"You must be high."

We laughed.

"And I also agree with you too. Upping her grade because she's Black? A sister knows better than to come at me like that. Students are lazy and want everything spoon-fed to them nowadays. She has to get up off her butt and do the work like we did. Ain't nobody gonna gift me a PhD. These trifling students can be on Instagram for three hours but won't study for three minutes. They fail and come to me like it's my fault. Living off federal funds. Mad because they need to be spoon-fed. They plagiarize. Invent dead relatives to get extensions. Lying about everything. I tell them day one that writing-spelling-subject-verb agreements are a must. Adhere to rules of grammar if you want full credit and I'm called unfair for sticking to the law."

"They come to us like we're a shortcut."

"Shortcuts will leave you cut short. Ain't no shortcut worth taking, not for us. We still have to be twice as good to be seen as half as bad. We don't hit the Peter Principle and still keep getting promoted. Obama's excellence versus Trump's profound ignorance. Prime example."

We nodded in agreement; in strong agreement.

She said, "You've kept late nights and early mornings lately."

I shrugged. "Insomnia."

"Last few weeks I've seen you up practicing noctambulation around your front room, and I'd be up listening to music and walking around my house in the dark before I get ready to get my run in. On the days I don't run I'm still up and used to wish we could meet outside and stroll around the block together. I'd be smart and carry my gun."

"Shit, we better carry three or four."

She opened her parasol to block the sun, made it twirl, told Mo Fo, "Tell Pokey 'nem I'll be by later. Or to come over to my porch for some lemonade. Bring me some cake, if she can."

"Will do."

"Know what? I have a much better idea, Mo Fo. You need to keep your kids tonight. Me and Pokey can get cute and go out to East Memphis to the comedy club with my girls. I have enough free passes."

"Fatima, you know I never have a problem being with my kids. Take Pokey out on the town tonight. Just tell her when to be ready."

"You don't mind babysitting?"

"Babysit?" He laughed like what he heard was ludicrous. "A man can't babysit his own kids. Those my children just like they're hers."

"You're a good man, Mo Fo. Pokey got her a damn good man. God bless her. These brothers I meet are something else. You're making me want to go out and find a good white man. I love my chocolate, but I've always thought mixed babies were beautiful. You can hardly go wrong with a mixed baby. Keeping it real. There are exceptions, but the odds of them being beautiful by American standards are in your favor. Would have to be a Brad Pitt. Can't lose with a Brad Pitt."

I said, "Jennifer would beg to differ."

"So would Angelina. He need a sister." She laughed. "I'm going to do like Serena Williams. Get me a *foine* white man who respects Black women. Make my Brad Pitt wear a Black Lives Matter T every day."

I asked, "What you gonna wear?"

"He Brad Pitt fine? Nothing. If I wear anything, I'll be wearing him out both day and night. He'll be all the wardrobe a sister need."

We laughed.

She said, "But even Brad Pitt would have to pass my test."

"You have a test?"

"A one-question test to determine if we can go on a first date."

"What's the q?"

"They used to have to answer a few questions to get an afternoon date at a coffee shop. What does *pellucidity* mean? What does *infirmity* mean? What does *impenetrable* mean? What does *solipsistic* mean? What does *laconically* mean? What is a glib person? Then I started asking just one question. If I ask them what *equally yoked* means and they start talking about a stupid egg, I walk away shaking my gosh-darn head. That's relationship over. Because that means we're not equally yoked in the mind at the start. Not spiritually. They're faking the funk big-time. We're in two different places already. I got a lot of wrong answers from churchgoing men. Lots of wrong answers."

We laughed.

She went on. "The other issues I have are marriage and babies."

"You're almost thirty, ready for both."

"Marriage and babies are probably eighth and ninth on my list. I'm lying. Actually, neither is in my top ten. I can be the neighborhood auntie and have no problem sleeping at night."

"You're the boss of your life and don't live it otherwise."

She told Mo Fo, "I'll get Yemi Savage to drive us in her Jeep. We can throw back a couple of prairie fires, chase it with a beer to make it a boilermaker, and see if someone can tickle our funny bone."

I asked, "Prairie fire?"

"Whiskey and Tabasco sauce."

I said, "Have to try that next time I go out."

"Goes good on barbecue too. Marinate some Q in that overnight, bake it a bit, grill it, and as it falls off the bone you'll thank me."

"Will definitely try that."

"I know what Mo Fo drinks. What's your go-to drink, Professor?"

I said, "Mimosas for breakfast. Jack and Coke at the club."

She waved good-bye as she took slow steps backward.

She nodded my way. "Have a good morning, Professor."

I replied, "Have a good morning, Professor. Where you off to?"

"Y'all know I always meander to Yemi Savage's house most of the time, but she usually comes down on my end of the block once a week or so for a Kaffeeklatsch. My house not messy like she keeps hers. My OCD acts up at her house and I start cleaning her house. We might watch CNN and talk about work, men, family, news, gossip, and sip her bland coffee. Might have to mix it with a little something to make it nice."

"Same thing me and Mo Fo do when we have the time."

She called back, "Mr. Moses Ford."

"Yes, ma'am."

"Be ready to have your wife come home drunk as a skunk."

He said, "We'll probably end up with quintuplets."

Again, we all laughed the laugh of neighbors.

She had a nice house and car and didn't come off as a scattergood. No one on this block could afford to be. We used digital coupons and hit the sales rack at the discount stores most of the time. We knew how to look good rain or shine if nothing else. We bought our watermelons and peaches from Watermelon Man whenever he drove up from Clarksdale, Mississippi. We ate sunflower seeds and spit the shells in the grass. And we looked good doing it in Trues, Nikes, and swag from the Gap. Being broke and looking broke were two different things. We were professional and blue-collar paycheck-to-paycheck people and we never stepped out looking raggedy. Even Mo Fo looked regal sitting on his front porch.

On my block we had old-school dignity. We had new-age pride.

The widow passed by Pokey's ride, then yelled a good morning, even though she couldn't see Pokey. Pokey yelled good morning back.

Mo Fo said, "She's something else."

"Your wife?"

"Her too. But the widow."

"Yeah, she's something else."

The widow waved and spoke to everyone she saw as she passed. She stopped in front of the Westbrooks' house, started a conversation.

I said, "Hope we didn't get too Blackity Black for your taste."

"You're sitting next to a white veteran from Who Gives a Damn, Mississippi, a white man who is married to a high-energy Black woman as tall as Simone Biles, and same said white man from deep in Grenada County came from a family of rednecks, and despite that he thinks fur himself and loves to wear his favorite blue Obama T-shirt. Said white man is doing that in a red state. That's me. Moses Vernon Ford. I live in a Black neighborhood in a two-bedroom home with six loud and lovable people and happy for it. I'm my own kind of minority here and across Tennessee. At times I feel like I'm a club of one."

"Bull. Er'body in 38109 knows you and your family and are straight up Team Mo Fo. We're all living in a red state where white people give Black people the blues."

"That's why when y'all get to talking politics like that I listen to learn so I'll know how to direct and protect my amazing kids. I have five beautiful Black kids to educate, raise, feed, and protect until they can do all that for themselves. Yessir. I get to sit and listen to some folks and because my skin is like theirs and I don't say nothing, they assume I think the same way they think. I get to teach that to my children as well."

"You get to see them in their natural habitat and hear things they'd never say to us in public."

"When I'm out by myself, especially when I cross the state line, they see me as just another white man. I hear conversations that make me angry and sad. They say things that make John Wayne's anti-Black interview in *Playboy* sound like a love letter to African Americans. I hear ugly conversations that make me afraid for my wife and children."

"Bet you do. To be able to infiltrate and listen to folks who want a second civil war, a race war, that would be an experience."

"I've been minding my own business and people have come up to me and said the ugliest things about Black people, Jews, Muslims, women, and Mexicans. Random folks just being their true selves. But the shocked and ashamed looks on their faces when they run across me again and I'm holding my beautiful wife's little hand and laughing with my rambunctious kids, how their mouths drop—that shit's priceless. Some come over to apologize, tell me they're sorry, ask for forgiveness, try to explain how they've been brought up. Some. Not many. A few call me names and want to spit in my face. A few. Most just go on about their business and never look my way again. I'm fine with that."

The widow looked back, saw me looking, waved. I waved back. The daylight hit the widow's skirt and the sheer material revealed the mathematics of her hidden figure, exposed the outline of her anatomy.

Mo Fo nodded. "Cut her grass. Centipede grass needs love too."

I said, "Her thighs don't touch."

"Cut her grass."

She was the perfect shade of chocolate. I grinned.

Comparing Black women to food—my last girlfriend was triggered by that and flew into a rage. It offended both her Blackness and her feminism. She told me that was contrived to a lot of Black women.

Mo Fo said, "She looked back at you twice."

I told Mo Fo, "Can't mess with a neighbor."

"Cut her grass."

I told Mo Fo, "I don't need one who could get mad and stand on her porch and throw a Molotov cocktail into my living room window."

He laughed hard.

Widow Fatima's up-the-street sorority sister, Yemi Savage, stepped out on Blair Hunt Drive. She was a few houses away, but was hard to miss her as she headed this way waving.

I stood and waved back.

Mo Fo did the same.

She was busty, more than six feet tall in flip-flops. Shredded jeans and Pippi Longstocking braids. Our neighborhood attorney met Widow Fatima halfway and the sorority sisters chuckled and headed back north.

Mo Fo said, "Pokey right. But Pokey always right. If the doctor from TSU leaves her lawn like that, he ain't no good for her. Sometimes her grass doesn't get cut for over a month of Sundays. Never seen him in the daylight. He ain't nothing but a backdoor man."

"Maybe what she wants from a man is inside the house at midnight."

"Woman her age sleeping with fire every night. Woman her age is restless. Maybe that's why she's up like you. Both of y'all be pacing the floor and peeping out the window. Itty Bitty is easy on the eyes. She's erudite. Went to Auburn and then came back to Christian Brothers for another degree. She studied epistemology. Went back to our local HBCU to disseminate knowledge. You write books. Teach. You're erudite. Teach at UAN. You're single, far as I know. Widow Fatima ain't got nobody worth having. You ain't had company in months as far as I can see."

"We're across-the-street neighbors. And she's never invited me to her front porch. I'm surprised she talked to me this long."

"That's why I let y'all talk. Your disquisition didn't need my assistance. She was talking to *you*. Felt like an interview to me."

"Nah."

"Cut her grass for her. She might make you a glass of lemonade."

"Bet she goes good with some corn bread."

Mo Fo slapped his long legs with both hands and laughed.

I said, "She probably so sweet won't even need honey."

"You put honey on your corn bread?"

"And I use vegan butter."

THE SON OF MR. SULEMAN   113

"Not even an erudite man would mess up corn bread twice over like that. Forget all I done said. Never mind. You're not good enough for her."

We laughed again, grown men acting like high school boys.

At the moment I didn't feel good enough to have a shadow.

Too much was being added to my lazy man's load.

My mind went back to Fat Man, and my anger rose to the brim.

My old man was going down slow, packing up and getting ready to leave on the next train. Told myself I didn't care. A coldness ruled my heart. My lips turned down. Komorebi had found out who my father was.

She'd widened an *uncloseable* wound.

These fucking green eyes.

This complexion.

Even with a beard, still doppelgangers.

Momma was a gym rat and looked all of twenty-five, no makeup, no exaggeration. Momma was in her late forties now but had been pregnant at fifteen by a married man who was twenty-seven then.

Based on math and law, my father was a pedophile.

He had been one for more than thirty-one years.

I was the undeniable proof of a crime he'd never been charged with.

A lot of unkind words regarding Momma were put in court documents back then.

If my father was drowning, I'd run to him, throwing the heaviest cinder blocks I could carry.

CHAPTER 15

MOMMA WHIPPED IN my driveway, testing my Nova, seventies music blasting, Sis riding shotgun. Momma was laughing her ass off; Sis scowled like she was about to blow a gasket.

I asked, "What happened this time?"

Sis barked, "It wasn't funny, Momma. Apologize."

Momma couldn't stop laughing. "Baby Doll salty because she had an app and asked me if I wanted to know what I'll look like when I get old, and I told her if I ever wanted to do that, I'd look her right in her face. She'll look old enough to join AARP before your momma will."

"*Wasn't funny.*"

"You tried to make Momma look ugly for shits and giggles, and Momma hurt your *wittle* feelings. Her face so bent out of shape and got her *wooking* so ugly Momma should start a GoFundMe for a face transplant to make her halfway pretty again. Put that on Facebook Live for a joke, Baby Doll. And don't snap back, because Momma been at this since snapbacks were called snappy comebacks."

I busted a gut. "Y'all look like Shits and Giggles, not saying who is who."

"Sweet Meat, et tu, big brother?" Sis playfully barked at me, then turned back to our laughing momma. "It's called a *clapback*. *Snapback* is a baseball cap. You be trying too hard to be relevant."

Momma had on fresh Nike leggings paired with a fitted sorority T.

She raised her right hand to block the morning sun and proclaimed, "We be hungry."

Looking like she needed five more hours of sleep, Sis asked, "Sweet Meat, you got food?"

"I always have food, if nothing else."

Momma said, "You better offer us more than a syrup sandwich with no bread and no syrup."

"You're chief cook and bottle washer."

"At my house."

"At everybody house. Go on in and hostile takeover my home like you always do."

"Wash your booty and get dressed so we can eat and go make dat money."

I showered again, put on faded and ripped-to-death straight-leg jeans by True Religion. I paired my Trues with an ironed CREAM T that hugged my biceps. CREAM: Cash rules everything around me. Was in a Wu-Tang mood. It was too hot for socks and tennis shoes, so I pulled on a pair of sandals. Momma and Sis were moving around my kitchen, the *Hong Kong Phooey* issue behind them, now low talking like besties.

Sis said, "Black Kevin, ain't he too young for you, Momma?"

"I'm tired of dating. It's hard to date and find a good-quality man at this age. Too many games being played. They are ten years older than me and wanna continue to be a serial dater. Still want to be the old man in the club collecting numbers. Dating when you are almost fifty sucks."

"Who was you sneaking off with before Black Kevin?"

Momma told Baby Doll, "I dated this guy, really nice guy, funny, smart. I said to him the next time I have sex will only be after I see my partner's HIV and STD results. The fool says to me he's not taking any tests. He knows his body and is fine. He is a brilliant anthropology professor who is outspoken about the fairness in academia. Smart people can be stupider than the stupidest of the stupid. Book sense ain't common sense. I was shocked. I asked him if he only went to the doctor when something was wrong. He said yes. Older than me. No physical. No colonoscopy. No prostate exam."

"So basically, he will sleep with a woman and use her to see if he has diseases by getting her STD report after she sleeps with him. He'd give her one hundred diseases and blame them all on her."

"As a friend concerned with him as a Black man, I told that fool he could have some underlying problems and doesn't know, and when the symptoms show, it will be too late."

"Men like him drop dead at the kitchen table during a good Christmas dinner."

"He started yelling at me like I was Celie in *The Color Purple*."

"No. He. Didn't."

"Shouted that he was healthy and didn't need to be tested. He yelled at me like I was half as young as I look. Showed me his real face."

"I hope his bitch ass got cussed out real good."

"Smart and dumb all at once. I'm not dating to suddenly end up being an old man's nursemaid. He's blocked every which way now. The rest is between him, his doctor, the CDC, and the pallbearer."

"Damn, Momma. Just damn."

"Your go, Baby Doll. Fess up before slowpoke Sweet Meat get done cleaning his hind parts. Tell Momma something Momma don't know."

"Before I was messing with this last crazy girl, I was talking to a guy on the phone for a month straight. Almost every night a three-hour conversation. Every night. We would text throughout the day. He was in graduate school at U of M and talking to me about his business plan . . . sharing intimate details about himself. And then, poof, he vanished. Was gone like a thief in the night. Haven't heard a word from him since. I called a handful of times and phone went straight to voice mail. Doesn't respond to my texts anymore."

"My age or your age, never gets better. Never gets better."

"Changing teams hasn't helped. Harder breaking up with a woman than it is a man. This one making me regret ever meeting her. Might change back."

Momma said, "I know you're just joking about changing teams. Besides, same players here now as when you left. Roster hasn't changed."

"I know. I've dated more women than I have men but I know how the breakup game goes on both sides. Well, I know how it has gone with me, specifically. Men get stupid. They want the perfume, any jewelry, and the panties back they bought you. I mean, to do what with? They want to be reimbursed for every meal they offered to buy, every birthday present they gave you, plus gas money."

"They're still doing that?"

Momma and Sis laughed until they cried.

Momma got her breath. "Roster hasn't changed and I guess neither has the game."

"Momma. Why did he stop communicating?"

"You do something with him?"

"No more than kiss. We went on a date. Horrible kisser."

"Man can't kiss, that's the man you gotta quit."

"He was aggressive. He rammed his tongue down my throat."

"Bad at kissing, then bad at everything else. Be glad that one gone."

"Still hurts the ego to be dropped with no explanation. Messes with your head. I'm supposed to ghost a bad kisser, not be ghosted."

Momma and Sis were biscuits and eggs. When they sang together it rumbled a room, and I'd swear an aggrandized Beyoncé and Rihanna 2.0 were duetting Coachella in my kitchen, live in concert.

I hummed, hit falsetto notes, and added Luke James and Maxwell spiced with D'Angelo to the morning show.

Momma called out, "Sweet Meat, you standing around the corner listening to us talk about things not your business? You ear hustling us?"

"Sure am. Er'day I'm hustling."

Sis laughed. "Always eavesdropping. Nosy ass."

"My favorite hobby. How else am I supposed to learn the truth?"

Momma said, "What we talking about ain't the business of no man."

I said, "Some days I can't tell which one of y'all is the adult."

Sis called out, "I loaded up my guns. So did Momma."

"Cool. We can hit the range last, right before they close."

Momma had cooked breakfast: veg sausage, egg whites with onions, tomatoes, and mushrooms, oatmeal waiting on a generous helping of brown sugar and nondairy butter. I made Mexican spiced coffee simmered with cinnamon, cloves, chocolate, and a raw sugar called *piloncillo*. The end result was a rich, indulgent, spicy drink made for kings and queens.

I called out my kitchen window to Pokey, told her to tell Mo Fo I was making coffee, and she sent her brood of five over with two big empty coffee cups. I sent two big cups of coffee back over to Mo Fo and his wife for life. Pokey yelled she was going to send a slice of chocolate cake later on.

Momma said, "Fastest Swimmers, let's eat 'fore Momma pass out with missed-meal cramps."

We blessed the food, ate, talked family business, about buying houses and one day being able to afford a big-ass crib in Cordova or Germantown. Sis got on her phone and flirted with a native of La Paz here on temporary work visa. When Sis walked to the front room so we couldn't hear her hustle, Momma and I exchanged worried looks. The eye contact, the silence, her shifty body language, our interaction in silence as we downed oatmeal and egg whites, was a conversation. Without words, just a simple nod and concern for me in her eyes, Momma told me that she knew that my father was dying.

Momma needed to know that her firstborn was going to be all right.

In a tender, serious tone she asked, "You going to Mr. Suleman's funeral if you get invited?"

Without hesitation I shook my head. "He'll be at mine before I go to his."

She nodded, no grudge for what he had done detected. "Momma done."

I swallowed like I was drinking resentment made of arsenic. "Pi done if Momma done."

Sis ended her call, washed the dishes, went to my closet, and came back wearing a T she had left over here last week when she came to do her laundry, a black T with her woke message of the day.

I said, "I know you're not wearing the T you wore buck nekkid all over the Internet today."

"To prove I do not look older than my momma. Let's see who turn the most heads."

"Baby Doll, if you have to walk around half-naked to try and beat me, Momma already won."

We headed to my ride. I took the wheel; Sis slid in the back; Momma rode shotgun. I headed out Kansas Street to Belz Boulevard, ended up behind a small Toyota stacked up with what looked like fifty feet of cardboard, heavy enough to make the vehicle favor its right side. Fools didn't want to make two or three trips and did a lazy man's load, this one unmanageably large. I changed lanes, moved around him. Momma picked up her phone, sent rapid-fire texts to my siblings. She was the queen of texting.

Momma said, "Er'body gonna meet us at the first listing."

I said, "I bet all three of 'em show up CP time."

"They were born CP time."

Sis moved so she could get all of us in a photo to send the Swimmers. "Sweet Meat, Imma need your hoopty tonight. You can go with me or stay at home. If you rolling, be ret by nine and you driving."

I ran my hand over my field of black cotton. Come-stained silk blouse was on my mind. I should have held the beauty queen's head, shoved her face in my lap as hard as I could, stabbed upward, and made her take it all at once. Should've held the back of her head until she choked to death, then left her on the side of the road and drove away, then stopped at Denny's and bought myself a chunk of pie.

But there still would have been a blouse with my DNA, enough evidence from the death of a Brownsville-born beauty queen for a black man from Memphis to be given the electric chair.

Even dead she'd have race, the law, and the Judge of all Judges in her corner.

The Judge of all Judges would still have won.

Momma got my attention. "Sweet Meat. Last time. Replace your ice cream with yogurt."

"Why must you take the fun out of life?"

"Show up for leg day this week. That goes for both of you. Y'all getting summertime lazy."

I turned on the music as the Steve Miller Band sang "The Joker," and her smile went to hell.

Sis playfully asked, "What's wrong? Why Momma frowning and upset all of a swudden?"

Serious, I asked, "What's wrong, Momma? Tell the truth and shame the devil."

Momma changed the station to an Elvis Presley tune. "Nothing wrong."

I asked, "We really gonna ride around doing Elvis Presley in the hood?"

Sis huffed. "'The only thing Negroes can do for me is buy my records and shine my shoes.'"

Momma shook her head. "Don't believe everything you hear. Don't let fools revise the man's history. He acknowledged his debt to black folks and the musicians who influenced him."

"*I repeat.* I heard he said all a black man could do for him was shine his gosh-darn shoes."

"B.B. King told me he knew Elvis and there was not a single drop of racism in that man."

"They said the same thing about Canada's president. How'd that work out?"

Momma changed the station again. That nineties number she loved came on. "Love Is a Rock."

Momma regrouped, and her smile went upward to heaven again.

Sis groaned. "Anything but that song. Anything. Slitting my wrists now."

Momma got CP loud, became pure joy, and made us join in. We did our best to conquer the rapid lyrics. Momma knew each word, had sung that ditty for decades, rapped it all out like she was the boss. We had car karaoke at thirty miles an hour. By the time we were at the four-way at Third Street and Southgate Shopping Center, my mind was stuck on my father's family, blood relatives I'd never met.

Fat Man had had the nerve to come to my house early on a Saturday morning, interrupt my yard work, and plant a seed. He'd done his damage and now weeds were growing inside my head.

Momma clapped, car danced, and sang while Sis did the same. She put on another Elvis number and soon we all had our top lips curled up and were trying to *outsang* the hell out of "Suspicious Minds." Then we did "Jailhouse Rock" so hard people in cars around us joined in.

Momma had seen the signs that death was coming to our family days ago. Once a man and woman made a baby, they became part of the same family tree, became the root, and like it or not, until the end, from that day forward, due to the child they created, they were family.

That was why Momma had seen the signs.

I wondered how many goddamn signs I had missed.

Sis had left me and Momma at the table in case we needed a moment. Now we ignored California. We were a jovial disassembled community, laughing heartily as a man slowly died.

In a concerned voice Sis asked, "Sweet Meat, you okay?"

"I'm good."

Momma knew. Sis knew. Momma had told her. So the Fastest Swimmers all knew.

They knew before I knew because I had been wrapped up in bullshit at UAN.

Sometimes I could get too anxious and be slow on the uptake, but I eventually figured things out. Which is probably why I jumped on figuring out Gemma Buckingham's right combination and permutation. Whenever served with something that either didn't feel, look, or sound right, eventually I would do whatever needed to be done to know what I didn't know. Any woman I'd ever dated who turned shady as Grady could stand up, stamp their feet, shout, and testify to that obsession.

Gemma Buckingham represented something normal.

Last night I was a regular boy meeting a girl.

I was a BMFM in search of romance and love.

We played a nice game.

Even if I never heard from her again, I'd needed to feel normal last night.

She took me from under the weight being imposed on me by the Bitch from Brownsville.

And with the news of my old man, the irony of a pedophile's intrusion wasn't lost on me.

But for now, for a while, they'd be compartmentalized, donated to the department of amnesia. Would fall away from that part of my reality and hide in some version of a Sunken Place. I'd live where America has kept too many of us trapped since its inception, in denial, as long as I could.

CHAPTER 16

SIX DAYS LATER Gemma Buckingham called and gave me her address on Tennessee Street. She'd lied and told me she'd lived in the heart of the most dangerous hood in the 901, only to find out she lived in a four-bedroom castle atop the bluff. An area that was pretty much a haven built for whites, the ones with old money who saw themselves as cultured and sophisticated. Gemma Buckingham had jaw dropping views of Tom Lee Park and Big Muddy. She had immediate access to top-shelf dining and shopping, could stroll and catch performances at the Orpheum, or throw on tennis shoes and walk to see ballgames or concerts at FedEx Forum.

I googled her address. Twenty-nine interior pictures came up. She was in a five-thousand-square-foot custom home. Exquisite kitchen filled with the latest in high-tech Bluetooth appliances and stonework. Beautiful wet bar, ideal for entertaining. The master suite was the size of my house, closets had enough space to park my Nova. Fireplaces all over, including in the bedrooms and the master bath. If she was tired, an elevator would carry her to any of the three levels, and I wouldn't be surprised if an electric scooter wasn't waiting to take it from there. The property at the address Gemma Buckingham gave me went for nearly 1.6 million dollars. I wondered who cleaned house and cut the Bahia grass once a week.

Her crib was fucking fabulous.

"Are we Fucking Fabulous tonight?"

"I'm wearing a different nighttime perfume."

"Nighttime? So, you switch it up."

"A sista can't walk around smelling the same sexy way every day and night. No mystery or thrill in redundancy. A girl has professional perfumes she wears for work and proper fragrances for the sensual martini hours after. Same goes for makeup, hairstyles, and clothing. And for our undies. All are a reflection of our moods."

"So, what kind of undies do you have on?"

"The kind made to be taken off after one shot, two drinks, and three kisses."

"Let's go find a bartender."

WE DRANK, WALKED Beale Street. Gemma Buckingham told me so many fascinating stories.

We ended up talking about her amazing Afro, and she told me she had it first done in Ghana, told me about how natural hair was coming back in Africa. That surprised me because I didn't know it had ever left. But they'd retrained local beauticians and hairdressers and taught them how to *Eurofy* and straighten Black hair, and now they were going back natural, reclaiming their birthright. That was why she had given up the perm and reclaimed her natural hair and roots.

I said, "Women and hair. Issues all over the world."

"Hair defines us. It's the first thing you see, your first impression of us, and us of each other."

"India Arie would disagree."

She said, "Yeah. Was surprised at the number of weaves in the West Indies. And many looked very *interesting*, to say the least. They used colorful yarn and crocheted it in with their natural hair. A weave of sorts. Horrible to me, but it worked for them. That material is flammable in my humble opinion."

Rooster crowing in my mind, anger hidden, I chuckled. "Women and hair."

"Almost as obsessive as some men and theirs. Yours is always on point. Beard too."

"Touché. I get this beautiful field of black cotton done each week, but might miss a week here and there, and I don't fret over it being tight every day like that."

"You're a guy. The rougher you look, at times, the better. Be handsome, but not too pretty."

"You're pretty all the time."

"I will stipulate to the fact that hair is a bit of an obsession for some." I frowned a little. "Know any woman who gets it done every day? Gets it fixed every morning?"

She frowned too. "I'm sure Meghan does. She's royalty. She is forced to maintain a certain image. At times a woman changes her hair to fit her mood, a way of transforming, of becoming someone else."

"She's lost that freedom. She's chained herself to someone else's tradition."

"We all need to be someone else, to be free, see what that feels like, if only for a while."

TUESDAY WE WENT to a Sun Studio tour, then the Stax Museum so I could teach London about Otis Redding, Carla Thomas, and Booker T. & the M.G.s. Thursday we rode the vintage Main Street trolley down to where MLK was assassinated, toured the National Civil Rights Museum at the Lorraine Motel, left emotional, angry, teary-eyed, then stopped by the Blues Hall of Fame and Center for Southern Folklore, grabbed coffee at a café, and headed over to Burkle Estate on Second to the Slave Haven Underground Railroad Museum. I took Gemma Buckingham to the Silly Goose. She had one drink. We hit Earnestine and Hazel's. She had two more drinks and we chowed down on hot wings.

I said, "You can eat some chicken. You don't leave anything on the bone."

"I learned the proper way to eat chicken in Nigeria; it's not enough to simply eat the flesh. We break the bone, suck out the marrow, and pulverize the remainder until there's almost nothing left."

I grinned, sipped, then asked, "Tell me something about you I don't know."

"Personal?"

"Not too. Save the hard stuff for the next six dates."

"We're dating six more times?"

"At least. I might have to get a second job, but we're going out a few more times."

"I don't want you going bankrupt putting a drink in my hand and a smile on my face. We could always go camping in Gatlinburg and the Great Smoky Mountains. Never been camping before."

"Black people? Camping? That's called being homeless."

"Movies at the Malco at Overton Square are fine."

"Yeah?"

"We can do an early movie. We don't have to be out all night."

"What kind of moving pictures you like?"

"I prefer sci-fi to rom-coms and horror to almost anything else."

"Do you?"

"There are, however, exceptions to every rule. What about you?"

I said, "I read comic books, always have, always will. I read novels, but I prefer comics. Grew up on comics. Learned to read by reading comics. Love graphic novels, the more adult-themed ones."

"Are you serious? Who do you like the most? Which comic? Superman or Batman?"

"Anything by Brian Michael Bendis."

"He elevates comics to a level beyond literature."

"Does a woman as pretty as you really read comic books?"

"Right now, I am loving *Saga* by Brian Vaughan, but the art by Fiona Staples drew me in. She makes war, sex, and space, in the sci-fi genre, utterly amazing."

"Comics are so fucking expensive."

"I spent over forty dollars to buy *Compendium One*, and it was worth every bloody penny. I'd guess it runs six bucks for about twenty pages. Page for page, costs way more than a novel."

I chuckled. "I buy a lot of indie titles too. Those cost more. Lot of talent out there."

"Ever written one?"

"Thought about it. Wanted to do this thing with DC. Superman's planet had an island of Black people that was mentioned in one issue, only one issue, and I think it's a missed opportunity."

"On an island." She laughed a little. "They put their Black people on an island."

"Vathlo Island. Their canon has Black Kryptonians, described as a highly developed and intellectual Black race. I could see Jor-El going to them for advice on building his son's spaceship, or see them forecasting the destruction of Krypton, but it's ignored the way the GOP ignores global warming."

"More like Wakandans. Was thinking stereotypical weed-smoking Jamaicans for a moment."

"Melanin-blessed people who would have unlimited superpowers under a yellow sun. Part of the plot, if I wrote that, would be them getting to that yellow sun. It would be their running north."

"Relegated to an island."

"Still described as immigrants."

"Cringeworthy stereotypes and same age-old tropes to say the least."

"When white people write your future, it's worse than the past they have already delivered."

She sipped. "I know you buy your novels here, but where do you buy your stash of comics?"

"Place called 901 Comics."

"Midtown's number one comic bookstore?"

"Yeah."

"No way. I used Uber to go down on Young Avenue last Thursday afternoon."

"I don't know many women who read comics."

"Deadpool, Lana Kane, Black Cat, Sailor Jupiter, Jessica Rabbit. I cosplay as well."

"That's something I'd like to see."

"Small world, my fellow nerd. Surprised we never bumped into each other there."

We left there and jammed at Electric Cowboy for a while; then we shut down Club 152 at three in the morning. The night ended with a ravenous French kiss that left me as dizzy as a kid his first time on an überspeedy merry-go-round. The honeymoon kiss ebbed and flowed. Lasted until sunrise. She aroused me to no end. Had never been so hard. Was difficult to let London go and head back to Blair Hunt Drive. Her skin was flushed. Her curls had an Afro Sheen glow. I smelled hints of coconut.

As I pulled away to leave, I asked, "What did you say you do for a living?"

"I told you that if I told you, I'd have to kill you. I'm beginning to like you so much."

I said, "I guess as long as it has nothing to do with human trafficking, prostitution, pedophilia, organ smuggling, or any form of Black slavery, you can remain a mystery wrapped in an enigma."

"None of those. But if you guess right, I'll have to kill you. And I really like you."

"Really?"

"Of course not. Always wanted to sound like a badass vixen in a James Bond movie."

"That body." I grinned. "I bet you know a lot of ways to make death come to town."

"Especially if I'm on top."

"I've been warned."

CHAPTER 17

ON OUR NEXT date Gemma rocked skinny jeans, trainers, and a Meghan as Queen T-shirt. We hit 901 Comics like excited kids. We checked out new comics, trades, superhero collectibles, statues, toys, action figures. Drifted into their back-issue room stocked with forty thousand silver-, bronze-, and modern-age comics.

"Where do you get your comics in London?"

"Forbidden Planet on Shaftesbury. It's a megastore. Very nice spot. Nerd heaven."

"Will google."

She picked up some swag. "So, would you prefer to shag Black Cat or Catwoman?"

"Black Cat."

She chose a sexy Black Cat top to buy. "Reverse cowgirl? Wonder Woman, Storm, or Harley Quinn?"

"Storm."

She chose Storm. "Doggie style. Vixen or Misty Knight?"

"Vixen."

"Sixty-nine. Rocket, Nubia, or Naskia?"

"Nubia. But line 'em all up. Sounds like Monday through Friday to me."

She laughed. "Could you handle a Monday-through-Friday cosplay on that level?"

While she bought a stack of graphic novels and tight-fitting T-shirts that totaled five hundred dollars, Gemma Buckingham told me about Black Brits I'd never heard of, people of African descent who were the first Blacks allowed to achieve what white men were born entitled to across the pond, and she educated me on a few who were the equivalent of my civil rights leaders: Trevor McDonald, Moira Stewart, Lord Paul Boateng, Trevor Phillips, Diane Abbott, David Lammy, Kanya King.

"Safe to assume neither you nor many Americans know much about my world across the pond."

"Outside of watching *Doctor Who*, *Luther*, and a royal wedding or two, nada."

"Yet I have been raised with immense knowledge of your history and heroes."

We stepped into Goner Records long enough to check out the coin-operated Elvis shrine. I dropped in a quarter and Elvis showed himself, sang "Thus Spoke Zarathustra."

"And this is your royalty."

"Their royalty. Al Green is my king. B.B. was my king before that."

We stepped into Java Cabana, a chic, retro-style coffee shop, its floors made from recycled wood ripped from an old bowling alley. Like most things on this side of the tracks, it was a shrine to Elvis mixed with local artwork. Gemma Buckingham had a vegetarian sandwich and I ordered a meatless sloppy Joe. She had a Lisa Marie, a dark roast flavored with cocoa and raspberry. I had a java shake.

She said, "Tell me more about your comic idea."

"I'd start it off with that island being taken by Brainiac, and we'd find a lot of his tech came from the Vathlonians. They won't wait for permission to be free. It will be bigger than Haiti's revolt, only they won't be forced to pay for their own independence. They would battle aliens and gain their own freedom, as a nation. Would run it parallel to the global treatment of our people, with a better ending. Each time they pass a different color sun, the radiation will impact them a different way, and the cumulative effect will determine what type of supermen they become. Would be political and have characters who want to be presidents and dictators. Wouldn't interfere with the present canon, so the fanboys won't be able to bitch too much. Ran that idea by the guys where I buy my comics."

We listened to live acoustic music that gave way to poetry readings while we mixed with neighborhood residents and musicians and browsed local artwork that decorated the walls. Saw people I knew from UAN, U of M, Christian Brothers University, Rhodes College, and Memphis College of Art.

"Would you care to go to church with me on Sunday?"

"Sorry, love. Not big on religious rituals. I mean, it's the same Bible each Sunday, for years, decades, the same stories. No one continues the same studies once they have the degree."

"It's always someone's first time hearing any lecture. Mine are on repeat as well."

"Not for the choir, I doubt if many'd go to church each week. Take away that aspect, remove the choir, have each week a recurring TED Talk, then who shows up, especially if Arsenal is playing? If you find that offensive and don't want to take this any further, I will understand, but I won't apologize."

"Atheist?"

"Raised Catholic, but now I'm agnostic mixed with heterodoxy. My opinions are based on traveling the world, on seeing over a hundred countries and just as many faiths, not by sitting in the same nest singing the same song. Politics and religion have become the same to me, both unable to change, and when confronted with truth, they cling to the same lies, reshape truth to fit their faulty agendas. One of my brothers had a bad experience with a man who claimed to be a servant of God. I can't reconcile how God would allow the clergy to do what he did to my brother, to other boys, or be a conspirator in all of those violations against women, if he were truly present."

"Be careful. This is the South, and racist or not, people hate it when you attack religion."

"Christianity isn't under attack, same as all criticism of Israel isn't anti-Semitic, and all comments about Black issues from Europeans aren't racist. People ask religious leaders questions in order to clear up things that seem highly improbable. We just want clarity. There is no attack."

"Didn't mean to piss you off."

She gave me a sardonic British smile. "Political or religious, I'm allergic to BS."

"Well, we're trained that way here in the South. We love to insult with positivity and a smile."

"Example? In case I have missed being educated in the perfect insult. I love insults."

"If anyone says God bless you, you were just cursed Bible Belt style."

"I've been told that a lot, especially by my neighbors. That and to go to heaven."

"Go to heaven can mean the opposite, depending on context and degree of smile."

Gemma Buckingham moisturized her pillow-soft lips. She licked and ate a piece of Cadbury chocolate, an aphrodisiac. I wanted that sweet taste in her mouth. We had enough wine to get that heady feeling, then had another glass of sweet wine and took it outside. We made out for a few minutes, until her Uber arrived, showing me there was no intention of letting things get more intimate later on.

I was pulling in my driveway when my phone rang. Gemma Buckingham.

She said, "What are you doing?"

"Just got home."

"I just showered."

"That's a visual."

"Do you have a woman?"

"No incumbent. Position open. Interviewing."

"Who?"

"You."

"I'm hungry for you."

"I'm hungrier for you."

"Can you return to my home by the river for ten minutes?"

"Ten minutes?"

"Yes."

"On my way."

"I hope you do eat. A man going down on a woman is the sweetest thing. Makes the sun come out at midnight and if done properly sends a smile to my heart and tears of joy down my face."

"As long as it's gluten-free."

"One of the best-known guides to ranking the best restaurants is called the Michelin series. One star means it's a very good eatery; two stars signify it's definitely worth a trip; three stars is exceptional, worth a special journey. Delicious is four stars."

"Can't wait to meet her so I can post my own review on Yelp."

"Don't worry, Pi. I won't feed you nothing I wouldn't eat."

"On my way."

"Ten minutes."

"No problem."

"And no talking. We've talked enough to last three lifetimes."

"Okay."

"Come take me all the way."

"All the way?"

"As they say here, I want to get rode hard and put up wet, be bedraggled and wake up looking like something the cat dragged in. I want a big smile on my pretty little face as I walk side to side."

"That's all the way."

"Then we pretend it never happened."

CHAPTER 18

FIFTEEN MINUTES LATER I exited the highway, passed the parks dedicated to slave-owning Confederates on the right, the Mississippi River and shores of West Memphis, Arkansas, to my left, let GPS lead me to her Buckingham Palace on the 'Sip. I parked my red Nova outside of her mansion on Tennessee Street. She was waiting, let me in her front door, double doors at least fourteen feet high. Lights were low, and the air conditioner had the room chilled enough to harden nipples.

She wore her new Storm from the X-Men tank top, mid-section cut away, and a thong, standing in just enough darkness to shadow the best physical parts of a woman. The Brit had a long white wig over her Afro. Had cosmeticized herself, her gorgeous face utter perfection. Even had in contacts to give her the proper eyes. She was Storm. Soon as the door closed, I pulled her to me, and our ravenous kisses took us to the carpeted part of the floor in the entryway. My candy kisses went south, verified her need and revealed my greed. I pulled her thong away, tossed it to the side, these the lips I craved. She felt my tongue, easygoing, yet strong. Filled with rich rhythm and blues and gospel music. Her breathing thickened. Ecstasy awakened in her face. I went down on her, put a zillion kisses on her swollen labia, then gently kissed her sex in the style of the good old French. She held my hair like it was her reins and rode my tongue like she couldn't get enough. Her moans rose as her eyes closed, allowed darkness to magnify the feeling of being stirred. Her hands fell to her sides and her pose was Jesus on the cross, crucified by pleasure. She became my church, the doors to salvation open wide, only she was wild, rebellious, gyrating her blues away. The goddess had needs. I was here to worship, to hear her psalms and chants, to witness the lustful song in her heart. She fought me, refused to sing so quickly, tried to not sing so loudly, but her breathing thickened and carried her down the road to glorious southern revival hallelujahs. I licked her lovely petals and she bloomed. She was so fucking beautiful, giving herself to me.

I was the writer Arthur Miller with Marilyn Monroe.

Her beauty made me a beast.

Her hands gripped the top of my rugged bro 'fro, and she tumbled into the heat of the fire, made wicked sounds like she was amazed at the power, texture, and strength of my tongue. My tongue made her speak in tongues. I held her ass, held that softness, then used my fingers, opened her up.

She shuddered, then sang and writhed as she squirmed and squeezed her breasts. It felt like she was no longer in control of what she did, of where her hands went. She licked one nipple, squeezed the other, and moaned and danced against my tongue. I remained consistent, patient, intense, the rhythm of my tongue a love song. Gregorian chants rose. She looked down at me. Her legs shook, lips trembled, and tears fell. I tasted her as if I savored her soul, used my mouth like a man unafraid, worshipped her in figure eights, consumed her honey in long swipes. She moved against me like she needed to be consumed. Her hips moved, did a hard grind, then a slow roll against my beard and chin. Her heat couldn't be contained, was strong enough to tan my face. She was feral. I added fingers, stirred her like coffee, rubbed her spot, sucked her spot, gave her head that made her grab my hair, pull my hair, then return to sucking her nipples, squeezing her breasts. Her arousal magnified mine. I was feral as fuck too. Her legs strained. I gave her my dank hand, fed her the honey on my fingers, and she sucked each finger like she was trying to make it come. Her body quaked and she set free a song in many ragged octaves, a song of madness, the exorcism so sweet. She was in her own universe.

I didn't back away. Tried to make her see colors never invented. My tongue persisted. Small circles. Up and down. As deep inside as I could go. My hands on her ass, pulling her back to me when she wiggled away. No reprieve. I was the greedy bastard. Insatiable. I licked her sex and refused to let her come down. Again pulling at her own nipples, sucking one and pinching the other, begging to suck my fingers, what she felt so overpowering I wanted to masturbate and come. She was almost there again, whimpering, riding a thousand waves as she held her belly, jerked, floated away, breathing expanding and contracting, making faces like it hurt to breathe, shedding more tears, having iridescent, kaleidoscopic, psychedelic, prismatic orgasms. The journey toward insanity was so beautiful. Her legs shook again, and she was one with the cosmos.

I ran my fingers through her sweat, heat rising like steam. She exhaled in spurts before she opened her eyes, took me in, frowned, then gave a mischievous grin, one that matched mine. She massaged the sides of my face, slapped my damp skin in amazement, pulled me toward her, and on the way I kissed her belly, her breasts, her nipples, and when I had moved from one pair of trembling lips to the next, she kissed me like she was so aroused she might never come down. She still couldn't talk. She adjusted her body, spread her wings, and I eased my weight on hers, kissed her breasts as I eased inside her. Musical inimitable moans. Barbaric lugubrious moans. She held me, made her nails rake my back as I slid inside a warm home. Felt like she came again, then patted my leg, needed me to stop. She was overwhelmed. I moved away from her, watched her suffer. When she calmed, she crawled right back to me, took me in her mouth, stroked me, sucked me, suckled me, worked me in slow motion, had me firm, then pulled me back on top of her, put the tip inside, the tip and no more, then rubbed it back and forth as she feverishly kissed me, her tongue tasting like me and mine like her. I pushed deep, filled her up in a way my tongue was unable to do, and she sang again, sang a wordless song as our tongues danced. I filled her up, pulled away, left her almost empty, then rushed to fill her again. She sucked my tongue, sucked my neck, bit my skin, gave me her nails, moved against me, not one word decipherable. She was losing control and I was on the same road. She felt my pain, my agony, my need to come growing and throbbing inside her. She looked in my face, in my eyes, studied my weakness, saw me trying to not surrender and journey to that other universe while she did the same. She made me turn over. Her turn to ride. We were wet, slick, and when I slipped out my absence made her groan. When she put me back inside her, it was the warmth of an ardent fireplace on a chilly night. She held my hands down, made me surrender to spiritual levels I'd never experienced before. The wicked movements of her hips ruled me. It was her turn to etch a look of desperation in my face. It was her turn to smile. She rode me to the edge of madness, then backed away, then took me to the edge again, a game she did over and over, turned me into a harpsichord that played both soft and loud sounds. I wanted freedom. She teased me until insanity owned my mind, until I was about to be one with the universe, until the conclusion was inevitable, then moved away from me, took me in her mouth, let my ebony run as deep as she could, gag reflex strong, made my back arch as my legs strained, my scream silent as she caused the catastrophic flood of all floods to rise and rush from my wicked soul. She quaffed, drank heartily with large sips, a parched vampire finally getting its desired nutrients. She snatched the soul inside my soul's soul. I died. Came back to life. We lay there forever, breathing like we'd been deprived of oxygen. She was panting hard, one hand over her rapidly thumping heart. In cool air that couldn't compete with heat rising from her amber skin, all fucked out, squirming, satisfied, her rough breathing calmed. Soon so did mine.

The raging storm had surged and subsided.

"Gemma Buckingham."

No reply. Her wig had shifted enough to reveal that her Afro was back in two long braids.

"Gemma Buckingham."

Again no reply. It was as if her name had no meaning.

"Gemma Buckingham."

She blinked like she was coming out of a trance, trapped in a dream where she was someone else.

She lay there like an infant so tender and mild, ready to suck her thumb and sleep in heavenly peace. I tasted her on my tongue as I pulled my wrinkled clothes on, our scents rising from my dank flesh. I left her there, on her floor, white wig half-on and half-off, smiling, ridden hard and put away wet.

CHAPTER 19

AS SOON AS my tires turned from I-55 onto South Parkway West and headed toward the north end of Kansas Street, my phone rang. The Bitch from Brownsville. She was calling me from the outskirts of Memphis where people were addicted to opioids and would never be treated like crack addicts. Her people did less time for the same crimes. Humidity became frost and my world covered in ice and snow in the summertime. I didn't answer the first ring, but by the time I had driven a mile and was passing Shady Grove, she had called back eight times in a row. Her picture had been on the front page of *The Commercial Appeal* today, same for UAN's paper, her with the Judge of all Judges as they prepared to fly to Washington to dine with our senator and Individual 1. Local stations had covered their trip. She'd been to the White House and was back. She had to be feeling pretty good about herself. She had to feel powerful.

I said, "You've returned from sipping champagne and eating sturgeon eggs on taxpayer dollars."

She said, "Tomorrow. After your morning lecture. Hampton Inn at Wolfchase Galleria. I need to see you for a couple of hours. So be prepared. The room will be paid for, in my hairdresser's name. I will send you the room number as soon as she checks in. I think it's time we move from cars to the bed."

I parked in the lot at Riverview Community Center. "You'll mess up your hair."

"Do as I tell you and my hair will be fine."

"At least until the rooster crows again."

"You know I really like you, right? I wouldn't put my mouth on you if I felt otherwise."

"Are there others?"

"No."

"Why me?"

"You remind me of someone. And I have to have you. I just have to."

I rubbed my temples. "What the fuck do you want from me?"

"Acceptance. Compliance. I'm married to a fat old man, for fuck's sake. I need vitality in my life."

I said, "I'm not doing a Hampton Inn down off Highway 64."

She whisper-laughed. "My blouse begs to differ."

Again, as I had dreamed since this started, I wanted to give her the third act of *Of Mice and Men*. "If I have to do this, take me to the Peabody. Not a second-rate motel that has a microwave."

"Not the Peabody. My constituents have lunch there. I would have to be seen at valet; then I'd have to pass the bar and lobby to get to the elevator. I could be seen by the judge's friends."

"Not my issue. I want room service. I want to eat like I'm at the White House."

"So arrogant since you've had that militant hairstyle. We will tend to that field of Black cotton."

"Get the presidential suite at the Peabody, not the side-chick special at the Hampton."

"That will be as much as two thousand dollars. Ten times a room at Hampton."

"If you can get your hair done every morning when the rooster crows, you can afford it."

"The judge can afford it. He'll pay for our playdate and never be the wiser."

I rambled. "Women like you never say no to playdates with a Mandingo. You've been obsessed for years, craving forbidden fruit since it was illegal to share a glance at us, let alone be bare-skinned in the same bed with us warriors. This terrifies me and excites you. Sucking Black dick was your secret desire even if it meant being thrown out by the family."

"That was uncalled for."

"Are you mad?"

"When I grew up, chicken noodle soup was a luxury. We ate beans and biscuits and there was no second helping. We prayed to have eggs, milk, and meat. Were too proud to let anyone in Brownsville know we were on food stamps, so we would go to other towns where no one knew us and beg for assistance. Couldn't afford cheese to make lasagna. We had seventy cows and from the time I could walk, it was my job to tend to them and clean up behind them. If we had a large pig, we'd have enough meat for the winter. That stench of poverty lives in my nostrils. Smells like hog jowls and black-eyed peas. I was nine working like a thirty-year-old. Was six of us and we made four thousand one year but had three hundred thousand dollars in debt. I prayed for deliverance. One day we were at a food bank. Man saw me and said I was the prettiest white girl he'd ever seen. Told me I should enter his beauty contest." Her breathing was jagged. "Look at me now. Educated. Beautiful. I wear the finest clothing. My hair is always perfect. I am the bitch every woman strives to be. I'm the bitch many men would love to have. I married smart, married well, and I'm rich. I'm offering you an affair that many would die to have. And yet you refuse to capitulate."

"You're not a Black woman. You'll never have her struggles. You're not from my side of town."

"I came from conditions beyond any poverty you will ever know. I sold my soul to the devil a long time ago. If you knew my life from the start . . . I am what *every* Black woman strives to be."

"No Black woman I've ever met. People love a white woman's rags-to-riches story."

"With the struggles I've had, *with my sacrifices*, I'll take that as a compliment."

"Dr. Helen Stone-Calhoun. Wife of Judge Zachary Beauregard

Calhoun, the racist who carries a shotgun named Thunder and sees his verdict as the final verdict in all matters, end this before the judge finds out and bodies drop."

"Tomorrow, Professor Suleman. The Peabody. Soon as your lecture ends, our fun begins."

"Presidential suite."

"Be worth it. And be prepared. Bring protection for that long black Cadillac."

We were playing cards and she had a hand filled with spades and trump cards.

"Why me?"

She paused. "You know I'm in love with you. You know I am. All the compliments I gave you, the gifts, the attention, with the risk I'm taking on my own behalf, you could tell I was fond of you. I want you. I desire you sexually, if nothing else. Plain and simple. And I always get what I want. Always."

CHAPTER 20

RACISM SAVED ME.

Alarms blared at ten A.M., panic rose, and everybody yelled, started running and hiding.

Another wannabe Dylann Roof had woken up mad and needed to show off his assault rifle by allowing his military-grade projectile emissioners to spit rounds of hot lead into warm Black bodies. This one had driven three hundred miles north of his home to shoot up the students at UAN because he heard we were the Pharaohs, an African reference, then assumed UAN meant University of African Negroes, and furthermore assumed we were an HBCU like Morehouse and Howard. He showed up locked and loaded, a lone wolf determined to start a race war and get the other lone wolves like him howling about how hard it was being a white man in America, no receipts worthy of being displayed. He charged onto the campus screaming but was thrown off when he saw all the snowy faces. His skinfolk were already yelling that another goddamn motherfuckin racist-ass terrorist was on campus, yelling for the Aggressive Six to come and handle this like their tuition was paying them to do, undergrads and grad students running and ducking and failing to remember protocol for an active shooter outside.

At the start I had taken charge, moved a frozen Professor Norberto Eli and Professor Arrickson to the side as both hyperventilated while students needed guidance. I jumped on a table, whistled as loud as a train, calmed the confused.

I gave orders to students and my superiors, and within ninety seconds, fifty-plus were hidden inside five rooms, in corners closer to the front so no one could get hit by bullets if they tore into wooden doors backed with metal plating head on. Under my orders doors were blocked by cafeteria furniture. Our only hope was the terrorist wasn't a UAN student who knew our protocol.

Panicked breathing, excited utterances, tweets saying good-bye to a cruel world, FaceTime calls to parents and Skypes to lovers, prayers to Jesus, Allah, Buddha, Moses, and others, I shut it all down. Calls could go out, I wouldn't separate a child from their parent, but they couldn't talk and give away any sign we were behind these locked doors.

We became tongueless church mice listening for gunshots in the distance, or the footsteps of killers coming our way. We waited for an unknown number of barbarians to be at our door.

Absolute chaos. Social media being checked. "I'm scared" texts sent to parents, family, lovers, and loved ones. East Memphis told to shelter in place. Dorms and student apartments on lockdown. Same over at U of M. Indiscriminate shooter as far as anyone knew. Psychologist called, sociologist called. Specially trained officers arrived. Evacuation meeting center and reunification center established. Bulletproof book bags were all over, but no one was allowed to go to retrieve a backpack. Law enforcement escorted students to safety, made them present identification. Students were questioned; many witnessed a shooter lugging guns and ammo. They were traumatized for life. Traffic was gridlocked. Roadblocks. Paramedics. News stations. Emotions high. Hugs. Tears flowed like the Mississippi.

The madness was broadcast live on all local stations and covered by two on the level of CNN. More coverage was given to UAN than to the HBCU LeMoyne-Owen. More news vans and higher-level reporters were sent east; the rookie reporters were sent to the other side of the tracks to do the same at our HBCU. I guess they thought the students at LeMoyne-Owen bled blood of lesser value. Not for Black Twitter, the attempted attack across town would have gone unnoticed.

Black folks had to depend on Black folks all the way down the line.

Momma and all the Fastest Swimmers had messaged our three-year-long family group chat on WhatsApp forty-eleven times. Momma was at the gym, watching it on their television.

Four hours and some-odd minutes later the all-clear alarm sounded: suspect in custody, no other suspects. That was two hours beyond the time I was supposed to be Mandingo at the Peabody.

Everyone got up: Black, white, Chinese, Hindu, Muslim, Iranian, indigenous, African, American; strangers hugged each other and cried. Black and white frats, same for sororities, held hands in a survivors' prayer, and though Twitter said no deaths had been reported they still prayed no one was harmed today as the devil made his rounds. Somebody should have played that seventies Coca-Cola song teaching the world to sing in perfect harmony, because that's where we were, bound by the trauma of the day.

I helped students to their feet, hugged each like a church member. One Hispanic girl shook head to toe, full-body trembled without stopping. For what felt like eternity, I was their shield, had put each student behind me as if I were made of Kevlar, like they were Momma, Sis, or any of the Fastest Swimmers. A group of brothers and sisters were terrified; one sister couldn't stand, needed to sit back down, because she had read live tweets while we hid, had seen on social that the lunatic was here for a Black attack. Her heart rate had to be in the 140s; someone majoring in nursing called a paramedic.

The nursing student stayed with her and her crew.

My phone rang over and over.

I answered.

She tsked. "Looks like I wasted over a thousand dollars on a hotel room at the Peabody."

She told me she was in the hotel room, in her Agent Provocateur lingerie, lingerie that was royal blue and made of softest silk material with a delicate lace. She had grown woman toys and whipped cream at her side, was watching this unfold on television. She was disappointed.

She said, "This room. My lingerie. I will add every last penny to your tab."

THE SON OF MR. SULEMAN   145

She hung up.

My phone buzzed right away. She had sent me a NSFW picture. I deleted it as soon as I saw it. She was in a pornographic state of mind. My people were being terrorized and she couldn't care less.

UAN HAD MADE history. We were the only university to have a second attack. The second armed racist was mad and motivated because the first terrorist had stolen the attention he desired.

Over in Gemma Buckingham's London, Piers Morgan said our name. Soon we saw UAN was both UK news and UK Twitter famous. The BBC joined in with CNN International and covered a dark moment in American history. University Along the Nile. The world knew our name. This was our world every day, magnified, tweeted, and retweeted. It was another day when people woke up anxious to kill Black folks.

All this was popping, and I was fucking glad I didn't have to go to the Peabody and get robbed.

There was a press conference; we learned that after the domestic terrorist leapt out of his pickup truck at UAN carrying an assault rifle and ammo, he didn't see anybody Black, just white folks. When shit went down, brothers and sisters became Olympic-level track stars. He couldn't catch anybody lugging all that weight. He saw the Aggressive Six running his way, guns drawn. The coward saw six men with guns carrying bullets with his name on them, men anxious to kill a rabid dog, and revised his plan.

He leapt back in his old pickup. The joke the dark hearts posted on social media was that he must've asked Siri where the closest Black college was. That joke was verified when the police eventually revealed that the madman's GPS sent him ten miles or so away toward our local HBCU, where Momma worked. He was spotted doing a screeching U-turn at McLemore and Mississippi. MPD caught him on Walker Avenue, two minutes before he made it to the edges of LeMoyne-Owen's campus.

He was sitting on six military-level assault weapons, riding in a filthy pickup filled with ammunition, and when it was all over, he was gingerly arrested, not one shot fired.

Too bad that motherfucker didn't have a loosie. He was allowed to leave breathing and probably ended up down at 201 with a full belly and his breath smelling like it was fresh from Burger King.

In the meantime, the Aggressive Six scoured my campus, went from building to building at UAN, had to make sure he was a lone wolf, not part of a pack, before the all clear was sounded.

We emerged from each hideout in the Little Pyramid having a hug-fest made for Woodstock, school mass shootings, especially the eleven mass deadly school shootings that happened since Columbine, on our minds. UAN Pharaohs, traumatized, checked on each other, hugged, cried, did a circle, joined hands no matter their denomination, and prayed no one here or at LeMoyne-Owen was hurt today.

My phone rang; Gemma Buckingham. Told her I was fine but didn't have time to talk.

As I exited the Little Pyramid, people thanked me, hugged me until I was unable to breathe.

Professor Thor exited from his hiding place, came out of the pandemonium of the day whistling Dixie like it was a sunny afternoon at Tom Lee Park. He spotted a Muslim girl consoling a dozen students and readjusted his course. He went directly to her, said something that caused her to freeze; then he smiled and strolled away with a victorious grin and even happier whistling.

Then the man in the Lansky Brothers suit saw me, came my way whistling that Popeyes jingle.

He put on that wide smile, and in that Don-Rickles-meets-the-Joker tone asked me, "Who won gold, silver, and bronze? Your people ran like FloJo Carl Lewis and hid like they're trained by none other than Harriet Tubman."

He was ten pounds of shit in a five-pound bag and couldn't smell his own stench. The tenured professor chuckled, then kept it moving.

I said nothing, a habit that had become too hard to break.

The never-crack-a-smile Aggressive Six had arrived.

Professor Thor had a conversation with their leader as if Schwarzenegger was his main henchman. Schwarzenegger saw me staring and shot me a look like he'd found out I'd had his wife and he was ready to double-pop me. Professor Thor roused them all. The Aggressive Six headed into the Little Pyramid as Professor Thor walked away, headed across a panicked campus at an unbothered pace.

I went to the Muslim sister, gave her my UAN card, asked what Professor Thor said to her.

"He said, 'Looking like a moose limb.' Instead of Muslim, he called me a 'moose limb.' Then took it further. 'Guess I should say Amma Sloppy Laker.' Amma Sloppy Laker. His debasing as-salam alaikum, which means 'peace be unto you.' Why would he insult me in such a way at a time like this?"

"I can be a witness if you want to report the matter."

"Would my reporting him or any racist to other racists make a difference?"

"Still, get it on his record."

"If I dared to put one blemish on his record, they will put a thousand falsehoods on mine. I will just add that insult to the rest. Despite my complaints, I still get called *Muslim* journalist, which always amuses me. I have never heard any of my colleagues in the industry introduced as *Christian* journalist or *Jewish* journalist."

"Keep my card."

She took it and read my name. "Your surname is Arabic."

I nodded.

She smiled a little, gave me the nod of an ally. She put it in her back pocket, then went to comfort those who needed it the most.

CHAPTER 21

I NEEDED TO see London. Needed her energy. I called her, asked her out on a last-minute date.

Gemma Buckingham met me at her front door, stood in her three levels of luxury on the 'Sip, kissing me in the style of the French. She rocked a wild and kinky pinkish Afro paired with a one-of-a-kind red dress made from African brocade fabric, plus high heels with red bottoms. Her clothes, her mood, were sexy. I had on slim Trues cuffed over my tan brogues and an X-Men T-shirt underneath a one-button suit jacket. I had an extra shirt in my car in case we ended up going to dance, and tennis shoes in case we went to the Malco Summer Drive-In.

She gave me the biggest hug, was glad I was okay.

She said, "I've been on pins and needles. So happy to see you face-to-face. I feel better now."

Her shaking body told me she'd been worried since news had broken about the madness.

She said, "Not much coverage regarding the attempted attack at the Black uni."

"Par for the course; par for the course. That's why we need our own media."

We watched local news and talked about the attack at UAN a moment. She said, "You are truly a hero in my eyes."

"Nah. Just did my job."

"No one from the news interviewed you?"

I shook my head. "Again, par for the course."

WHEN WE'D HAD enough of the news, I drove Gemma Buckingham to the heart of East Memphis to Novel bookstore, a well-stocked, beautiful spot that had a bar and a sweeter-than-sweet restaurant inside. We browsed books, moved from Tom Wolfe to Dostoyevsky to Toni Morrison.

She became excited. "They have physical copies of both your novels. I'm going to buy these."

"You don't have to. I have copies. At least two boxes of each are dry rotting in my garage."

"I insist. Wait. Is this author next to you with the same unique surname a relative?"

I paused as she realized who Komorebi had been talking about. "He's my father."

Overexcited, eyes wide, she asked, "*Your father* did the Forever series? Are you fucking serious? The Forever series are my mum's favorite novels. *Forever* was to her what *Harry Potter* was to me. I grew up watching her read them all, and she read each one at least a dozen times. She neglected us and spent our food money on books whenever he had a new novel."

"You don't say."

"He's your father. You have his green eyes, his complexion, and his face. You are unmistakably his. I am in Memphis in the company of royalty."

I said nothing as she held his book up to my face, compared my features to his. A feeling of agita overcame me as the storm inside my gut rolled in on a bed of shotgun thunder and Remington lightning.

She flipped that pedophile's hardcover open to the first page. "How are his books?"

"Wouldn't know."

"You don't read books written by your own father? Interesting. I assumed the opposite."

I kept it real. "Due to alphabetizing by surname, our books are stocked closer than we'll ever be. Too bad we don't use first names first, like they do in Iceland's phone book. Problem would be solved."

"This bothers you."

I said, "I should've used a pseudonym."

She flipped the book over, read my father's bio. "Your father lives in California."

"He's lived on the dark side of the moon all of my life as far as I know."

She paid for the novels, used a metal Amex charge card, and as soon as that was done, we saw two open barstools and hit the bar. She had a Manhattan, a southern man's brown liquor in a pretty, classy glass to make it look soft, feminine, and ladylike. That drink was a metaphor for a few women I'd known. Pretty on the outside, darkness within, and intoxicating. I had an old-fashioned. By drink two we were cozy. By drink three we were seated up under each other, touching a lot, all smiles, giggles, and laughs.

She slid the two novels to me, then extended a Montblanc. "Do you mind?"

I signed both to "The Lady from London," which made her smile.

We drank and talked, my mind on a man who was dying a slow death eighteen hundred miles away.

Gemma Buckingham was roast beef and fish and chips and bangers and mash and Yorkshire pudding and shepherd's pie and beans and toast and ploughman's lunch and the dirty Thames and corrupt Parliament and Big Ben and the Tube. I was blue suede shoes and highways and a collection of big towns that in the big picture were small towns. I was catfish, sweltering summers, and unbearable winters where Christians and racism had deep roots in the land of gospel music and the delta blues. I was W.C. Handy, Al Green, the Temprees, and the Bar-Kays played at family reunions in the shadows of trees in Chickasaw Heritage Park. And when I was on this side of town, I was as much Marc Cohn jamming "Walking in Memphis" as I was Bobby Blue Bland crooning "Memphis Monday Morning" on mine.

She was British. I was about as South Memphis as a Black man could get.

She had grown up with her mom and dad in the same house. I was raised by a single mom. Gemma Buckingham was from London and seemed to know a better world. All I knew was that I knew Memphis and Memphis knew me. Familiarity breeds contempt. Was hardly a place I could go without running into someone I'd gone to elementary, middle school, or high school with, or bumped into someone I knew from Piggly Wiggly, FedEx, the University of Memphis, UAN, or one of the few clubs, or attended church with. Couldn't take a date to the Delta Fair on Walnut Grove or the Mid-South Fair in Southaven without bumping into a half dozen girls or women I'd dated since I was twelve or thirteen. It always felt like eyes were on me, like I had to be accountable.

At times I felt trapped, like I had to be a version of me approved by all.

Gemma Buckingham was free, had no such connections, no such liability, everyone she passed a stranger to her, each place a new place, a foreigner in a strange land, not tethered to religion or culture. In a new land, the woman had no history and got to become a virgin all over again.

She was a woman who'd traveled the world, and I'd barely left the racism embedded in the DNA of the Bible Belt. I rarely left the South. We stayed where we felt safe, despite the danger.

Her history was different from mine, but it wasn't a history that made her equal to her oppressor. Back where she came from, she probably wasn't a unicorn, and I wasn't a unique man here in the South, but my South Memphis swag and style had her attention. She wasn't rooted in Harriet Tubman and underground railroads. Downtown, in front of the MTA building, surrounded by crape myrtle trees, there was an unpreserved, poorly marked slave auction block. I'd never heard of slave auction blocks in London. Only had heard about slave ships being built there.

She was Black; I was Black; yet the difference was astounding.

Still, no matter where our histories converged, I knew the attraction was palpable.

I said, "We keep drinking like this, we won't make it to a dance club tonight."

"I am interested in you. Only you. No dancing tonight."

I asked her, "What about your parents? You never said."

Her lips eased up methodically. "My mum is English; my father is Zambian."

She had mentioned *Nigerian* roots when I met her, but I didn't question it because nobody I knew was from one spot. We were the by-way-of people. Our roots were shaky. Older Black people were in Memphis by way of Mississippi, or in Chicago by way of N'awlins. Maybe Africans had it the same way.

With that thought I hummed, "Interesting."

"Word thief. All writers are thieves of words."

"You can't steal what's free. Words already in the dictionary, alphabetized at that."

She touched my beard, that contact electrifying. "Which blogs or novels do you recommend I follow or read so I can become savvy in things political, Black, and American?"

"Blavity. The Grio. The Root. Reddit. Any novel by AM Joy. What blogs you follow?"

"Who's for Dinner. Hey, Dip Your Toes In. It's All Bee. Just Go Places. Wonderlusting. Mostly travel and beauty by Nigerian and British bloggers. Also a few on being mixed race. Charnelle Geraldine. Colour Me Courtney. Sincerely Sainabou. Nothing I love exists on this side of the pond."

"Who are you, Gemma Buckingham?"

"At this stage in my life? A joy-seeking woman filled with never-ending curiosity."

"You're my kind of Black woman, accent and all, and I want you to know that."

She chuckled, sipped, and shook her head. Somehow, I'd fucked up.

I dialed it back, asked, "What happened? I say something wrong?"

"We're being honest? Yes, you did. Pet peeve of mine was activated. Sorry. I usually do a better job of hiding it. I didn't mean to react in such a negative manner. But you do it incessantly."

"The accent? You've had enough of us southerners teasing your accent?"

"No. Hate being called *Black*." She became flannel-mouthed. "A major pet peeve."

"Seriously? A Black Brit hates being called a Black Brit?"

"In London the wankers call you Black and scream for you to go back to Africa."

"Do like I do. Tell them there is no return policy on stolen goods."

"Across the pond, was called Black as a pejorative more times than I care to remember. It's not as loud as is it over here, but it happens in a way that makes it hard to respond."

"In London."

"Nothing good comes with being called Black. Makes me smile a harsh Brixton smile. Black means nasty, dark, gloomy, obscure, sad, tragic, disastrous, terrible. Fight me on that, American."

"Lady from London, over here black also means debt-free, solvent, fiscally sound, able to pay one's obligations, creditworthy, of good monetary standing, rock-solid, secure, moneymaking, profitable; in other words, my Blackness means I'm spiritually in the black and I don't owe anybody of any race, creed, or color a goddamn thing. I wear my Blackness like it's the best suit I own."

"Best suit you own. Love that."

"Baby, my Blackness is dripping swag, is better than an embroidered fur jacket made by Gucci. My Blackness is a goat fur, mink, lambswool, and silk-embroidered fur jacket, an unambiguous example of high-class craftsmanship and expert tailoring. My Blackness is priceless and twice as stylish as a white man's coat made with long sleeves, sequin embroidery, a spread collar, a straight hem, and cross-stitched details laced with diamonds and trimmed in gold from the rooter to the tooter."

"Black and proud, say it loud as you buy me another drink. Bartender, the same for us, please?"

"Black means power, fear, mystery, strength, authority, elegance, and sophistication."

"Right on, right on. A man after my own melanin. Say it loud."

"Then scream it louder for the ones that hate us because they know that one drop of this melanin cancels that white-power-Euro bullshit they've been peddling. That moratorium will happen at the ballot box, and then we need to set term limits, get rid of the career politicians."

"Some seem so angry, and I can't understand why."

"Tides are changing, one election at a time." I shook my head. "They're so desperate to up their numbers that white men with political power are forcing their beloved women to have rape babies. Their women. That's as amoral as it is draconian and desperate."

"Let me turn on my psychogalvanometer." She made a whirr noise. "Brexit detects no lies."

"White men are desperate to maintain their overseer status and political power."

"I guess the unwanted children of Great Britain escaped their oppressors but clung to their savage ways, brought it here, Bibles in hand, and became to Blacks what the UK was to them."

I sipped the last of my drink, stuck on what she'd said: "You hate . . . being called Black."

"Hated. Past tense. I've been redefined."

The bartender put fresh drinks in front of both of us, smiled, then walked away. His smile told me that he felt something here, that the energy of possibility existed between me and my exotic date.

She asked, "How did Black folks get all the negativity?"

"White has a better publicity team. White owns all the media and bookstores. With that power you can revise history, spread lies over and over until they become the gullible, ignorant, and naïve man's truth. The White House is where the most amoral laws came from the get-go, laws written by white men to subjugate Blacks, laws that made the life of the Black man and woman pure hell."

She said, "White is the color you turn when terrified. White is the color of surrender."

I nodded. "You can mix anything with my beautiful Blackness, any race, and it still comes out Black. Takes a lot to make Black look contaminated. White, you see all the stains right away."

"Time to change gears."

"Yeah?"

"Time to clock in."

"Clock in?"

"Rhymes with."

I gave the bartender my UAN-branded Visa, and while he ran the charges, I turned to my date, touched her beautiful face. Her lips touched mine and we put some French on our kissing.

She put her soft tongue deeper inside my heated mouth. "I want you inside me like this."

We eased off our barstools and prepared to confront the humidity sitting on East Memphis.

I held her left hand with my right, carried the books she had bought in my left. "I'll be pleased to meet you."

She asked, "Pleased to meet me?"

"Rhymes with."

CHAPTER 22

RESONANT AND DEEP in sound, the orgasm shook me as I quavered. The raging currents of the Nile emptied into the warmth of the Mediterranean Sea. It was a symphony in three movements that quickly took her to the everlasting. Pornography and poetry, an alternating between the harshness of fucking and the kindness of making love. London came hard, grunted, squealed, a library of long moans, skin slapping, sophistication gone, feral, primal, face so tight when she busted a nut looked like she was mean mugging, then finished with giggles, covered my face with her hand to stop my watching her.

I chuckled. "I came too fast."

"No faster than I did."

"Came hard."

"No harder than I did."

We were on her living room floor, clothed, splayed out, five minutes of hard sex behind us.

She eased up, went to a bathroom a few feet away, cleaned herself, then came back with a warm towel, wiped me down as I lay on my back. She cleaned me then took me in her mouth.

I said, "It was beautiful."

"It was as elegant as it was devastating."

"Those faces."

"Hush."

She suckled, a mewling baby with a pacifier. I massaged her soft hair, wished my life felt that way, hummed and watched her, grew in length and girth, hardened, groans escalating as she worked me.

She smiled. "I think we're ready again."

She gave me her hand and pulled me to my feet.

We took the elevator to her master bedroom. It opened on the 'Sip with the view of all views.

She said, "Take your shirt off."

She went to a shopping bag, threw me a Captain America T. I pulled it on. She pulled away her dress, pulled on a Black Widow T, nothing else. She—in nothing but a twenty-dollar T—was a showstopper. Voluptuous woman, thick hips, rounded backside, small waist, an hourglass.

She said, "I have a red wig. But I'd have to braid my hair. Next time."

Her softness hardened me. She licked her lips, grinned at her power.

I tried to get my balance, pull and kick away my Trues, but they bunched at my ankles. She wanted me right then, as bad as I wanted to be inside her. I pulled her T up over her breasts. Gemma Buckingham's gorgeous face was pressed against her floor-to-ceiling glass. We shagged in slow motion, at the easygoing pace of the slow-moving river, unhurried, kissing, nibbling, moaning, swimming, with the view of all views from Gemma Buckingham's Buckingham Palace. Then we fucked each other like it might be our last time fucking. We laughed because we were determined to be the last one bucking or stroking. She threw down like a woman afraid of nothing and ready to try anything. I had my T-shirt wrapped around her waist, used it to rein her back into me over and over. We changed positions. Long legs opened wide for me, my body eased on her gifts, and she took control of me, guided me to the space she wanted me to fill, panted, cooed, and showed me a new her as I broke the skin in slow motion.

Gemma Buckingham's hands clasped my ass, pulled me, raised her ass toward me for more. I put that Memphis funk in her Brixton soul, gave gliding strokes, and she responded with circular motions. She gave up tenuous hallelujahs. I clung to her as she pulled me deeper, demanded more. She became a loquacious lover, a moaner who narrated each emotion, proclaimed what I was doing, sang her arousal, told me what she wanted me to do to her, then did things to me that had never been done before.

Her phone rang, and she threw it to the side.

She put me back inside her, and I held her British-born ass in my hands as she went to town.

When London was getting worn down and could barely breathe, I took over, got my second wind, and stroked the drunk out of Gemma Buckingham. I slapped her amber ass, made her beg me not to stop.

I gave Gemma Buckingham the hate that was inflaming my heart, and she mistook that hate I gave for something else, told me to not stop fucking her, said the way I was fucking her was perfect.

As we lay dehydrated and exhausted, her phone rang again.

In a voice that didn't hide how spent and parched she was, she struggled to say, "Sorry, love. I won't be returning for a weekend as planned to attend the West End production of *Death of a Salesman* with a prestigious and acclaimed African American actor in the leading role. So sorry I won't be able to host Wendell and Sharon after the performance as promised. I'll be here indefinitely."

She held my dick in her hand, kissed the head, suckled, tried to get me to stay hard enough to mount me again.

"Yes. Indefinitely."

Black Widow eased enough of Captain America inside her to make her eyes roll.

She huffed. "Nothing contained in the e-mail I sent shall be considered a legally binding agreement. Need to be clear because I will not be available to discuss it any further. The way I feel at this moment, I may never return to London. Memphis. In America, not Africa. Has everything I need. Everything. So, indefinitely. Summer cold. I've come down with a summer cold. Let me get my medicine."

Black Widow killed the call, threw the phone across the room, made it fly.

CHAPTER 23

GEMMA BUCKINGHAM'S VOICE burst up the stairs, startled me awake. "Then why did you follow me until no one could see us and go out of your way to hug me at the bloody conference when I'd never met you, which was uncalled-for as well as totally gross, then proceed to push yourself against me and whisper in my ear that I had been very unfairly treated during negotiations because I am a *Black* woman? *Not with your bloody hand on my arse.* I'm no bloody scrubber. You were reported. I had the pleasure of having to sit through twenty very uninteresting speakers over four Vegas days so hot I saw the devil sitting by the pool drinking a glass of ice water, and then you assault me, touch me as if it's your right to put your hands on me because you like the way I look? *Naff off.*"

Five minutes later Gemma Buckingham danced off her elevator singing a Sam Smith song, the one he did with Normani. I pretended I was just waking up. She stood over me with breakfast. She fed me a two-egg omelet done with egg whites and spices that woke every part of my palette, spinach, blueberries, walnuts, a boiled egg salad with Italian dressing, along with a cup of Earl Grey tea.

"This omelet. Damn this is good. Might have to ask for the recipe."

"I'd never give up my recipe. I keep my secrets to myself."

After breakfast, I moisturized her scalp for her, used coconut oil, played with her incredible Afro. She touched my penis, aroused me, gave me head again. Gemma Buckingham tenderized me, gave me another sloppy blo' in a shower rocking eight showerheads. The bathroom was cavernous; each moan reverberated in an echo chamber. There were his and her sinks on opposite sides of a gigantic bathtub big enough for six. Over the bathtub was a chandelier hanging from a recess in the twelve-foot ceiling. I had her down on the marble floor, scooting backward each time I thrust. Made the songbird's legs tremble. I felt her fire. Gemma Buckingham pulled my face, made me look in her eyes, worked me from the bottom.

She had me good.

She whispered, "Cosplay."

I nodded.

"Stroke it for me. Like that. So meaty. That wanker is so meaty."

She disappeared, went to her T-shirt stash.

She called out, "Would love to record us. Watch it. Delete it, of course. Never had a sex tape."

"By now, I assumed all women under thirty had secretly done a Kardashian."

"Late bloomer here. Certain things I'd never do in London."

She came back. Green wig over her Afro. Fresh green She-Hulk T. She had transformed.

With a wink she softball-tossed me a new red T. I pulled it on and became a masturbating Deadpool.

She took over, stroked me, kissed me. "American. You are seriously representing your country."

"African American. Black folks are only American on passports, and most of us don't own one."

"Because America, in its own ignorance, thinks it is the world and all should come to her."

"I resemble that remark."

"If sex gets better than this, I might fly you to Barbados to eat at Just Grillin' restaurant."

She put me on my back, had my legs up, knees pushed back; she squatted over me, worked me inside her sacred space, mounted me as if she were the man. I had never been in that position before.

Being in a woman's position, pinned down by her weight, it intimidated me at first. I could barely move. She had the power, all the control. She found her balance, was on her haunches, moved up and down. It got good and she took that real estate round and round, worked me until I trembled and moaned hallelujahs. She got into it, held my ankles, worked me like I had worked her. I relaxed into it. She turned me into an opera singer, kept me under her weight, her strokes, and I surrendered, melodic, majestic moans from beginning to end. She took it all and sang at the same time. A duet that reverberated in the cavernous bathroom like an echo chamber.

She led me back to the bedroom.

While we cooled down, she turned on the seventy-inch curved television, started watching a program she had saved. I checked my phone. Momma, then Sis, had called in the middle of our opera.

I texted both of them back so they wouldn't think the worst; then I checked Twitter.

My last name was trending.

Seeing my surname jolted me, and I put my phone down.

My father was trending.

Gemma Buckingham snapped at an American reality show, "Iris, for real? As fine as Keith is, I would be shagging him every night twice a night and again in the morning. Shag the man already."

I cuddled up against her for a half hour, unwanted people heavy on my mind. She reached for me, gave me intense kisses as she crawled her right hand between my legs, tested my recovery. Enough time had passed; she wanted more Pi. Outside her floor-to-ceiling windows, there was a glimmering, road-like reflection on Old Man River. There was no such view from my queen bed on Blair Hunt Drive.

The green wig was gone, but she was in She-Hulk mode. I was in another mood. Enough with being dominated. I held her ankles, took her like she had taken me before, hand around her throat, mild choking, hard coming. As soon as that five minutes of funk was done, as riverboats passed her riverside mansion, while neighbors walked dogs, I rolled away from her; she pulled her wavy hair back and fanned herself, sweated as she did. She tugged at her soft hair, hair soft like the lives of people who took that level of existence for granted, and raised up on her elbows, made her booty move in circles, made each cheek move separately, made it shake, moved like she was grinding hard on the softness of the bed.

I applauded her sensuality, pretended I was caked up and made it rain. "Twerking your ass off."

"Not twerking. It's an African dance. *La danse du fessier.*"

"Translate."

"The dance of the behind."

"Still twerking."

"All about moving the bottom. The Côte d'Ivoire government tried to ban *mapouka* at least a generation ago, when I was a baby in nappies, long before they had invented the word *twerking*, because it was too damn sexy. Can you imagine? A booty dance too sexy for Africa?"

"A shag by any other name."

"*La danse du fessier.*"

I repeated, "Still twerking."

She showed her joy, performed the *mapouka* like she lived underneath a double rainbow. Double rainbows were beautiful and significant, a symbol of transformation, a sign of good fortune in Eastern cultures. The first arc was all about the material world, which it seemed like she had conquered before thirty. The second arc signified the spiritual realm, another place she seemed to control. She was an ass-popping goddess come to life.

She had beautiful rainbows in her world. I had black butterflies dancing in mine.

My father was dead.

Needing to get away and deal with my darkness, my black butterflies, I said, "I have to go home."

The dance ended and so did her joyous smile.

"So soon? Is some tristate skank eager for you to get home so she can get the last drop?"

Her history, the harsh reason she fled the UK, was there, hidden behind an odd, jealous smile.

Her unspoken past collided with the secret life of Pi. Tension entered the room, watched us.

I considered the time, the heat, my responsibilities, as an excuse to get the fuck out of there.

"Have to cut my grass before it gets too hot. We like our yards to look good before we go to church on Sunday, at least I do. I have to open a portal and grade about thirty papers."

"Grade the bloody papers tomorrow."

"I don't work on Sundays."

"Best day for work. It's calm. Peaceful. No telemarketers calling all bloody day. Easier to focus."

"I won't work on the day I've been taught Jesus rose from the dead."

"So far as the yard, you don't have a professional gardener to keep you sorted out?"

"Everyone on my side of town self-gardens."

"I have a cleaning service, handyman service, gardener, and a cook on standby, if needed."

"Lucky you. Under my roof I'm the chief cook and bottle washer. Only one on payroll."

"I have no idea what that means, but okay. What's your address?"

"Why?"

"Hiding something? Are you another mendacious man wasting my precious time?"

"Not at all. Nothing to lie about. At least not yet, but give it some time."

That truth got a laugh out of her. "Your address, please. I'm a problem solver."

With an uneasy smile I told her my address.

She made a call, rang up a service called Lopez Landscaping, the same hardworking people who took care of her pristine property year-round, and a two-man team was going to head up Horn Lake Road to Kansas Street, turn right on Blair Hunt Drive, cut my grass and pull my weeds.

I said, "It's the white house with black awnings. Hedges around the front. I'll need those tended to too. Blair Hunt Drive is right off the south end of Kansas Street right after they pass the train tracks, some apartments on the left, Joubert on the right, if they come from the south.

If they come from Parkway, they can hit that end of Blair Hunt and follow it to my crib. They won't be able to miss it."

"They want to know is there a gate?"

"It's not locked."

"Dogs?"

"No pets. Neighbors have rottweilers and German shepherds, but they're fenced in."

I liked her, had to think of this as being loving, not a red flag, not as her being controlling.

Besides Momma, not many times in my life could I remember a woman doing anything like this for me. Even this gesture was messing with my manhood, my ego. I'd been mowing lawns since I was twelve years old, had cut more yards between Kansas Street and Riverside Boulevard than I could remember, had been cutting my own since I bought my little house under the best shade tree on the block. It was downright awkward having another man going to touch a blade of grass in my yard, like I was being irresponsible, like I was giving permission for him to slow dance with someone I loved. We were serious about our land and property in the South. That was why I had never gone across the street and cut Widow Fatima's grass. To cut a man's or woman's grass, first there had to be consent.

Gemma Buckingham repeated, "Blair Hunt Drive? Postal code . . . I mean *zip* code, please."

I nodded: "38109."

"Blair Hunt. Someone famous?"

"Blair T. Hunt was the principal of Booker T. Washington High School during the civil rights movement, while America was practicing being Alcatraz for the Black man. He was the pastor of Mississippi Boulevard Christian Church for fifty years. World War I vet. Fought for equality in Memphis. Did his studies at LeMoyne-Owen Institute, Morehouse College, Tennessee State, and Harvard."

"Impressive."

"Knowing about him made me want to do better. I used to secretly wish that somehow, he was my real father. Admired him so much, as soon

THE SON OF MR. SULEMAN   165

as I saw a house on Blair Hunt on the market, I jumped on it. I was living around the corner but finally had my own space."

Gemma Buckingham hadn't heard what I said since she said, "Impressive."

My volatile history meant nothing to her. My heroes were just American names with no weight, no sacrifice. I'd been talking to myself, reminding myself what it meant to be a Black man from Memphis.

I was explaining a crucial part of who I was, but she wasn't listening.

She ended the call, enthused, problem solved, smiled. "You can stay a lot longer now."

"The papers. I still have to leave soon. Need that done before I go to church in the morning."

The booty dance started again, her signal for affection. "Anything else you need to get sorted?"

"Standing appointment with my barber this afternoon."

"Who's your barber?"

"My sister."

"You're more than welcome to come back and do your work here. I have Wi-Fi. It's iffy in a couple of spots around the house for some reason. My bloody calls drop as I'm going up the stairs."

"You need a range extender."

"What's that?"

"It improves your Wi-Fi signal. This house is huge. You probably have a lot of dead spots."

"You know how to put one in, or should I call an expert right now, and have it done forthwith?"

"For better Wi-Fi, get an Eero or Linksys, something that covers three levels. I'd have to install the main one with your router, then use the extender to create a new Wi-Fi to attach each level."

"Xfinity never told me I could improve my signal. I told them I was having issues and all they did was try to sell me a more expensive package, which didn't help. Those arses will get cursed out."

"I'd need good Internet to be able to do what I have to do. That and some privacy to focus."

"I can give you a bedroom to use as your private office, if that would work for you. If you want to crash a few days, I can swap out bedroom furniture for office furniture. Had thought about doing that anyway. Hell, with this space, I could let you two rooms for free, one for work and one to masturbate in, if you want space. If you are on one side of my palace and I'm working on the other, we won't disturb each other. And I promise not to disrupt you. Well, not often. But it would be worth the distraction."

"You don't have to do all that. I could sit at the ten-chair kitchen table. You have two dining areas and I could just spread my papers out there in the informal one, connect, grade papers, return e-mails."

"Right now, you have me in a glorious mood. Shagged me well and I want to make you happy."

"The happy ending that was heralded by another happy ending was more than enough."

"The way your tongue makes circles like a figure eight, how you make Delicious smile."

"She smiles?"

Gemma Buckingham made her ass show me why certain dances were banned, laughed. "I know I can be a bit much, moody, snarky, tend to go after what I want with a passion, but don't be afraid of me. Don't be afraid to share your feelings. A man who shares his feelings is like a woman who has balls."

"This from the woman who reveals nothing about herself."

"You shagged my face. With that meaty meat you shagged my face practically to your balls."

"You put your honey on my tongue."

"You put a copious amount of nectar in my mouth. Down my throat."

"I know I was unhinged and got carried away for a while."

That ass wagged faster. "I want that again, me on my back, head hanging off the edge of the bed, face shagged until I can harvest all your sweetness, and it was indeed sweet. Sweet and oh so thick."

"Delicious was delicious. Will post my Yelp rating in a few."

"London Bridge has come down in America."

She had to take another call. I did some ear hustling. She was talking to a corporation in Delaware. The top businesses prefer to use the state of Delaware as their home address. It was the home of the Fortune 500 because the tax benefits there made it like having your trade in the tax-friendly Cayman Islands. Up there the citizens were outnumbered by corporations. Whatever she did, she was the chief cook and bottle washer in charge of more than a few top-salary chief cooks and bottle washers.

Strange men would be on my property, cutting my grass, touching what was mine.

Anxious, I checked my messages again, saw six more e-mails from Komorebi, all marked urgent.

Then I saw a message from Brownsville, a mandatory invitation to meet her for pho at a place in Bartlett at sundown to *socialize* for two hours, to pho and fuck, said our last conversation about matters regarding our famous institution were never completed to her satisfaction.

She was ignored too.

I checked Twitter again.

#RIPSuleman was listed at number one.

Forever series was at number three.

He who died on social media was alive to the world.

CHAPTER 24

MY PHONE RANG as I held it, scared me, made me blink and jump out of the insidious clenched-jaw trance I had fallen into. I was suddenly in a sinkhole so deep no ladder or rope could pull me out. My mother's lovely image flashed. Didn't answer her, didn't answer my hero, the teenage girl who had refused to seek an abortion for what had been done; the brilliant, gregarious, loquacious, and erudite teen who changed her life from what it could have been for me. I didn't answer the woman who still rose despite the odds, despite having more children, despite more sacrificing, and I guiltily sent her to voice mail, something I rarely did. I always answered my momma's calls, no matter what time, day or night. She'd know my behavior was different today, would hear it in my strained voice the moment I answered, and she would know why. I guess the town crier had alerted the village, because Sis called, and the rest of the Fastest Swimmers hunted me down, left messages. Then an urgent call came in from Beverly Hills. That was fat-ass attorney Carlton what's his face. Suleman's messenger.

I didn't answer anyone, didn't check any more texts or voice messages. I turned the phone off. I turned away from the world I knew, let this place be my Vathlo Island, my paradise away from an exploding civilization. I could hide from the world, but not from my own thoughts. His inside children got to see him live, were privileged to see him die; they were allowed to know him, to choose to like, love, or dislike him. I had been given no such options. I had only been recognized on Wikipedia, what in the end would be the online obituary for us all. But regardless of what had been done, I'd never speak ill of the dead. Wasn't raised that way. Had to bury this ish deeper than six feet in the ground. Was time to compartmentalize decades of pain and disappointment. I wanted to break down like Will Smith did in the famous daddy-issues episode of *The Fresh Prince of Bel-Air*. His dad had abandoned him. I related, knew that episode line by line, beat by beat, and that crucial scene played in my head as if someone had looked in my life, knew what was hidden, penned it just for me.

Anger would rise, but no tears would fall from these eyes.

Not for a man who had damned my mother, then cursed me with his shame.

CHAPTER 25

FROM WHEN I first learned my truth, learned that my father was not dead, learned that my father was a four-hour plane ride away, that I wasn't the oldest, that I had siblings I'd never heard of, that shit hurt. The age difference between him and Momma came up, and I learned categorically what a pedophile was. I saw the legal papers; Momma had them in a folder in the bottom of a drawer. They were supposed to be hidden. On that day of learning, I sat and read them all. My momma had been painted as a gold-digging girl from Memphis trying to get his Los Angeles money by babying up. I told myself I'd forgive that motherfucker when dogs started to meow, cats began to bark, and the moon outshined the sun.

You don't treat my momma like that. There would be no forgiveness hug between us.

He'd had more than thirty years to fall on his knees in front of her and try to get one.

I showered, washed my face, found coconut oil in one of the cabinets and moisturized my skin, included my hair and beard, then found some eye drops, cleared the red from my eyes. I went back to the only distraction I had worth having. I had to stay here longer, needed to hide a while before facing my new reality. I went back to playing the role of the rebound man, only with this turn of events, with this watershed moment, Gemma Buckingham was being used as the rebound for these feelings.

Of all the superheroes to transform into, she had chosen to be Thunder, Anissa Pierce, the eldest daughter of the superhero Black Lightning. Couldn't do Thunder. I had her change, and she came back as Harley Quinn, the quintessential villain. She tossed me a Joker tee, which was fine because that fit my temperament, darkness, and mood. I squeezed into the tee as I had done the others, became rough, pulled her to me. Had her on her back, pretty mouth opened, gave her face and throat that which it desired. Again, her softness hardened me. Now she was my accoutrement, the accessory I needed to complement this outfit of agony. She was the vessel I dominated, the orifices I took charge of and used to release my torment and ache. I dug deep, made the *Titanic* rise from its depths, had her facedown, ass up, gave her pain and pleasure. Misplaced anger, when given in slow, profound, measured strokes, felt like honeymoon sex and fairy-tale love, made a common woman feel like a princess. Two hours later she was Catwoman and I was Batman, my final ire a supernova, an imploding sun. Whatever lived inside her was volatile, a new kind of fire, as hard to extinguish as the wrath inside me. Secrets lived inside her as secrets lived inside us all.

When the shouting was done, when sanity returned, I wanted to be with her the rest of my days, let her hold me in the absence of talking, in the absence of sex, have her possess me, keep me.

Bess had loved Porgy, but she knew she couldn't stay there with him forever.

CHAPTER 26

I WATCHED GEMMA Buckingham get dressed in a very nice blue sleeveless dress, then checked her out when she was putting on perfume. She sprayed it in the air and ran, laughed through the mist. I watched the transformation from a woman who had woken up looking like she'd had the roughest of rough nights to a professional woman who looked like she'd never had drunken sex. She took a short East Coast call. The domineering tone of her voice and the augmented vocabulary was like hearing a dignitary at the United Nations speak a foreign language. It was intimidating. She put on a different, softer voice and called her white mother in Europe. She lied, told her mum she was about to catch a flight, told her mum she loved her as she sighed, rolled her eyes. She lied to her mother with so much ease.

When the call ended, she walked me to the door. "Pi."

"Well, I swan. That's my name."

"Mr. 3.14 times three-ish. Plus, girth. You were a challenge. Hope to see you again, soon."

"Same here."

"Before they start growing grass in Greenland."

"Would hope so."

"Would love to do this again before global warming gets us all."

"You have my number."

"I saw the aurora borealis."

"I saw London."

"You have core muscles in your selfie stick."

"Selfie stick?"

"Rhymes with. It gets hard like it's been doing all kinds of sit-ups and has a six-pack on top of a six-pack. I can barely stand up. It fills this blank space so perfectly. You broke me."

"How so?"

"The wicked way you shagged me. I'm broken. Won't walk straight for hours, if not days."

"We call that being sprung."

"It's this one bit you did; got me tripping. That one thing you did."

"A man who grew up on hog maw and chitlins ain't scared to eat nothing."

"I was talking about the other thing. That was the one thing that has me tripping."

"What's that one thing?"

"You know. I'm not saying. It was wicked and nasty. I had no idea I'd ever be down with that."

"Oh, you were down with it."

"I'm afraid I've gone from loving meat pie to craving Pi's meat."

We laughed.

"Had no idea a church boy would do the things you do and them so bloody well, well, well."

"I'm an usher, not an angel. Don't get it twisted."

"Inside me it feels like it grows longer than Hong Kong's Central–Mid-Levels Escalator; and is definitely a challenge for a *Black* Brit's gag reflex."

Again, we laughed.

She took both of my hands in hers, kissed me. "This is a special moment. I'm not a slag."

"Slag?"

"Slut. Every negative thing a man says to reduce a woman after the deed is done."

"Well, Miss Fo-Twenty, I don't think you are any of those things. If you are, then I am the same."

"I've been shagged, educated, and conquered. By a Black American."
She grinned. "Don't pat yourself on the back as you leave. At least wait
until you are in your car going down Riverside Drive."

She touched my beard, played in it, and I did the same with her damp
Afro.

She said, "You have a certain je ne sais quoi that charms me, charms
everybody."

"Not everybody."

"Your wicked sense of humor. Sense of self. The way you aren't afraid
to taste my arousal. You make me feel beautiful. It leaves a woman feeling
totally enamored. I've never met a man like you."

"Shimmy shimmy ko ko bop."

Her laughter made her breasts dance. "The things you say and how
you say them."

"I hope to see you soon."

She refused to set me free. "I'm too fond of you. Too fond for my own
good."

"How do you know?"

"I'll know when it's serious for me."

"How?"

"I haven't let you see me with my hair in a bonnet. Do you know what
a sister has to go through with this massive hair when I don't wrap it at
night? All for you. We'll get to the bonnet phase, I hope."

"Baby steps."

"The bonnet stage is when things are getting serious for me, you
know?"

"I thought that was the blow job phase."

"A woman will get cute and blow you, but not let you see her in an
ugly bonnet."

"Okay. Learning."

"Remember, I'm a struggling demisexual."

"A very sexual demisexual with sapiosexual needs to make it all come
together."

"The way you made me come. You broke me. You really did."

"How broken is broken in this case?"

"Makes-me-fantasize-all-day broken."

"What fantasy?"

"On a rainy Saturday, we rest in my master bed, do this, that, and the other, order Grubhub and listen to *Stamped from the Beginning* on Audible. We get comfy and buy a stack of comics each week. We buy novels each week. You finger me while I read to you and then I suck your fingers clean, then push you up against a wall, get down on my knees and practice my sloppy blo' technique to completion."

"Treat me like that and by the time Christmas lights are up I'll be all but living on the shores of the Mississippi with you. I'd only be popping by my place in South Memphis once on the weekends, long enough to check my mail, check on the neighbors, and rake the leaves from my lawn."

She laughed. I did too.

I said, "Yeah, I guess if we do all that, I could easily be broken too."

CHAPTER 27

A REPRESENTATIVE OF Blue Lives Matter popped up out of nowhere and tailed me as soon as I left Gemma Buckingham's upscale community on the Big Muddy. BBQ Becky or a copycat Zimmerman had spotted my black cotton standing high and it looked like pro-Blackness had come to promote Black Lives Matter in the wrong zip code. They stayed on my bumper down I-55, their ride close enough to impregnate my Nova with a good money shot.

Cars and trucks filled with lawbreaking white folks zoomed by me busting the speed limit. I stayed in the slow lane doing five to ten below the limit. Johnny Fun-Spoiler stayed in my rearview and on my ass.

In my rearview I made out one cop hunting me down at fifty miles an hour in ninety-degree heat. I was the runaway of the day.

My phone rang. Sis. I answered. I said, "Sis?"

"Sweet Meat?"

"Busy. Let me hit you back."

I hung up.

I eased off the highway doing five under the speed limit at Parkway, made sure I signaled one hundred feet before all turns, and hit the street doing under twenty-five. As soon as I started my left turn, Johnny Law hit the sirens. I signaled again before I pulled to the right.

The slave catcher parked his flashing lights thirty billy-club lengths behind me. In the direction of Slumber Products and the start of Martin Luther King Riverside Park. The boy in blue took his gotdamn time getting out. A power move to disrespect my relationship with time.

A two-bit psychological move.

I told Siri to play country music, Johnny Cash on repeat. The Man in Black sang his ultimate hit, "Hurt" as six feet of armed local law approached my unarmed driver's-side window in the heat of the scorching sun. Humidity made the air too wet for a fly to lift off, and mosquitoes were grounded until further notice.

Gravel crunched underneath his military-style boots.

My window was down. Air on high.

Johnny Cash crooned the melancholy ditty like he was telling me that misery loved company and I'd be feeling the same pain soon.

Johnny Law saw I was alone. Looked disappointed. Wanted to fry bigger fish. He took in my hair. Spat. Always the hair. Same for my clothes. Grinned an ugly grin of superiority and demanded respect under reflective glasses. I didn't say a word. Speak when spoken to, never before.

"Know why I pulled you over?"

I didn't answer, but I stared.

He asked, "Did you hear my question?"

"It sounded rhetorical to me."

"What was that?"

"That was a rhetorical question."

He didn't like that ish at all.

He expected Tupac and got Blair Underwood.

"Officer, I know some nescient people believe in magical Negroes, but I'm not clairvoyant. If I were, not only would I have known yesterday that you'd be so intent on pulling me over today, but I'd know why."

The hashtag maker didn't like that either.

He clenched his jaw. "Aren't you a smart one."

"I'm a UAN graduate. Same for my master's degree. Maybe for my PhD. Currently I'm an adjunct there. I teach hundreds of students who are in university bettering themselves. Yourself?"

He had no idea what clairvoyant meant.

Or adjunct.

Or rhetorical.

He was probably from a small town that made Memphis look like Times Square when they dropped the ball on New Year's Eve. From a place that still held a racist name like the place that used to be called Dead Negro Hollow, Tennessee; Wetback Tank, New Mexico; or the area once referred to as Runaway Negro Creek; or what was Dead Injun Creek.

Today he was the mayor of Dead Negro Draw.

"A white Chevy Nova was reported stolen thirty minutes ago."

"So you think someone stole a white Nova from around here thirty minutes ago, took it across town and got a top-of-the-line paint job at Maaco ten miles out east on Summer, deliberately painted the white Nova get-a-ticket red to not look so obvious because nobody ever notices a red car, then somehow drove back in time to get to thirty minutes after it was stolen in order to get pulled over and have a conversation filled with prevarications and mendacities with you, Officer . . . *Cockburn?*"

He hated I'd read his badge and said his name out loud.

He kept his hand on his holster.

The man with a name that sounded like a raging STD clenched his jaw and power-stared at me for thirty seconds, called me a nigger with his hidden eyes at least frice every aggravating second. Sweat dripped from his temples as he again disrespected my relationship with time.

Officer Cockburn looked like he'd been force-fed motor oil.

"Let me check in and see if we're going to let you go this time."

"Let me go?" My nostrils flared. "Officer Cockburn. What law was broken? How are you deciding if you're letting me go? You've followed me for five minutes and five miles from downtown riding my bumper, so I know you ran my plates. You've identified who I am and know where I live. The tint on my windows isn't too dark and meets the side and back allowance for thirty-five percent of light transmission. You know this red-as-red-can-get Chevy Nova is registered in my government name, has never been white, and hasn't ever been reported stolen. My head-light's not out and I don't have a busted taillight. I was driving under the speed limit. And you're not letting me go? What's my offense, other than the obvious?"

He spat and headed back to his paddy wagon.

I mumbled, "Motherfucking bitch-ass cracker redneck."

He had my goat and he knew it. But I held it in for now.

This bullshit.

My damn phone rang. It was Gemma Buckingham.

"I was about to send you information on London's Windrush generation . . . logged on . . . just saw . . . Pi . . . do you know . . . then my mum called crying . . . she follows your father's social . . . and . . ."

"Your *mum's* favorite writer died."

"Anything I can do?"

"Will call you. Bye."

"Are you sure? I could—"

I killed the call, my mood darker than the darkest dungeon.

After Gemma Buckingham had made me feel so gotdamn good. On the day my father finally died. I put this on my freshly dead father.

The riled cop sat behind me in his patrol car, seething, lights still flashing to warn that a nuclear power plant was ready to melt down.

Eight minutes and forty-six seconds went by.

Barney Fife came back with a glower that said the only way he could calm his throbbing hand pain was by firing his weapon at an unarmed BMFM until content. Then he dropped the largest tree known to man, the General Sherman Tree, on top of my fuckin nappy head.

"Judge Calhoun said have a nice day. And if he dials your number again to not be an ugly disrespectful nappy-headed bellicose nigger. Your honorable Judge Calhoun said considering the tragic events of the morning, you can go. Enjoy your day, Professor Pi Maurice Suleman. And the Judge of all Judges said to say he's sorry for your loss. That's the only reason this ends here. Would've been a good day for Thunder to roar in Riverside Park. Thank your ugly pappy for dying today."

CHAPTER 28

THE PATROLLER WITH a name that sounded like a bad STD shot me a hard look as he pulled away. He hopped back on the highway, lights flashing, siren screaming, doing twice the speed limit toward Tom Lee Park.

My heart was a drum thumping at 140 beats a minute, but it was still able to beat. What mattered the most was my momma didn't have to end up on TV crying for her son while she planned a closed-casket funeral at Shady Grove. After systemic racism was gone, I pulled away, cut down a side street, Pennsylvania, ten levels of anger at the point of exploding.

I parked at the curb in front of what had been Carver High and screamed. Thought no one could see, but just as the cursing and shouting got hallelujah good, a familiar sports car limped by me. A Nissan 370Z coupe with the club colors of the Las Vegas Raiders. The Volunteer State tags on the back were framed in an Auburn University license plate holder. A worn flag from the islands dangled from the rearview mirror.

Breathing hard, I took in the injured sports car.

She was too busy screaming herself to see my madness.

The rear passenger tire was flat, damn near coming off the rim. Car crippled, it hobbled by me, then pulled over like she had given up.

She pushed open her car door, then eased out. Widow Fatima Martinez-Bowman stood by her car door, then raised her right hand to keep the sun out of her eyes. I knew the car but almost didn't recognize her with violet, turquoise, and blue mermaid hair, long hair, layered, in a bob, full, curled with loose spirals.

She sighed. "Morning, Professor."

I nodded. "Professor. Yeah. Morning."

Her negative energy could scorch the sun.

She'd gotten up on the wrong side of somebody's bed.

She wore trendy sugar-and-spice-colored joggers paired with a harlequin-green summertime hoodie. The hoodie hung low and loosely around her waist the way a woman did when she tried to hide her butt.

She evaluated me. "Looks like you're in a foul mood."

"Just got pulled over by a douchebag cop on Parkway."

"Let's not insult douchebags. At least they have a purpose."

Her singsong Caribbean voice was saccharine. Each word sounded lyrically intelligent, even when her check-engine light was flashing.

I exhaled my angst. "Your mood looks worse than mine."

"Unless the moon falls into the ocean, can't get any worse. I need those black-eyed peas I ate New Year's Eve for good luck to kick in."

"You and me both."

We were both parked in front of Carver High across from two-bedroom single-family homes, a few with well-maintained yards on the same level as mine. Widow Fatima inhaled and exhaled hard, then took measured steps toward me. I closed the door on my Nova, walked the narrow side street toward her at the same pace. She frowned down at her flat tire as she took her reluctant stroll in my direction.

I asked, "What happened? Wait, that's a stupid question."

"Matches how I feel right now."

"Outside the axiomatic, you're jacking up your expensive rims."

"Well, Professor Outside the Axiomatic, I caught a flat tire on the way to the interstate, then pulled over to call Mo Fo 'nem tire company, saw my stupid phone was dead, and realized I left my doggone charger in the kitchen, so I can't call Mo Fo 'nem or AAA. Was going to slow-drive back home, at least get close enough to walk. Got to Pennsylvania and thought taking side streets toward Majuba would be better."

"No one coming?"

"Can you drop me at home? I'll charge my phone, then have Yemi Savage or Pokey 'nem drive me back over this way and meet AAA."

"It's just a flat. Let me check out your spare and change it."

"You don't mind? I mean, you're dressed real nice this morning."

"Where you headed?"

She paused, sat on some hard thought, a hot feeling. "Smackover. Needed to do a quick turnaround business trip to Arkansas."

"Two-hundred-mile road trip. Four hundred round trip."

She kissed her teeth and rode her thoughts.

Some bad news was there, but I didn't get into her business.

I looked behind me, checked to see if more cops were coming.

I was rattled. Deeply rattled.

My fuckin phone buzzed. The death of my father irritated my life.

I nodded, too busy reading condolence messages from Four Ds and forty-eleven others who knew Suleman was my absentee father.

I took what I needed out of the trunk, and she reached into her car, took out a parasol, this one kiwi and off-white. She opened it, made her shade.

She cranked up her radio, covered us with Caribbean music.

I asked my across-the-street neighbor, "What song is that?"

"'Sak Pasé.'"

"Reggae?"

"Soca."

"I'm not hip on soca. I know hip-hop, R and B, blues, gospel, country, pop, soft rock, Elvis, and Al, but nothing about soca."

"You never been to a Why Nots Friday at Cloud Blu?"

"Never evah."

"Don't sleep on Caribbean music." She dabbed her brow like her thoughts were too many and disjointed. "I should go buy some sorrel."

"Sorrel? Never heard of that."

"West Indian drink. Sorrel. A Christmassy lemonade."

"Heard you make a real good lemonade."

She paused, twirled her parasol. "Where's your lemonade maker?"

"Ain't got one."

"You be out all times of the night."

"Partying with Sis."

"I don't see your car come morning when I go run."

"Sure you ain't making lemonade for somebody through the night?"

"As of today, only one mason jar resting at my kitchen table."

"Sounds like you have a story to tell."

Her nostrils flared again. She wanted to talk to not explode.

She said, "Don't repeat my business, Professor Suleman."

"I won't, Professor Bowman."

She struggled, swallowed. "Not a word to Yemi Savage and Pokey. I really am going to feel like a fool when I tell them the fool I've been."

"Okay."

"Between you, me, and the bedpost, this morning I found out the good doctor from TSU was being bad with a heifer from Smackover."

"And you were going there to kick up shit?"

"Heifer was kind enough to ring my phone at two in the morning and now I want to smack her silly butt over and over. Nerve to dial my number looking for me. Skank went off on me. Now you know. He went to Smackover, Arkansas, and got him a new glass to drink from."

"Sorry to hear."

She twirled her parasol faster. "Don't tell nobody my business."

I started changing her flat tire. She came and stood by me, waved away traffic when a car came. Her energy said she had more to say.

Widow Fatima ranted, "Smackover was about to get sheself a new edjumacation. She brought that frama to my house over my phone."

"Frama?"

"Last part of the word *drama*. First part starts with an eff."

"Frama."

"Had me lose my religion and cussing too. At two in the morning. She's going to mess around with the wrong one and need to get resurrected to see another tomorrow."

"You're definitely off to a bad morning."

"I ran after to calm down. Couple hours later. She had me so upset I got dressed and ran from my house through Riverside Park, came out up here and went down Kansas Street back to our end of Blair Hunt."

"How many miles is that?"

"Ten, eleven."

"When I travel that far I take luggage and book an Airbnb."

She laughed a little and shook her head at my joke. "Now I'm in my hurt feelings and talking too much. I done put anger and hurt feelings in charge, let them run my silly mouth, and testified to you now."

"Smackover triggered you."

"Childhood issues. I can't stand a bully, won't take it like I did when I was a teenager, and this gave me too many gosh-darn flashbacks. Don't call my number acting crazy and wake me up calling me out of my name and kick the hornet's nest and don't expect to feel a few good stings."

"Yup. Someone got triggered high and can't come down."

"Smackover, Arkansas, can have the doctor from TSU. The doctor from TSU won't park in my driveway or eat supper at my dinner table ever again. Right now, if a tree was uprooted and fell on his two-timing butt during a tornado, I'd feel sorry for the tree and forgive the tornado."

"That would be an act of God."

"She was still blowing up my phone after I ran. He did the cheating and she's mad at me. Embarrassing. I just posted I was no longer single and now I gotta change my status on Facebook again. Like a fool."

"I'm done changing your flat tire."

She moved her parasol to her other hand. "That was fast."

I put her jack and flat tire in her trunk. She went to her car and came back with napkins and bottled water. I cleaned my hands the best I could. She wasn't rushing to leave. We stood in the shade. She was still twirling her parasol, fired up and not ready to let go of the disturbance in her heart.

I said, "Everybody thought you were happy over there."

"Said I worked too much, was too independent, didn't eat enough, jogged too much, and based on the pictures of the girl who rang my number at two in the morning, I guess I'm a bit too skinny for his taste."

"Smackover."

"For an old-ass used cup with a bunch of Bébé kids. Well, she ain't old, ain't but twentysomething, but she has two kids."

"That's mean."

"I'm mad. This has to run its course. I'll be nice tomorrow."

"He's coming back like 'Return of the Mack'?"

"His Mercedes ain't welcome on Blair Hunt unless he wants me to get my matches and go Angela Bassett in *Waiting to Exhale* on his ass."

"What she do? Doctor like him? Professor like you?"

"Her Facebook page said she works at Walmart. Cashier."

"Damn."

"On EBT too. She posted a complaint about her EBT being late."

"Somebody's trolling big-time."

"Like I said, I'm mad."

"She ain't got nothing on you."

"A bigger booooooooo-tay."

"Bigger don't mean better."

"A fat ass ain't always where it at."

"Oh, fat shaming."

"She fatty with a batty and called me out of my name, and what she said was the foulest thing a woman can say to another woman, at two in the morning, and fat shaming is where you're drawing the line?"

"What did she call you?"

"Anorexic. Cunt."

"Oh. Damn."

"Was she *cunt* shaming, pardon my French? Does she know my *cunt*? Can she see it? I saw her photos on Facebook. Her booty so big when she leaves a room it takes it ten minutes to catch up with her body. This anorexic cunt was going to be on her like a duck on a june bug."

"Two wrongs."

"This wrong was going to whup her to make it right."

"You're old enough that your wants won't hurt you."

"She started it. He prefers her to me. Maybe I am jealous but she a big girl. Miss Big Bones got a Bertha Butt Boogie booty that could put Betty Butt, Bella Butt, and Bathsheba Butt to shame on Baby Got Back night at Mollie Fontaine and I can't say she got a fat ass? Black man always leaves a Black woman for either a bigger butt or a white woman. He got both. She's white and I called her white. That shaming too? I guess I can't get upset and do no yo-momma snaps no mo' either, huh?"

I laughed. "Why are you going off on me now?"

"She called me an *anorexic cunt.* If I called her a snowflake would I be snow shaming the snow bunny on a sunny morning? And you know white folks say way worse things about us day and night on the Internet. That's where you draw the line? You siding with my enemy, neighbor?"

"I stand corrected, Professor. Team Fatima all the way."

"And, Professor, you know when a sista mad, she gonna say what she gonna say the way she wanna say it, then ask Jesus to forgive her when she done acting up. Don't get all fake East Memphis PC at sunrise and censor my well-earned pisstivity. She started it. She. Started. It."

"Stop shaming folks."

"Besides, cain't nobody hear me and ain't nobody out here but me, you, and God, and I know he's laughing. He made her fool butt and she ain't nothing but a joke. And like I said, neighbor, she the one started it."

"Stop shaming."

She mocked me. "Stop shaming. Stop shaming. Stop shaming."

I said, "Neighbor, be glad you didn't make that trip."

"I know, I know. I act stupid and she wins ten times over."

"That's how it always plays out for us with too much to lose."

"All I can say is he left me for a centipede. Centipedes are evil caterpillars, mad because they will never become butterflies."

"You are a butterfly."

"And I am a very rare butterfly getting degreed up."

"Can't argue that."

"I might be slim in the thighs but I'm easy on the eyes."

"You're a gorgeous woman."

That disarmed her. "Wow. I would settle for cute."

"Gorgeous."

"Never knew you thought . . ."

"Charming and stunningly beautiful."

She stopped twirling her parasol. "I'm just gonna say thank you."

"I guess he's blind in one eye and can't see out of the other."

She sighed. "They say a way to a man's heart is through his stomach. I cooked him some of everything. Oxtail. Peach cobbler. Candied yams. Smothered chicken. Barbecue chicken. Baked chicken. Greens. String beans. Mac and cheese. Rice and peas. Flying fish. Gumbo. Mashed potatoes. Patties, ackee and salt-fish, jerk chicken, salt-fish fritters, callaloo, breadfruit. Curry goat, cabbage, plantains, red snapper. Bombay duck. Bread pudding. Roti. And gave him my lemonade. Gave it to him too soon."

I let that rest a few seconds, tried to do a mild redirect to calm her down. "So, you're from all over and ended up here in Memphis."

"Started off on Highway 48 West in McComb."

"Mississippi. Lived there with your folks?"

"Parents split."

"So you had two homes."

"Nah. Not even close. Both remarried other folks, had new families. Momma moved to Iowa to be a nurse. Daddy moved to Utah and opened a used-car lot. That divorce made me a Little Orphan Annie."

"Where they put you?"

"Grew up with my grandparents from when I was four or five. The West Indian side. When I was a teen, stayed with the African side in Brooklyn half a summer. Then got sent down to Grapeland to stay with other relatives a couple weeks. A time or two they sent me to the islands for a month, or to Africa for two months. I was a soccer ball."

"You got shuffled around a lot."

"Mostly state to state with one old, raggedy suitcase I had to wrap tape around to keep from falling open on the bottom of the Greyhound."

"That's rough."

"Never really unpacked. I *stayed* places but never felt like I *lived* anywhere. *Stayed* in a lot of houses. Slept on more sofas and floors than I care to remember. Never felt like I had a home until I bought my little house. Now I feel settled. Not as anxious. I could finally unpack."

"That's a journey."

"You?"

"With my momma and siblings. Same house since I was born, then moved down on Blair Hunt Drive. Same neighborhood all my life."

"Must be nice."

She spun her parasol again. Perturbed. Her emotional tell.

I said, "Like your new hairstyle."

"Flew to Vegas and had it done."

"Said no Black woman in Tennessee to me ever."

"I love your hair, too."

"Freedom."

"Absolute."

In a few words, we said a lot regarding our history of hair.

I'd seen her rock many natural hairstyles over the years: Bantu knots, bald with big earrings, short and texturized and colored salmon, or colored dark green for St. Patrick's Day. I'd seen her in a Mohawk, braids to her butt, short and happy to be nappy, caramel curls, wash and go, coiled, teeny-weeny 'fro, French braids, blond with sides shaved.

Each style was a statement of freedom. White folks didn't get that. They lived in our history without noticing what was happening to us.

Back in the day when folks in the tristate area bought $5.50 tickets at Goldsmith's to see the Beatles, the Ronettes, and the Remains at the Mid-South Coliseum, white folks controlled our hair. They still haven't let that go. Our children were being kicked out of school for growing Black hair while Black. Dreadlocks, braids, and Mohawks were part of our little steps toward freedom. It felt like loss of power and lack of submission and rejection to the ones comfortable with seeing my folks oppressed in any way they could think of. When Momma's momma was growing up, damn near every Black hairstyle was forced assimilation, the Black version of a famous white woman's hairdo that undid everything Africa. It was what white people accepted. If you wanted a job, break out the hot comb or the creamy crack.

They controlled our hair.

They controlled our self-esteem.

Black people from sea to shining sea destroyed their natural hair in hopes of garnering a white man's approval that would come when hell froze over and the devil went ice-skating with Judy Garland.

I thought about all of that because that beauty-queen Bitch from Brownsville Dr. Stone-Calhoun wanted to cut mine to feel empowered.

The widow asked, "Were you screaming when I passed by you?"

"Was aggravated because of the police harassing me for the forty-eleventh time and was singing out my pain in the key of G."

"I guess I'm not the only one who wants to smack somebody."

"This morning, no, you're not."

"Hope we can keep this moment in the sun between us."

"You don't scream, I won't holla."

She chuckled. "I'm acting ugly and you called me gorgeous."

"I take it back."

"Too late now, handsome. Too late."

"Oh, you think I'm handsome."

Her cavernous dimples came to life. "My handsome across-the-street neighbor called me gorgeous and I don't even have my face on."

Music flowed our way from up Fields Avenue and disturbed our conversation to distract ourselves from the world. A commotion had started up that way. We fanned ourselves and watched a few people from this two-lane street in the 38109 exit their homes, hurrying off that way.

She wasn't ready to leave. I didn't want to go back to reality.

I latched on to the wicked beats, rapped along with the hard lyrics.

She chuckled. "Oh, you're a rapper now? UAN know about this?"

"That's one of Memphis's best groups. You better recognize."

She said, "When I was in middle school, I wanted to be a rapper. I made up my intro to this horrible song."

"Spit some bars."

She threw down. "Little titties, little waist, little booty, pretty face; long legs, slender thighs, eyes that get you hypnotized."

I laughed like death hadn't touched my family this morning. I laughed as if I hadn't been threatened to become strange fruit.

The widow motioned at the commotion. "We need to investigate."

"Lock your car."

"We ain't going far."

"On this block I lock my car when I'm inside it."

She did and I did the same; then we crossed the two-lane street.

Midway up Fields Avenue, music by Moneybagg Yo blasted. A crowd had congregated outside a yellow wooden house where the zoysia grass needed a makeover and some landscaping love. A dozen folks were on the patchy yard of a two-bedroom home. My people were pumping fists in a circle around two shirtless teenage brothas. The bros were swinging at each other like Ali and Frazier back in Momma's day.

The widow said, "We're just in time to watch a good one."

We joined in, cheered the playful street fight.

A slim, bald guy my age waved at me. BoJack. We went to Carver together. Hadn't seen him in at least five years. He had on his work uniform. I waved at my classmate and we both went back to eyeing the morning entertainment. Slaps in Cobraville echoed like gunshots, and the crowd encouraged the slap boxers to take the blow and dish two more, the n-word flying free like birds in the blue sky.

This was part of the ritual. The upbringing. The toughening.

She asked, "Professor, do you know what we're witnessing?"

"Slap boxing."

"More than that."

"I know."

Nothing else needed to be said as we took in the sport.

We understood the world we lived in.

Some folks were armed, dressed like yuppies, marching at rallies, waving tiki torches, and openly calling for a race war, so we did what we had to do to stay ground-level tough.

We had to learn to not be afraid on our side of the tracks before we stepped on grass and concrete where we were unwelcome.

My people dressed smart and sat at lunch counters across the tracks and were spit on, slapped, punched in the face, treated to water hoses and billy clubs, shouted at like we were less than human—Black man, woman, or child. Every day was hell week when you lived encased in Black skin.

Every time we were knocked down, we cursed, rolled over with the pain, nodded, spat bright red blood, and made it to our bloodied knees in prayer, nodded again, returned to one knee in resistance, then smirked, looked evil in the eyes, nodded three times, and got back up on both feet with dignity. Be the abused a Black man, colored woman, or Negro child, we always got back up on both feet.

My phone buzzed. Didn't bother to look down. I knew who it was. Not answering infuriated her.

Once away from the lies they lived, once they had ditched their judgmental friends, hypocritical peers, and two-faced peers, people like the Bitch from Brownsville exhaled and surrendered to the burn within. Those types capitulated to the secret them. To their authentic selves. Evil to us by day, they craved to be inside the warmth of Africa, needed to have the profoundness of the motherland live deep within them . . . quenching the desire inside them . . . from first darkness until they trembled and sang *nants ingonyama bagithi baba* at sunrise. I just never pegged Dr. Stone-Calhoun as being that type. She fuckin fooled me.

Slap boxing had a winner, but it wasn't about winning or losing. It taught my skinfolk to get in the fight. It taught us to fight back. Even if you lost you were respected for not backing down. It looked physical, but it was mental preparation. It was us pledging one another and getting ready to cross the burning sands put down by white folks. That toughening up was the Black man learning to stay in the fight even if the odds were stacked against him. The boys we cheered on were the next Malcolm, Martin, and Marcus working it out in boot camp. The girls were the next generation of Black women refusing to capitulate to water hoses, German shepherds, and church bombings. The people before us had gotten in the ring and slap boxed their way from slavery through Jim Crow and beyond civil rights into the Black Lives Matter era.

Very few victories, lots of blows taken, but we stayed in the ring.

We had to learn to not be afraid here before we marched over there.

It was a sign.

I had to stay in the ring.

Take the blow.

Fight back.

Against people like the Calhouns. I just didn't know how.

The widow said, "They're showing off for some girl. Not sure which one, but they're acting silly when the sun too high."

The two teen boys ended their round, gave each other some dap, and stepped aside, both sweating profusely. Two teen sisters stepped into the front-yard ring; both were stretching, talking smack to each other, each anxious to have the same fun and win bragging rights for this street.

My phone was still exploding, had never stopped while I was changing the flat tire. Gemma Buckingham was calling back to back, sending texts.

I sent her calls to voice mail. The Fastest Swimmers received the same fate. My father was dead. Reality reeled me back in.

The widow had seen enough, and we headed back to our rides.

She said, "Funny."

"What?"

"I never come down Pennsylvania."

"Same here, not since high school."

"We're in the same odd place at the same exact time early on a random morning. Feels like we'd been directed this way by the universe."

"Sometimes a coincidence is just a coincidence."

"Right. Just a coincidence you're parked where I broke down."

When we made it back to her car, she adjusted her top around her waist, closed her parasol like it was the period at the end of a sentence, then in a professional tone said, "Thanks for saving me."

The way she said that, she was talking about more than the flat tire.

I said, "We all need saving at some point."

She eased in, started the engine, made it purr, put the air on high, then let down her window. "How much I owe you, Professor?"

"Go back home, Professor, and we're even."

"You're heading home?"

"We pull up at our houses at the same time, folks will start talking."

She paused.

I asked, "What?"

"You are excessively handsome and have an amazing smile."

"All right, now."

"You started it. Called me gorgeous. You're the one started it."

Her new hairstyle. How her clothes fit. If Innocent and Sexy had a baby, then she was their only child. She was a lusty song in a Baptist church on Easter Sunday, what you'd get if Walt Disney made soft porn.

I asked, "Done being mad?"

"Done. For now."

"Now, take your narrow ass home."

"Ass shaming? You can rank on mine, but I can't talk about hers?"

We laughed again.

She thanked me, waved, then cruised south in her two-seater sports car. Soca music faded as she drove south at an easy pace. I watched her disappear, then composed Gemma Buckingham a courtesy text, told her I enjoyed her company last night, was busy now dealing with my father, and I'd contact her when I was able to. I hit send as I eased in my warm Nova, my father's death trending higher on Twitter. I went back to reality.

Went back to seeing if slave catchers were still on my tail.

They had come as far as my exit.

I doubted they would come into the heart of Blackness.

My phone rang. It was Dr. Stone-Calhoun. I rejected the call. She called right back. I rejected it again. Again. Again. Again. Again. Again.

CHAPTER 29

KANSAS STREET AUTOMOTIVE was the small shop for the neighborhood. Our mechanic had been there at least fifty years recycling Black dollars. As I headed south, I saw a shiny black VW Beetle with yellow roses on the dash parked out front. I slowed down and turned into the small lot just as a 31 Crosstown Kansas sped by going north, a teenage boy chasing the bus as if he were trying to catch his freedom. As soon as I pulled up, I saw Momma talking to the owner. The owner was laughing.

I waved at our mechanic, a light-skinned septuagenarian with sweet gray hair, said I'd missed him at church the last month of Sundays. He laughed and waved me away. I always told him that.

Momma finished with him and came out to my car, waved the invoice at me like it was an extension cord made for whupping me.

She barked, "As far as anybody who knows you enough to care knows, you were on the side of the road somewhere dead, or some woman in a police uniform had come to the wrong house shooting."

"I was busy last night."

Momma raised a brow. "With whom?"

"You haven't met her."

"Where she from?"

"She's not from M-Town."

"Boy."

"London."

"How you meet her?"

"UAN event."

"Since when these shenanigans been going on?"

"Known her a couple weeks."

"Oh, she one of them fast girls."

"Momma why do you talk so fast?"

"Stupid people talk slow."

"And Momma ain't stupid."

"Now, was you with that fast-ass from UAPB?"

"Nah."

"Hope you wrapped it up."

"Drawing the line."

"Line undrawn. I wanna be a momma once removed, but not by some out-of-town heifer I ain't met. Have your fun but you know she has to stand before me and see if she can handle this family."

"I'll ask her over for a Sunday dinner. Give me a few days to see how it goes."

"It went last night. Why won't it go in a few days? Anyway, Sweet Meat, answer your Momma."

The condom question was in the air, and the look on my face didn't lie. "Well."

"No babies before a wedding, no matter what I have done."

"Women nowadays don't want a wedding before the baby."

"She pretty? Don't need no butt-ugly grandbabies. I'll love 'em but won't look at 'em much."

"Not coyote ugly."

"Dark-skinned?"

"Not so much."

"Brown?"

"Other side of the paper bag, but not as far as Kanye traveled."

"Boy, don't make me have a WorldStar moment. I'll dog-walk you on Facebook Live."

I beat my chest like a drumroll. "Bring on Sister Colorism, the first cousin of Brother Racism."

"Bringing Momma Factism. Outside of Lena Horne and Halle Berry, they don't age well. I dated yellow men. They looked real good young. When I see them now all the white blood in them done bubbled up, come out. They look like they need to drop their bodies off at the gym and don't pick it up until it's ready. They're eating bad food, done let themselves go toward diabetes and hypertension, got all Porky Pig and look more like Mr. Charlie than Charlie's legitimate children. The ones that passing, they start to look like the Black side of their family if they live long enough for the real hair born in Africa to reveal itself. They perm it every day to not look like they came from where they come from."

"Momma."

"Sweet Meat, don't interrupt me. Where you say she from?"

"She's from the UK. London. Some area called Brixton."

"Big Ben and queens and kings."

"Momma, please."

"Momma Nike talking, shut your trap and widen your ears. If she single, she's single for a reason. For every single pretty woman, especially a yellow gal, there some broke man glad she gone to hunt for gold somewhere else. Takes a man a long time to see the ugly in a pretty woman that can pass because a man sees that kind of pretty and he stop thinking straight. Bring her by the house so Momma can get her liquored up and look in her face until I can see the nature of her soul and give you a report so you can see what she is hiding under that pretty. Pretty woman can't hide nothing from your momma. I ain't ready to see my boy brokenhearted and crying the tears of a clown like his momma used to when she was a fool."

"Sis dates all races and you don't complain."

"That means all races think my daughter pretty, and that means they will think I'm gorgeous if she brings one back to Sunday dinner. Bring home another Abby Phillip, Genevieve Nnaji, Karine Jean-Pierre, or a Mara Rose. I promise not to run the next one off. Momma got issues, and Momma pretty as they can come. Being called Black and ugly by a daddy who'd been brainwashed into thinking he was Black and ugly didn't help, not one bit. Everybody had the same mentality. When I grew up Hollywood would ugly up pretty dark-skinned women in movies and make

Miss Ann look prettier than she will ever be first thing in the morning. There were a lot of Jayne Kennedys. People still missed the pretty in a dark woman like me until Lupita came along, now they Wakanda saluting us and hollering at your momma *everywhere* she goes. Grew up being called ugly, while ugly, funny-looking, light-skinned girls were called pretty. By my own people. Colored girl grows up witnessing that, first boy tells her she pretty, don't know how to act. Momma a brown-skinned grown-ass woman now and ain't worried about being liked. You can't control if folks like you, so if they don't, let them go kick rocks. Momma done double-dipped in her feelings now. Momma gonna take a chill pill and downshift from fifth gear."

"Momma Nike done talking?"

"Mouth still moving; come to your own conclusion."

I said, "Momma not done."

She hummed. "Can she run a lawn mower?"

"No idea."

"Momma Nike done talking. Bye-bye, conversation. Time to roll."

Momma fanned herself and headed to my car.

I eased us back on Kansas Street.

Momma looked over her invoice. "Need to replace both dang control arms. Leak from stupid oil pan, no idea how much that will cost yet. SRS light on but he can't figure out why, not yet. Air pump mounting bolts missing. Need to rotate tires. Plugs, timing belt, and water pump will be about six hundred. Rear brakes another two hundred. About fifteen hundred to make it whole again."

She took in my face, my green eyes.

My face was his face.

She'd had to live with that all of my life.

I came out of her womb looking like a man she couldn't stand.

He'd been as inescapable for her as he was for me, my face in her eyes every day, his novels everywhere I went. She regretted meeting him but loved me. She loved me as hard as she hated him. I was her positive, her negative, her good, her bad, her contranym.

Momma whispered her thoughts, "Mr. Suleman gone."

She never called him anything but his formal name, as if he was still her elder. She had put his last name as my surname back then, for court reasons. She was called the gold digger from Memphis, shamed in court, the home-wrecking Black girl, but everything was handled behind closed doors. She could've been very twisted and bitter from that encounter, or from being treated very badly by her parents, but she struck out on her own, a brown-skinned girl in a white man's world, made a few mistakes, and still turned out to be amazing.

I asked, "You okay?"

"Are you okay? That's my concern."

I said, "I'm okay if you're okay."

She pulled her lips in.

I said, "Momma?"

She shook her head over and over.

Momma wasn't okay. I pulled over.

I said, "Momma?"

"Mr. Suleman has gifted me with bad memories this morning."

"Momma. I'm listening. It's just us."

She took a moment. "We live in a nation of unplanned pregnancies. A nation of accidental babies. America would almost be an empty parking lot if we were populated by intentional babies. Welfare office is wall to wall with white girls. Food-stamp lines nothing but rednecks. But they came after me. They came hard after a Black teenage girl from Memphis almost thirty-two years ago. They said ugly things in those court papers because I was pregnant by a famous man and didn't get rid of you to make his life with his wife and other brand-new son easier. It read like they were trying to ruin any potential future I might have, and they hated you before you were born. A woman can't forget or forgive certain things. He had a bunch of babies by different women after, and I bet a dollar to a doughnut hole they all received the same ugly treatment in family court. Those nasty and amoral people tried to get me to get rid of my baby. Said I wouldn't finish school. Wouldn't be anything. Wouldn't have anything. I've outlived him and his bullshit. Momma won. I was in the hospital by myself in labor for thirty-six hours and they still induced labor because you didn't want to come out. I notified his attorney and then I was the fuckin problem. He's still your daddy even if he's about to be in a coffin and dead in the grave, but six feet under or six away, dead or alive, your father will never be my friend."

I held her hand and she squeezed mine. Her being hurt made my anger grow. I wouldn't kill for me, but I'd murder for her.

"They talked about me like I had no ambition whatsoever. The stereotypical view of all Black women in America had my name on top, that unwarranted and unresearched assessment of me filed as a legal document like it was my truth. I went to see him because I was a fan. Wanted to be a writer at the time. He left a bitter taste in my mouth so I changed ambitions just so people wouldn't accuse me of riding his jock. I was a country girl from Memphis who wanted to be like Zora Neale Hurston. He stole that from me. He was international. I knew me and Mr. Suleman had a moment but never had a chance. Not for you, he would've forgotten my name thirty-two years before he died."

We'd gone to see Mr. Suleman once. A book signing in Nashville. We drove two hours and parked outside, were going to go into the packed event, stand to the side, let him see us, then walk away. That was five or six years ago. We didn't get out of the car, the same VW Momma had left at the shop to get made whole. We watched people go in in swarms, at least four hundred fans, then made a U-turn back to Memphis.

Mr. Suleman never did literary events in Memphis. I guess he did what he had to do to avoid us. Checks were sent from his accountant like he was forced to pay monthly extortion for racketeering. My guess was that checks were sent so if it ever came out, he would have seemed like less of a criminal. In the land where Jerry Lee Lewis married his thirteen-year-old cousin, that was how I felt about it.

Momma wiped away her tears and I started driving again "So. A yellow gal."

"Afrocentric. Not hiding the Blackness."

"She bet' not be a mud duck. Yellow gals can be mud ducks too. Especially when they start acting a quarter past white."

When we made it to Momma's house, a black SUV was parked out front, engine running. Fat Man was back to give it one last try. I saw him and became as unstable as nitroglycerin, was on the verge of exploding.

I parked in Momma's driveway. Eased out of my Nova like a cowboy easing off his horse to put on his six-shooter for a showdown at high noon. Fat Man stepped out of his ride the moment we did, sharp as a tack, nervous as hell, his hands up in the don't-shoot position, knees shaking. He saw the no soliciting sign, understood he was trespassing on private property, kept his hands up in absolute surrender.

"I just got off a plane. I don't know if you heard . . ."

Our expressions let him know we had heard.

"Five minutes. I was there when he left, and all I do, these are his final wishes. He regrets you didn't come. Five minutes, then I will be gone, back to catch a plane to California to arrange his funeral."

Momma looked at me for a decision, and I nodded at the CEO of the only family I knew. We went toward Fat Man. I took the lead to protect my momma. No MLK in my heart, I marched like I was Malcolm X on steroids. Momma walked like she was twenty feet tall.

We stormed through a raging sun and unrelenting humidity to see what the fuck the Fat Man from California wanted this time.

THE SECRET LIFE OF
MR. SULEMAN

CHAPTER 30

THE FIRST TIME I saw Mr. Suleman, he was suited up, boxed up, ready to be eulogized and buried six feet under. I stood over his extravagant coffin and told him hello, was respectful as I had been taught by Momma, said it was nice to finally meet him, but he didn't loosen up his formaldehyde-filled scowl and say anything back. Two thousand people, fans, friends, family, were at the event. When I turned around his teary-eyed widow saw me and leapt to her feet. The woman pointed at me, petrified. She was beautiful, skin high-money smooth, complexion as dark as ink. Her legs wobbled and her eyes rolled into the back of her head as she fainted. She fell fast; nothing caught her except the colorful carpeted floor. Her black dress flew up and exposed her black thong, which went unnoticed, because everyone was staring at me, the stranger with the dead man's face.

The deceased man's legitimate sons and daughters rose to their feet. Fat Man had told me that my West Coast siblings' ages ranged from midthirties down to early twenties. We were all adults, at least by the definition of the word. Jaw tight, I evaluated the choir of privileged Sulemans.

They mean mugged and I returned the favor.

We all resembled him, but I was the closest to being the doppelganger of the dead man in the extravagant dead man's box. I stood over a dead man dressed like I was coffin ready. He was no longer clean-shaven, had grown a beard in his final days, became me as he died in slow motion. Salt and pepper, more pepper than salt. His suit the same color as mine. That was why my appearance was next-level shocking. I was his ghost. He was what I'd look like, lifeless, no spirit, worm food, in years to come.

Everyone from the choir to the pulpit to the congregation became a gathering of bees buzzing. My presence confirmed a more than thirty-year-old rumor. I adjusted my necktie, put on my black shades, and left the rumbling church, stepped in the nasty air smothering Los Angeles, California.

Had to get in my rental and meet with a well-tanned fat man at a nearby coffee shop.

CHAPTER 31

MADNESS CAME DOWN out of the clouds and I got distracted. I missed a right turn when I saw five helicopters had swooped out of nowhere and were flying low overhead. The whirlybirds roared like thunder. Sounded like they were damn near on my roof. News and police were cutting through gray air and smog hunting for a runaway. Down on the streets traffic kept moving like no one gave a hot damn.

This harsh energy. This was not the Bible Belt. Not Memphis, West Memphis, or Hernando.

Right after GPS said I'd crossed congested West Adams Boulevard and made it to the other side of the intersection, three lanes of arrogant, lane-swapping traffic going north came to a hard stop.

I had made it across the intersection while the traffic light was fresh yellow. The fool behind me floored it to make it through the same yellow light. The idiot didn't realize traffic had stopped. They slammed on their brakes hard enough to burn rubber, then smashed into the rear of my leased SUV with enough force to raise the back end up toward the heaven my dead pedophilic father would never see.

I threw my rented SUV in park and let three dozen cars speed by, each passing close enough to rip my door off, before I stepped out on traffic-filled La Brea, a street name I wasn't sure how to pronounce. The driver broke away from their deployed air bag, struggled to get their door to open, waited for a short break in the madness of California traffic, then staggered out of their fucked-up vehicle. The front end of the car that hit me was annihilated, hood folded like an accordion, smoke rising to polluted clouds, fluids leaking and the scents peppering the carbon-monoxide-filled air.

That wasn't what was un-fucking-believable. Blond ten-inch curly Afro on a Black woman in red-bottom heels. It was Gemma Buckingham dressed like a French model rocking a new hairstyle.

As traffic backed up behind us, I exploded, "You're following me?"

"Pi, don't hate me."

"How did you know where I was?"

"Your father died. I came to offer condolences on behalf of myself and me mum."

"You were there?"

"I followed you when you left the funeral. Tried to catch you, but you were practically running."

"You've stalked me from Memphis to Los Angeles?"

"Not getting one caring, concerned message returned felt like I'd been shagged and ghosted."

"When you bring your UK driving here?"

"I arrived yesterday."

"I landed a few hours ago."

"I've reached out to you a dozen times since I heard—"

With madness over our heads and crazy traffic at our side, a Black man and a Mexican suddenly bolted from around a corner in panic mode. Both were in their early twenties. They scowled at us, saw our vehicles were in an act of congress, then sprinted by us. They yanked a woman out of her car. The Black guy yelled he saw a mu-fuckin' kid in the car. The Mexican tossed the baby and its seat on the filthy pothole-ravished streets with its mother and sped away. Took all of ten seconds.

Gemma Buckingham trembled in my arms, terrified beyond belief. Police sirens magnified; now it was a bona fide high-speed chase, with the bad guys running folks off the road and breaking red lights.

The carjacked mother's knees had road rash that showed her skin to the white meat. She bled from being thug-handled and thrown to the ground like she was trash. She screamed for the world to help her, but folks only looked at her, recorded her for social media, or shrugged and raced to the bus stops like that was her problem. A swarm moved around her like she'd been dumb enough to ride with her door unlocked, so you get what you get. She flagged down the LAPD. A couple of cop cars at the end of the Soul Train of sirens stopped to tend to the traumatized family. It looked like the baby was okay, crying, but had no idea what had happened. The Asian mom was fit to be tied.

New traffic came from three directions, passed the congestion, had no idea what was going on and didn't slow to find out. Gunshots sounded in the distance. Gemma Buckingham jerked. Frozen, we watched this ish like tourists. A carload of millennials cussed and told us to get our fucking cars out the goddamn street so they could go to fucking work. Parents cursed in front of their kids, blew horns, yelled at other folks to speed up, change lanes, or get the hell out of the way. They acted like fools right in front of the police as they assisted the assaulted mom and child. West Coast people had places to be and they were ready to peel a cap to make sure they got there. This was my first morning in Los Angeles.

This city was a foreign language.

With a shudder, I pried Gemma Buckingham away from me. "We're about to get run down."

Her voice trembled. "These wankers, these bloody rude wankers."

I moved her to the curb and pulled her ride to the side, parked it in the Chevron station lot where gas was damn near five dollars a gallon, more than twice and a half what I paid in M-Town.

Gemma Buckingham called her rental company and within thirty minutes a AAA truck came, carted it off to the land of damaged vehicles. We got into my injured SUV, eased away.

Would deal with my accident later.

My insurance would cover me, and she promised to hit me back the thousand-dollar deductible.

The steering pulled to the left. She had jammed my rear, damaged the bumper, and messed up the suspension. The smooth ride was now rough. The on-ramp was packed. A light was allowing cars on one at a time, so we went nowhere fast. We crept along like we were getting on a ride at Six Flags on its busiest day of the year. We were trapped. My GPS said it would take twenty-six minutes to go three miles. Back home that was a short road trip out of the city.

"Pi. What is your destination?"

"I'm going a mile down to the next exit. Have to meet a fat man to get the skinny on what other bullshit I have to do next."

"Aren't you going back in the direction you came from?"

"I went too far north, and now have to go east, then go south again."

"North, south, east, west, none of that means anything to me out here."

"I misread the GPS, took the wrong street, and let it redirect me. All the streets have funny names, a lot of them are in Spanish, and I don't speak Spanish, so they look like gibberish to me."

"The helicopters scared me, made me slow and take my eyes off the road."

"We saw a gotdamn carjacking."

"We almost got carjacked."

"Not for the accident. They had their roughish eyes on our rides."

"That poor woman. She was all of five feet tall, if that. Did they have to be so brutal?"

"At least her kid is too young to remember this ish. You gonna be okay over there?"

"I am traumatized. My fingers are numb, heart palpitating, can barely think straight. Hear it all the time and see it in movies but you never know how real and terrifying such horrific atrocities are until they happen before your eyes. I'm scared of driving or walking down a street in this city now."

"One morning in Los Angeles and we both need counseling and an oxygen tank."

"This city. I've never seen this part before, only the beaches, Santa Monica, and Rodeo Drive."

"Welp. Not impressed."

"I'm missing the snarky comments, British classism, and occasional stabbings in London."

As we made it to the top of the on-ramp, I saw traffic that went on for miles. Moving like a snail, I looked at the lumps of debris scattered on the side of the road, then saw a little billboard that proudly announced that this part of the nation's coast-to-coast highway was sponsored by Atheist United.

I said, "No wonder we're seeing what we're seeing. Your people have adopted this section."

"Agnostic, not atheist."

She pulled down the visor, used the mirror to check her hair and makeup. She looked amazing and smelled fucking fabulous.

I said, "Like your new do."

She grinned through the anxiety. "Didn't want to arrive looking busted."

I glanced north and saw the edges of mountains hidden by smog. Maybe the city was beautiful from a distance, but I came from clean air and skies with a color that envied Carolina blue. Here nasty air covered everything beautiful. Layers of filth so deep I could use my finger to write out a grocery list.

This town was a pretty woman in dirty drawers.

Gemma Buckingham took a hard breath. "Why didn't you stay at your father's funeral?"

"I said I would come; didn't say I would stay. Did as I promised to honor his last will."

Gemma Buckingham said, "Was an odd moment. You look so unique to me, then we came here, and I saw your siblings, saw rows of men and women with green eyes, saw people who looked like you."

She had an obituary in her hand. I saw his face again, his eyes, the face I would have if I lived as long as he had. She saw my expression and tucked the obituary away, eased it in her black purse.

"This city is loud, as pleasant as the scream from a tuba. Air so thick it looks like it's smoldering. If London's air looked like that, so smoky and gray, there would be a dozen fires across the city."

We were almost run off the highway by a lane-changing busted-ass Civic with a coffee-can exhaust. Fool drove that piece of shit for ten feet like he was at NASCAR going for the checkered flag. Traffic stopped him cold; then the six lanes moved at between two and five miles an hour, stop and go, more stop than go. Fifteen minutes and one exit later GPS told me to exit at Crenshaw Boulevard, commanded me to turn right.

We were greeted by a carnival of homeless people hustling and living at every corner of the off-ramp, hands extended for donations. A street artist had redone a billboard for *Once Upon a Time in Hollywood*. Leo DiCaprio's face had been replaced by Jeffrey Epstein's. Brad Pitt's face had been replaced with Roman Polanski's. The billboard had been re-titled *Once Upon a Time in Pedowood*.

That billboard was a sign.

Crenshaw Boulevard was a three-lane street with potholes unmatched in undeveloped countries.

We exited and were greeted by gas stations, worn strip malls, and the scent of barbecue. It didn't smell like Memphis Q.

Gemma Buckingham jested, "We are definitely heading toward the get-toe now. The get-toe."

"You sound disappointed."

"The name Crenshaw sounds regal. I had anticipated a village-like area of grand Victorian terraces and colorful town houses. Upmarket delis, chic eateries, gastropubs, and tea rooms, like Camden Market."

"Looks African American, African, and Caribbean."

"And Mexican. I think those are Mexicans over there."

"I thought those were white folks with deep tans."

"No, love. Those are Mexicans. Or South and Central Americans."

"Couldn't tell. And wouldn't know the difference."

"We must get you a passport and fill it with stamps at some point."

"I guess my ignorance is showing. I sound like a southerner."

She took it in. "Architecture in America is immature compared to London. Sophomoric. Can't compare to Westminster Abbey, St. Paul's Cathedral, or Houses of Parliament. Structures along Crenshaw are drab, yawn-worthy, seriously lacking. Speaking of lacking, that applies to the use of bidets over here. How can a country as rich and prosperous as yours not have bidets in every bathroom, public or private?"

"Priorities."

"Americans are a tad bit disgusting in that department."

In the sky pollution, hovering behind a gigantic ten-foot-high BLACK LIVES MATTER billboard, was another spectacular advertisement thrice as large. It exclaimed BLACK LIVES MATTER SO LET'S QUIT KILLING EACH OTHER. The second billboard's intent was to checkmate and give a stiff middle finger to the first.

Gemma Buckingham read the signs, frowned. "All lives matter."

I sighed at the woman kin to white folks. "Gemma Buckingham."

"Yes?"

I hesitated. "Nothing."

She fluffed her Afro in her mirror. "What, love?"

"Nothing. Love."

"What do you believe in, Professor?"

"I believe in equality of all people, especially in political, economic, and social life."

"So, then all lives matter, love. All lives matter, not just Black lives."

"Tell that to the white man."

"I could always quiz my white mother."

"Black Lives Matter is an issue for you?"

"Obviously not for the Black people who are killing each other."

Irritation rose, but I didn't have the bandwidth to debate the issue. I'd just seen my father for the first and last time. The pedophile who had created me was dead. I'd seen a dead man who looked so much like me I wondered if seeing him in a big-ticket coffin was a deadly sign directed at me. I saw myself dead and that fuckin bothered me to my testicles.

We hit more traffic, got stuck at every red light for up to ten cycles.

She said, "I wonder what the architecture of the home in Windsor Hills where Meghan Markle grew up is like. I have the address to her mum's residence. I did my research, and where she grew up is one of the wealthiest African American neighborhoods in America. By my Google calculations, we're only eight kilometers, or five miles away. We happen to be heading in that direction at the moment. It's locked in my GPS."

"Why do you like Meghan Markle so much?"

"When I see the Duchess of Sussex, I see myself. Can't help it. She's my mirror. I need Meghan Markle to win both in love and her professional endeavors, need her to succeed as a mother and woman regardless of her husband, and win for all of the little girls who look like us, especially the mixed-race ones here in London, girls who grew up like me, with an emotionally weak European mother like mine, with an emotionally abusive African father like mine. The shit Meghan endures now living in a family who are rumored to have once supported Nazis, to be the only Black woman in that circle who isn't a maid, only certain people can understand, and not enough are empathetic to her emotional plight. I get it. I've always been more a fan of Princess Margaret than Lady Diana, but Meghan came along and it was like seeing myself and all I've endured all over, only it's written on the cover of every tabloid newspaper and classless magazine and retweeted online by the daft and bigoted. All most see is a woman who is not pure white living what to them seems like a luxurious life of taxpayer-funded privilege that is alien to most civilians. I see a human being, a woman, mistreated."

I nodded, still didn't get it, but changed the topic back to LA traffic, said, "Cold molasses moves faster going uphill in a blizzard."

"I have no idea what that means. Like the other day I asked you how you liked your cereal, and you responded, 'Drylongso.'"

"I sho did."

"I still have no idea what that means."

I chuckled. "Means same way I like you. All by yourself; naked, nothing added, no accoutrements."

"Well, in that case, can't wait to have you *drylongso* again."

In one section, tattered tents were up for a quarter of a block. Vagrants, junkies, veterans, pedophiles, the well-tanned homeless.

Each man, woman, or child was a story.

She mumbled, "This is shocking. Reminds me of the unpublicized parts of London. London isn't all kings and queens and Big Ben and Buckingham Palace."

"Y'all gots sum po' folks too."

She said, "There are so many homeless people under palm trees."

"My church does a lot with the homeless. A lot of them are veterans and/or addicted. We try and help, find them jobs, places to stay."

"Women need better protection. A lot have found themselves suddenly in crisis, desperate, and need a little help before all is lost."

Gemma Buckingham was in a new mood, stern now. "They all need to be inside from the elements, preferably in a place that ministers to their physical, spiritual, and emotional needs. I mean, if your country can afford to go to Mars to see what's there, this shouldn't exist anywhere."

"What's the situation in London?"

Gemma Buckingham became smaller, shook her head, mumbled like a child, "Hostels and squats. Brighton Beach. Hostels and squats."

"What was that?"

"'Please, sir, I want some more.'"

"What?"

"Nothing. Nothing at all. Just a line from *Oliver Twist*."

"The song?"

"No, no, no." She was irritated with me. "From Dickens. From a novel. *The Parish Boy's Progress*. A tale of artful dodgers, pickpockets, chins criminals, and sordid lives. Street children. Unfortunately, I can tell you're not familiar. It's been in movies. A musical play in the West End."

"Been years since I was forced to read that in middle school. Never connected to that novel. I know we mispronounced your cities and stuff."

"'Please, sir, I want some more.'"

"What's exactly a hostel? A hotel, motel, Holiday Inn situation?"

"One step above being homeless. So close to the homelessness we are witnessing as we crawl in traffic one can't tell really the difference."

"You're triggered."

"Meaning?"

"In a mood."

"Blow your horn, please?"

"What?"

"Please, blow your horn."

She'd spotted a homeless woman. She called her to her window and handed her a one-hundred-dollar bill. The woman thanked her and ran back to her cart filled with plastic bottles before she was jacked.

Trancelike, in a tiny voice Gemma Buckingham whispered, "'Please, sir, I want some more.'"

"You okay?"

" 'Please, sir, I want some more.' "

"Maybe I'll get you to moan that later on."

She rubbed her nose but gave no reply.

She wasn't amused by this strip of the Crenshaw Strip.

It felt like she'd lived a silver-spoon life from the moment she exited her white British mother's womb and saw that poverty was disgusting; she was only happy and comfortable around luxury.

Gemma Buckingham took a call as I drove, her voice shaky, rattled by the topography, but trying to be professional. I got my ear hustle on. She talked to someone about the BCA, which was the Black Cultural Archives, across the pond in Brixton. She mentioned some Notting Hill networking event at Tileyard, then told them she was very busy at the moment, was in Los Angeles, attending a funeral.

She said, "You want to know who died? Besides my feelings for you? My *boyfriend's* father passed. Yes, American. Black. You expect me to be Billy no mates? Of course he satisfies me, to no end. Comprehensive. Well, fuck you too, pathetic wanker. If you can't be professional moving forward, then we will have to sever all business as well as personal ties. You were the one unfaithful yet anytime I was out of eyesight for ten bloody minutes insisted on sniffing my Victoria's out like Tanqueray. I was naïve enough to be every kind of faithful, while you were every kind of unfaithful imaginable."

Whoever was on the other end got loud, took over the conversation.

She snapped, "I didn't need to tell you I was bloody moving. Our affair should have been a bloody one-nighter, you blighter. Let's look at it this way, honey. If it costs more to fix a bloody car than the car is worth, then that car is considered totaled. The moment you put your wanker in that girl, you wrecked us beyond repair."

He shouted something in a British accent so thick I couldn't make out a word.

Gemma Buckingham put on her version of a southern accent and said, "Yo momma."

Then she hung up. You learned a lot about people watching the way they treated others in your presence. The unkind way they treated other people was the harsh way they would soon treat you.

I gave her a moment, then said, "So, businesswoman, I'm your boyfriend."

"I was just saying that."

"You seem unflappable, but he sure got your goat."

"Lost the plot. Sorry you had to bear witness. Will be more discrete."

"'Yo momma'?"

"Hope I said that right. Been standing in the mirror practicing."

"Oh, you said it like you grew up eating pickled pig feet for breakfast and souse for lunch and had a big fat dill pickle with a red-and-white peppermint stick down the middle as a snack."

"As my sisters say here in America, I'm a grown-ass woman paying my own bills and don't have time to be playing with other folks' children, let alone entertaining boo-boo the fool."

A beat passed before I asked, "You still love the guy?"

Her jaw tightened and she sighed, spoke just above a heartbroken whisper. "Enough."

"He saw you in a bonnet?"

She turned her body away, annoyed.

My phone rang and I answered too late, so as we sat in my ride, I checked the message.

"I changed my mind about letting you get on top of me. I can't stand looking at your face, so get behind me. Get as mad as you want to and become so riled you spank my bottom over and over because you think I'm a bad girl, if that will make you feel empowered; do whatever you like but you better not touch my hair. Takes too much effort to make it perfect every morning. You will be behind me, in your place, and you will keep your paws on my sweet little ass and never touch one strand of my hair. Return my call after you bury your pappy."

Then my jaw was tight; I was the one annoyed.

Gemma Buckingham tentatively put her hand on mine. "You okay?"

"Another condolences call."

"I'm sorry for your loss. My mum is devastated."

"They ever meet?"

"No. He was in London several times, but she never met him. Why do you ask?"

"Want to be sure you and I aren't related. Would hate to find out I was banging my sister."

"Inbreeding. Isn't that what you Americans are infamous for in your notoriously racist Bible Belt? You get married to a first cousin and both families sit on the same side of church sort of thing, right?"

"You have us mixed up with the royal families in your England. A lot of y'all have that Habsburg jaw look. Especially Prince Charles."

"Funny you mention the Habsburg jaw, a well-documented defect created by incest."

"Why so?"

"Your royalty, the huge white man I saw with his wife the night I met you. The couple everyone applauded when they entered the room."

"The Judge of all Judges and his former-beauty-queen wife."

"He has the Habsburg jaw. Without a doubt he has it."

CHAPTER 32

GPS COMMANDED ME to turn left, into a strip that housed a Denny's, Walgreens, Starbucks, and Goodwill. Back stiff from the crash, I went inside the coffee shop and looked for Fat Man. He wasn't there. Gemma Buckingham yawned hard, looked jet-lagged but strong. Gemma Buckingham's phone rang again. Had become irritating as fuck.

She answered, then told whoever was on the other end, "Do not upgrade to Catalina. It forces the sixty-four-bit compliance and breaks every program I use. That's what the system tech guy told me. No idea. I'm only repeating what he said. Sort it out. Carry on. All the best."

That ear hustle told me little more about her. She was still an enigma, more now than before.

She put her phone away as I checked the time, then turned to me and asked, "Tea?"

"Coffee."

"Black?"

"Cream."

"Sugar?"

"Please."

"Kind?"

"Raw."

"Vente?"

"Vente."

"Find us a seat."

A white woman rushed in like this was her zip code as much as anyone else's. Real pretty for a white woman with orange dreadlocks. Her T-shirt declared she was an intersectional vegan feminist.

She grabbed a preordered beverage, spoke to a dozen sisters, cheek-kissed two, then left.

Gemma Buckingham came back with our orders.

I asked, "How does it feel driving on the opposite side of the road?"

"Leaves me a bit unnerved. Have to really focus when changing lanes and you don't have any bloody roundabouts to make it easier."

"The way you drive can kill folks. No wonder you Uber every-dang-where."

"If my old back injury from my days as a dancer flares up again, I'll need morphine and hydrocodone until the damage is manageable. If I end up on the poisonous opioids, I'll be back to living on stool softeners and having terrible, nightmarish hallucinations, ugly dreams that are in color and so real that it feels like I've been transported to another psychedelic dimension."

I nodded. "Our adrenaline level is high, so back pain won't kick in for a day or two."

Gemma Buckingham studied my face as I rose from deep thoughts. "Are you okay, Pi?"

I was worried about my momma.

Soon a loud faux Katt Williams type walked in poppin' off. Red Air Jordan sweats and blue Fila sliders. He grabbed a preorder from the counter, then copped a squat at the bistro table next to us. He ranted on his phone like sitting in peace offended him to his core.

"Big-ass billboards. On Crenshaw. Black Lives Matter ain't stopped Black-on-Black crime. Yeah, nigga, my opinion. Naw, nigga, you have to leave the hood. Leave bad for good. Or leave bad, for good. Howsoevers-never you want to take it, all the same. Get some paper and the hood will get resentful of your success and haters from the hood will kill you in the streets. Malibu nigga. You gots to move to Malibu. Fuck Hyde Park. Fuck

Compton. Fuck Watts. Only motherfucker doing a drive-by in Malibu is the goddamn postman."

A blond white-woman cop came in. Her LAPD uniform was pristine. That gun changed the energy; the room jumped tense.

A sister in the back stood, started chanting, "Jury says ten. She'll do five. Unarmed brother, dead. Never again alive. No justice, no peace. No justice, no peace. Hands up. Don't shoot. Can't breathe."

Lady LAPD grabbed her preordered drink and skedaddled.

The room went back to its emotional segregation.

"It's uncanny how you resemble your father. Like in the movie previews I've just recently seen online showing a young Will Smith and older Will Smith in the next movie he's doing, *Gemini Man*. Even with your beard, with those green eyes, hell, you are him with a beard."

Lips in half a smile, as she made it sound as if she were regarding a man who had taken the vow of poverty, chastity, and obedience, I sighed as I responded, "Enough."

"You're in a dark place."

"Filled with helicopters, the homeless, and music by Snoop."

"Pi, I noticed your name wasn't listed in your father's obituary."

I let that hang.

Legs crossed, she dabbed her eyes. "No worries. Hurts my heart, that's all."

My phone rang. It was Dr. Stone-Calhoun again.

"When you return, I may have two friends I want you to meet for lunch at the Peabody."

"For what purpose?"

"Maybe from time to time you can be their friend."

I asked, "Why me?"

"Why not you?"

I nodded. "Sure. Set a meeting."

I hung up.

Gemma Buckingham asked, "All good?"

Again I nodded.

Gemma Buckingham tensed; "Pi?"

"Yeah?"

"Pi, I saw your social media. Saw your exes. I see there is a certain type of beauty you prefer."

"Wait. Hold on. You have social media now?"

"I created an account to look at yours."

"Who does that?"

"Demisexual women from the UK who are enamored by a green-eyed man from Memphis."

"You really want to have this conversation right now?"

"Tell me about your ex."

"Which ex?"

"The tall and slim brown-skinned girl with the stunning dreadlocks."

"She got a better job in a bigger city and a small-town boy like me no longer fit the bill. If you had scrolled through her Facebook feed, you'd have seen her with her husband."

"The basketball player from U of M, your rival university. You went behind enemy lines."

"How do you know about K-Wolf?"

"Went to her page."

"Trolling. Would think that would be beneath you."

"I'm human. Was curious. Needed to know. She is Afro-Barbadian, Afro-Guyanese, and Irish."

"All I know is she was from Horseshoe Bend and went to the uni on a full ride."

"We seem to have time. To kill the boredom, play nice, tell me about your fling with her."

I took the reins, controlled the matter. "Tell me about your ex. How'd you meet?"

"Once upon a time, when my hair was shorter, they saw this Black nose, these full lips, and I was pulled out of line at Heathrow by cops, a line of at least two hundred where I appeared to be the only Black Londoner; once they heard my accent, they realized I wasn't Nigerian or Ghanaian or whatever, but that meant nothing. They saw my British passport, took the time to ensure it was authentic; then the officers threw my passport back at me. No explanation. No one obviously white and

Euro was stopped. Then I noticed the other man. A Black man. They harass all Africans. We started a conversation about that after, then exchanged numbers, and eventually—"

Without warning, an invisible Mack truck slammed into the building. Nobody stopped typing into their laptops, nobody stopped talking on their phones, no business meetings at metal bistro tables outside by Walgreens paused, the latte machine didn't hiatus, the cappuccino kept on humming, and no one missed taking a sip of overpriced products.

White boy saw my wide-eyed WTF expression, laughed, picked up two cups when his name was called, and as he passed me, he chuckled, "Whoa. Dude. Chill, bro. Just another earthquake."

He exited the spot, hopped on a motorized skateboard he'd left with his Big Booty Judy.

White Boy and his BBJ sped away sipping lattes, unbothered by dull skies or traffic.

The ground had shaken, and mofos drank coffee like it was nothing. Gemma Buckingham became the loudest one in the coffee shop. "An earthquake. What's next?"

I answered, "Locusts."

A custom painted '72 drop-top Chevrolet Chevelle roared into the lot and took one of the angled spaces facing the crater-size potholes on dilapidated Crenshaw. That muscle car was a wicked SS 454. Ruby red with dual white rally stripes running from hood to trunk. Black bucket seats, console power top, tachometer and gauges, and raised white letter tires. Gorgeous. Waxed bumper to bumper. Drenched in chrome. The Fat Man from Beverly Hills jumped out of that car and hurried inside.

CHAPTER 33

FAT MAN WAS in a mood and fit to be tied. This time I stood in another man's territory, I was the trespasser, so I showed my manners, extended my right hand, and shook with him for the first time. This was his land, his drab stucco castles, where he was the king of all he litigated.

I said, "Mr. Carlton, you're an hour late."

"Mr. Suleman, you're at the wrong Starbucks. Took me an hour to figure that out."

"You said on Crenshaw."

"North. North of the 10 at Washington, closer, two or three lights toward Wilshire."

"I did like GPS told me and made a right-hand turn off Crenshaw at Highway 10."

"Interstate. It's called an interstate. Nobody would say Highway 10. The 10, the 405, the 110, article and noun, whatever, so you know. I try not to come down to this part of Crenshaw."

"Why not?"

"Before you label me as a racist, Crenshaw that way goes to the beach, stops below horse ranches and mansions. I just don't like going through a million red lights to get here."

"One Starbucks showed up when I asked Siri to help a brother out. This one."

Fat Man growled, slapped his forehead. "My mistake. That Starbucks is on Washington at Crenshaw, not Crenshaw at Washington. I fly down Crenshaw and turn in from the main entrance on Crenshaw, but the front door with the address faces Washington. I got so tied up in phone calls and legal documents and trusts and book rights that I was distracted. Dealing with this fiasco . . . your old man . . . disorganized until the end . . . and your siblings . . . I was all over the country flying from city to city. I loved your dad, but I need to get this buffet of bullshit he left behind off my table."

I introduced Gemma Buckingham as my girlfriend, did that as a little dig for what she had done.

I opened the glass door like a gentleman, took in the ticktock of her sweet ass as she shimmied by. Michelin star, exceptional cuisine that was worth a special journey. If she'd stalked me this far, no matter who her broken heart loved, I guess the M-Town meat I was slinging was on par with Michelin as well. The stressed fat man overtook us and my Straight Outta Memphis it'll-be-there-when-I-get-there pace. We moved fast to keep up with the overworked fat man, the messenger for the dead.

He said, "Crazy day here. In Westwood, hundreds of ICE protests have blocked Wilshire and in downtown LA the activists are calling for changes at LAPD. That protest is happening outside of LAPD Headquarters and it's damn near the peak of rush hour. Plus there was a bank robbery at Wells Fargo. There were five suspects out there jumping from backyard to backyard. An app on my phone said there's a lot of police activity going on off of Hyde Park and Marlton. Looks like a raid is about to happen. Traffic is being redirected up Hillsdale, so we're in the middle of everything wrong in LA right now. It'll take an hour to drive four miles."

"I'll follow you."

He thought about it. "Ride with me. I'll send someone for your rental and send it back."

"It was in an accident."

"Unless there is a dead body in the trunk, consider that handled as well."

"With Gemma Buckingham's car. She rear-ended me trying to keep up."

"Get me both your rental info, and it's all taken care of. Now, to one of the Suleman homes."

CHAPTER 34

WE ENDED UP in Hancock Park. Smooth, unblemished road. Gated mansions off a snaking street were beyond impressive. Definitely a CREAM neighborhood—cash rules everything around me. In my mind that track from *Enter the Wu-Tang* supplied the theme music on hard repeat.

We passed an empty lot between two mansions.

I asked, "How much that lot cost?"

"A million. As much as two. Twice that much next year, as is."

"Ain't no house on it. Didn't have grass, just lumps of dirt."

Fat Man stopped in front of a large home, three levels, contemporary, all white. He put in a code and the double gates hummed open. The six-car, two-motorcycle garage was a combination of luxury and classic cars. He who dies with the most toys on display wins. A 1960 Chevy Corvette met me as soon as I walked into the car lot. It was a four-speed, Cobra red and Carver white, like Momma's high school colors at Carver High. A white Chevy ZR2 Bison, brand-new, waved at me, then smiled. It was next to a black two-door heavy truck, maybe made in '62, and it looked like it had been built fresh this morning.

Fat Man saw me eyeballing at the Vette again, a car made to be driven along a beach on Sundays, and said, "Trying to dump that for sixty. Would take thirty to get it off the books."

"I can't even afford that scooter over there."

"It's a Znen. Better quality than most. When you PDI it, make sure you clean the jet with a needle. Maurice bought a lot of things the last year, cars he'd never drive, clothes he'd never wear. The car I'm driving is his. I have to keep it with me to keep your siblings from stealing everything not nailed down."

"Why act like Big Money Grip and buy shit knowing you're leaving on the next train?"

"He tried to do normal things, even if it was him sitting up in his bed, popping pills, and online shopping for crap half the night. He probably slept two hours a night for the last six months. He bought all this shit to tell himself he wasn't dying. Maybe it was his way of keeping from being depressed."

"When gods are bored."

"You know, you and he are same build, same size, and he has so many unworn suits."

"Don't jinx me like that. Would never wear it, no matter if it's brand-new."

"Wasn't offering. It's part of the estate. Everything down to the last paper clip."

I motioned. "That John Deere. That's an E180. Best lawn tractor around. What happens to it?"

"It'll probably all end up at Goodwill. I think Maurice put that in his will. Out of spite."

"Sounds like he was a vengeful man. Not a nice man at all. His reputation precedes him."

"The rich don't have to be nice. He was different before he became famous. He was almost likable. Fame changes them all."

CHAPTER 35

FAT MAN SAID he was hungry, so we went to a New York–style bar nearby in Hancock Park. He ran ahead of us to the eatery, had to see a man about a horse, and left us strolling at my Memphis pace.

When Gemma and I stepped inside, a burly white guy bumped into me. He muttered something that told me that ish was intentional. He went to his seat, frowned back at me, gave me a daring up-and-down like he wanted me to react to his slight and start some cross-burning shit.

Gemma Buckingham asked, "Did we do something to offend him? Am I not dressed properly?"

I checked the room's demo. White people, Asians, Latinos, people from the Philippines, and East Indians. That fool had body-checked me like this was a hood club off Merton in North Memphis.

"He's mad because the cargo in his slave ship appeared on deck and eclipsed his sunlight." I gave him hard eye contact. "If we need to work this apology out outside, let's go."

"I bet he has one of those bloody assault weapons."

The room had picked up on the energy, what felt like the start of a schoolyard fight.

Fat Man came back from the john, felt the new energy, took in the way people stared at me.

He asked, "Okay, Suleman. What the fuck did you do?"

I headed toward the asshole, M-Town *skrong*. "Mothafucka, you betta 'pologize."

Gemma Buckingham got in front of me. "Violence is the way of the unenlightened primitive."

"And that primitive needs to be enlightened."

Fat Man grabbed my biceps and snapped, "Mr. Suleman?"

"Playing pussy gonna get his ass fucked."

"You can't come into a business acting like you've lost your mind."

"*He bumped into me.*"

"So what? People bump into me all day long."

"He didn't apologize."

"Jesus. Don't be one of them."

"What does that mean?"

"Not like he stepped on your Jordans."

"That offends me."

"You're offensive. Let me de-escalate this thing before it ends up on Shaun King and DeRay Mckesson's Twitter feed and this gets put on a new level. If you don't want me to apologize, then apologize to the owners for the noise. Look, I have a headache and need to get me something to eat."

"Let me check my pockets for fucks to give; sorry, all out."

"My blood sugar is low, I am hypoglycemic with diabetes, and I need to eat, dammit."

"He assaulted me, did it like he was calling me a boy, and that's worse than being called . . ."

"Another fucking hashtag moment. He's recording. Don't need this."

Gemma Buckingham was so scared she was already shaking her head and hurrying back out of the place. I stormed back out of Fat Man's favorite haunt before I caught a case. Fat Man struggled to keep up, ran behind me calling out my name like he had been demoted to tote-and-fetch guy.

He got in his car screaming at me like I was wrong.

I cursed him out.

Fat Man exploded. "I need some fucking food so shut the fuck up with that shit until I eat."

"Fuck you."

Like Sis, I had my triggers, moments that could drag me toward a blackout. Mine were an accumulation. The strongest camel's back could take the weight of only so many straws.

CHAPTER 36

IN FAT MAN'S swank office, one with stark white walls, a gazillion legal books, hundreds of novels, and pictures of him and every celebrity known to man, the starved and irate fat white man chomped on Nigerian food he had gotten delivered. Jollof rice, sautéed spinach, and chicken.

My rage at being straight-up disrespected, then given the blame, remained strong.

Fat Man snapped, "I get it. *Jesus.* How many times do I have to hear this trite speech in my lifetime? Your ancestors were treated abysmally, slept in their own filth and waste while lying arm to arm in cramped spaces, suffered a lack of food and water, were injured with no medical attention, and if they didn't die from the heat, starvation, or scurvy, if the enslaved didn't find a way to kill themselves in the Middle Passage, if they didn't find freedom in the arms of death, they landed in a hell they couldn't pray themselves out of. The Africans' new hell was the rich white man's new heaven."

"It can never be said enough. We'll only stop when the right people start listening."

Gemma Buckingham's phone rang with a call from somewhere overseas, and she needed to use a private room for a hot minute so she could put out a blazing fire regarding her secret job.

"Let the angry-Black-man routine go for once. He bumped into you two hours ago."

"I was assaulted, and you tell me I should apologize. How fucked-up is that? Your people continue to do fucked-up shit and at every turn you find a way to flip it and blame it on the victim. I'm angry, but I'm not an angry Black man. It's white people who are angry, not us. Your people are doing the assaults, not us. Angry because we exist without either being bed wenches or serving their whims. White people are fucking with us. Angry white men and angry white women. You think Black folks were born pissed off? I was a Black child, born happy, then abused by a racist nation to a point where I might not ever recover from the PTSD it has forced me to tread in on a daily basis. I've been forced to get used to the temperature for over thirty years; that doesn't mean I'll ever feel comfortable in this fucking cesspool."

"Yada yada yada. I don't need to hear about it once more in my life."

"No one tells the Jews to stop telling their stories."

"I get it. Ease off the drum."

"The Ashanti, Ewe, Wolof, Malinke, Yoruba, Ibo, Balante, Kissi, Hausa, and Fulani, all stolen because the white man who claimed he was genetically superior was too lazy to put down his weapons of torture and destruction to pick his own cotton, tobacco, and sugarcane."

"Mr. Pi Maurice Suleman, don't dare and try and make me feel guilty for some shit that happened before my time and I had no control over and would never have approved. On this trying day, I'm your ally, here to protect your inheritance. If you don't want to be left in the cold, don't make me your enemy. Let's review and see who is wrong in this scenario. I grew up having to hear this shit, be attacked at every turn for being white with money. I'm fat and can barely walk up a flight of stairs; you don't think people bump into me without apologizing? You don't think I can drive down Crenshaw and not get looked at like I'm on the wrong side of town? I get it. Your old man drank and called the white man locusts on a rampage, terrorists in a land that for them had no rules. Said they turned God into the devil. Said with insurmountable evil in their hearts, Bibles in their hands, crucifixes around their necks, righteous scowls on their pale faces, the barbarians at the gates called the victims of their destructive manifest destiny savages. I get it."

"Enough."

"Take that diatribe to a Farrakhan meeting and get back to me when you've worked enough of that shit out of your system so we can sit down and conduct business like men. Running around shouting out your grievances like a louder-than-loud-mouthed Stephen Smith won't do you any good. There is an inverse ratio between the volume in which an argument is made and the quality of its logic."

I capitulated. "Your city. I digress."

"I mean, fuck, alligators and crocodiles coexist in parts of the world, but people."

"I said I digress."

"Your people need to stop having complain rallies and do like Tyler Perry."

"My people?"

"Don't. Just don't." He bit the last of the chicken, tossed the bone, sucked his fingers. "Tyler built an empire. That's all I'm saying. Study his business model and maybe all ships can rise together."

"A rising tide lifts all boats."

"You get the point. Tyler basically said complaining makes no money. Guy used to be homeless."

I took it down a bit. "You were my father's friend."

"When I see him on the other side, we'll argue again, say the meanest shit to each other."

"What was your last argument about?"

"Trump. He'd answer the door naked, except for a MAGA hat. He thought that was funny. Then he'd put on a suit and go into his office to write. We argued every damn day. Even in the end, when he was in a dreamlike state that had him acting bat-shit crazy until he needed three caregivers, I was here, watching it all, and we argued."

Fat Man cried. The final messenger set free a lazy man's load of emotions, let all the boxes tumble from his cart.

"In the end, I don't know shit. I'm another passenger. Who's right, who's wrong, all I know is hate is taught going in both directions. Your cause needs a real leader, only one, with many advisers, not dozens with bad advice. I told your father, from my point of view, your people need a leader with a hard mission statement and not all of these random groups contradicting or trying to overshout or outblog or tweet all day at each other. You have economic power and that can do a number on capitalism. Get what works from Garvey, MLK, and Malcolm, and present with the profoundness of Baldwin. You can set up a network and have all of your own businesses and keep most of the green dollars in the hands of those you want them in. Just my opinion. I'm a born-rich, gonna-die-richer white guy sitting in the bleachers watching your people in a losing game. You're training wrong, in my opinion, because you don't have a decent coach. Most of the leaders, especially the self-appointed ones on social media, are opportunistic. Even if they have good intentions, they aren't good enough to play Civil Rights, the Sandlot Edition, but they think they're at pro status, better than MLK and Malcolm. Counting followers means nothing. People who hate you follow. In sports, losing teams pack stadiums. Losing teams sell jerseys. But they are still losing. Don't be a marquee player on a losing team. I'm talking to you the same way I used to talk to your father. I can be wrong about all I say; it's just one man's opinion. But if I say any of that out loud, your old man always warned, then I'm forever branded the racist. So, it was me and him, the unbendable against the unmovable, sipping scotch and arguing. Despite what you think, he wasn't always bad."

Fat Man wiped away his tears, regained his manhood.

I asked, "What kind of man are you?"

"A man, a human being, trying to figure this shit out, but throwing in small bits of the towel every day. Kind of jealous your old man got to stop paying taxes before me, but my day will come."

I nodded.

He said, "I read your books. Both of them. Well, did the audio version on a plane trip."

"Okay."

"You're a better writer than he ever was. I told him that. It pissed him off. I bought him copies. He read paperbacks and collected first-edition hardcovers."

"He touched my books."

"He read both of them over a weekend, one each day. I can't read that fast; it takes me six months to do a book. He was pissed but agreed you were the superior writer. He told me to find first editions of your works. I already had and was happy to give them to him, gift wrapped, on the spot."

"Why?"

"Why? That was the only argument I ever won against that man. Years of arguing, and he only capitulated to one argument. He had produced at least one child worth his weight in gold."

"Question."

"You have an audience."

"When did he grow a beard?"

The fat man wiped away tears as he laughed. "After he read your books. He read them more than once. The pages were bent back, words highlighted. He was really into what you had to say. Professionally he was impressed, but I think he was prouder of what you'd done than anything. He hated when he first saw your name in a bookstore next to his. You had an end cap at some big bookstore, and he kicked one over and stormed out. They took your books off the shelves because of his complaints. He came around. He read your two books like they were new books to the Bible he'd needed all his life and talked about you off and on. Did it so much your brothers and sisters out here put two and two together and he confessed he was your dad. Jealousy ensued."

"Well, at least they got to spend time with him and know him well enough to not like him."

"When he was dying, he had that Steve Miller Band song on repeat walking around singing, 'She was the sweetest thing, I evah did see, really like her peaches, had to shake her tree.' You know it?"

"Not the right lyrics, but I know it."

"From the era of the great singers and songwriters. Not like the trash you hear today."

"Grew up listening to that song almost every day with my momma."

"Your old man's name was Maurice."

"No, it's not."

"His middle name was Maurice."

"Maurice."

"He loved that Maurice part of the song. Called himself the Space Cowboy back in his day. We never knew what the hell the lyrics 'pompitous of love' meant, but he sang that gibberish from his soul."

"Space cowboy. Gangster of love. Maurice."

"Maurice sang he was a picker, grinner, lover, and sinner writing his books in the California sun."

"Maurice."

The fat man sobbed, laughed, and sang, "You're the sweetest thing . . . I ever did see . . . really like your peaches . . . wanna shake your tree. Great. Now I'm going to have that stuck in my head until I die."

I struggled with the revelation. "That's about my momma."

"I know. He showed me her photo not long ago. A bodybuilder? She looks impressive. Looked like the clock went in reverse for her, because she looks as young as the pictures of her daughters."

"He looked at her social media? Since when?"

"I'd guess maybe since Myspace."

"Why?"

"If not for him being married, with kids, and his age, and the fear of damaging his reputation . . . he met your mother and wanted her more than he did his wife."

"She was fifteen and he was married with children."

"People said Jerry Lee Lewis married a thirteen-year-old. Elvis Presley met Priscilla when she was fourteen and had her living at Graceland when she was about fifteen. B.B. King sang about a girl who was sweet sixteen. Jim Croce sang about sleeping with jailbait. The Beatles sang about jailbait in 'I Saw Her Standing There' and all the underage chased them back to their hotels. Sting and the Police sang about jailbait in 'Don't Stand So Close to Me' and young girls wanted to be picked from the bunch. Spinal Tap had lyrics that went 'You're too young, and I'm too well hung, but tonight I'm gonna rock ya.' On 'Stray Cat Blues' Mick Jagger made millions singing about a thirteen-year-old. Rebellious young girls were everywhere chasing fame. Bill Wyman from the Rolling Stones dated a thirteen-year-old when he was damn near fifty. Steely Dan had a song about showing pornographic films to kids in his goddamn den. Don't judge *then* by the standards of *now*. Well, do. Talk about the behavior of men, yes, but talk about the behavior of the girls back then too. Springsteen sang one too. 'I'm on Fire.' 'Walk This Way' by Aerosmith. Also remember that thirty or fifty years ago there was no MeToo and that lifestyle was idolized, accepted, played every hour on the radio, danced to in all genres of music, and publicly romanticized."

"You sound like you're before a judge trying to get Polanski sent home with no charges. I'm living proof that a lot more than singing or dancing was done. I'm the motherfuckin evidence of a crime."

"Look, you're in your emotions. I'm merely presenting the facts. A lesson in history. I know the situation was fucked-up. It was messy for everybody, and I was a part of it from beginning to end, protecting him. He did some things in his youth that he carried to the end. We all do."

"Won't argue that."

"We went to Lakers, Rams, and Raiders games. He was UCLA and I was USC and we went to the battle and hoped the other's team lost. USC never let me down. Small victories went a long way against that stubborn fool. Bunch of wives who had kids to get a guaranteed income. Seems like every time he shook a tree; a baby peach would come rolling out nine months later. Hate him all you want. He was no worse than the man he voted for. Individual 1 has more assault cases than Bill Cosby and thirty million people and evangelists are still supporting that dictator-loving tax-evading racist. Go figure."

"That's how we judge each other nowadays? By who has reaped the most and raped the least? By who had the most fun at the Playboy Mansion, then watched Magic Johnson get a triple-double?"

"What happened between him and your mother, from the bit I saw, it was consensual."

"How would you know?"

"She called up, said she was in a book club, and he told her to bring the club up to get their books signed. Opened the door, she was alone. No book club. Only a dreamy-eyed fifteen-year-old girl holding a hardback. I think she had saved her last dime to get that novel and sneak from home to come meet your father. She had on starched blue jeans and a high school T-shirt. It was red and white. Had a red cobra on the front. She was surprised to see me and thought he was going to be alone. I took the hint and left."

"That was wrong."

"It was the way we did things thirty years ago. It was. How women did things thirty years ago."

"She wasn't a grown woman. She was a girl, still a child, not old enough to give consent."

"That was the way things were then. I left the room when she was all over him, looked comfortable. Nine months later you fell from the tree he shook. But he didn't leave her high and dry. He paid child support from day one. My wife was his accountant and has the receipts. She cut the checks. My wife's sister was his literary agent. Most of his families and my family, for thirty years, same picnics."

"He left my momma behind as a pregnant teenager and moved on to other heifers."

"There was more to it than a one-night thing. He liked her. He took her to the Shell Shack in Mexico Beach, Florida, because he said they had the best local seafood in Mexico Beach since 1965. He said he met a free and gentle flower growing wild and couldn't fight ignoring his brand-new wedding ring for a couple nights. Your mother ignored it too. Girls always sing they want to have fun, damn the consequences. They had a good time, ate shrimp, scallops, and oysters, bought T-shirts and novelty gifts. He took her to LeftBank Art Gallery and they rode horses along the beach at sunset. He told me he showed her the marina, then almost got caught having a quickie in St. Joseph Point Lighthouse."

"So the fuck what?"

"He was married, but he wasn't happy, not the real kind. Might be hard to feel that kind of happy when a woman you barely know rushes you to marry her because she manages to get pregnant four months after she learned the size of your checkbook. He told me that it never took much for a lonely man to fall in love, a kiss from the devil or a hug from an angel, and it felt like he'd had both."

"Don't try and make this some sort of Humbert Humbert–Lolita thing."

"I have no idea what that means. Can we be real here a minute? Mind if I am as blunt as I feel right now? Don't make all the girls and women saints. There are no saints. A lot of women are out there Tarzan dating, swinging from dick to dick, not letting one go until they have a good grip on the next."

"Jungle reference. Okay."

"See? No matter what I say, no matter how innocent, your mind is stuck on that channel. Next time I'll say Miley Cyrus dating and take the chance of being attacked by her fan base. Fucking Christ."

"His married-with-child-and-pregnant-wife ass made himself a pedophile, got on a plane like nothing had happened, and flew first-class back home to his family, left me growing in Momma's womb."

"He said your mother was mature for her age. Girls mature faster, stuff like that."

"'Girls mature faster' is the mantra of pedophiles, said to take away accountability and give blame. She looked like this, walked like that, had this on, so she made me do this, couldn't help myself. And white boys. They get caught in the act of rape in July and are home with a clean record by September. They always use 'he's not a man, he's a boy' as an excuse for shitty white men to absolve themselves of their responsibility for their crimes by suggesting they're too immature to know better."

"He tried to do right after. He paid your momma's expenses. You were taken care of."

"Not on this level. I bet a moon pie and a crate of RC Colas that he did the least he could."

"But you were taken care of. I mean, you were in Memphis. Cost of living there is way less."

I nodded. "Here ten thousand dollars' worth of dried-out desert costs two million dollars."

"The cost of gas is outrageous, probably to you, by the prices I saw in Memphis."

"Five dollars a gallon out here. Costs a lot to be poor in this city."

"I was tempted to buy a tanker of that two-dollar gas in Memphis and send it back here."

I took in this world, compared it to mine, where people made sure they washed their dishes at night, so they didn't wake up with roaches at their table waiting on more food in the morning.

I said, "My momma deserved the same palm trees, smog, bad traffic, and ocean views."

"I repeat, she was taken care of each month."

"So the fuck what? Of all he had, he hired someone to send my momma the least."

"Take it down a notch. Right or wrong, I'm trying to be reasonable and offer some explanation. I am . . . was . . . his attorney, friend, white brother, and protector. Even now I refuse to let his name be sullied. He needed me to help steer him right at times. I did my best to be a good example for him."

"You look like a man who does everything so right, but you ain't doing nothing but wrong."

"Are you perfect? You moonwalking on water? You able to change California's hard water to sweet wine from Martha's Vineyard? What kind of man are you in your personal life, Mr. Suleman?"

"Nah. Don't flip this. Don't you dare try to make me sympathize with the devil."

"Trying to give you some insight on who your father was. He was just a man, that's all."

"Playing devil's advocate."

"Look in the mirror for a moment, not out the window."

"What kind of man are you to have a man like him as a best friend for thirty years?"

"No matter what you say, or feel, you're still his son. His blood lives in you. Again, I put it on the table, in a calm voice and in a curious way, partly professional, but man-to-man, what kind of Black man are you? You know his faults. You're the living proof of his biggest weakness. You're the proof of some weakness your mother had on that day too. You're a peach that rolled off a tree. You look like him. Same tone of voice with different accent. I'm looking at a ghost right now. Again, what kind of man are you?"

"How much crime rich and powerful men like y'all have to commit to qualify for jail?"

"Y'all."

"Your people."

"I don't have any people."

"Those who represent your people, regardless of the hue of their skin. You stood up for your people in Hancock Park. You showed your hand with your cousin, and you showed it big-time."

"Always back to something I had nothing to do with or ability to control, making me a coconspirator in all evils simply because I'm a white man, and that works my motherfucking nerves."

"Always finding a way to Hancock Park us every chance you get."

"Mr. Suleman, I've been nice, and I'm running out of nice. So shut the fuck up *in my office* for two minutes. Don't fucking turn into Kamala Queen-of-the-Clapback Harris and start Joe Bidening me when my record has always been on the side of good, even when I had no option but to swim in this swamp and work with the bad. Good people are forced to work with bad people to give good people a chance. Stop making me your monster simply because I recognize the way things were, and, yes, needed to change, and yelling at me and not actively listening. Why keep attacking me? Asking for a friend."

"Because."

"Because Maurice is dead, and you can't attack him, so you're trying to kill the messenger."

"What's your rate? About two hundred or three hundred an hour to be the keeper of men's darkest secrets?"

He laughed. "I'm charging a measly six fifty an hour. Some clients are hit for twice that. This view of the marina has a price. Only charging Maurice six fifty an hour, half my normal rate, as a final favor."

There was a knock at his door, two soft taps.

He told them to come in.

A fifty-something svelte woman entered, phone in hand, and marched over to us, grim-faced.

She froze, gazed at me like I'd stolen something, took me in head to toe, then gradually smiled, tears in her eyes. "Maurice kept your handsomeness tucked away on the other side of the country?"

CHAPTER 37

THE SVELTE WOMAN had toned legs and skinny arms, paired with an almost yoga-flat stomach, pearls, silver bracelets, and a ginormous blood diamond. Her skin sparkled, a lotion blended with glitter. She had papers and a novel in her hands. *Sex Power Money.* She carried the book like it was her mantra.

She said, "I swear, Carl, sounded like you and Maurice were in here going at it for a moment."

She smiled like she had a heart as pure and loving as that of a nun, stood like she had the elegance of royalty.

Fat Man nodded. "This kid is definitely Suleman's even if he had doubts about any of the others."

"Most definitely his kid."

"If women had men who cared and would fight for them way he's fighting for his mother, the world would be a better place. I think the problem is men raise men, so fools raise fools."

"Duh."

Fat Man introduced me to his svelte wife, another keeper of my father's secrets. We shook hands, her grip professional. Her aroma was sweet, soft, and disarming. Smelled like floral top notes of orange blossom and neroli. The well-tanned woman looked like the epitome of California living, like her soul was everything tofu, farm raised, and gluten-free. I doubted if she'd ever been to the lupus, diabetes, and high blood pressure side of town. Dripping. Well-to-do. I doubted if anyone in her family had ever heard of asthma or boarded a plane and sat crammed in a middle seat back in coach.

Fat Man said, "Mr. Pi Maurice Suleman from Memphis, this amazing woman and mother of my three children is my lighthouse, shining bright; she led me away from being a fool and into love."

They laughed and looked like perfect love, like a young love that would never go cold, not even in Siberia, a love that wouldn't sweat on the most humid day in Brownsville, Texas.

Her phone rang and she waited for it to go to messages, then checked.

Svelte Wife said, "The rest are here. I'll keep them separated until we get the big room set up. We're using the room away from everyone in case it gets loud. Security will be in the hallway. I have my secretary making everyone adhere to the seating chart to avoid this becoming a Red Wedding."

"Did everybody get searched?"

"No weapons. I went over the rules of engagement with each one."

"Who came?"

"All of the Motherfuckers except one, the one who was the hardest to track down."

"Language. In front of a client."

"What did Maurice call them with his every living and dying breath?"

"Motherfuckers."

"Then Motherfuckers they shall be called, same as they are referred to in his legal documents. Motherfuckers. They are all sitting out there with hands like cups. Outside of the last wife, there's not a tear in the building. But when they hear his wishes, they'll cry rivers."

"Every last Suleman that Space Cowboy created, even the ones who skipped the funeral?"

"You know them. Every ex-wife showed up in her own limousine. Mistresses did the same."

"I bet every spoiled child or bastard child came in his or her leased Lamborghini or Mercedes."

"They're after every dime, complaining about having to pay twenty dollars an hour to park."

"A tree is known by its fruit. Room will be filled with green eyes."

"In more ways than one." She laughed. "We really need to Facebook Live this shit, for kicks."

"Is that in his requests?"

"Fuck, I better double-check. If we had embalmed him how he wanted . . . tell him, baby."

"Maurice wanted to be embalmed with him in a suit, sitting up in a chair, signing books, or in front of his typewriter. That was the funeral he wanted. Would've had, but he skipped signing that page. So, I used my own discretion and kept it simple. *Hilarious.* A dead man in a chair signing his last book."

They laughed so hard they had to leave to go get cooled off.

Lots of books by my dead old man were around me, made me uneasy, so I stood up and browsed the Fat Man's collection of never-read novels like I was back home walking through my favorite bookstore. Saw some random novels by people I'd never heard of, then halted when I saw what was tucked away on the bottom shelf, hidden in plain sight.

My lips moved with surprise as I read each book title, but no words left my mouth.

For White Folks Who Teach in the Hood . . . and the Rest of Y'all Too.

How White Folks Got So Rich: The Untold Story of American White Supremacy.

This was the attorney's stash. CNN smiles covered Fox News hearts once again.

The door opened and Gemma Buckingham came back. Her face was so red it looked like she had finished an hour-long shouting match. Something was off, but she masked it with a coarse smile.

"Sorry that took so long, love. Didn't mean to be rude. Won't happen again."

I led Gemma Buckingham to the secret stash and showed her the books in question.

"I don't see a reason to be concerned. Aren't there a lot of books by

African Americans with the word *nigga* or *nigger* in the title? Do you have any idea what these books are about? Don't judge a book you haven't read by the title and race of the author. Those titles are humorous to me, if gimmicky. You have come to some illogical conclusion upon first glance the same way some people, including Black folks, arrive at some stereotypical conclusion and prejudge you before they get to know you. You're exhibiting the same behavior of those you demean."

"Was asking your opinion. No need to rip me a new asshole."

"Well, how about this one, honey: *How Not to Get Shot: And Other Advice from White People.* It's by a Black man. That is the literature I think you should be reading at the moment. If we're being honest, I see a Black writer called that side of my family white people. Should I feel slighted on their behalf? Does the white-folk title offend the other side of my family? Does that arouse the loudmouth in you as well? Will you lose the plot and fight in public and risk incarceration to prove your point? Is this the thing you are willing to risk everything you have achieved over? Including your life and possibly mine?"

Gemma Buckingham sat down, crossed her legs, hands on her knees, nostrils flared.

It felt like she was aggravated by something else, something outside this room, maybe beyond this country, yet was giving that hostile energy to me as she simmered and vented, "Doesn't it exhaust you? Your very existence, your *Blackness*? Today it seems your every response is relative to your being Black. Being Black in a white world. But that's the America I've seen. Almost every movie you make, well, the ones you win awards for, has the same oppressive theme. Lauded for how well you play the role of a slave at a whipping post, or if it's modern, then accolades for portraying a socially abused person. Almost every popular book you write is about your relationship to whiteness and white power."

I nodded. "That whiteness is the smog that covers us the way smog smothers LA."

"Doesn't it feel overwhelming to not be able to let go? That in and of itself is a mental slavery."

"They kidnapped us. They still rule over us. They've determined not only where but how we live. We can't drive while Black, breathe while

Black, deliver UPS packages while Black, barbecue while Black. The list of offenses we've created while minding our own business is endless. Having a hairstyle that suits either our fancy or the texture of our hair is offensive. We're being shot or incarcerated for minding our own business. Like them, Gemma Buckingham, sounds like you see the Black man and woman as the problem. We've lived our lives compromising as a culture. I can't walk across campus without the same professor insulting me because I'm Black. A fucking flea in my ear. He does it over and over, just enough to irritate, just enough to make me look like a fool if I phone it in. I speak up and I'm the problem. We are always the problem. The Negro problem. The problem Lincoln failed to fix because he couldn't figure out how to send the freed slaves back to Africa. And, yeah, they had established an emigration committee and tried. History skipped over that and made the man a saint. I really need to visit London and see how kind and royally Black folks and Africans are treated. Need to see your political power structure and members of Parliament."

"Let's not fight."

"Let's not because we'd have to tell the truth."

"Emotions are high today."

"And I'm fucking tired."

"Welcome to the club, population at least forty million here, another two million in London."

I exhaled. "I need a couple folks to stop fucking with me. I need them to stop Hancock Parking me. This lazy man's load will get a straw too many. One Hancock Park too many . . . the moment I snap . . ."

"Enough."

Silence paid us a little visit and took over the room.

She winked. "You need to widen my aperture and test its limit."

"For both of us to calm down."

Gemma Buckingham touched my hand. I held her soft fingers.

Fat Man and Svelte Wife came back in, all lovey-dovey.

Svelte Wife asked me, "What's the conversation?"

I said, "Reparations and a global effort to end racism across all cultures and systems. Join in with your checkbooks open; any check you write make payable to Johnny Cash, without the Johnny."

They laughed.

Then Gemma Buckingham improvised so smoothly I believed the lie she told as the gospel truth. She said, "We were also talking about police brutality in London. Pi asked me about it. On my side of the world Sean Rigg was murdered by police in a Brixton police station. Across the pond, where I was raised, it's Joy Gardner, Smiley Culture, Roger Sylvester, Mzee Mohammed-Daley, Trevor Smith, Sarah Reed, Cherry Groce, and Jimmy Mubenga. Many more names. Many more hashtags. I was telling the professor that the UK's list of Black and brown bodies being brutalized by police in clear cases of excessive, unwarranted force is just as long. We hear of yours, but not a word of ours is mentioned here in the USA. You're the sun and we're Pluto. I watch your news. People here skip over BBC channels and our news. We're all connected, you know? We were debating that as well. I told the professor that it seems America believes everything revolves around America. Just my observation and conclusion from overhearing conversations in Memphis. You think that if you're extinguished, then so goes the world. So terribly closed-minded and myopic here."

Svelte Wife nodded. "Bingo. America only looks in the mirror, never out the window."

Fat Man added, "Unless we're dropping bombs. Have to open a window to drop a bomb. And if someone near suffers from flatulence."

Again laughter.

I was amazed at how easily Gemma Buckingham had lied. She made me believe we had actually had that conversation. She had smoother-than-warm-butter lies.

Fat Man said, "Ready to get this show on the road, Mr. Pi Suleman of Blair Hunt Drive?"

"Whenever you ready, boss man. You know me, white folks say jump and we ask how high."

"Stop it. You're becoming a walking cliché. Just . . . for once . . . put it on pause."

"Anything else I need to work on?"

"Mr. Pi Suleman, stop saying hello to everybody you pass by. We don't do that here."

"Nothing wrong with acknowledging other people exist."

"Like I said, we don't do that here."

"So it's like *The Sixth Sense*. I'm dead to them, can see everybody, but no one can see me."

"Welcome to LA."

CHAPTER 38

AN ANXIOUS WOMAN in strappy high heels and jeans that had no alibi rushed our way, then saw us and halted like she was intimidated. She had whitish skin, light hair that bounced below her waist, and pallid eyes. Her lips were as full as Gemma Buckingham's lips, ripe with features of a Black woman.

The albino saw us, tensed like she was going to run away, but Gemma Buckingham told her good afternoon. That London accent stalled the colorless girl, as it had stalled me when we'd first met.

The albino was a deer in headlights, didn't know how to respond. She nervously looked the Londoner up and down, seeking something nice to say, and told Gemma Buckingham, "I like your shoes."

Gemma Buckingham replied, "Wish I had yours. Those are gorgeous, like you, love."

Her body language relaxed. "Thank you for saying that."

The woman with pallid eyes eased on a pair of sunglasses as if that hid both her eyes and unique skin; then she hurried to wait for an elevator with three dozen people. She stood by a well-dressed Black girl who looked like the singer Normani and another woman in ragged jeans built like the rapper Cardi B. Both women saw us as we passed, but nobody said good afternoon or hello. They evaluated me, silently wondered if I was somebody, realized I wasn't a movie star, looked away.

I was as dead to them as Suleman was dead to me.

Fat Man huffed and puffed and directed us to his private elevator.

A small smirk combined with a nod told me Gemma Buckingham was impressed.

Ten floors later, we walked out of the private elevator and were almost trampled by the same albino woman again. She apologized for almost running into us. Then she was in a hurry again. Her heels clapped a mean song as she ran. She looked back at us twice before she disappeared.

Fat Man said, "That is one of your sisters. She's older than you. She had never heard of you until two days ago. You look like your dad; that's why she keeps staring. He was harder on her than the rest of the brood, and she loved him the most, until she didn't. Let her go in and get her assigned seat."

"She wasn't at the funeral. I would've noticed her."

"I'm surprised she's here now."

I hummed, confused. "I didn't know I had an older sister and an older brother."

"Mr. Suleman, that sister used to be your oldest brother."

CHAPTER 39

FAT MAN AND Svelte Wife had set the stage, had done as my father had requested in his manifesto, had me enter the room last, like I was the most important, for dramatic effect.

A mini horse was in the conference room. It neighed at me. An ostrich was in the room too. Both were therapy or emotional support animals. There were dogs in the room too, most of them too big for me to feel comfortable, but I faked the funk and acted like stepping into a mini zoo was no big deal.

Black and beige faces saw me and turned a whiter shade of pale.

I was a millennial haint, an angry dead spirit that scared the bejesus out of them all. While I lived a rough public-school life in a blue-collar area, while I spent countless days walking miles to work or chasing the 31 Crosstown Kansas and transferring funky buses in rain and freezing cold, they'd been warm and dry, in new cars and popping rubber bands at private schools.

Not one Motherfucker said hello. They'd slug me before they hugged me.

They regarded me the same way I had Fat Man upon first meeting.

Defensive, as an act of self-preservation and ego, I reciprocated tenfold to the power of pi.

They'd never met me and already resented me. The outside kid. The bastard child.

This lot knew nothing about food stamps. Had never had to eat ramen noodles or had hot dogs for breakfast and canned sardines for dinner. Never had to walk two miles in the heat of summer or cold of winter to the laundromat carrying bags of clothes. Never used a gas oven as a heater. Never had to boil hot water to be able to take a warm bath. Never depended on school breakfast and a free lunch program to get help from Monday to Friday. Getting something dry-cleaned was a luxury for me.

The scent of cupidity perfumed the room, its stench eye watering, thicker than swirling black toxic smoke from a nine-alarm fire on an oil rig. Eyes and frowns focused on me. Green eyes like mine.

My brothers and sisters.

Suleman's wife burst into tears and upset her ostrich. The horse neighed again; dogs barked.

The drama queen wanted to come to me and grab me and make me be her husband, but her legal counsel held the wild horse back, and soon she calmed. They all had legal counsel. This felt like a tribunal. My eyes went to the ones dressed in Louis Vuitton, Gucci, Prada, Off-White, Chanel, Burberry, Dolce & Gabbana, Balmain. That wasn't the swag of my kinfolk, but the drip they had on their well-fed therapy dogs. Samoyed. English bulldog. Lowchen. Rottweiler. Tibetan mastiff. Saluki. Akita. Irish wolfhound. The sister next to me rolled her eyes as I sat down. She was holding a ten-thousand-dollar baby chow chow, a dog she held like it was a newborn baby and kept kissing on the mouth. The dog had slim thighs and a booty and wore designer jeans that her canine body didn't understand.

Outside of the ostrich and mini horse, every wife, daughter, or mistress had a dog dressed for the runway. The women were dripping in name brands I'd never heard of and came in a mixed bag. The energy said they were either afraid of the dead man, loyal to the dead man, or idolized the dead man. A couple checked their watches and their shifty and aggravated body language said that they had waited impatiently for him to die, had waited too damn long, and were ready to get what they were going to get so they could get gone. They all looked like they lived to impress, and I wasn't impressed.

Black people down south learned to read a man in the blink of an eye as a survival technique. A man had to learn to read men, Black or white, redneck or hood, rich or poor, because they could all bring handshakes followed by ill will. This lot was transparent, as easy as reading a Dr. Seuss book.

My brand-new siblings were green-eyed psychopaths sipping vodka from designer bottles and thinking the quiet brother from down south was dumb as a two-dollar masonry brick from Home Depot. Dark, untrusting looks from each rang volumes. Cold-blooded stares said they knew I was too stupid to know what was up. I was nice, but if push came to shove, I'd go *Pulp Fiction* on their asses.

My sister who used to be my brother was the quietest, said nothing, was invisible to all. I found it hard to not stare at her. We made eye contact that lasted two blinks. She sat back. I looked away.

Fat Man reached in his bag, took out a brand-new red MAGA cap, eased it on his head.

With a shrug, he said, "Maurice has this written in, first line."

My pallid sister began rocking back and forth, struggled with some inner thought. I recognized that body language because oftentimes it was my own. None of the Fastest Swimmers did that. My anxiety rocking had to have come from Suleman's blood. She rocked and looked at this shit show, eyes going from sibling to sibling, seeing no love for her in the room, and she nodded like she'd come to some conclusion based on something grander than money, maybe based on the peace she needed in her life. She stood without a word and left, did a quick walk away from any inheritance, back to her own life.

As cool as Matthew McConaughey chilling in a Lincoln Navigator, I did what I had been told to do by Fat Man and Svelte Wife in a fancy-swanky office high over the Pacific Ocean.

I was to say nothing. I was to answer to no one.

I had to be my dead father's spirit come to life in the room.

Fat Man would do the talking.

Fat Man said, "He wants his favorite song played as we go."

Everyone groaned, including the high-maintenance horse, ostrich, and pedigreed mutts.

The attorney took out his phone and told Siri to play Steve Miller Band, "The Joker," on repeat, the live version. Again everybody groaned and shifted.

"This is a lot of complicated legalese on paper. So I don't come across as grandiloquent by using pretentious words, complicated legal terms, and phrases, I'm going to keep it simple for everyone. Will say it all in laymen's terms, so we're all clear on what's being ordered, directed, yada yada."

The Suleman will was read, and from the start, what was ugly became atrocious.

The first rule of order was to split the rights to his hundred and one novels, to all of his labors of love, some written under various pseudonyms, not all in the same genre. I would be given two months to decide which forty-five would go exclusively to Pi Suleman, Memphis, Tennessee, Blair Hunt Drive. I would be allowed to choose which books I'd obtain rights and royalties to for the rest of my life, the rest to be divided among the rest, choice of remaining novels going from youngest born to the oldest.

A madhouse of voices snapped at my messenger like he was someone they had known for decades, saw as a life-or-death ally, and now he had reneged and sold out the Kurds.

Fat Man said, "Here it is ordered, if any one protests aloud, just one of you, or displays negative body language of the same effect, and that is what we have witnessed, as this session is being recorded for legal purposes, the next section supersedes the aforementioned and the rights to all of Maurice Suleman's novels, any unfinished novel or short story or memoir, yada yada, yada, movies, theatrical production, foreign rights, in forms now known and in the future unknown that produce a revenue stream of any kind, et cetera, et cetera, it shall all go to Mr. Pi Suleman from Memphis, Tennessee, yada yada yada. Congratulations to Mr. Pi Suleman, Memphis, Tennessee, Blair Hunt Drive. It shall be for him to decide to keep it that way, or if he wants to disperse it in some other fashion to a relative or relatives of his choice. All of this was prepared months ago, when the disease first started, drafted immediately after a psychiatric evaluation proving he was of sound mind and capable of making this sort of thing his last will and testament. Twelve attorneys and I worked this for the last year."

The room rumbled, dogs barked, and the clients were flabbergasted. Opposing attorneys conferred, did that for thirty minutes as we took in the view. They capitulated. It was on lock for now.

My attorney said, "Same rules apply as we move forward regarding other assets. We have to go over the houses, the rental properties, the automobiles, personal effects, investments, yada yada, yada. Anyone who wants to walk can, and what was left to you, be it vague, shared, or specific, shall also go to Pi Suleman of Memphis, Tennessee, to keep or pass along to his relatives based on his own discretion."

The league of counsels read the papers, talked to one another, and there were no loopholes.

On another matter, my counsel read, "I leave it all to the visionary writer Professor Pi Maurice Suleman, the Ta-Nehisi Coates of the Suleman family. I hereby crown my second-born child the next Black aesthetic, and my word adoration can be used as a quote from his father in all publicity materials."

Every green-eyed Negro face tightened like they had stomach pain, migraines, and constipation. The sister with the cute dog in the stripper booty shorts had had enough. She jumped to her sky-high heels so fast her chair turned over and her secret bottle of vodka spilled across the table. "That's the product of a deranged mind right here. This is bullshit. It's one more example of why this will should not be allowed and we split everything evenly. One of his caregivers called and told me he was walking around naked thinking he was the next president of the United States when he died. He had lost his mind. Oh, I'm president. Emperor doesn't need new clothes. She said he'd laugh then cough and his neuropathy would make his hands and feet cramp up so bad he couldn't stand up. He took twenty pills a fuckin day. Not only was he constipated; he was full of shit. He was insane and you know he was."

Fat Man laughed. "Only shit I smell is the bullshit you're peddling. You'll end in a defamation-of-character lawsuit, and so will the so-called caregiver, especially with an NDA in place, unless said caregiver has video, and we know there was a no-phone policy on premises . . . so, Motherfucker 6, try again."

No one else said a word.

Fat Man nodded. "Thank you. With that outburst, you have been disinherited of all, and your part, as stated before, now belongs to Professor Pi Maurice Suleman, to be returned to you if that is his will, to be distributed to any other relative, if that is his will, or to keep, if that is his will. What say you, Mr. Pi Suleman?"

Legs crossed at the knee, infused water up to my lips, game face on, I said nothing.

She marched out knocking shit over, dog barking, crying over the milk she had spilled. The rest chilled. They knew who had buttered their bread for decades and they were nearing the end of the loaf.

My father's attorney stayed calm. I watched him, tried to read him. He came across as a man who watched the way the wind blew and adjusted his sails to the ride. He was a fixer. That meant he believed in nothing but the bottom line. I doubt if he'd ever voted a day in his life. He didn't need to vote. Not for equal pay. Not for his rights. Men like him were born with a ninety-yard head start in a hundred-yard race. He didn't have my struggles. His people never had to march across any man's bridge for freedom. There were no pictures of his kinfolk hanging from trees. Compared to mine, his was a world of comfort. His world was the prize. A poor man could get confused here looking at seductive palm trees and yachts. A Black man could get access to this lifestyle and forget his history, or detach himself from his truth until the police chased him down the 405 in a white Bronco. With enough money, he might believe he could make himself over, be a new Jack Johnson, and own any white woman he desired.

I was a BMFM and the Bible Belt reminded me who I was and told me the truth about where I fit in the world. But high above the Pacific Ocean, letting Fat Man run this meeting like we were in his oval office, I felt a surge of energy from being in a spot that let me know what the powerful felt like.

Up in here I was the judge of all judges.

Up in here I had the final word.

CHAPTER 40

A MIGRAINE THE size of Atlanta's Stone Mountain was in my head, so Gemma Buckingham drove. Our new rental SUV had been delivered to the office. She said she needed the practice. I needed a break. We rode with traffic on Wilshire, ended up in Westwood Village, then drove the campus at UCLA.

Gemma Buckingham took in the Bruins architecture, then looked at me, worried, said, "Pi."

"I'm fine."

"Pants on fire."

"I know where the fire is."

I put my hand in Gemma Buckingham's lap, rubbed between her legs to calm my mind.

"I want to see what Delicious tastes and feels like in Los Angeles."

"Whenever you're ready, come and get it. She wants and misses you like crazy from the moment you pull out until you're back inside. She's purring and throbbing for you now."

I tried to finger her. What was warm started to get hot.

"You really going to wake up Delicious while I struggle to drive?"

I stirred her.

Gemma Buckingham bit the corner of her lip, squeezed against my finger and hummed.

She put on her right signal light and pulled into a five-level parking structure, drove to the top level. Each level up had fewer cars. Level five was practically empty. She saw an empty area, whipped that way. The moment she stopped, she undid her seat belt, then reached into her bag, took out lotion. She fished me out of my pants, went to work, had me holding on to the oh-shit bar, back arching. She put a hurricane inside my body, then leaned over, used her mouth and made a tsunami build.

Pleasure left my body like a storm. She paused when she felt the surge, hummed with the taste, sucked and suckled until I had to tap out to get her to stop. She licked me clean, took a final lollypop lick, kissed the tip, wiped her mouth, sucked her fingers, made sure no love droplets were left behind.

She said, "Amazing how that thing is like those expandable and retractable water hoses. Gets so freakin' huge and once it gets drained it suddenly shrivels back up like that, into a bloated worm."

"Damn, that was funky. Like nine cans of Magic Shave, that was funky."

"Whatever that means."

"I owe you one. Damn I owe you."

She patted herself on her back and laughed at her naughtiness.

I kissed her. "Right now I want to put you on a table and eat you like you've never been eaten before. It woke the beast in me."

"I'll be more than happy to collect that debt later."

I whispered, "Get in the back seat."

"Not in a car park."

"Car park? What's that? A parked car?"

"Here a car park is called a parking lot."

"Car park sounds like an amusement park."

"Don't want to mess up my hair and makeup or sully my dress."

"Cool. We won't park a car in a car lot this time."

Gemma Buckingham going down on me had left her breathing hot and thick, nipples hard, face flushed, her voice sultry, completely turned on. I bet she was wet. Wanted to finger and kiss her. She looked happy with herself. That blow job was probably more for her than it was for me. This kind of sex excited her. I smiled a relaxed smile. I'd been given brain in a parking lot on the campus of the prestigious, world-famous UCLA. This BMFM and the UAN were honored. It thrilled me too.

Aroused, Gemma Buckingham said, "We can go dogging later tonight if you like. Never did that across the pond. Could be interesting. Would be lovely if we were near a beach. Maybe Malibu. Could walk around and get a bite and drinks at a sidewalk café when we are done."

"I don't have a dog."

The Lady from London paused, looked at me, and tilted her head. She asked, "Are you serious?"

"I haven't had a dog since I was nine. Had a mutt name Butch."

The Londoner laughed, turned forty-eleven shades of red.

I asked, "What just happened?"

"I asked you to go dogging and you told me about your dog."

"Calling my dog Butch is funny?"

"No. Not at all."

"Had forgot about Butch. Not into dogs anymore. Guess I don't like dogs as much as my siblings."

Again she burst into laughter.

She informed me, "This dogging would be more . . . more like doggy style. And in a public place. Common thing in London."

"Dogging. Never heard of that."

"Makes me wonder how much of what I say isn't understood by you. Or anyone here. I had no idea what a parking lot was. When I was at the UAN event the night I met you, I politely asked someone how they found the event, and they told me they took I-240. That left me perplexed. I was asking if they were enjoying themselves and they gave me directions. Magnum over here is a condom but at home it's a Belgian ice cream bar. I went into a 7-Eleven and asked for a large Magnum, and all I can say is that when he threw me a box of prophylactics for ginormous wankers, the experience was embarrassing."

"I'm still stuck on dogging."

"And I'm stuck on Butch. Imagine inviting you to go dogging and you actually showed up with a German shepherd. I wouldn't know what to think. Will never be that curious."

We got out of the car, paused at the trunk to kiss again, kissed a while, then changed sides. She rode shotgun while I took the wheel. I left the parking lot and rejoined traffic with her redoing her lipstick.

"Did all of your exes bless your wanker? At this point, I think I have earned a right to ask."

"Slow your roll, London. I haven't seen you in a bonnet."

"That's a few phases away still. Seeing me without my face on and in a bonnet is the last exit before Mexico, as they say."

I answered her question. "Everybody I dated had their own way of bringing the worm up."

"Better than me?"

"Not better, my struggling demisexual. In or out of bed, no one has been better."

"I know I can be a bit much at times. I'll do better, I promise."

"What do you mean?"

"What attracts you to someone can become the very thing that pushes you away. Love and over-the-top passion can become the thing you despise."

"Love can be its own contranym."

"In my life, love has always been the ultimate contranym."

"Hence the sudden over-four-thousand-mile move to Memphis."

"Love pulls or it pushes, creates or destroys, never at ease, always in action."

She paused, felt the weight, the heat, the truth, the past, the uncertain future. I did the same.

"Pi?"

"Yeah."

"You gave me a hysterical, weeping, joyous, tender, violent, beautiful orgasm. Even now that energy has me fidgeting, licking my lips as my nostrils flare. After sex with you, I feel like spinning, leaping, doing grand jeté after grand jeté. But let's not get to the bonnet phase. Hard enough handling the physical without the mental."

"Getting off before that last exit."

"Would hate to have to suddenly leave Memphis."

"Your modus operandi when it gets to be too much for you."

"Survival skill."

"Nice to have that as an option."

"No one runs back into a wildfire."

"Can't argue with that."

"We can still do many other things, as much as we can do in Memphis. We can do road trips. Show me more of Tennessee, Mississippi, and Arkansas—what you call the tristate area. We can have fun like we're a real couple, but be sure to pause before the exit, park there, engine idling. We can enjoy what this is, listen to Audible books on long trips. I need to visit the house where Harriet Tubman hid the enslaved. I desperately want to see ATL. I heard about a place. City Winery. We could go see Miki Howard. See a play at Southwest Arts Center. Ashamed to admit I got ahead of myself and planned it all out. Imagined us driving across the West Memphis-Arkansas Bridge with *The Miseducation of Lauryn Hill* playing. I'd get us a room in Midtown. We check in, have lunch at Slutty Vegan, nap, then do dinner at Bacchanalia. Back at the room, I dress up like Big Barda, and you're Mister Miracle. The next morning, I get my hair did at Hair Be Poppin in Ellenwood."

"You put some serious thought in this."

"When I'm all cute again, we visit Titan Games and Comics. Barnes & Noble. Lenox Square, then back to the hotel room. In my mind, days later we talk about economic bifurcation on the way to a casino in Mississippi. I do want to see more of the South, so I rent a fancy car and we go back toward Birmingham, do a wee layover there, eat at Five Points, go bowling at Woolworth Recreation and Refreshment, then keep going up I-20 East toward ATL. That time I'll be driving, dressed like a country girl in Daisy Dukes like Beyoncé wore at Coachella, radio loud and singing 'Sweet Home Alabama.'"

"That's a lot of miles on the tires."

"When we are done, we go back to the Four Seasons, drink wine, use a phone to record us, go at it like feral rabbits, have soul-mate sex and sweat like we're trying to blend with the southern humidity. Then we watch and reenact the wicked movie we made. If they put a blue light on the room, artist Jackson Pollock will see our incredible artwork and give us a standing ovation for the creativity."

"We get real nasty."

"You exhaust me, but I dig deep, keep going. My body is hungry; around you my body is always famished. You make me sing Kapaichumarimarichopaco and rattle the walls. Delicious becomes the meal you can't get enough of. Your face lives between my thighs. Anything to make me sing in that British timbre. It will feel like a love supreme, the kind of love that makes me forget all the times my heart has been broken, makes me forget all the disappointments, all the times I have been let down. Back at the hotel room, I sneak into the bathroom and come back dressed like Uhura from *Star Trek*, only my outfit will be much tighter, have amazing cleavage because what I'm wearing will be sexier than anything from Victoria's. I ask you if you're ready to beam up, and you are so ready to beam up."

"You're a planner."

"I live my life organized."

"That's many road trips."

"But we can do as much in Memphis, since you have to work all week. If needed, to save time driving back and forth from your home to mine, I can spare a drawer for you to leave a few things in for a bit, and if it comes to that, give you your own walk-in closet. I can spoil you. Treat you like no other woman ever has. But no bonnet. I'd rather not go that far again. If only our timing had been better."

"Okay. The way you keep vacillating, plus my mood, my new era, I was thinking the same."

"We're going fast, but let's keep it right here. Not too much, not too little, just right."

"You sure? We don't have to have sex. We can still hang out. Dance. Hit the bookstore. Buy comics. But be done at a decent hour. Hugs and handshakes and maybe forehead kisses at most."

"Goldilocks is enjoying sleeping in Baby Bear's bed."

I said, "Back shots and sloppy blow jobs. Hard to give that up, even for Lent."

"Away from London, I am truly someone different. I'm exploring here. I feel more sexual. Awakened. I have no problem doing more creative things, being daring, doing a few off-the-beaten-path things."

"As long as you're comfortable."

"Enjoyed the naughty bit I just did in the car park."

"Me too."

"Dared myself to be a porn star, gave in, and surprised myself."

"Me too. Surprised me too."

"And I don't need you so comfortable where you keep on your socks and sliders during sex."

I laughed. "Somebody's been watching Black porn."

She grinned. "That wicked thing when you put my feet on your chest and went so deep inside me in slow motion, that bit broke me, could use that twenty minutes a day as therapy, but I don't want to cross the line to being so comfortable and hopeful and drunk from orgasm that I drop my guard and allow myself to be seen walking around in my everyday ugly underwear wearing a rainbow-colored bonnet that makes me look like a circus clown."

"I like clowns, as long as you don't go Pennywise; then I'd have to become a clown killer."

"Can't do too real. Need the illusion and fantasy to keep me in a certain altered reality and away from all roads that lead me back toward heartbreak. Living in Heartbreak Hotel is no fun. I'm finally back on smooth roads and not anxious to meet the start of rough roads and unfamiliar potholes that I'd have to learn to live with or choose to circumvent daily. I don't have the emotional bandwidth for that now. But I still enjoy being a nurturer. I can afford to spoil myself, but it's no fun spoiling myself alone."

"So, all that to say?"

"Culturally, we are different enough to find each other exotic and interesting; have enough in common due to melanin and global oppression to not have to strain to find things that allow us to bond. Our intellectual and emotional maturity encourages us to connect on both academic and spiritual levels, bond in a way that most others would never be able to comprehend."

"But no bonnet."

"No bonnet."

A soft beat passed before curiosity made me ask, "What was your heartbreaker's name?"

"Lennie."

I almost chuckled when she said the name from *Of Mice and Men*, as if that was an omen.

She said, "Nigerian. From Lagos. Works with Dangote Group."

"Lennie."

"If he had loved me as much as he does fantasy football, we might've had a chance. I was nonexistent to him when a game was on. Then he met a girl from Nairobi with the same obsession."

"Lennie."

"The law of diminishing returns applies to relationships as well. We were beyond a point at which the benefits gained were less than the amount of money and energy invested."

Her phone rang and she whispered it was a 212 area code, number unfamiliar, but she answered. "Who is this? From? When did we meet? Theater? New York? *Hamilton*? Oh, that was quite a while ago. Refresh my memory on that moment? Oh, surprised to hear from you. Well, I am no longer available as I am seeing someone now. Serious enough. Romantically involved, yes. Well, I was single when I met you, or I would not have given you most of my digits. Well, I'm not going to be apologetic if you had to dial almost a thousand numbers over six months to find me. Maybe you would have made contact sooner if you had done them sequentially and not randomly like you said you did. Sorry, love, you were interesting at the moment, but I've moved on. A very handsome writer, professor I met. After I met you. Yes, after. Well, I'm not running a bloody queue. Well, it's hardly my fault. You had the head start and he took the initiative and broke the code before you did, which was impressive. In less than one day. Must we become so indignant? Why must you know that? Are you that fragile? He says it tastes sweeter than maple syrup and makes me sing more symphonies than Mozart created. As often as I can, every day if possible. Hate the game, not me. Don't bother a ring back. Wanker, you'll be blocked. Yo momma."

She hung up and my phone rang with a call from the 901.

I answered and Momma took off talking: "Don't be alarmed, but Sis in jail."

CHAPTER 41

"Sis in jail?"

Momma chuckled. "I finally have a reason to bake a cake and hide a file in it. She would be so mad at me for laughing at her."

I chuckled with her and asked, "What done happened now?"

"She kicked some pretty girl upside her hard head for disrespecting her. Girl started it, came here and assaulted her, spat in her face, and Sis finished it. The girl blamed it all on Sis when MPD showed up. They sent the whole police force over. The girl got her feelings hurt and called the police lying up a storm. A big no no. You know we handle things internally. She better be glad I was at the gym. Baby Doll is nicer than I would have been. Momma don't play that. Gonna attack Baby Doll then tell po-po a bunch of lies. And she knows my child is a second-degree black belt out at Kang Rhee. She had that kick coming. She only kicked her once. Just to put some sense in her head. Not too hard. Baby Doll could've knocked the silly girl out if she wanted to, but she didn't kick her too hard, was just trying to show her who she was messing with."

"Jesus. Can't leave y'all for one day. What went down?"

"All the neighbors were out in the streets. The Ballards. The Whites. The Kendalls. The Boatwrights brought Cokes and the Smiths brought hoecakes. Reverend Johnson ran down from his house and was there to keep it calm. We all held hands and prayed a good prayer."

"Stop laughing."

"When something funny to Momma, Momma gonna laugh. We famous here this week. Everything gonna be fine. Caught the lying heifer on Ring. They took Sis because we Black. Police come this way they ain't happy until they got one of us sitting in the back of their car."

"You sure?"

"We posted it and her IG following went up by five thousand. She catching up with me."

I started laughing along with Momma. It was a Black thing. Our humor a family thing.

"What funny to Momma, funny to Momma, and I don't care who don't think so. We're gonna tease Sis a long time over this one. A real long time, Sweet Meat, like we did your barbecue that time."

I said, "I wished you had come, but now I'm glad you didn't."

"I had a ticket to go with you, same flight. They sent me one."

"Why didn't you come?"

"Those people don't want to meet me, and I don't need to meet them. Never said one thing nice about me, not once."

"This is about you. This is a chapter in your book as much as mine."

"This yours. I closed that chapter in mine. Now tell your momma you love her so she can go get her oldest daughter. Got me a Bruce Lee–kicking daughter. Mad at her, but proud of her. Never let folks do you wrong. She put that jealous girl in her place. That Dominican won't be back on Kansas Street carrying nothing heavier than roses and an apology the size of a big bucket of KFC chicken here on out."

"You cross us, you get what you get."

"What else you have to do out there? I need you back home."

"He wrote in his will for me to attend a few events."

"Events?"

"Funerals."

"He out there having two and three funerals?"

"More or less."

"Bet he is doing like Aretha Franklin. She had three outfit changes for her viewings and funeral. Can't die but once, yet er'body trying to get buried forty-eleven times with a seven-hour funeral."

"He's over-the-top."

"How he look? They do him up good?"

"He looked better dead than most folks do alive."

"Hate you by yourself out there."

"My friend came out."

"Yellow gal?"

"Yeah, she right here in the car with me."

"Sweet Meat, I'm running my mouth and you didn't say a stranger in the room?"

"She can't hear you."

"Fool, I hear you and if she sitting right next to you, she can hear your part of the conversation. Sweet Meat, politely tell your friend I need a word with both of you and put your phone on speaker."

Chuckling, I did what Momma said, no hesitation.

"Good morning. This is Miss Infinity Molyneaux. I'm Pi's mother."

"Miss Infinity Molyneaux, my name is Gemma Buckingham. Nice to meet you despite the circumstances."

"Likewise. You from out of town, I hear."

"I'm from London."

"I wanted to thank you for taking the time to go out there to be with my favorite son at his time of need. I don't know you yet, but he likes you, so I will like you until he stops liking you."

"Miss Molyneaux, it's my pleasure to help him get sorted."

"So you single, separated, divorced, or widowed?"

"Wow, well, if you must know, I'm divorced."

"How long?"

"I married at sixteen, like a fool, and was divorced the same year."

"Why you go off and do that?"

"Married to get away from my parents. They consented. He married me for citizenship."

"Any babies?"

"No children and in no rush."

"Where your peoples?"

"My mum is in Manchester and my father is in South Africa."

"They divorced?"

THE SON OF MR. SULEMAN267

"Not at all."

"Well, come by the house when you get back in town. We only bite people we like."

"I'll make sure I come for a visit as soon as possible."

"I'll make you a Sunday dinner. Tell my son to text me what you like to eat. When you come don't dress fancy. Wear your slippers if you want to. If you come in your pajamas, nobody gonna care."

"I look forward to meeting you."

"One more thing."

"Yes?"

"My son special. Want you to know that. But you his secret friend, and already know you are with a good man. Never done wrong a day in his life. When they made my son, they broke the mold. He ain't never going to brag on himself, cause that's my job. Momma was sick a little while and my son worked three jobs, did that when he was in high school to help all us out. Smart boy but that load had him struggling with his grades. Never complained, not one time. Grades got low, but he stuck to it and he made a comeback. Then he worked over at Southgate at Piggly Wiggly the third shift so he could go to classes at UAN in the day. U of M missed out when they turned him down. He used to walk from here to work in the dark, in the middle of the night, because the buses stop running at ten, would sleep a couple hours, then get back on the 31 Crosstown Kansas by seven, be on the back of the bus asleep before it took off."

"Had no idea he had struggled to achieve so much. Your son is truly an amazing man."

"Send a selfie right now so I know what y'all look like; that way if y'all go missing I can tell the police what you look like today and show 'em the clothes y'all had on."

We did.

"Oh, you yellow for real. Real yellow. You yellow enough to own the color. Not for your hair I'd swear you was skinfolk with Miss Ann out here in Germantown. You kind of pretty."

On a disturbed exhale, Gemma Buckingham whispered, "Wow."

"Y'all dressed real nice, look good together. But everybody daughter looks a little bit better when she's sitting next to one of my boys. Okay, pretty yellow gal. Bye."

Momma ended the call.

I asked, "You were married?"

Gemma Buckingham shifted. "That was interesting."

"Your word again."

"In this case 'unique' might be a better word choice."

"Momma is unique."

"You must be some momma and son."

"You okay?"

"Yellow gal?"

"Southern thing."

"Rude."

"No harm meant. Red bone, red, high yellow, you'll get called that and more here."

"So, since Meghan Markle grew up in an African American neighborhood, she had it just as bad on this side of the pond."

"Never heard of that actress until she married royalty."

"Yellow gal. Own the color. Miss Ann in Germantown. Bet Sunday dinner will be a riot."

"We okay?"

"You don't understand what it is to be biracial."

"No, I don't."

"Yellow gal. I assume your mother isn't a yellow gal, so Sunday dinner will be interesting."

"No harm meant."

"The damage is done."

"I'll call her."

"No need for a second traumatization."

"I can have her call you up and apologize, or do it face-to-face."

"It's cool; it's cool; it's cool; it's cool." She shook her head, chuckled. "Should be used to particular ways of thinking, but I'm not. I get all the crap Black people get from non-Blacks, plus the bigotry that Black people have. I'm the dumping ground for all that is wrong in the world. Everybody seems to think that my complexion makes it easier, that I don't have real issues, so they remind me of their issues every chance they get. You know how much it stings to catch a wanker you been spending your time with . . . in the arms of a woman who looks three shades closer to Africa than you ever will?"

She rubbed her temples.

Then she tossed in a laugh. "Shit, sorry. Maybe I am overreacting. I mean, I have been called worse. I guess that came out of nowhere, didn't anticipate that happening while I was in a car riding down a bloody freeway in Los Angeles. We've had a long day and it was a long trip to get here. I'm sleepy. Couldn't nap on the plane because I was too worried about you. Sleep, I need sleep."

"So, I lay the pipe one or twice real nice and we good?"

"We'll pretend it never happened. At Sunday dinner, it won't be an issue."

"Be yourself. If you show up in booty shorts and slippers, they will like you right away."

"She talks fast."

"People who talk slow stupid; Momma not stupid."

"So, do I come across as a dimwit, love? Should I talk a little faster?"

"It's a joke. She's always been a fast talker. When she lectures she makes herself slow down."

"At least she called me pretty. Mind showing me a selfie of you and the lovely woman, honey? I'm sure you have a ton of them in your phone. Hand it to me and I'll take a quick look-see."

"You used to be married."

"You have a sister in jail."

"Interesting."

"To say the least."

"You were married."

"For seed money to start my business, no other reason."

"At sixteen?"

"At sixteen. It was a business transaction."

"A business transaction."

"Which defines marriage. At some point, all relationships evolve and involve business."

CHAPTER 42

HAIR STYLED LIKE Misty Knight with a T as her cosplay uniform, eyes wild, Gemma Buckingham panted, craned her neck, looked back at me in my Power Man T, focused on my green eyes as she touched my hands, hands choking her neck harder, harder. She nodded she wanted more. In Luke Cage mode I stroked her at a steady pace, the cadence of a rapid heartbeat. Skin slapped, the bed rocked, the walls shook, and her wild hair bounced same as mine. I grunted like a man losing the plot one stroke at a time. She twisted her body, brought her tongue to mine. I added deep, wild kisses to the mix.

Orgasm frenzied her, its riptides yanked her under, had her stressed for drops of fresh air as her body shivered head to toe. She tensed against its power but was consumed by the surges of electricity, the crashing waves. She fell away from me, left my beard dank with honey from London. I watched her. Waves died down, became twitches, then spasms that lessened. She needed a break. I washed my face and came back. She was still panting, sweating, twitching. I got on top, took her missionary.

"Pi . . . Pi . . . oh, Pi . . . I . . . I . . . I'm going to come again."

Soon she was on the suite's plush sofa, on her back, legs hanging over the edges, open wide so I could tongue love Delicious while she worked her gag reflex at the same time. Her phone was on the table, recording our session. I changed positions, gave her big daddy long strokes, put her feet on my chest, sucked her toes, then pulled out as she was at the end of body-quivering, Jesus-calling, Afro-pulling orgasm eleven, because I was calling God too. With a caveman grunt I grabbed her 'fro and brought her mouth to the fountain to have communion; she greedily hurried her full lips to my erection. Stroked and sucked and stroked and sucked until I grunted louder and moaned and lost control and tried to feed it all to her, made love to her face the way she liked it, the intense way she demanded it, this her ultimate challenge, to take it all, and I came so hard I almost fell off the sofa and passed out.

"Jesus, what was that all 'bout and can you please do it again, but not now."

I didn't want to leave here.

We were in the London West Hollywood at Beverly Hills, ordering room service, smashing up the place. We could've been at a Motel 6 somewhere on a dusty section of Route 66 for all I cared.

All I wanted to do was avoid the lazy man's load I'd left in the 901.

"You're bloody different here too, Pi."

"How so?"

"Uninhibited."

"Like you're different in Memphis than you are in London."

She fluffed her magnificent Afro. "No one I know in London would recognize me here."

"You said you want to see more of the South."

"So much to see here. America is so bloody large. Did some research. You can drive for days and still be in America. You can drive for twelve hours and still be in the same state."

"In at least three states, yeah."

"And each of your fifty states has its own laws, which makes it sound like fifty countries."

I said, "You'll have to show me around London one day."

"That's about all it would take to see most of London, one day. Compared to here. We could walk from the Eye to Buckingham Palace and see everything from St. Paul's Cathedral to Parliament."

"I would love to take a selfie walking across the big London Bridge."

"I think you have the bridges confused, as most Americans have done.

That Victorian, gothic monstrosity is Tower Bridge, named for the Tower of London, where they had bloody executions. Americans think that's London Bridge for some reason."

"Where is London Bridge?"

"Two bridges away. Next to Parliament. It's a very boring pedestrian bridge."

I asked, "What's the best hotel you've stayed in?"

"Lanesborough back home. No, maybe the Langham in Central London."

"Outside of London?"

"Saxon in South Africa was nice. I've traveled extensively and stayed in some nice ones."

"Top five here in the States?"

"Southernmost House Hotel, Key West, Florida. Grand Hotel, Mackinac Island, Michigan. The Plaza Hotel, New York, New York. The Miami Biltmore, Coral Gables, Florida. The Peabody."

"Jesus. How many places have you been to? Do you even remember?"

She named at least fifty spots around the world. "I'm sure there are more."

The Lady from London was next to me, warmth to warmth, cuddled and calm, her body sticky, a Rorschach of come stains all over her skin, the bed a Jackson Pollack. She knew me, had known me over and over during more sessions of congress than I could count, her skin against mine, and she still had no idea about my secrets, the secret life of Pi, as I had no idea about the secret life of Gemma Buckingham.

My phone rang and she handed it to me as she got up to go to the bathroom.

It was Four Ds.

"Mane, I fucked up. Mane, I'm about to lose my job and my wife."

I knew Four Ds, so I had a gut feeling what foolishness had happened. I had a gut feeling who had happened. I hoped I was wrong.

I told him, "Not now. Nothing I can do, so not now."

I hung up.

When Gemma Buckingham came back, she mounted me.

CHAPTER 43

THE NEXT MORNING, three hours after the rooster had crowed back in Tennessee, I wore straight-leg Trues and a black T that proclaimed KILL-MONGER WAS RIGHT. My golden UAN zip-up hoodie was at my side. Gemma Buckingham had on jeans and a colorful Camden T, her hoodie Brixton branded. Fat Man met us in the lobby suited up like he was ready to do battle in court. Gemma Buckingham didn't want to come upstairs into the office. She told me she had no problem catching an Uber and riding around.

I said, "I'm not comfortable with you going out into LA alone. Wait a bit."

"I've seen over one hundred countries. Most of those places were developing countries where I traveled alone. I can handle myself in LA."

As we stood at the private elevator I asked, "You sure?"

"Meghan grew up in Windsor Hills, not far from Hollywood, maybe nine miles or so. I want to see if I can find her mum's home, take a picture out front."

"Now I know why you really came here, for Meghan Markle, not to console the accoutrement."

"I know how to multitask. It will take you hours to sort your affairs. I won't be missed."

I kissed her on the cheek, playfully gave her two dollars, and let her go on her way.

When we were in his office I stood in front of Fat Man's contemporary bookshelves.

He asked, "Did you ever read any of his books?"

"Never. Knocked a few down if I saw them at the bookstore, but never picked one up."

"He worked on a memoir."

"Was it published?"

"Unfinished. Few pages. It's part of the stuff you will inherit. To dispose of or sell or publish. Up to you. You can burn it in a barrel but be warned that might be like burning a barrel of money."

"I have matches, a can of lawn-mower gas, and a barrel sitting in my backyard."

"Last thing he worked on was the memoir. All the success, the women, the children, and he was dying all by himself, hoping one of his Motherfuckers would call to see how he was doing, or stop by to see if they could order him a meal from Grubhub. To occupy his mind and not feel so alone while his life was winding down, he started his memoirs."

I didn't add anything, but I wondered how my momma's reputation was presented.

"Your father did the Forever series. That was what elevated his career. The Forever series."

"I see them in your office. Have seen them everywhere I have gone. He's inescapable."

"That was twenty of his books. Ten years of his life on the same theme."

"I heard."

"On each dedication page, he only wrote that word, Forever. His publisher always wanted to know why he dedicated a book to itself, and readers would ask him that at events. That was the one question he would never answer."

"So what?"

"Synonym."

"You mean pseudonym."

"I mean synonym."

"You have your words mixed up."

"Forever is a synonym."

I was confused. "Where we going with this?"

He paused. "Forever means infinity. Forever is Infinity."

He said my mother's name and I paused, tried to read what he was saying.

He repeated, "Forever means infinity. Forever is Infinity."

My eyes went to the line of books in the Forever series, seeing them clearly for the first time.

He went on, "The Forever series, that was him writing about Infinity Molyneaux."

I dismissed it. Had to. It didn't fit my beliefs. But once a thought has been planted, it became part of a man's yard, another weed to pull.

I whispered, "Forever means infinity. Forever is Infinity."

"I'm not trying to upset you; I just wanted you to have all the information. To be considered and valued and judged as you see fit."

"I'll never drive my red Chevy to the levy and give those thoughts another think."

He nodded. "One more thing."

"As long as it's under one hundred words. Edit as you go."

"Suleman had me reach out to your mother one time. He had an event in Boston, away from the wife, kids, and drama he had at home. He offered to fly you and her up there first-class so he could meet you after his event. He wanted her to come early in the day with you and enjoy herself, then meet at the hotel so he could meet you. Miss Molyneaux told me to tell Mr. Suleman that if he wanted to see you, be it the next week or the next spring or the one after that, he knew where she was, same address the checks went to, so he knew where you lived, and then said bye and hung up the phone."

"I'll almost believe that one."

"She called back the next day, and it was the last time she called."

"How'd that go?"

"Miss Infinity Molyneaux of Memphis, Tennessee, told me to tell *New York Times* bestselling author Mr. Suleman that he might've been a picker, grinner, and midnight sinner, but she wasn't a rambling woman. Said if Mr. Suleman can't offer to bring his son to where he lives and wants her to come to some far corner of the world so he can sneak and meet you when there wasn't anyone around, he had mistaken not only the kind of mother but the kind of woman she was. Requested me to never contact her again with foolishness. Told me to tell Mr. Suleman's angry, betrayed, and heartbroken wife of that trying era she apologizes for all the confusion she unintentionally helped cause. She accepted her part in all that happened and apologized, then hoped and prayed Mr. Suleman found time to go visit his other kids in public before it was too late. Said if not then may God bless him. Said bye. Hung up."

"That's my momma."

He nodded. "I knew the man best and I'm still learning about him. Things he didn't want anybody to know while he was alive are popping up left and right, like little brush fires, easy to put out if handled right away, but can be a wildfire if ignored. Nothing stays hidden forever. If not disclosed while aboveground, death will reveal all."

"All of that and he still died alone."

"Kid, we all die alone."

"Not when you have loved ones at your beside."

"You might have an audience, but you're the only one doing the dying."

CHAPTER 44

THE NEXT MORNING we were at West Angeles Cathedral. They told me my old man had come back to church in the end, was baptized again. But I knew not even holy water could wash away all the stains.

We moved into the crowded auditorium, one big enough to hold a midsize concert. The photos in the program showed my father had run in the company of prominent authors like Toni Morrison, Colson White-head, Salman Rushdie, and former FBI director James Comey. Tickets were sixty-five a pop.

The man referred to in the program as "The Divine Griot" and "The Michelangelo of Black Literature" would be laid to rest in an aboveground tomb, an elaborate house to honor those who died with the most toys.

There was a still on the wall with a picture of my clean-shaven father holding one of his novels. Images of my dead father played on a screen and a brother next to me got on his phone loud-talking to somebody, overexcited.

"Nigga, you ain't going to believe who the hell I'm seeing right now. I am up in this book service thing for this nigga and I swear to God I'm standing right next to a nigga who look like the nigga who died. Naw, nigga right next to me. If this some faked-death Tupac-and-Elvis bull-shit, I want my coins back for this bootleg ticket. A little indica-sativa for my glaucoma, but I ain't that goddamn high. Hold on, nigga, hold on."

He leaned in and took a selfie with me, touched my sleeve, went back to talking.

"He ain't no ghost because my hand didn't go through him like it would a real Casper. On the church big screen, the dead nigga is drippin' in finesse and sitting up in a chair made for a goddamn god, signing a stack of his books like he's writing a new Bible, and the nigga next to me looks like that nigga, only his suit ain't as nice as the ballin' nigga I came to see about getting this ton of books signed. Because they worth a lot more money when a nigga dead, that why. Nigga next to me looks like the dead nigga spat him out his nuts. Nigga, if I looked that much like that rich Black nigga who wrote all those books, I'd be down at the bank first thing in the morning holding a book up to my face as my goddamn identification to steal his coins and run my ass up to Malibu. No drive-bys, nigga. Not unless it's the motherfuckin postman."

THAT NIGHT FAT Man drove me around in a drop-top, chauffeured me from property to property.

Gemma Buckingham was with Svelte Wife. They went up to the Geffen Playhouse to see a production called *Black Super Hero Magic Mama*. London just wanted to have fun even if she had to dance in a few mourner's tears. She'd ride away any grief or anger or anxiety I brought to our hotel bed later, more than happy after they were done with theater, bar hopping, and meeting celebrities.

I said, "Two of his cribs are ten miles apart."

"Ten miles here not the same as in Memphis. It was in case traffic was bad and he didn't want to drive another two hours to get to a bed. Each bed had a mistress, the largest one, his wife."

"He was doing the most."

Fat Man said, "He would move into a house, get lonely, move a woman in with him, get tired of her, and leave her in that house while he moved to another one. This Hancock Park house is where he went to write. None of the women were allowed to visit him here. Other than houses, had a lot of depreciating assets, things that had less value every day, or had no value to anybody but him from the get-go. Cars were stacked up like trophies. Fancy suits were lined up like in a clothing shop."

I made sure Fat Man walked to the houses on both sides and in the front, had a white face in a suit introduce himself and tell the neighbors, people my father had never met, that a new, younger Black man would be coming onto the property. As they came out, I made sure they saw me, knew what I looked like, and informed them of the colors I would be wearing when I came back by here tomorrow. One house had enough furniture to fill up the houses of all of Momma's Fastest Swimmers, furniture that looked like no one had ever sat on it long enough to break wind. Every sofa or chair was comfortable enough to sleep in. Not that I'd take any of it, but most of it was too big to even fit in a house small as mine. The garage was larger than my entire house.

Fat Attorney said, "The dead leave a mess for the living to straighten out."

"I've seen smaller messes. This is like a big-ass business shutting down and having a fire sale."

"This will take six months, at least, if those idiot Motherfuckers don't fight this in court. When I die, I'm not doing it like this, not leaving a heavy load like this on my family."

"At six hundred fifty dollars an hour."

"My friends-and-family rate."

"You turn your lips up at six hundred and fifty an hour like it's below minimum wage."

"Suleman's Motherfuckers are complaining about that too."

"Not like you're shoveling shit."

"Would smell better than the shit he left behind for me to sort out."

"You're going to be sitting in a nice office, with a view of the ocean, sipping scotch as you work, and you make it sound like you'll be in the noonday sun digging six-foot-deep holes in a graveyard."

"My pen is my shovel and I've been digging people out of deeper holes for decades."

I said, "Mr. Suleman called his children the Motherfuckers."

"All day long to his dying breath. You don't want to know what he called their mothers."

I was going to tell him Momma called us the Fastest Swimmers, but that wasn't his business. I had two families now. The Motherfuckers had no love, wanted what they could get. The Fastest Swimmers, we never had much, but each swimmer had been loved from the start.

He asked, "Want to drive one of these drop-tops or other new cars down PCH?"

"PCH? Publishers Clearing House?"

"Pacific Coast Highway. By the ocean. Go see the perfect sunset. Smog makes the skies a really pretty color of orange and yellows. You'd get some fresh air. Could get good seafood along the way."

"How long would that take?"

"PCH stretches about 150 miles along the coast."

"A nice little road trip if you don't mind sitting in traffic going slower than I can run."

"You'd take your time and pass all the beaches."

I looked over the car lot. "Which one would it be okay for me to get in and take for a test spin?"

"All of them. It might not have sunken in yet, Mr. Suleman, but legally these will be yours."

"All of this?"

"To dispose of as you wish." He nodded. "Which one you want to test-ride first?"

I pointed. "That one. It's a beast."

"The Harley?"

"Next to it."

"The *lawn mower?*"

"Yeah. Can I take it around the yard a couple times and put some straight lines in the little grass he has? Whoever has been doing the yard needs a few classes in how to do this kinda grass right."

"Well, this is going to be your yard, if you want it, so go right ahead."

"Probably safer for me in here than out there."

"What you mean?"

"Man of European persuasion, it's safer for you in the streets. My people are safer in their homes. Even if this will be mine, these folks will see my brown face and send the cops to the front door to either kill me or charge me with trying to steal what legally belongs to me to dispose of as I wish."

"I worry about it out there too. It impacts my life too. I have kids. It's not safe in schools."

"They're after people who don't look like you; you're the collateral damage for a larger cause."

"I have kids in middle school. It's not safe in our place of worship either."

"You go to church?"

"I send money. Tax write-off."

"You cut your own grass?"

"I cut checks."

"You've never cut your own grass?"

He laughed like that was the dumbest question ever, walked away shaking his head.

"Ever cleaned your own toilet?"

He found that hysterical.

"You don't get up early on Saturday mornings and clean your own house? Who cleans your gutter? Bet you don't have an idea how to change an air filter or change your dryer lint vent."

"Mr. Suleman, your mother did a good job raising you. Too bad she didn't raise the Motherfuckers. Half of them have never bothered to learn how to flush a toilet, let alone clean one."

CHAPTER 45

MY PHONE BUZZED before the sun and kept buzzing while we were in the crowd at Hollywood Forest Lawn Cemetery. I had left Memphis for a moment but it didn't mean my daily issues had boarded a different plane and gone off to become someone else's shit to deal with.

Dr. Stone-Calhoun was Hancock Parking me with every call, even when she breathed heavily and hung up. A come-stained blouse could have me locked up the moment I landed in Memphis. My side of the story would be too incredulous for any jury to believe.

Gemma Buckingham whispered, "What's wrong with my boo?"

"Work stuff."

"Don't they know where you are?"

"Do you think they care?"

"This is why one should be self-employed at all times."

"Shit has me stressed."

"I'll fix that for you back at the room, like I did last night. I'm here for you."

BACK AT THE room, Gemma Buckingham dressed up like Wonder Woman. She'd bought gear for me, dressed me in a tight Superman T, my guns popping. She became a goddess, and the deity Gemma Buckingham trembled under this mortal's touch when I kissed her heavenly pillow-soft lips. My touch took her breath away. She wanted me. I felt her swirled flesh, her amalgamation of two worlds, of two continents that lived in my ignorance, and almost lost my mind. Wanted to know her and stroke and kiss away every angst percolating inside me. I wanted to cover myself with Gemma Buckingham to erase the abuse from the Bitch from Brownsville. Wanted to not care that Four Ds was in dire straits. Wanted to fucking forget everybody and never go back to Memphis.

My old man had a house up in the Black Beverly Hills, a four-thousand-square-foot number he bought thirty years ago and had rarely used. After another event at Eso Won, a group of international Black writers had another gathering in a house that would be mine to dispose of as I saw fit, another three-level house I could chill in and be selfish and live better than most other folks, or give that corner of Black Beverly Hills to the relative of my choosing. It was an upper-class Black area. A rarity in America. Populated by well-educated people who looked like me and my family. My people have always been educated, just never allowed to have real estate and community on this level. I felt safe. Told myself I could live here.

CHAPTER 46

GEMMA BUCKINGHAM AND Fat Man's wife bonded, talked business tactics more than fashion, compared their travels around the world, had conversation that would make the Bechdel test folks stand up and clap ten times. After ten minutes of whispering and giggling like new best friends, they called a car service and scheduled a girls' trip over to Rodeo Drive, Century City, rich folks zip codes and beyond.

I had to deal with Fat Man and a dead man's business, things unearthed as Mr. Suleman was given back to that same earth, and I didn't want Gemma Buckingham all up in Suleman business, so I was glad my lustful Londoner and Fat Man's Svelte Wife went to shop until they dropped.

I was okay for a while, cooler than Matthew in a Navigator, until I saw more ish on CNN. The news had set me off. A special report had come on. Another Black woman had been shot and killed by cops down south. She was unarmed, dead in seconds because she looked suspicious.

Fat Man chuckled and groaned. "Get it off your chest."

I grinned. "You're learning my moods."

"You're easy to read."

I motioned at the TV, at another crying, irretrievably broken Black family being interviewed.

Exhausted, I said, "We have to explain to the same people over and over what's going on. I've tried. I've been trying to explain to white folks about Black folks since I learned to say words."

"You're not screaming."

"We scream because when we whisper, no one listens. You're listening."

"Okay."

"Yeah, we scream. You do that when you're talking to someone deaf. You talk louder, you scream for their benefit, not yours." I sighed. "My people always end up dead. It doesn't matter if we march turning the other cheek like MLK or kick open doors by any means necessary like Malcolm, we end up dead. We're treated wrong in broad daylight, arrested for doing nothing, killed, and the police hold a press conference saying nothing wrong has been done and expect the dead to apologize."

"Okay."

"I scare you."

"Trying to understand you so I can save you and people you come in contact with."

"You don't know me."

"Tell me who you are."

"I am a man made in the cargo hold of ships destined for the shores of America, a man deemed free only because it was sanctioned by the government as an amendment, a man whose freedom was written as an afterthought, yet the cause of a war between the conflicted values of white men. I am a man with family history that has been marinated in four hundred years of racism."

"Okay for me to say something, or you're going to keep doing what sounds like spoken word?"

"Your office, your house, your rules."

"I accept and agree with all you said."

I said, "I am a Black man born in Memphis. That's shaped me in all ways. We had to carry signs saying 'I Am a Man' and beg for equality as MLK was killed in our backyard. Who are you?"

The Fat Man said, "I was supposed to be named Roger de Groot the Fifth."

"Well, at least your family knows what their true family name used to

be. Black man's last name isn't about his family tree; it's about the tree of
the family who used to own his stolen, kidnapped, and enslaved family.
Our last name is the name of those who erased our history and forced us
to believe what they believe. Our surname is *their* brand, a designator of
their property. Edna *owned by* Johnson. Edna Johnson. John *owned by*
Smith. John Smith. Even his surname is a reminder of the oppressor. My
skinfolks were kidnapped and enslaved by rich white Christians, and
even if they broke free, it was impossible to swim home to Africa. America was our Alcatraz. America was the Rock the enslaved Africans couldn't
escape. America is still the Black man's Alcatraz. With draconian laws."

"Stop doing that. It's irritating."

"Stop doing what?"

"When a man tells you that he's been hit by a car, don't upstage him
and say you were run over by a train. The pain might be different, but it's
still pain. My pain. Everything isn't always about you."

I nodded, waited to see where he was going with this new round of old
bullshit.

"For every crime a white man or woman commits, it comes back at me
too. I have no connections to your part of the country, but the moment I
landed there, I might as well have been a plantation owner and supporter
of the KKK. Never understood that part of America and its obsessions.
My people came from the Netherlands. They were pacifists and lived on
a farm in the province of Drenthe."

"Part of those welcomed with open arms at the Ellis Island experiences."

"They came here, worked hard, labored sunup to sundown, and things
worked out."

"They came on the top of a ship, as human beings, not as chattel, not
in chains."

"Pi, my car, not your train."

"Keep driving."

"Anyway, instead of being Carlton Jones, a name I've never cared for,
I'd be the fifth Roger de Groot living in America."

"Took your family four generations to rise to this level. Your family did all this in about a hundred years. Mine have been here over four hundred years, worked harder than yours . . . all this in four generations."

"I know. It's unfair."

"All they had to do for us was give us the forty acres and the mule as promised. But doing what was right will always seem wrong to certain people." I shook my head. "All this in four generations."

"We didn't arrive at this level; my people came here with a nickel in their pockets."

"At least you had a nickel."

"They forced my people to change their names at the island, into something the illiterate men in America could pronounce. So, since de Groot looked or sounded funny and not American enough, they named us. My people had long hair, the men all had dirty beards, and they all wore old clothes. None had been to school and the story is the men hadn't been to the barber for over nine years. Back then my family had been living in isolation waiting for the end of time. It's not much, but that's part of who I am."

"In the end your people were allowed to get by. You were allowed to be white. Get land. Buy houses. If America had apologized with forty acres and a mule, it would be better sea to shining sea for everybody, but that would be too much like right and America loves to wake up doing wrong."

Another moment passed.

"Well, I'm glad the American dream worked out for your skinfolk."

My cold delivery shook him to the core.

I said, "I'm sorry, man. I just get hot under the collar."

"You upstaged me."

"Didn't mean to run over your car with my bus."

"You hit me with a Union Pacific five-engine train that time, then backed it up twice."

We laughed a little. No matter how hard he thought his family had it, until I saw images of his people as strange fruit hanging from southern trees, or being sprayed by water hoses while the police sicced German shepherds on as many of his people as they could, until he showed me they had a Black Wall Street burned down while his people were being arrested and killed because a cracker could, I was dialing 1-800-BULLSHIT on all he had to say. What I felt showed in my eyes and body language.

He asked, "Are you always intense? When I met you in Memphis the first time, that was a scary moment. I know this is a lot, but take my advice, it's not worth a stroke. Take a few breaths, calm down. Looking so much like your old man it scares me. But let me talk this time."

I nodded.

He said, "The lawyer in me gets irked when I don't get an answer to a direct question."

"What question?"

"Who are you? What is your motivation? What makes you behave the way you behave, what makes you make the choices you make? What's the real backstory?"

"Didn't you hear me answer?"

"I heard the same old speech any Black man in America can regurgitate ten times a day, and rightfully so. But saying the same thing over and over, it becomes cliché, and the ears start to numb."

"America does the same cliché shit over and over, so we redeliver the same message."

"I mean, who you really are beyond that, that part of you that creates the fuel to be able to put that much fire to your words, that much passion."

"You don't want to hear all that."

"No, I do, I really do. Will help me a lot. What's the biggest issue you have in your life? What's the most personal? Where does the anger start? Not the part that wakes up when some idiot bumps into you, but what makes that type of anger possible to catch fire and make you want to implode?"

"Why are you asking?"

"I'm a pacifist. The only fight I've ever been in is a legal fight. I've been hit by people, bullied as a child, but I have never raised my hand to swat a fly. Maybe it's part admiration that you are able to do that."

CHAPTER 47

I GAVE HIM my main issue.

The source of my anger and why I kept repeating mydamnself like a song put on repeat. No one on the other side listened. They talked. Never listened. It didn't matter if I was blunt or wrapped my medicine in sugar, motherfuckers on the other side of the railroad tracks refused to listen. Students didn't listen. I told him about Komorebi, a couple others.

At least two of my coworkers felt it was fun to say stupid shit to me and when I let them know what was pissing me off they didn't change direction, didn't listen to my complaints, not the white ones.

A few of the Black ones were just as stubborn, expected what I had worked hard to achieve to be given to them for free.

The only place I felt safe was in my house on Blair Hunt Drive early on a Sunday morning. Only felt I was listened to and respected by my family, and that was when they were in that kind of mood.

He had no comeback, no rebuttal for that.

In a calm tone I pointed up at the ongoing news conference on his big-screen curved television, explained the obvious once again. "That could've been Momma or one of my sisters. The barbarians are outside our doors, not yours. They've been Hancock Parking my people without apology all of our lives. So, my reacting to that bump was the sum of my history finally set on fire. He did it to me in front of Gemma Buckingham. Fucker tried to emasculate me, then sit down for shots."

"I get it. I'm not in denial regarding my privilege. To be honest, it has kept me alive."

"Tell the truth and shame the devil, Roger de Groot."

"That should be my official nickname. Call me Roger de Groot moving forward."

We sat and watched the grieving family.

He asked, "Need anything?"

"Brown liquor, Roger de Groot. Brown liquor."

He opened his desk, took out two glasses and a bottle of scotch, poured us drinks.

He said, "Macallan. Twenty-five-year-old Sherry Oak."

We touched glasses. I sipped. Honey and fruit. Had never had liquor this delicious in my life. Wondered how many house notes I'd have to forfeit to be able to buy a bottle of this truth serum. Like Gemma Buckingham it was mature; it had layers of flavors, smooth and sweet, got me high.

He said, "Looks like a lot is on your mind. Been that way since I first met you."

"You're an attorney. The keeper of secrets."

"That's the rumor."

"Maybe I should run this issue at work by you. I guess Sulemans have this in our DNA."

I sipped my scotch. While I worked on getting my head right, there was a soft knock at the door. A millennial with tattoos from her neck to her toenails came in dragging carryon luggage behind her.

The attorney said, "Shit, is this my day, Angela?"

The rail-thin, yellow-and-purple-haired woman asked, "Should I come back?"

"No, no, it's fine."

He moved to a side chair and Angela set up shop, put a drape over his upper body, then took out her barber tools. She cut the attorney's hair as he sipped his scotch to smooth jazz. This was an echo of the privileged life the Bitch from Brownsville had each morning as the rooster crowed.

THE SON OF MR. SULEMAN 291

He asked me if I wanted a haircut. It would be his treat.

I laughed. "Thanks for the offer, but I'm letting my 'fro grow 'til it won't grow no mo'."

I sipped scotch almost as old as I was and secretly admired yachts down below headed out to sea. Twenty minutes later he peeled a knot out his pocket, about two grand in walking-around money, and without any pain being shown with parting with his money, he nonchalantly handed her three hundred plus one hundred as a tip, and she left like she'd earned less than twenty bucks, not one cartwheel turned.

He stood in front of a full-body mirror, checked himself out, nodded in approval, then refilled our glasses. He sat down with a serious face, one meant for 650-dollars-an-hour business.

"You say you have an issue at work?"

I sipped my scotch again, inhaled notes that included honey, vanilla, and ripe apple.

A moment passed before I responded. "I can't afford your rates."

"Pro bono."

"I can afford that all day long."

The truth serum had kicked in; that warm, fuzzy sensation made me trust the man across the table. The attorney studied the Black man from Memphis who had been a loudmouth since he landed. He saw that even though I stood my ground, something had me scared from the inside.

My voice shook as I opened Pandora's box and confessed, "Her name is Dr. Stone-Calhoun. She's married to the most powerful judge in Memphis. Eats lunch with senators, does dinner with presidents."

"You're scared."

"As Emmett Till was on his last day on top of soil. I'll be treated like one of the Scottsboro Boys. White women are dangerous. I knew better. White women are fully aware of their pedestal, and use it."

"Who knows?"

"Nobody. I haven't told anybody. Was hoping it would just go away at some point."

He saw the unseen luggage courtesy of a white woman at UAN I had brought with me on this trip, saw my lazy man's load. By the next hit of top-shelf scotch, I had told him everything. It was cathartic. I clicked on the lights and revealed my personal boogeyman. He nodded, sipped as I sipped, then steepled his soft hands for a second of hard thinking, took that Chevy to the levy, took a disturbed breath, set free a troubled exhale, then leaned in, patted my leg like he was getting ready to give me a long legal talk.

I'd said too much, told a man who could have a CNN smile covering his Fox News heart more than I had intended to, had told a man who had a book on white supremacy in his office my shame.

CHAPTER 48

IT WAS TOO late to turn back.

My tipsy attorney said, "Sexual violence against men is treated differently and—"

I interrupted him. "You sure this is pro bono? If the meter is ticking, stop it at two hundred."

He nodded. "I know people who know people who know people, coast to coast."

"When I get back home, soon as I set foot on UAN campus and walk by all the statues of the pharaohs, I'll end up escorted by the campus police. I feel it. They will walk me out in front of everybody to make a point, a message to the other Blacks on campus. That rock I kicked is moving and is about to turn into a boulder rolling down the road at top speed. White man does the same, it's about his individual action. I do the same, they will blame every Black man alive. I don't want to bring any shame on my family. And, yeah, the big part of it's a Black thing. Blacks teaching at UAN, U of M, Christian Brothers University, LeMoyne-Owen, Southwest Tennessee Community College, men who have worked hard, came up from nothing, were the first to graduate in their family, they will all be given a hard time. Over me. Because if one of us did it, we're all guilty of the same crime. That's the unwritten rule."

He nodded. "It can't be undone, but I can minimize the damage."

"Sure you want to try and do that?"

"You're part of my life now. I've met you, argued with you, and respect you as a man."

"I'm part of your life. That means now you're part of this ugly page in mine."

"Let's minimize it to a paragraph. You see me here, in this light, as an attorney, but I'm a busy man and I have a lot of other stuff going on in my life. Dealing with this, these days with you, this isn't my main story. I guess if I did memoirs, it might get a mention, but no more than a paragraph, because I have a life that is as layered and complicated as everyone else."

"You're right."

He poured himself another glass. "Can I try and talk the way I see this in a book-talk kind of way? Your father used to do that to confuse me, but let me see if I learned anything from him."

I extended my glass for more of the same. "Shoot your best shot."

"Even when people are in the same book, in our own ways, we still remain our separate stories. You said you were the sum of your experiences. I get it. You're that book. That makes me the sum of mine. I'm the sum of my existence, and I'd write about my life from my point of view. It would probably sound like bullshit to you, but it would be my life and my truth. Your mother is the sum of her own trials. The man who had planted the seed of life in your mother, he is . . . was the sum of his. This was where we all gather and meet for a few days, but then the living go back to writing our main stories."

I sat and stirred.

He said, "Love him, hate him, cremate him, and shit on his ashes and throw them flaming in the middle of any given freeway, that's up to you. It won't change the facts. You are his son. You have so much of his DNA it made his wife faint when she laid eyes on you."

"I'm not him."

"That's not what I'm saying. But in the end, no matter how you judge his actions, you are his son, and you get to tell that part of the story any way you want to. Consider all the information and keep it real. Don't apologize for the fucked-up things he did, but don't let my best friend's story read like propaganda, don't make it sound like you're an angry little boy with a need for vengeance against a dead guy because he never called or spent time with you while he was living. He fucked up; he knew he fucked up a long time ago. Look at his kids out here. He did the right thing keeping you away from those Motherfuckers. Look at his ex-wives and his mistresses, look at all the shit he owned that served no purpose, and all you see is the signs of a man who was a workaholic so he could have an excuse to not be around people, a man no one loved outside of a paycheck, a man who was crying out for love, could get fucked by a groupie in a heartbeat, but was unhappy until the day he died. He did your mother a favor when he went away and didn't call her to come be with him. If he had run to her, gave up that writing shit and lived where she lives, he might've been a better man. He'd've learned something unteachable from your mother. See this shit show and how everything else he touched turned out? You've only been here a few days, but try to imagine this bullshit every day for the last thirty goddamn years. Sometimes when you really give a damn about someone, when you love them more than you love yourself, you man up. You let that love for them drive you to want the best in life for them no matter what; you don't drag them deeper into your shit so you have to break your own heart and go the other way so they can have a chance. Your mother was a country girl with a big smile, innocent eyes, and smart as hell. She was the kind of person the world needs. Use your Memphis eyes, open them wide and see how people here are living. Good people come here and get all fucked up. This West Coast life would have destroyed all the good that was left in your mother. Open your eyes. Look at your mother compared to the women he had out here. Your mother won. She won this fight a long time ago. I guess you could say he had you come all this way to collect her first-prize trophy or distribute it to others as you wish."

Like a drunken man, I wiped tears from my eyes.

"I mean, out here you have a sister that used to be your brother. No judgment, but I can't imagine the shit that kid had to go through. Nobody had heard from her for ten years. She was hard to track down. Then walked away from it all."

"Yeah. No one would look at her. She was dead to those Motherfuckers."

He handed me a tissue.

I took a moment, looked up at that line of novels again, whispered, "Forever."

I wiped my eyes. Roots had been planted too deep to yank out all at once.

I said, "My fucking life was already an episode of *Black Mirror*. Then he died."

"Now you're being honest about the root of your current anger. It's not about Suleman."

"You're right. This is the luggage I can't put down. If I try, it follows me."

"Talk to me."

"What if I'm not only the fool but the bad guy? What if I'm the monster in this scenario?"

"I minimize the damage, if you want. Won't leave this room, not by my mouth." He made sure his door was locked. "Tell me again the professor's name you're having that issue with. While you're having your moment, I'll make some calls. I know a few lawyers who can help. They owe me a few favors."

"She threatened to take away my classes if we don't hook up soon as I get back."

"Makes no difference. I've been in this profession for decades, and you have no idea the people I come in contact with but can never talk about. I can make it so that everybody doesn't need to know."

I was exposed, cornered, vulnerable. "Let me have the room for five minutes."

"You can cry in front me. Your dad did it all the time, especially the last six months."

"I'm not my dad and you're not my best friend."

A moment went by.

He asked, "So, how do you judge a novel? By one chapter or by the entire book?"

"Back to that."

"Humor me."

"Chapter by chapter as I go, I guess, then at the end, critique it as a whole."

"That's the way people get judged too. Some judge people by the parts, and judge them on one single fuck-up, and that becomes the review of their life. Some are judged in the whole, as a book."

"You made that up?"

"Nah. Your old man did. While he was writing his life story, he told me that."

"You're his walking and talking memoirs."

"I was there. Yeah. You can measure a man's life, his value, by the parts, or by the whole. For me, even though I don't read more than legal papers, it's hard to tell how good a book is by one chapter."

He got back up, moved like a sober man after a good night's rest. He shook off any trace of being turned up. He popped a mint, used a mouth spray, signs that he was a highly functional alcoholic.

"I'm going to miss him. I complain, but in the end, it was worth it."

"Now you're the angry one."

He nodded in agreement. "Now he's gone and I'm mad, need to argue with people."

CHAPTER 49

TWO MINUTES LATER he downed another scotch, made me another drink, then made a third one and sat it to the side, serving someone nobody could see but him. He whispered something to the dead.

"You okay?"

He nodded.

He said, "Before we take the meeting, I need to be clear. She contacted you, asked you out from a position of power, pursued you, followed you, and when you told her no over and over, continued her demands, threatened your job, and then assaulted you in your car after an event she insisted that you attend, and when you tried to end it, continued to call you, sent e-mails and texts not related to work demanding you respond to her threats."

"Yeah, sounds like the biggest lie ever told when you hear it said out loud."

"You have the texts and e-mails, that's a start. Anything more substantial?"

Then I remembered. "Shit. My phone was on. I thought she was the police pulling me over, so I started recording as soon as I pulled over, in case I didn't make it back home. I had forgotten it was on, but when I pulled away I realized."

"You sure you recorded it? Her face and voice and her vehicle are on the recording?"

"It's on my phone. Never looked at it, but it's saved on my phone. I never delete anything."

"Is it clear?"

"Like I said, never looked at it."

"That's the new iPhone?"

"Yeah."

"Show me the video."

I scrolled back in time, handed him my phone.

He said, "Let me step away and determine what we have."

Reluctantly I added, "And I saved a message she left earlier. She's been blowing my phone up."

"I changed my mind about letting you get on top of me. I can't stand looking at your face, so get behind me. Get as mad as you want to and become so riled you spank my bottom over and over because you think I'm a bad girl, if that will make you feel empowered; do whatever you like but you better not touch my hair. Takes too much effort to make it perfect every morning. You will be behind me, in your place, and you will keep your paws on my sweet little ass and never touch one strand of my hair. Return my call after you bury your pappy."

Roger de Groot reassured me that I was in the right all the way down the line. He was eager to move forward. No one had seen any of the evidence, it hadn't been on social, so we had the advantage. People would be destroyed as others smiled all the way to the bank. He asked me if I had any questions. I had only a couple. No amount of money would be worth the volcanic pain if the lava ran wild and destroyed others. My self-esteem was deader than Elvis and my BMFM confidence had left the building.

I imagined the Motherfuckers dying in laughter while the Fastest Swimmers drowned in grief. Then I imagined being kicked off the usher board, excommunicated, being the next big sermon at church.

I inhaled sharply, exhaled slowly, asked Roger de Groot, "Will my family find out about this?"

"I will minimize the damage."

"Will it end up on the front page of *The Commercial Appeal*?"

There was no answer, just a look of uncertainty.

I chuckled out my angst. "If it gets out, the Motherfuckers will experience schadenfreude."

"What's that?"

"Pleasure taken from the misfortune of others. A desire to see others suffer. Schadenfreude."

"That's a normal day in Los Angeles and Hollywood. Now I know what to call it. Schadenfreude."

He walked out and eased up his door.

The office door opened a second later and Gemma Buckingham and my attorney's wife came in laughing like best friends, carrying two dozen bags of swag.

Gemma Buckingham dropped her load of bags and hurried to me with her phone. "Look, I took a selfie at the Hollywood sign from the car park at Griffith Observatory. I saw this in that *La La Land* movie. I literally stood on the spots where the stars danced around. Look at this. Wait for it. I took selfies with not one, but five top celebrities. There is a hiking area by the observatory and celebrity after celebrity was out walking around looking busted like they were ordinary people. Oh, let me show you the bargains we found. Everything in America is so much cheaper than things on any high street in London. I would never do this much shopping at one time on Bond or Oxford Street. Well, there I would have traveled by the Tube, not inside a car with so much trunk space begging to be filled. Overdid it a bit, love. I have to stop and purchase another suitcase along the way."

I downshifted from the mood I was in, put on a smile, joined in the fun the best I could. This was one kind of trip for me, another for Gemma Buckingham. I was here on family business, and she had come to help, but even now this was an adventure, and she wanted to sight-see, have fun, have sex.

Now I had gotten scotched up, opened my big mouth, and involved Roger de Groot in my drama with the Bitch from Brownsville.

Gemma Buckingham asked, "Pi, are you inebriated?"

"Had one drink."

The attorney's wife laughed. "Not in this office. No one has one drink in this office."

Gemma Buckingham asked my attorney's wife about what a Londoner had to do to emigrate here. She had no idea what the new rules were here, and she'd come over planning a short stay. Sounded like business, so I stood, tested my legs. Gemma Buckingham grinned and winked at me in that special way. Later on she'd be ridden hard and put up wet.

But for now, she was lollygagging and drinking like it was happy hour in midtown. Her laughing that hard bothered me a bit; it felt as misplaced as busting a gut at a funeral. While the women stood in the window making plans to do more tonight and tomorrow, I looked back at the books in the room. A cemetery with literary tombstones. I needed to step away from this graveyard because, like me, my bladder had had more than it could stand.

Gemma Buckingham laughed at me. "You can barely stand up straight."

"I'm good."

Gemma Buckingham laughed so hard she almost spilled her drink. "You need help walking, Professor? Should I get you a cane or maybe a stroller like the old people use, love?"

"My husband has drunk everyone who comes in his office under the table."

"Love, you sure you can walk, or should I find you a chauffeur on an electric scooter?"

I waved them away and left the office, went to the lounge and found Cokes and other sugary drinks, gave myself a caffeine infusion.

When I was in the marble john sending water to the river, I saw myself in the mirror.

I touched my wild hair, hair that certain folks would prefer I cut so they could feel more comfortable in their biased shoes, then laughed at the idea of my attorney offering to let a tattooed white woman I had never laid eyes on before cut a nappy lock from my beautiful hair. Trust had to be earned with any barber, no matter the color of their skin. A white woman cutting my Negro hair. I'd never get that goddamn drunk. Some barber chairs were not meant to be sat in, not by a man from Memphis. Tattoo woman did a good enough job on a white man's hair, but Sis could do a cut better than that with her eyes closed. Three hundred for a dull-ass basic cut. I would've spent half the money in my pockets, then wound up on a plane and going home looking like who done it and what for.

Two things it took a long time to trust: white people and the barber.

If either was having a bad day when you showed up, you would leave looking fucked-up.

My phone rang with a 901 number and I answered with a smile. "Mo Fo."

"Erudite man. You good?"

"Yeah, I'm good. How y'all?"

"Good as rain so I can't complain."

"Tell everybody I said hi."

"Saw 'em talking about your daddy back here on the evening news. Saw it on CNN too. Sad for you he died of long-standing health problems last Thursday morning. We praying for you back here."

"Thanks."

"Back soon?"

"Lord willing and the creek don't rise, I'll be back soon."

"I'll run the mower across your front lawn while you gone."

"You don't have to, but thanks."

"Well, need anything, call me directly or tell your momma."

"You know I will."

"LA traffic? Bad as they say? It that bad out there?"

"Freeway looks like a tailgate party rooter to the tooter."

"Seen anybody famous yet?"

"Katt Williams."

"Was he in a limo?"

"Big enough for a hundred people."

"So, they traffic moves slower than the Mississippi flow."

"If the Mississippi moved this slow it would be considered a lake."

"Can't even imagine."

"If you remember and have the time, take my trash cans out."

"Already did that. No need coming back home to full cans."

"Thanks."

"You have the nicest yard on Blair Hunt Drive. That why I like sitting on my porch and looking at it."

"I do my best."

"Widow Fatima was looking at it too. She was here visiting Pokey. Pokey told her you had a nice backyard and had did your patio up real good, and then Widow Fatima asked me to show her how you did your patio up real good. That surprised me. Me and the kids took her over. Widow sang your praises. Hope you don't mind we all went out back and looked at the set you made. She was very impressed. I like all the solar lights in the ground. Lights up real pretty every night over there."

"Widow Fatima actually came across to my side of Blair Hunt Drive and went to my house?"

Mo Fo laughed. "When you get back, think about cutting Widow Fatima's grass."

"I'm sure that pretty, erudite woman ain't got no problem finding a man with a better lawn mower."

"Don't be out there in California putting honey on your corn bread. Molasses go with corn bread."

We laughed. I had somebody familiar on the phone, had someone trusted with my house and yard, and I didn't want to let go.

Mo Fo said, "Mind if I ask you a favor?"

"Shoot."

"Okay to sit out on your porch? Gets so noisy over here I can't hear myself think."

"My porch your porch, same as my kitchen yours to use when you need."

"Pokey hear that she'll be over there cooking in your nice double oven like she live there."

He thanked me again, and he was gone, happy to be able to go one house away and chill out. To Mo Fo that would be leaving to go on a private vacation. Not everybody needed to cross a pond first-class or sail the seven seas in a superyacht to smoke a joint, have a beer or two, and be content.

Widow Fatima had crossed to my house. She'd never been in my yard in five years. I guess since I fixed her flat tire, since I saved her from Smackover, she was more comfortable with me. That or my West Indian across-the-street neighbor wanted to make sure the man who paced his floors all through the night wasn't a Memphis-born lunatic burying dead bodies in his backyard all through the night.

WHEN I STEPPED out of the bathroom, the man who had been denied the right to be Roger de Groot the Fifth was waiting. He led me to a conference room. He had a big-time Nashville civil rights attorney lawyer the level of attorney Ben Crump about to get on the line.

The Nashville attorney was only one of six waiting on the line.

He'd assembled a dream team on my behalf.

CHAPTER 50

BE IT STARBUCKS, a restaurant with a racist waiting on my appearance, or in a professional setting, Roger de Groot the Fifth walked in every room like whoever was waiting needed him.

Because they did.

He might have had to wait in line to get second-rate food at a place with third-rate service, but away from the common man he had enough influence to make other powerful attorneys clear their overbooked calendars and be ready for a meeting in thirty minutes with one phone call.

Six attorneys were on the video conference. A half dozen strangers to my eyes.

My iPhone was Bluetoothed to a 120-inch projector screen.

Dr. Stone-Calhoun's beauty-queen face was clear enough, her southern voice loud enough.

"Hurrying off to a new midnight lover?"

"What can I do for you? This is past my office hours."

"Time for some quid pro quo."

"No."

"You know that at this point you don't have a choice. This horse has been let out of the barn. Quid pro quo, I spent money to get you a ticket so I could see you, and now I'm entitled quid pro for my efforts. Think of all I have done for you; the lunches, the presents. Let's be reasonable."

"No."

"Be a man. Park. Turn the air on high. Let me get inside for a moment."

"Where is your husband?"

"He's up there. Drunk as a skunk and snoring like five hogs, as usual. Past his bedtime."

"We can't keep doing this. I told you that the last time was the last time. Too much to lose."

"You want to get tenured or stay adjunct, or lose that position as well? Would be a shame if all of your classes were suddenly canceled. Would be such a shame, for a talented writer like you."

"Anything else?"

"Cut your hair, shave your beard, and look more professional, like you did last year."

"Dr. Stone-Calhoun. Most of all, Mrs. Calhoun, wife of Judge Calhoun, that's racist."

"I gave you the tickets to the coveted event. You met the star. This set me back a pretty penny."

"Your note said you wanted me to come socialize."

"Socialize, that was a metaphor."

"A metaphor to meet you for . . . what exactly?"

"Don't make a lady beg to get socialized one more time. Pull over there. Open the door."

A police car passed by. I had forgotten that had happened.

"Don't get me in trouble. I get caught with you like this and Johnny Law will find some old miscegenation law still on the books and give me life but see two of your tears and send you home."

"Today is Steak and BJ Day, and I'm all out of steak."

"With your husband in the car?"

"Over there. Under that shade tree. Before the drunk drivers take over the road."

"You'll get a suspended sentence while they lock me up for twenty years' hard labor."

"Over there. Socialize for a few minutes. Gimme some sugar when I get done."

Powerful men and women watched my courage atrophy.

They paused the video, said a few things back and forth, then resumed the assault.

"I'll make you rise like the sun and roar like Tom waiting on Ole Miss on a Saturday."

"You know it takes me a long time to come."

"Take as long as you need. I have mouth tricks that can keep my jaw from gettin' tired."

Fat Man saw my anxiety, stopped the presentation, and put his hand on my shoulder, gently massaged. Humiliation swelled inside me, a balloon that wouldn't stop growing. An unseen poisonous, gaseous, noxious cloud shortened my every breath. Strangers would watch me in my weakest, most disgusting moment. It was evil turning into a cheap roadside show made for an Internet porn site.

"Whenever you're ready, Mr. Suleman."

They were about to witness me at my weakest. Strangers who charged a house note an hour were about to watch a strong, intelligent Black man get assaulted by a Brownsville beauty queen on the side of the road. A moment passed with me shaking my head, rocking, wishing I'd deleted that video.

I'd never looked at it. No one wanted to relive being raped.

It was too late to turn this around. Too far gone to back it up now.

The cat was out the bag and the feline had let the horse out the barn.

A different video played in my head, the video of my future. The way things worked in my world wasn't the same as they worked in the rich or white, not on any level. Even with her initiating this bullshit, even with her threatening my job and controlling this, I knew I'd be found guilty and they would find a way to lock me up at 201 so fast it would make my head spin. I'd be arrested the moment my plane landed in Memphis, dragged away while Gemma Buckingham looked on in confusion and horror. That would be the last time she'd see me standing on the freedom side of plexiglass. My Timex would be swapped for handcuffs. I'd become a new slave. Black men were sentenced to more time for committing the exact same crime as a white person, and what she did, after ten white-woman tears, wouldn't be seen as a crime. White women killed their own babies, dressed in conservative clothing, and cried themselves to freedom.

I'd be criminalized, same as a boy minding his own business after buying a pack of Skittles, called savage and other terms used for wild animals while the ugliest, roughest photos of me were shown on all white media. Respect was earned, love was gained, and loyalty was returned; with this reveal, I could lose it all, join the world's largest prison population, go where the Judge of all Judges could arrange to get me shanked to death in a shower, raped, or hanged in a jail cell. I could lose all I was starting to achieve. I would no longer be welcome on the other side of the railroad tracks where the skies had the perfect shade of blue and Trader Joe's was the place to go. I'd be seen as an educated thug. The video would somehow be leaked. People would laugh. I'd trend on Twitter. No institution or publisher would dare touch me. Morality clauses. The Suleman name, I would be attached to the famous dead man, and with this as perfect timing, all would be magnified and exasperated. My Vathlo Island idea would be a pointless endeavor. Then, my family. My mother could die of heartbreak.

There could be a domino effect.

And the cycle of generational trauma would continue.

I felt both stroke-bound and stupid as fuck, worthless, unlikable, and had made a gotdamn fool of myself. Wanted to scream and kick until my anger left the building. I rocked a while, then sat up. Nodded I was fine. Took more scotch. Needed a brand-new bottle to wash this down.

"I'm ready. Play it until the end. Ignore me. Just play it and get it over with."

A dishonoring moment in the secret life of Pi resumed.

Six strangers watched as she robbed me.

I held on to the desk in front of me same way I had gripped the steering wheel, tense.

"*Relax.*"

"*Okay.*"

She gurgled, was bobbing, bobbing, gurgling, gagging, bobbing, gagging, bobbing for an audience. My hands gripped the steering wheel hard enough to rip it away. Attorneys took notes like this was a documentary. They watched what I wanted no one to see. Including me. The slurping sounds, her greed, her quick, short movements up and down, her determination to rob me of an orgasm played in surround sound. It was a horror show. My heartbeat was fast. Breathing was curt. This was taking a toll on me and my mental health. Angst burned away all the truth serum and liquid courage in my blood, left me wide-eyed with tears of anger flowing from my green eyes, hot lava over volcanic rock.

In that moment, to not have this moment, I wished I had killed her.

"You taste like a hot drink of port, sugar, lemon, and spices. You're my negus."

"We have a problem."

"I want you to go again. I'm still thirsty. You know I'm a please-a-man-two-times kinda girl."

She tried to raise the *Titanic* again. I squirmed with the sensitivity and she refused to stop, my discomfort her pleasure. I saw things either I didn't remember or wanted to forget; saw what crime had been compartmental-ized; heard a conversation that didn't sound familiar yet struck a chord. *"Dr. Stone-Calhoun, I came like you wanted. And now your husband is coming."*

Off-screen, the Judge of all Judges screamed out to his wife. I hadn't remembered that part.

"This so-'n'-so. I should whup his tail right now."

"Fuck. He sees us. He's looking right at us."

Without realizing it, I was rocking back and forth like a kid on a hobbyhorse.

Fat Man rubbed my shoulder again. Handed me a tissue.

"Bless his heart. He's as drunk as Cooter Brown. His glasses are off and the headlights are in his eyes. That's why I parked in front of you. Look at him. Would be a shame if he walked in front of a car."

"He's coming this way."

"Slower than molasses."

"Here comes the judge; here comes the judge; everybody knows that he is the judge."

"He won't remember. He'll wake up first thing morning sipping coffee and trying to get dirt on the Democrats."

"He's going to fall face-first and mess up some good concrete."

"He won't remember. Now, next time I want dinner on you and the rest of the night on top of me."

"*No.*"

"*Quid pro quo. Don't be stupid and lose all you have achieved. Quid pro quo. We both win.*"

"*For. The. Last. Time. No.*"

"*No? A hard no? Well, in that case, as a start, would hate for your check to get lost in the mail.*"

"*I use direct deposit.*"

"*Or get deleted from the UAN system. Funny things can happen when you push the right button on the Internet. God knows how long it would take to resolve that matter, if ever. Poof. Paycheck gone.*"

"*Quid pro quo.*"

"*You're catching on. Had me worried, Professor. Was starting to think you were a slow learner.*"

"*Look, cut me some slack. You're the same age as my mother.*"

"*But I'm not your mammy. It's okay to suck my titties, these ain't never been nor will be momma titties. Man up and play with one next time we quid pro quo.*"

THE MOVIE OF shame ended. Lights were turned on. Everyone could see me now. I was unhidden. Embarrassment and guilt ruled me head to gotdamn toe. I was ready for all to say I was in the wrong, and the men in the room would laugh hysterically at the BMFM, an educated man still green compared to the way they lived in megacities.

My phone was blowing up. I picked it up.

I cleared my throat, said, "She's pissed off and texting me over and over right now."

They read the messages as they came in real time.

> *Professor Suleman. Quid Pro Quo.*

> *Six times I have called you to no reply.*

> *I have left voice mails regarding setting up a date we can confer regarding certain matters.*

Days have gone by with you ignoring me. Funerals don't last twenty-four hours.

Remember your station.

Answer me or not, there will be quid pro quo.

They heard her tone, her attitude. They failed to understand my fear and reality. The power of ten upset and petulant white people in America was more powerful than a million Black men marching.

CHAPTER 51

TWO HOURS LATER the meeting ended, my shame was being put in legal documents, and it was up to the man who had been my dead father's fixer to do the same for another generation. Roger de Groot had become the farmer who showed up and planted a lot of seeds in my yard. I stood in the window, unsure about what I'd just done and with more scotch in my body than blood.

He said, "Your university had two terrorist events. Not good for their bottom line."

"Yeah. The world is looking at UAN right now. Might scare a few folks off. Big-money donors might take their checkbooks and generational wealth next door to the U of M."

"They won't want this additional negative publicity. It would become international as well."

I asked, "What now?"

"If we get there, then a detective conducts interviews with you and brings in Dr. Stone-Calhoun while gathering and evaluating evidence. She was so arrogant she got sloppy. It gets messy. They can drag it out. Six months maybe. When the case is finally pulled together, it's sent to the prosecutor, who decides what the charges should be. This is obvious. That video is unambiguous. Her face. Her voice. She stops you. Gets in your car. You said no over and over. She made threats. She left a message saying she wants to farm out your services. Disgusting. Everyone needs to hear her. She needs to hear herself. If it goes all the way, she could be looking at five to ten years. Long trial. She'd still end up doing Felicity Huffman time. She'd get sentenced to years, but once it died down, she'd be home in months. Unless it's settled expeditiously by UAN. In a way that kept her out of jail. They can open a checkbook and make it vanish. Universities do it all the time. Black man assaulted by white woman. Goes against every stereotype they've perpetuated. That's a CNN story that could run two weeks. The pundits would go mad. Again, unless it's settled expeditiously. With an NDA and a wire transfer. But overall it's your call."

"Gemma Buckingham can't find out about this. I want to go on being as normal as I can, do the shit Suleman requested, escape here until I have to go back to Memphis. I don't want to get off the plane and end up in handcuffs. I don't want to be slave-walked on television and have that played in an infinite loop on social media. Stranger things have happened to Black people. Always guilty until proven innocent, then still looked at like we are guilty but got away with the crime. The Calhouns are nobody here, but that's not the case in Memphis. They could buy me ten times over. I'm somebody here, today, in this office, but in the 901 I'm just another Black man. Compared to here, my life ain't much, but it's my life and I don't want to lose it. I hope I didn't just fuck up. Hope like hell I didn't."

"Sit."

"Okay."

"Listen."

"Okay."

Roger de Groot talked to me, a Black man from Memphis who felt like he was on trial, in the clandestine way wise men talked to naïve men over scotch and in the absence of women, maybe the honest way a father would talk to a son about the ways of the world.

"Pi, you know the fact that the woman who assaulted you is white, rich, educated, and beautiful works in her favor the way being Black works against you. Her rise from poverty in the shadows of the antebellum South won't be seen the same as yours from slavery and Jim Crow."

"Still a Black man."

"The Black-white thing is always the biggest obstacle."

"Same way it worked against Anita Hill. Same way it worked for Felicity Huffman."

"Your assaulter will hire ten conservative Gloria Allreds and try to dig into your past."

"All else fails, she'll appeal to religion. She'll blame it on the devil."

"They'll try and flip it and make you that devil. You had an orgasm so you must have wanted it. Your language said no yet your body betrayed you. Victims can orgasm during nonconsensual sexual violence. Experts will testify to that. But to many it's still confusing. The trials I've seen. Anyway. Black men are always vilified through their actions or the actions of family members. They might even try to tie you to things your old man did; a few bar fights are in his record. It's irrelevant because you didn't grow up with him, but don't put it past the desperate. They will scrutinize your work performance at UAN. Find disgruntled students who don't like you for some reason, quote them. Any issues there?"

"Students who think they deserved a better grade for mediocre offerings."

"Same for any ex-girlfriend who has a gripe."

"All exes are exes for a reason."

"Babies?"

"None."

"Abortions?"

"None."

"They will quote things you've written in your novels. Out of context."

"The sex scene I wrote."

"They'll attack your mother, bring up that she was a teenage mom, now unmarried with five kids, criminalize her, but we'll turn that into a story of perseverance and survival. Educator. Champion bodybuilder. All of her children are college educated with no prison records. None of you have babies out of wedlock. Your family is the true American success story, yet they will try to spin it and your character will be assassinated ten times over. But we will do the same with your abuser's character.

Everyone from a small town is running from something. We will dig into her past, see if she's hiding anything. It can get as ugly as they want it to be. But none of it will be more powerful than the ten-minute video a jury could see. Once seen it cannot be unseen. Or unheard. The jury will have a transcript in hand. Her words. The video showing her debasing you, the video of her stopping you and making demands, threatening your livelihood, the images of her sucking your dick when you objected, her not giving a fuck as her drunk husband called out her name, her going to him and coming back to you demanding more; that can be leaked to the press and then social media can be the judge."

"It would be all over Black Twitter. News reporters would be outside my home."

"They'd be after her more than you. The beautiful white woman, the beauty queen, the woman who married well, the Christian, the doctor at UAN. They will see her true character. She was drunk and aggressive. She did it in front of her husband. She said she hoped he was run over by a car. That's cold-blooded. She can end up on Redtube and YouPorn until the end of time. Once that hits the Internet and gets uploaded to interracial sites like Blacked, it can never be erased. That can be her legacy. Each time her name is dropped into Google a link to her sucking your cock and laughing like a giddy schoolgirl when it was done will appear. The shot of after, as she laughed and wiped it away, undeniably her and clear as day. It will end up in her Wikipedia page like it's part of her living obituary."

"Jesus."

"That's worst-case scenario."

"Best case?"

"With your permission they can write a check and poof it's gone, Wikipedia page scrubbed. And when all is said and done you can sue her as well as sue the university."

"Can they fire me?"

"Least of your concerns."

"One of my top concerns. I busted my ass to get where I am. This defines me. I don't see myself winning. Not without shame. I'm not sure shame is worth it."

"This isn't your fault."

"Black people are taught everything is their fault, even their own enslavement. We're taught to forgive even when we're the one done wrong. Brainwashing runs deep. Especially in the South. We are turn the other cheek, more MLK than Malcolm. And that forgiveness train does us in every time."

"That video is the bloody glove, only it's still on her hand and it fits. The bloody glove fits. It fits and they won't acquit the bitch because your shit is as legit as it gets."

I trusted Roger de Groot, of Netherlands extract, attorney in California. Same as my father had done for more than thirty years. My father's best was the only friend I had for the next two thousand miles. He was my Kevlar. I wouldn't miss shit about California, but I'd remember him when I went back home.

"Want to hear a story about your old man?"

"Not really."

"You owe me."

"You said my part was pro bono. I'm planning on making you keep your promise."

"One remembrance. I'm in pain too. It's kind of funny. It would make me feel better."

"Keep it short."

"It was in the nineties. He had a rival when he first started. This guy used to shit talk about your daddy every time he got onstage or was on the radio. It became vicious, to the point where people were getting served for slander. I had never heard of writers acting like rappers, dissing each other so hard it was beginning to sound like Ice Cube going after NWA with 'No Vaseline,' with ten-dollar words."

"The ancients against the moderns. Tom Wolfe dissing Norman Mailer. Vidal fighting Mailer."

"If you're saying it was like Tupac and Biggie, it was that over-the-top. Your old man would release a book; then the other writer, the loser who will remain unnamed, would release a book the next year with the same goddamn theme. It went on for five years. It didn't start out that way. Your dad and the unnamed loser used to be friends. But when a man thinks another man is interfering with both his fame and his bottom line and ruining his business, things change. The loser who will remain unnamed started five years before your dad, was doing good for a couple of years, but then your old man showed up, handsome enough to sell forty-dollar books with blank pages as long as his picture was on the back, and in three years your old man stole almost all of the loser's spotlight. Your old man used to be happy for the loser as a writer, sent him Christmas cards, used to tell people to buy the loser's books, endorsed one, sent congratulations for making some prestigious list your old man had made three years earlier. The jealous loser mistook genuine congratulations as shade."

"Wait, you did an on-point Ice Cube, NWA, Tupac, and Biggie reference."

"That's the music I listen to when no one is around to judge me. Say I appropriate, but I'm still going to listen. Cube had the best diss track hands down with 'No Vaseline,' so far as being in your face. But I'd give Kool Moe Dee's 'Let's Go' an A-plus for creativity. 'No Vaseline' sends shivers down my spine each time, but I have a family and I can play the LL diss track in the car on repeat. I have to put on Cube and rap the words I am allowed to rap without being called a racist when the wife and kids aren't around. That's my go-to when I've had a fucked-up day; I rap it out of me while I'm stuck in traffic trying to get home. Hell, when I met you, you pissed me off so much I was riding around Memphis playing Cube until I left. In case you want to know, no, I don't say the n-word. Never have. Not even in my dreams. I change that offensive word to *brotha* and have a good time looking like a suntanned fool. Anyway. Your dad had a hard-core hater. All a man has to do to create a new enemy is be successful. He was jealous of your old man's accomplishments, felt he was supposed to be in that position. Other guy had a lousy business model. Mind you, this was before Myspace, so social media like it is now was a long way off. People barely had cell phones with cameras back then, thank God. If you wanted to take a picture you had to invest in a Kodak camera and hope you ended up with a decent shot six months later when you finished a roll and got the film developed. Anyway. Back to the story. There was a big event for writers in Chicago. I will never forget that place, or that day, because that day changed the trajectory of your old man's career."

"How so?"

"They got into an argument on the main stage, in front of five hundred women. That belligerent fuck got on the mic and called your old man a third-rate writer in front of five hundred Nubian women. They were in each other's faces, cursing, and I mean they cussed at least nine hundred times, way more than Lil Jon and the East Side Boyz did on 'Roll Call.' Way more f-bombs and n-word usage. I was standing in the middle of a riot. Security pulled them apart. When that was going on, this woman was so disgusted with two Black men fighting like thugs, she went up and grabbed the microphone and yelled, 'Why don't y'all put your dicks on the table. Let's get this contest over with, dammit.'"

"You're good at your hip-hop references but bad at pulling my leg."

"Yup, her exact words. 'Why don't y'all put your dicks on the table.' Back then they had their wars face-to-face and fist to fist, not by throwing words back and forth over social media while using the toilet. Anyway. 'Why don't y'all put your dicks on the table.' I will never forget how that scream shut down the auditorium. Your old man *slowly* unzipped his suit pants, and the room came to complete silence. Five hundred women had stopped talking and were easing closer to the stage like zombies. They knew he wasn't going to do it. But that girl yelled again, 'Put your dicks on the table and get this over so we can decide which moron's books we gonna buy before I get my ass back home.'"

"And?"

"Your old man slammed his Jamaican cock on the goddamn table. *In front of five hundred women.*"

"Get the fuck out of here."

"He stood up like he was the man, nothing scared him, and slammed his anaconda on the table in front of five hundred women, slapped it like he was beating a drum, and each time he whacked it down it sounded like thunder was approaching. That idiot grabbed the microphone, his dick still on the table, and did a line from a Richard Pryor routine he listened to all the time, yelled, 'And it's deep tooooo!'"

"I ain't going to take time to burn gas driving my Chevy to the levy and believe that ish."

"Sounds crazy, right?"

"That sounds as believable as Naipaul fighting Paul Theroux, while Mary McCarthy and William Giraldi double-teamed Lillian Hellman and Alix Ohlin, then the winners tag-teamed and helped James Wood get a piece of Jonathan Franzen on a Monday night at the Mid-South Coliseum."

"I have no idea what that means."

"Means I don't believe you. To LA folks I might look green, but I wasn't born yesterday."

"I was there. I was the one who had to rush the stage and pull him away. The room was so loud the building shook like they were having earthquakes and aftershocks during a hurricane in Chicago."

"He was vulgar, humiliated himself, and was thrown out in front of five hundred women."

"You wish. We came outside and his signing area had the longest line on record of any book signing people had ever seen. They sold out of over a thousand books, then had workers running to every bookstore in Chicago to bring back all the books they could find. The line went around the building two times. He signed books for over twelve hours. It made me want to invest in Sharpies. We had to shut it down. When we finally made it back to his room, a groupie had broken in and was in his bed waiting."

"Now you're lying and trying to sauce up a lie that don't need any more flavor."

"I was there. We walked into his hotel room and candles were lit. The room smelled sweet, like strawberries and champagne. A woman was there. She looked like a scaled down, low-budget version of Miss America Vanessa Williams with fire-red hair. The groupie was on the bed, a fire-red feather boa around her neck and hanging down across her breasts, already naked to make her intentions clear."

"That's pretty extreme to get a book signed. Nobody in their right mind would do that."

"She looked at your daddy with a smile, patted her vagina, and said, 'And it's deep too.'"

That was when he lost it with the laughter. He laughed so hard it made me laugh.

"Before I could leave, there was a knock at his door. I opened it and it was a tanned woman with short blond hair parted down the middle. She had the world's biggest smile, a Julia Roberts–ish grin that took up ninety-five percent of her face. I'll never forget her face when she saw my fat ass and not Maurice. She said her name was Maria Amanda Hiltunen. A professional woman, an aeronautical engineer wearing heels that probably cost more than all the clothing I have on right now. She was holding at least six of his books. I told her Maurice was going to be occupied for a couple of hours. She told me she'd wait, then sat down on the carpet outside his door."

"How big this lie going to get?"

"Just letting you know your old man didn't take shit from anybody."

"What would he have done if a man in Hancock Park had bumped into him on purpose?"

"You invited that man to have a fight. Your old man would've been dragging that man across ten freeways. Nobody bumped into your daddy like that. You insulted him, two seconds you'd be on the ground, and thirty seconds after that, in the back of an ambulance. No matter how young or old. If you were fifteen or a hundred and five, start shit, and be ready to suffer the consequences of your actions expediently and expeditiously."

"He didn't let nobody get away with pushing him around. Nobody Hancock Parked him."

"Women Hancock Parked him. Around women he became a lamb, smiling and laughing. But never weak with another man. He could make a man feel small by using his vocabulary. If that verbal humiliation didn't do the job to his liking, he would beat you up and never take off his suit coat."

"Black, white, or otherwise, no man Hancock Parked him. He made men apologize."

"I had to make a lot of things go away. I spent days and nights keeping his Wikipedia clean."

I measured myself against a man I'd never met.

Fat Man went on, "Just because you fuck up or commit what the religious have categorized as a sin, which is practically everything, it doesn't mean you're evil. It shows you're human. In my humble opinion it's how you fix yourself or deal with the fuck-up that matters most. Suleman did his best. Guy was pretty much on his own from age fourteen. By stats a guy with his background should have been dead before he was twenty-one. You judge him by his relationship with one person. You're judging him by one chapter while I've read the entire book. So we won't see eye to eye. And that's fine."

The lawyer was a teacher, and a better one than I would ever be. Each story he told made a point, was a lesson. He knew how to wrap the bitter in sugar to make it taste sweet going down.

I said, "Tell me one more lie from back in the day, and we're done for the night."

"You want to hear me ramble my heart about that rambling Space Cowboy?"

"Let's see if you can spin a yarn better than the last Moby Dick–size lie."

"Let me tell you about when we were in New Orleans at Essence, Fourth of July, and we were walking down Bourbon Street, sipping on hurricanes, and somebody stepped on his Air Jordans."

One lie gave way to the next, and four hours later when the sun stood up, he was still lying.

Curious, I asked, "You have any siblings?"

"One brother. He left here in his right mind, but when he returned from the war, he came back half past crazy. I take care of him by sending checks. I guess your old man took up that empty space."

I nodded, wondered what kind of man I'd be if I'd grown up with him in my reach, calling him my daddy, grown up with the Motherfuckers on the Pacific and not the Swimmers on the 'Sip.

I wondered how Memphis and the Swimmers would look to me from this direction.

Roger de Groot said, "Many idolized him. In the end he idolized you, the man he saw you became, and he admitted that you are the one thing, maybe the only thing, he felt he did right."

"I won't waste gas money on driving to the levy to think on that lie."

"Let me show you something. You'd look right at it and never see it, and it's obvious."

I followed him to a walk-in closet the size of a two-car garage. It was well organized, had an inch of space between all hanged clothing. Shoes. At least thirty watches on display. Mouth-watering swag.

"Mr. Pi Maurice Suleman, all the clothes here are brand-new, your size. New. I think he bought them for you. Very stylish. What is your size shoe? They're your size. His foot was a half size smaller. Your dad was a half inch shorter. Yes, he researched you. He idolized you. He'd created a man better than he."

I was stunned. It was seductive. I could change clothes and change lives right now. This was what Momma and the Fastest Swimmers were afraid of.

I asked, "What's real? Can't tell. Memphis feels like a dream, this my new palm-tree-lined reality. All I have to do is not go back. Do like Gemma Buckingham and pick a palace here. Start over."

"You have options."

"I've never had options before."

"How does that feel?"

"Perplexing."

I took a breath, browsed the swag.

I said, "Tell me another tall tale about my old man."

I didn't hear the rest, was looking at a pair of Wayfarers mixed in with the swag in my sizes.

Lured by something I couldn't explain, I was trying on new clothing and shoes bought for me by a dead man I'd never liked and could never love, a kid at Christmastime in the summer.

I TOOK GEMMA Buckingham to Ima Beverly Hills, where meals started at one hundred and forty dollars. It was an elegant Japanese spot.

Gemma Buckingham wore skinny ripped jeans in the hue of heather gray. They were painted on and pimped her curves harder than Iceberg Slim did his women. She paired it with red-bottom heels and a tight white Grenfell United T-shirt, a political number that spoke of a tragedy that had happened in government housing across the pond in London.

She explained, "It was a devastating fire which ripped through the Grenfell Tower block in West London. There were no smoke detectors. Universally the poor are treated with the same neglect. The government said we were left with seventy-two dead, but we knew the real number was in the hundreds. Hundreds burned beyond recognition and hundreds of the poor suddenly left homeless. Nothing substantial has been done to rectify their loss, pain, and suffering to date."

"Horrific."

"I knew Grenfell like the back of my hand. It was personal for me."

She gave me the details. It was something I knew nothing about and felt no connection to. There was empathy but no painful connection, not like when I saw the same here on American soil.

It was foreign to me on all levels.

She said, "Americans know nothing about my country, while we are force-fed your history starting at slavery. We are taught all Blacks here are the product of slavery, not Africa. So, there is a disconnect. And at the same time, we know more about your Harriet Tubman and Rosa Parks than we do our own African and Black British heroes."

I didn't interrupt. She talked and I listened.

IN THE MIDDLE of the next night, as Gemma Buckingham slept in her Batwoman outfit, I adjusted my Green Lantern T and answered my phone. Four Ds had called me forty-eleven times.

I walked to the other side of the suite, looked out at the city's lights and landmarks.

"Mane, I've been trying to tell you how I fucked up. Komorebi got me. Mane, I'm about to lose my job and my wife."

"You're loud, Four Ds. Take a breath. Slow your roll. It's two in the morning here."

"She asked me to meet her and see the ducks march from the elevator and get in the pond. I hadn't seen the Peabody ducks in years. We had drinks. Got flirty. Then she had me so hot and bothered I couldn't cool off if two hundred helicopters did waterdrops at the same time. Then we went upstairs."

"Mane."

"She got me on her Samsung clear; tall as I am, ain't no doubt it's me because Wilt Chamberlain ain't in town this week. She says she'll take that funky little Samsung video to my wife today, to UAN for breakfast, and post it on IG by noon tomorrow. I'm done. My career. My marriage. She is trying to send me to divorce court, to the unemployment line, and down to 201 in one fell swoop."

Four Ds was stressed to the max. "Mane, she recorded us."

"Mane. How?"

"Mane, she wouldn't say, but sent the video, had to delete it, cause Melissa goes through my phone like a company doing random drug tests. Looks like she had a friend with a camera hidden in the room."

"You done bumped up her grade?"

"Done did that already."

"What else can that maneater from Manassas want from you?"

"She will meet with me to try and settle, told me to bring an arbitrator if I wanted, and I am choosing you. Come help me talk some sense into this fool's head before she contacts my wife."

"Did you choose me, or did she choose me?"

"She suggested you, now that I think about it."

"Things here are complicated. Like I said, I won't be back for a few days."

"What should I tell her?"

"Tell her she has to fuckin wait. Tell her my gotdam father just died, I'm busy as fuck, and the mu'fuckin line starts to the left and grab a lemonade from Soul Fish Cafe and wait her gotdamn turn. And in the meantime to get off her butt and do the work. Do the gotdamn work."

THE NEXT DAY I stood in the enormous master bedroom where the man who planted my seed of life had died. A chill ran through me. Forty-plus bottles of death-delaying pills were at his bedside, some two thousand dollars for a single dosage. Had cost him thousands a day to stay alive long enough to die alone.

I needed to feel his spirit, needed to ask him a million questions, wanted to argue and fight with him the way he had done with Roger de Groot. The thing I wanted to argue about was the thing that would have caused me not to exist. I stopped fighting, lowered my walls, and had a moment, wiped my eyes. I became Will Smith, the Fresh Prince, letting the beast go free, inhaling, exhaling, in pain, in denial, coming undone. If anything, I should have been calling Momma and seeing how she was, if she needed consoling, but I couldn't. This plane was going down and I had to put my own air mask on first before I reached out to any other survivors. Tears of anger came in a silent torrent. I realized things that had never been dealt with would never be dealt with. I cried and laughed at myself, felt like a fool.

He had needed me and I had needed him.

I apologized for not coming to see him before he was gone, for not being his final audience.

I had home training, even if I disliked him, so I thanked him for sending Roger de Groot my way. I knew that wasn't over. This would be resolved in Memphis, where nothing would be in my favor. The Bitch from Brownsville would get called out by UAN, offered a shot at arbitration first. The Judge of all Judges was a vengeful man. This was the eye of the hurricane.

So when I got back home Lightning would have to stay loaded, ready to herald thunder. In the meantime, I did something I had to do.

Dressed in another expensive suit, under a half-moon on a chilly night, I stood by the Olympic-size swimming pool and dropped the older Suleman's MAGA hat on the outdoor grill. Doused it with lighter fluid. Tossed a burning match. Stood warmed by cremation. Smiled.

CHAPTER 52

GEMMA BUCKINGHAM AND I booked a four-hour red-eye flight back from dealing with Suleman business in California. We were reading over newspapers we'd picked up: *Final Call, LA Sentinel, LA Wave, The Epoch Times,* and *LA Focus. The Epoch Times* had been ripped in half and stuffed in the seat back. We compared Cali news and politics to Memphis's concerns, and she did the same with London.

She was disturbed, and in the end there was a point she wanted to make, but not before I found myself too excited and made mine. I'd had a watershed moment, had left a secret meeting with a league of expensive-as-fuck lawyers and was heading to another set of money grabbers when I made it back home, so I was on edge, my smile and words soft, but my lazy man's load heavy from being reloaded.

Soon she put her hand on mine in preparation. "I worry."

"About?"

"You've scared me, just a tad."

"How so?"

"You have a bit of a temper."

"When provoked."

"I saw that ugly side of you come unbridled in Hancock Park."

"I was assaulted. You saw me get assaulted."

"I saw what transpired, had a front-row seat, and to be honest it has left me a bit concerned about a Black man from Memphis."

"I was minding my own business. He assaulted me. Baited me."

"Don't end up being the victim of someone's rite of passage."

"Doing my best. Doing my best. But they are making it hard."

"I was with you. If they killed you for some reason, they would do the same to me. I've seen videos of how they treat Black women here. They drag teen Black girls in bikinis across concrete with no remorse. I don't want to be bloody murdered or shot by a racist because a racist bumped into you and suddenly you forgot how Americans have guns."

THE SECRET LIFE OF
GEMMA BUCKINGHAM

CHAPTER 53

SAMMIE-LYNN SIPPED HER Coke and lowered her voice to a conspiratorial whisper. "Not saying who said what to whom and when or why it was said, but *The Commercial Appeal, Bartlett Express, Collierville Herald,* and every blogger in the tristate is trying to find Dr. Stone-Calhoun."

Professor Quarry whispered back to his excited wife, "Channel 5 and channel 24 reported from outside of the Judge of all Judge's twelve-bedroom plantation home. He refused to comment."

"Heard the newspeople are still whistling Dixie and waiting outside his mansion down by Wolf River. She did something. Had to be illegal."

"They want to know the state of their marriage, if nothing else."

"Rumor for the morning is she met with a divorce attorney today at Dowden, Worley, Jewell, & Olswing. Met as soon as they opened."

"Once again the Calhouns are a front-page, pictures-above-the-fold story in the tristate area."

"She was abruptly fired from UAN and fled to her so-called sick momma's raggedy house in Brownsville. And now a divorce. I guess that's her Heartbreak Hotel until she finds gainful employment."

"The queen of Memphis now qualifies for unemployment."

"Escorted from campus in front of everybody and their momma."

"By the chancellor herself."

"Big fall from grace."

"She has gone from meeting the president of the United States and pooping in the Lincoln Bedroom at the White House to once again fighting mosquitoes in the crummy bedroom she slept in as a child."

"Her sick momma lives in a run-down two-story log-and-chink home constructed of white oak on what was once a nice plantation."

"Dilapidated, from what I heard."

"It has a nice wraparound porch."

"She never talked about her Brownsville living."

"She came to the city and didn't look back, but I heard she's been supporting her sick momma since she left and married the judge."

"When I get the address, I'll send it so you can drop it in Google."

"What else we know for certain?"

"She became a ghost before her constituents could question her."

"The mayor didn't take her calls."

"Neither did the senator."

"Nor the White House."

"Our chancellor had her blackballed lickety-split."

"And not a word from the judge."

"He approved this, then; otherwise, heads would be rolling."

"Oh, checking my phone and this just in."

"What now?"

"Rumor is the judge cut off her access to his family money."

"She's become a rich pauper too?"

"She's gone from eating caviar to eating potted meat on saltines."

They weren't too far off the mark. I was hanging with the gossipers to get a feel for what the rest of UAN might know so far. Was worried that my name would come up, despite the legal arrangements.

Professor Quarry said, "What-some-ever happened had to be god-awful because the judge couldn't fix it by threat, by check, or by ringing the mayor, the chief of police, or the governor. She was escorted away like a common criminal. Students posted multiple videos across social. The Aggressive Six approached her first thing in the morning with the president of UAN as their lead. He is never here before ten in the morning. He got out of his bed early, so this is beyond serious. Without a hello to anybody, he ordered the professor thrown off UAN campus immediately. Heard she had quite a hissy fit on the way out the door. She was carrying on like a fool in public. This is the wife of the Judge of all Judges. He had to green-light it as well. He had to have."

Sammie-Lynn leaned in, chuckled. "Heard she took those big ma-chest-ic boobs over to U of M seeking employment. That betrayal is far worse than the judge becoming a Yankee."

"Ten times worse in my book."

"The Tigers wouldn't let her in the front door. Our fallen pharaoh did something bad. She has been ostracized. Persona non grata."

"Don't worry. Give it time. The truth always come out in the wash. Might take some time, but I always find the truth."

Sammie-Lynn rolled her eyes. "Sick mother in Brownsville, my behind. This is too much drama for a sick momma."

Then the lovebirds noticed me sitting there, eating and checking social media and texting Gemma Buckingham about hooking up later, head down as if I wasn't paying them any attention. I became relevant.

Professor Quarry leaned in and spoke to me in a hushed whisper. "You act like you're not excited to hear the news about our dear sweet Dr. Stone-Calhoun. While we were in New York and you were in California, her office was being cleaned out."

"I've been too busy to check the rumor mill. What's going on?"

"Professor Pi Suleman, didn't you hear what we just said? Or have you been too busy playing on your phone to listen up?"

"Not playing, multitasking. My father's death, people are still messaging me, and I was a bit preoccupied with work issues."

"They say she *suddenly* resigned, claimed she needed to *suddenly* move back to Brownsville so she could take care of her sick mother. Hogwash. If her sweet little mother is that ill, common sense says she would've brought her up here to her plantation house, not move back to that dilapidated home she grew up in. To top it off, she claims she's thinking about moving up *north*. I know for a fact it's true."

"How so, Professor?"

"Sammie-Lynn is her real estate agent. Her people contacted my wife regarding finding long-term accommodations for Dr. Stone-Calhoun up there with the Yanks, near Ithaca, where nobody will know her name."

Sammie-Lynn pondered. "Tenured professors are fired for one of four reasons."

"True."

"One is incompetence."

Professor Quarry shook his head. "Which she wasn't."

"Refusal to do their job."

"Which she did."

"Now, the third is moral turpitude."

"Fraud? Perjury? Hit and run? Domestic violence?"

Sammie-Lynn slurped her Coke. "I'm betting on embezzlement."

Professor Quarry disagreed. "UAN is paying millions to make it go away."

"The only thing left is hanky-panky."

"It has to be something to do with sex."

"Dr. Stone-Calhoun . . . and sex."

The newlyweds laughed like it was the punch line to end all punch lines. My cellular rang, and I excused myself from the circulators of news unproven by raising a finger like I was in church, stepped away.

Soon as I answered, Four Ds' panicked voice rolled out as fast as Eminem doing a high-speed rap. "Mane, she knows you're back. Said after today if you don't come be my arbitrator, she's going to take the video to UAN and send copies to my wife late tonight."

"Let me minimize the damage. I can be there in a couple of hours."

"Can you meet a nucca a couple of hours sooner?"

"Got shit to do. Text me the meet spot. Two hours."

Taking hypocritical breaths, I ended the call and went back to my seat, my cold onion rings, my warm coke.

They had no idea why the UAN had settled a lawsuit that would've rocked M-Town like a 10.0 earthquake. Even if they had heard what had happened, they'd never believe it was with a Black man from Memphis.

Sammie-Lynn asked me, "Well, what do you think of all this mess between the prestigious Calhouns and the UAN, Professor Suleman?"

"Well, I have no idea what to think, but it sounds like she blew this job."

"It has been verified she can't get another. At least not at U of M. She might have to go teach high school in Ithaca, New York, if they can tolerate her nasty better-than-you attitude for more than fifteen minutes."

I said, "She was definitely a credit to her people. God bless her."

CHAPTER 54

THE SAME WAY a student had stalked me, after I had finished lunch with the gossipmongers, I got comfortable and chilled in the shade in front of the sculpture of Rameses the Second. I waited for his stale lecture to end to set this straight. Professor Thor came out of the UAN music building thirty minutes later than I had anticipated. My problem smirked when he saw me, then changed his course so he could pass by me and look me in the face with a smile made by the devil.

"Well, if it ain't Shaun DeRay Malcolm X King Smith Mckesson with nappy hair by Angela Davis."

He chuckled like he had come up with the most mashed-up millennial insult ever.

I smiled but wanted to slap the taste out of his mouth and make him kneel before Zod. That was the straw to topple a lazy man's load.

I trailed my rabbit at a fast pace, then turned and stood in his face. That move startled him. Professor Thor tried to go around me and I moved with him. We did that dance over and over like a comedy routine. He chuckled, thought I was putting on a minstrel show and trying to get him to laugh.

I bumped into him head-on and his blue eyes went wide, reacted like he'd been shot.

He asked, "What was that?"

Perplexed, getting mad, he tried to walk around me again.

Where he moved, I moved. I kept getting in front of him.

"Ain't you the Jesse Lewis Carl Jackson today, rushing like there is a BOGO at Popeyes. Why y'all love that Popeyes so much? Ain't as good as Chick-fil-A, but you people lined up like you were trying to get on a ride at Libertyland to get ahold of that Popeyes chicken sammich. The way your people were acting like fools, you'd think the people were seasoning their dead birds with menthol."

Every pejorative, every insult, the way he said them, you knew it wasn't the first time. These were his scripted lines, lines he had practiced in the mirror while working on his Don Rickles delivery and innocent smile. This was what made him feel empowered. But today was not going to be his day.

White men gave Black folks a lot of bad days, but it was a worse day for a white man when a Black man was fed up. This Suleman was the son of another Suleman who took no prisoners.

I let him stroll a little while; the next thing the old man knew I was back in front of him.

"Why you meddling? Your nearabout tripped me up. Stop larking. I need to air up my car tire before my long trip home. Behave that way again and you might find yourself in a heap of trouble."

I Hancock Parked him again.

He tried to stroll faster and get away, but I stayed on him like I was tailgating, driving in LA, switched lanes and cut him off, gave him some more Hancock Parking, a lazy man's load being unpacked.

He asked, "Is there a problem?"

"Is there?"

I was smiling, so in his mind this melanized dog was wagging its tail, couldn't be angry. A kicked dog was gonna holla, and that was what I was here to do, holla about being kicked, tail wagging with a smile. I Hancock Parked him one more time, the ultimate Hancock Park, and he toppled to the ground.

He was terrified. "Professor *Suleman*."

"So you do know my given name. Thought you had me confused with somebody else."

"Of course I know your gosh-darn name."

"You have called me out of my name forty-fuckin-eleven times, but that's not a problem, right? If I knew your name, knew how hard you had worked to get a little respect and still called you out of your name every time I saw you, if I called you David Duke, Strom Thurmond, or Theophilus Eugene Connor with a chuckle and a knee slap, if I did redneck jokes, old white man–cracker–potted meat–man from Mississippi jokes while I pointed out white-on-white crime, I reckon that would be called a problem."

It was in his wide, unblinking eyes that he knew what he had been doing. This had been his safe place, where he was allowed to get away with his microaggressions, insults he had probably done year after year unpunished, but all of a sudden, when called out, he reverted to being a terrified country boy.

"It was some harmless teasing. A little harmless fun."

"A rope is harmless until it's around a man's neck. Your insults have strangled me."

He was an aged soldier with no army, too scared to get to his feet.

He sat humiliated as his crotch grew wet as rain.

"Professor Thor. Professor William Archibald Spooner Thor the Third, of German blood, a man who acts like he owns the day Thursday and is the god of thunder. You. Ain't. Shit. This has been a waste of time. You're nothing. Here I am thinking you have me at a disadvantage. But you know what? I won against you a long time ago when I conquered every obstacle all the George Wallace–and–Bull Connor–praising honkies like you created to hold me back. I graduated from UAN, a Black man from Memphis educated in an underfunded public school in a neglected zip code, became a professor at a school that was forced to integrate my skinfolk during civil rights, when cotton was no longer king because they couldn't force us to pick it for you, and you can't stand it because you couldn't stop us from rising up beyond your level. What's hilarious is that you lost that battle a long time ago, but you still think you can win. Losing is beyond your way of thinking, especially since your ilk thinks the Old South will rise up again. Loser, you lost. Hear ye! Hear ye! Your childish Don Rickles insults are impotent to me from here on out. You ain't shit to me. Bruh, I'm moving on and leaving your and your pappy's ways behind, because people like you never change, even when learned a lesson by mouth or a good ass kicking. You're old, set in your ways, and won't change, but you will do this one favor because it will be good for your health. Next time you see me coming, run the other way. You're not bred to run like Usain Bolt, but you see me smiling and whistling your way with my tail wagging, you better run like Forrest Gump. Hope you see me before I see you. I'm done being nice. Next to what I might do next, this right here will feel like I'm tap-dancing and singing 'Oh Happy Day.' Even if I smile at you, don't mistake my Martin for Malcolm the way I did your Fox News for CNN. I know you're probably a black shoe polish Justin Pierre James Trudeau copycat after dark; that's okay, long as it's done cowardly, behind my back, and not during the hours of the sun, inside your home. I can't control you and won't waste my time trying. But I got friends and they got friends. We be watching. One more thing. Be a good Christian and call everybody you come in contact with by our given Christian or Muslim or East Indian name. Stop crying. There is no crying in racism. This is me being as nice as I'll ever be with you moving forward. Stop crying. Man up, dust off your britches, go find some good lemonade, and enjoy the rest of the gotdamn day."

My bodacious shit talking came to a screeching halt when I saw the Aggressive Six storming my way. They saw me Hancocking and were coming this way fast to break my glasses and stomp my plates. Not another brother or sister was in sight to hold up a phone and record me becoming the latest hashtag.

CHAPTER 55

THE AGGRESSIVE SIX surrounded us.

They asked him, the white man, not me, if everything was okay.

We waited for his response. He was sitting in urine, thinking.

"Lost my daggone footing and this gentleman, my coworker, came along and out of the goodness of his heart took the time to help a fallen man back to his feet. Due to his assistance I believe I am able to walk straight now and will be careful how I walk from here on out."

Professor Thor was a leaf shaking in a storm. He regarded security, then pouted down at the river he'd made in fear, put his wide eyes on the wet spot on his suit pants, struggled to his feet and skedaddled.

I turned to walk the other way, but two of the campus police blocked me, extended their hands out palms first, the police move that told my Black ass to stay the fuck where I was, because it wasn't over for the Motherfucker who had stood his ground.

Schwarzenegger mean-mugged me, hand on his holster, same as the rest of his cronies.

"We saw what happened. We saw it all from the beginning. You pushed him to the ground."

He looked toward the professor's retreat until he was sure he was out of sight. When Schwarzenegger faced me again, his face was red with so much anger the pain made his eyes fill with tears. Barely able to speak, he stepped inside my personal space. He extended his right hand. Palm open. Confused, I did the same, knowing he was going to do a move that twisted my arm until pain took me to the ground. He surprised me, gave me a firm handshake, shook my hand vigorously as he choked up.

He said, "Auschwitz-Birkenau. Belzec. Bergen-Belsen. Buchenwald. Chelmno. Dachau."

Confusion owned me until I read his name tag. Surname Rosenthal. Jewish. Then I understood. Thor was German.

"This morning he came over to me. 'Hotter than an oven out here.' Every time that bastard passed by me this week, he laughed and said it was hotter than an oven and he bet that being in an oven made it hard for me to concentrate."

"I don't get it."

"Ovens. Concentration camps."

"That's disgusting."

"If I could've shanked him, I would've."

Schwarzenegger was shedding tears for six million of his skinfolk lost in concentration camps the same way I cried for the at least two million Africans lost in the Middle Passage. I sat on my excited utterance this time. When a man told you that he'd been hit by a car, you didn't respond by saying you'd been getting run over by the 31 Crosstown twice a day since 1619. As his tears flowed, I let him have the floor.

One by one, most of the Aggressive Six spoke up, became witnesses testifying at a trial.

Schwarzenegger's lips trembled as he mocked Professor Thor, hardly able to repeat the anti-Semitic slurs. "'Well, don't you look like the type who'd Jew a Christian down over a nickel. Tell me, Hymie doing this morning, and I'll tell you how you are doing.'"

The Rambo showed his disgust. "Moose limb. Amma Sloppy Laker."

I nodded. "I've heard those before."

Each told the insults they'd had to deal with on the clock, when they had been powerless to do anything more than grin and bear it, lest they lose their jobs. It wasn't just me. Not just brown people.

I said, "His caucasity won't end. They don't know how to let it end. It's a mental illness. Racism is a mental illness."

"But pissy boy will think twice."

"One would hope."

Schwarzenegger smirked, then laughed. "Thor pissed himself. The scaredy-cat let out more piss than the 'Sip."

They all laughed.

A code squawked on their radio and the Aggressive Six rushed to their rides without a good-bye. Six Segways took off like cowboys on electronic stallions, headed to save the day.

Pyrrhic victories.

CHAPTER 56

WHEN I CROSSED UAN's Pharaoh Road, five thousand pounds of anger came at me full throttle. I jumped back. The foldaway side-view mirror of a large SUV slapped my right arm as death came at me hard. The Grim Reaper had been waiting. It didn't slow down. Would've run me over and left me to die. It was a Cadillac Escalade, platinum edition, hundred-thousand-dollar SUV being used as a two-and-a-half-ton lethal weapon. The motherfucker who wanted me dead made a rubber burning U-turn and sped back my way again.

I thought it was the outraged Bitch from Brownsville, but the oversize figure was as huge as it was unmistakable. The Judge of all Judges was behind the wheel, his Confederate face a ball of rage. He had taken the SUV back from his wife. He spat out his window, tried to rattlesnake spit a fistful of phlegm into my eyes. He had seen the video, had seen his wife bobbing for a nappy-headed Black man's elixir.

He showed me Thunder was riding shotgun, ready to damage a head of cotton. The sound of a double pump heralded my way. He cocked Thunder as a threat. Unarmed, like a fool, I stood my ground.

Again I asked myself what would Suleman do.

I walked to my enemy's door. Not running shocked him as much as my tone. "You saw the video. You heard her wish you staggered in traffic and died, and you're coming after me. She bitch slapped you in your drunken face with the same unwashed hands she'd had on my cock, yelled and spit chunks of me in your face, and you're ready to run me over and threaten to shoot me? Say when and where. Old-ass peckerwood. You're coming at me like you're Billy badass when I watched her beat your ass for touching the precious hair on the nape of her neck. Twice. She did it in public at the Pink Palace, then beat your drunk ass in front of me when she put you back in this truck. Am I supposed to be afraid of you? Put the shotgun down, get out the truck, come this way, and learn something about yourself."

"Nigger."

"Mr. Nigger to you. You're a thief to say the least."

"I was the one robbed."

"Not more than me. I was robbed of my dignity."

"Nappy-headed nigger, I know the president of the USA. Smart-mouth nappy-headed nigger will learn his last lesson soon. UAN might have sent you nine million, but your final lesson will be paid in blood."

He was triggered by my presence, the most bitter white man I'd ever met. On the hottest day this side of hell, we locked humid gazes in a silent, furious battle of equipollent wills. He gripped Thunder like he needed me to fear him. I stood tall, hands in fists, demanding he respect me. Neither was going to happen, not on Pharaoh Road, not in this lifetime.

"Nine million dollars to an ugly nappy-headed nigger for violating my wife in the goddamn mouth, for tricking my wife and secretly record-ing it. Just happened to have your camera on. Just happened to forget it was there until you ran to Los Angeles and showed it to your fleet of out-of-town attorneys. You knew no attorney in his or her right mind from Texas to West Virginia would've entertained your little trick. They would've reported to me first. Scheming ugly nigger. No way you didn't set her up and do that on purpose. You followed us, saw I was indisposed at the moment, quickly took advantage of a drunk woman, and expect me to pay for your criminality. Nigger, you must be crazy."

Then my jaw was tight, voice dark, unhinged. "You'll pay. Civil suit yet to come. You have no verdict here. You heard your unfaithful wife,

Dr. Stone-Calhoun, that wayward and corrupt beauty queen from Brownsville, *you heard the bitch in her own gotdamn words.* She'll pay. Or you will pay on your wife's behalf. Same bank account."

"Another smart-mouth bellicose, uppity, nappy-headed nigger that needs to relearn his place. Had my inebriated wife in the mouth and now the nigger wants to get deep in my pockets and have me pay an arm and a leg for his concupiscence. The ugly nappy-headed nigger was already unjustifiably given millions in a rush to judgment, and now the nigger-rich nigger real eager to stand in the streets and fight."

"A shotgun-carrying cuckolded motherfucker who is aggressively hostile and as belligerent as his pugnacious cocksucking wife."

"Better take that UAN money and leave town for good, or you won't get a chance to spend one thin dime of that money. If I was you, boy, I'd pack up and leave before the next sunrise, if not sooner."

"I'm not running. I'm not hiding, I didn't do shit wrong."

"Leave town before sunrise and you might see another sunset."

"Not before the civil suit. I'm not done suing. We have a few million to go before this is done. Keep your checkbook open, motherfucker."

"Ugly nappy-headed nigger standing in my noonday sun acting real bellicose. He don't know I can have my boys come up from Hernando or over from Pine Bluff and do my dirty work. He must not know how this goes. Ain't but one way for this to end for him. Ain't but one way."

"That supposed to scare me?"

"Be careful, boy. Be real careful. Not unheard of for a South Memphis nigger to answer the front door and get shot multiple times. And it goes unsolved. Or a South Memphis nigger is driving down Lamar, gets pulled over for a busted taillight, car is searched, next thing you know they downtown on serious drug charges. And when a South Memphis nigger is in jail and manages to find a brand-new noose and commit suicide in a few hours, not unheard of, not at all."

Angry sweat ran down my back. "If we need to meet somewhere out by Lakeland or in Shelby Forest at high noon, let me know. You can bring Thunder and I'll bring Lightning and we can kick up a storm. Just remember that in a storm lightning comes before the thunder."

The Judge of all Judges sat in his oversize SUV and toyed with his shotgun, held Thunder in a firm right-handed grip, his irate disposition screaming he wanted to shotgun me in the face right here on the edge of UAN in broad daylight. To salve his ego and feel like he owned the ultimate control over all he vowed as genetically inferior, he wanted to shoot an unarmed Black man right then and test the law as it applied to him. Anger made him palpitate like me. His fury dripped into his blue eyes. My heart was feral inside my chest. Hands in fists, Suleman blood afire, I mean mugged him like we were in opposite gangs about to embark on a two-man civil war. Inside his seersucker the old man's chest rose and fell, became a balloon about to pop, his huge frame barely able to contain his delirium. He sat in his SUV like he was on his imaginary bench and stared me down in judgment. I was ten feet away from him, on the sidewalk, the defendant in my own life, unjustifiably put on trial.

UAN had put me on trial.

It had felt like UAN had paid to protect Dr. Stone-Calhoun's whiteness. They had a gag order that let me know they only cared about their reputation.

He nodded. "I'll have the last say. No matter what's rendered in the court, last word is mine. I'm the final verdict, for you and my wife."

"Not this time. Kunta Kinte won't become Toby. Not this time."

"Blair Hunt Drive. Right below Kansas Street. Big tree out front."

I took a step closer. "How you know my place?"

"Opposition research. Boy, you are an amateur at this."

"All you had to do was drop my address in Google to see that."

"I might be able to tell you what you had for breakfast."

I took another step, snarled, "Get out the SUV, Judge Cuckold. We can fight this shit out right here and right now with God as the referee."

"Maybe I'll do like I did growing up and do it myself, wake one morning before dawn in a nigger-shooting mood and render the final judgment on a nappy-headed nigger and all like him, man or woman."

"Remember that lightning comes before thunder."

"Blair Hunt Drive right below the south end at Kansas Street. That's where you live. A community center is around the corner by your momma and one of your sisters' houses. She's the sister with her ugly face on a few billboards. Your momma is a professor at the little Black college off Mississippi Boulevard. Your funny-talking girlfriend is half-white."

My heart triple-timed.

He said, "Biscuits. Turkey sausage. Egg whites. Glass of juice."

The motherfucker told me what I'd had for breakfast.

It jarred me. Then he told me what I'd just had for lunch.

I wanted to charge his SUV, yank the door open, pull him out, then drag him from the back of the machine he'd threatened to kill me with until his body came apart up and down Pharaoh Road. He saw my fed-up face, my nonblinking eyes. Read my body language, and when I was about to take a step, he pulled Thunder to his lap, barrel aimed my way.

In an Old Testament tone, he growled, "Wish a nigger would."

Dozens were on the road. Dozens who would see me attack him.

It would be a crazy nigger attacking an old white man.

This scenario was a lose-lose sitch for a Black man from Memphis.

Sun high over our heads, both of us shaking with choler, we kept our eye contact. We were two emotional men. In a country that had more guns than people, an emotional man was a deadly man.

Black man from Memphis. White man from Bluff City.

We lived under the same sun and moon but existed in different universes. We had two different upbringings. Upbringings that happened generations apart. He got his law degree and fought against any freedom my skinfolk fought for. I was his bad guy and he was my antagonist. Two different brainwashings. Two different realities. Two different gods.

"On the bench I've met gangsters, swindlers, thieves, and killers. I know some good killers. Real good. One phone call and they're all heading in your direction to do my dirty work to stay on my good side."

"Do it your fuckin self. Bitch-ass. Man up. Fuckin do it."

Our murderous midday glares were interrupted when another group of melanin-blessed Panhellenic students moved through dozens of white students and came up Pharaoh Road. The judge turned up his nose like he smelled too much patchouli, coconut oil, and shea butter. He saw what was coming our way and his murderous frown curved down and touched the sun-blistering ground. Afros. Braids. Mohawks. Dreadlocks. Fades.

A league of educated nappy-headed niggers. It was a T-shirt culture and most of my woke and ready skinfolk were walking billboards with pro-Black messages in bold letters from their chests and backs.

The judge squinted and read messages as they got closer.

He snarled, "Black Lives Matter. New Black Panther Party."

The judge didn't let his hand off Thunder.

More Black students came through the crowd to catch up.

The T-shirts with names of unarmed Black men and women turned into hashtags meant nothing to him, but the cuckolded Judge toyed with Thunder and snarled at pictures of Black heroes. Harriet, Rosa, Angela, and Assata. Martin, Marcus, Obama, and Malcolm. Juneteenth. Free-ish.

He clacked his teeth and flared his thin nostrils again when a brother wearing a YOU'RE LUCKY WE ONLY WANT REPARATIONS AND NOT REVENGE T-shirt passed by. Judge was deep in his feelings.

He said, "Christianity will again have power. Remain belligerent and bellicose. Your mockery will end. We'll have the final verdict."

The parade of politically and socially conscious billboards ended.

The motherfucker grumbled, "Once upon a time. Once upon a time we'd handle this nonsense. We would've showed you what matters."

Our hate resumed.

It was too fuckin late to be civil.

For mules like him it was probably too late in '68.

He took a half-empty bottle of Jack Daniel's from his suit pocket, took a hard swig, called me out of my name, spat again and hit the tip of my shoes as he toyed with Thunder. It was in his eyes. He was crazy, unhinged, in dire need of some psychiatric help. The madman spat at me again, but missed that time.

He growled, "Blair Hunt Drive under Kansas Street."

"Your wife did this. We keep it man to man. Between me and you."

"This is beyond my control now. It's in motion. Lots of recipes to making dead-nigger soup, lot of options with no penalties worth mentioning."

The Judge of all Judges revved his engine, shot me a gesture of contempt, put his four-wheeled assault weapon in gear, raced away, broke the speed limit while a crowd of students scattered, broke the law in front of both campus and MPD police, his verdict of all verdicts yet to come.

CHAPTER 57

FRANTIC AS A man on death row, I looked behind me, looked around me, checked thrice before I crossed the street, tried to see if someone was tailing me now. I couldn't stop sweating. My mind screamed; body trembled. Only a fool wouldn't feel some kind of anger dancing with fear. Both emotions were in a zip code where they had to be controlled. We had been trained to not back down and sit on our fears. Being verbally assaulted didn't stop me from moving on. My options. On the move, I thought this ish the best I could, with too many tabs open, looking for options. Only one made sense. I should've done like the league of white women assaulted by Roger Eugene Ailes at Fox News did for years. I should've just gone along with the program and dealt with the perverted Bitch from Brownsville, so I didn't get my wings clipped.

I hustled to get to Four Ds with too much on my mind.

Two days after I got back from LA, the judge had been forced to sit in an emergency courtroom on the campus of UAN, irritated at our arbitration. It was a morning that exposed his personal life to other powerful southern men and Bible Belt women from our alma mater.

UAN was its own world and wasted no time. It had had enough bad publicity, too many incidents, and didn't want this one going public. Roger de Groot had sold wolf tickets and demanded a quick and speedy trial; otherwise it would first be settled in the court of public opinion.

The power of a white man who was a Beverly Hills attorney.

Dr. Stone-Calhoun wore UAN colors, the judge a seersucker suit.

Her lead attorney was a middle-aged white man with Dylann Roof eyes. Her second attorney had a James Eagan Holmes smile. Very Aryan. The third was a double for Edmund Pettus. All were pale as ghosts.

The Judge of all Judges had them on his payroll in case of emergency. His tag team of Tennessee- and Mississippi-born Roger de Groots. They looked at my side of the table like it was an NAACP convention, only my team was made up of four Black women who'd graduated from Ivy League schools. Roger de Groot's strategy.

Like it had done in LA, the rape video played like the porn of the day. The room crackled with life-changing power as the truth played.

No one was affected more than the Judge of all Judges. He heard his wife demand I capitulate. The Black women at my side and the reps from UAN heard the same, all shocked, all shifting and scribbling notes.

The judge cringed with his wife's every word, then sat in his seersucker suit, tense, unmoving, deliberating. He was next to his wife, but he didn't hold her hand. I saw him in my periphery. His nostrils flared as he watched the sweet country girl he'd married demand that I let her blow the fuck out of me. He leaned away from her. None of his hired help looked directly at him. Southern humiliation was taking root.

The Bitch from Brownsville gaslighted the room, called the video fake news, said it was a fake recording. She said a gentleman would never record a God-fearing Christian woman like that, not unless he was on the side of Satan and planning on blackmailing her. She was flabbergasted and blamed me for taking advantage of her while she was drunk, stabbed my character, had a hissy fit, and rapidly told a lazy man's load of lies with the same Dixie antebellum tongue she assaulted me with.

Until that moment they had seen her as heartfelt, eloquent, and truthful. They had seen the Calhouns as the power couple of the South.

The judge showed his anxiety, was breathing like he had immense chest pressure, had a face of impending doom, but the doom was not for him. The judge stood so fast the polar bear flipped his high-back chair. The gun lover went into his pocket. Everybody jumped to their feet.

The judge pulled out a half-empty bottle of Jack.

He refused to accept what he'd seen. He refused to accept what he had heard. The truth was cold. For a moment he was frozen in a block of ice. A relic frozen in time. He took a step, legs unsteady, disoriented, first blinking, then closing his eyes tight, cringing like he was being attacked by a military-level strobe light. He defrosted, pulled it together the best he could. The giant looked at the men on the side of his table, frustrated, silently asking if this was the best the cotton-picking attorneys could do for the exorbitant price he was paying to protect his wife and his reputation. After what they'd seen, his crew looked at him with sorrowed eyes, the expression a man owned when questioning another man's value as a man, questioning his virility. Her sexual greed was undeniable, yet she denied it, ran the gaslighting bill up, said we hadn't seen what we thought we had seen, said the video wasn't authentic, and that wasn't her voice we heard. Everyone looked at her. No reply. She shouted at UAN's representatives, said I'd gone to Hollywood and during my father's funeral had hired professionals to create that disgusting fiction.

They reminded her the tape had been authenticated and done so by her own people. Her team had a copy. It was copied but undoctored.

The judge did a dramatic pause, shot me a deadly look, nodded a half dozen times, clacked his teeth, and issued a silent verdict, my verdict, but didn't look at his wife. Frankenstein drank Jack in a no-drinking zone and didn't look at his blond monster. But he talked at her. Talked down to her. After she had been both fired and publicly disgraced by being kicked off campus at UAN, he told her to not return to his home ever again. Right then she was told to not come back to the judge's home of three generations, a property that rivaled the Annesdale Mansion.

She rejected her eviction. Dared him to even try to keep her out.

The Judge of all Judges faced off with me. I understood his hard expression. This wasn't about money, not for us. This would end suddenly and violently with one of us reading from the Book of the Dead.

The judge left like a petulant god.

Dr. Stone-Calhoun acted like she was obsidian during Egyptian times, rare and to be treasured no matter what. Shit was uglier than a blobfish. She yelled that I was trying to ruin her career, her marriage, and rob both her and the UAN blind. She barked that I was from South

Memphis, came from a broken home, was lucky to get admitted to UAN, didn't meet my daddy before he died, momma had kids by multiple men, and had been a problem since I was hired at UAN as a lowly adjunct.

So many ways to call an educated Black man a basic nigger.

She did them all.

She didn't recognize me, and I didn't recognize her.

I had left Memphis as Pi Maurice Suleman, an adjunct at UAN who had few options, and returned as the son of Mr. Suleman, a man who could suddenly afford attorneys on a level that made all others shake in their wing tips and struggle to regroup. I'd worn one of the suits my father had bought as a metaphor. A thousand-dollar suit. Professional. Black with golden necktie. Monk-strap shoes. One of my father's Rolexes. I didn't show up to get Hancock Parked. I was next level, showed no hints of growing up depressed in the 38109. The Bitch from Brownsville argued a pointless argument, was in full gaslighting mode, said from her perspective she saw nothing wrong that had been done to me or her husband. I was a man and men couldn't be raped. A blow job wasn't rape. She was a goddamn beauty queen. She didn't need to rape a goddamn man. She'd married a powerful man to keep men like me from raping her. Sounding convincing. The rich. The beautiful. The entitled. She threatened if one second of that video, one taken without her permission, said it with tears in her eyes and a threatening tone, seethed as if she had somehow been raped by it being recorded, menaced that if that showed up on social media she was going to sue me and UAN for defamation of character and about two dozen other offenses. I was nothing to her. I was just another invisible man living among three million invisible Black men who secretly wanted her. All the passion and desire she'd claimed to have for this BMFM, how she'd savored the flavor of this child of Africa and greedily imbibed his precome, guzzled my come, and licked the draining after-come like it was the special of the day from Area 51 Ice Cream in Hernando, all the hate she had for the Judge of all Judges and lust for a BMFM on the video had done a hard one-eighty, the kind that burned rubber and left smoke so thick you choked half to death and couldn't see for half a mile. She loved her husband. Nobody was buying her bullshit. Truth was exposed among her peers, but her lies were recorded as her version of the truth for the legal record. I'd exposed her, a man telling on an affair, and was treated like a jailhouse snitch. Her bottomless fear was hidden behind anger that could've started a race riot, had my home and every Black home and every business in my zip code burned down a hundred years ago. She showed her ass. If the Bitch from Brownsville who could slap around the Judge of all Judges couldn't exercise her white power and control the body of a South Memphis Carver High School graduate, if she couldn't Mandingo and own an adjunct at the USN, if he was a tattletale, then this BMFM was nothing to her. I was a flea in her ear. She had been a tick in mine.

I was still a poor man, but I had access to Suleman money now. I had access to power. I had Roger de Groot. Her whiteness, status in the tri-state area, and position at UAN were a ripped-up food stamp to me.

Days ago, when I was leaving Cali, she had left messages demanding we meet at the Peabody. Threatened to fuck me good and shave me bald.

There was nothing else pho us to say to each other.

No reason pho her to call me pho nothing at all.

I thought about my family. My neighbors. My reputation.

She Lee Harvey Oswald'd my character, then loaded up an assault rifle and did her best to James Earl Ray my dignity. Her ego was tall enough to be a UAN power forward. Like I had done days before in LA, I sat as cool as Matthew in a Lincoln Navigator. She had her ten-minute temper tantrum, her diatribe undisturbed and on the official record.

Dr. Stone-Calhoun had flipped the script and put me on trial.

I didn't offer a rebuttal.

The bitch had no receipts.

I had a cocksucking video narrated by come-stained Russian Red lips. That was better than finding a golden ticket in my chocolate.

The way she cut her eyes at me, that, too, rang of murder.

UAN protected its legacy and Dr. Stone-Calhoun's whiteness.

They cared about their reputation.

They said it was business, not personal.

My people replayed the video, went over it point by point, then slid the UAN family a number, the cost of making this go away.

The cost of suffering for a BMFM.

UAN demanded a gag order.

A gag order over a blow job.

The irony.

Just like the gossipers at UAN had heard rumors, so had I. Big small towns didn't keep secrets too long. The Calhouns were white folks who only hired Black folks and Mexicans to clean toilets and do labor.

They talked.

The judge went home drunk as a skunk and ordered his workers to pack his wife's shit. The Bitch from Brownsville returned to home and he wouldn't let her inside the gate. The workers saw her, then looked away, made her invisible as they pretended to be busy but were recording what looked like another WorldStar moment in the making. No one responded to her commands. Landscapers ignored her. She had been dethroned and thrown out of a twelve-bedroom mansion situated near Wolf River, the privileged life as she knew it stripped away. She called the police. The cops pulled up and, shotgun in hand, Judge Calhoun sent them away. He barked and reminded them never to come back to his property uninvited by him. He'd call the chief of police directly if he needed assistance from MPD. Same if he needed the Shelby County sheriffs. He'd call the men at the top. He didn't deal with nigger women, not today. Both cops were women of color, neither African American. The police bodycams recorded footage to be leaked as retaliation for being insulted.

From inside his gate, the judge barked at his wife, "You are a bed of vipers and lies. You are the one wrong, so move on. Get off my property."

"My belongings. The things for my hair. I need everything."

"Came from my money. I'll give you what I want you to have."

"You're cutting me off?"

"At the knees."

"I'll sue."

"Walk away."

"Let me back in my house."

"I've kept your little secrets this long, from the day I met you, from the day I made you somebody, so don't worry, keep your mouth hush, and I'll add this one to the pile. This secret is the last one. I've had enough."

She exploded. "I know your secrets too."

"Walk away while the walking is good. Run to the niggers."

The cops said he told his wife that all of her hairdresser appointments had been canceled, and she had a conniption fit. The judge rattlesnake spat and said someone else would have to tend to her morning lies and daily deceit and do her hair as the rooster crowed.

She demanded to know where she was to sleep. Told him she could stay in her west wing of the home and no one would cross each other.

The judge carried his Thunder like a hunting rifle and polar-bear walked away, no room for her lies as he headed toward a mansion that had been in his family since slavery, paid for by slave labor, a home with more chambers than the Bates Motel had rooms. Halfway he stopped. He screamed to the skies, a man on the verge of going psycho. That should've ended it. The judge should've dealt with the Bitch from Brownsville, not me.

CHAPTER 58

As I CAREFULLY moved my humid body and anger through the coolness of UAN's underground parking lot, the lot all but empty, Four Ds' voice echoed, "Please, baby, please, baby, please, baby, baby, baby, please."

A ten-year-old white-and-gray Smart car told me the troublemaker who'd gone from Manassas High to UAN had shown up early.

"Please, baby, please, baby, please, baby, baby, baby, please."

Four Ds' four-door Dodge Ram 2500 was here too. He'd driven his weekend ride today. My best friend since Riverview Elementary had parked deeper in the underground lot, six car lengths from Komorebi.

Komorebi commanded, "Again, until you say it the way I want you to say it. I'm your Spikella Lee right now. Camera rolling, Action."

"Please, baby, please, baby, please, baby, baby, baby, please."

Her crassness echoed in the recesses one hundred feet before I saw them. What I saw looked ridiculous. Four Ds was damn near seven feet tall, and Komorebi was all of five-foot nothing, but today they were the same height. DaReus Danian D'Angelo Darellson was on his knees begging Komorebi DaShiarra Regina Devin Jackson to not show the video of him breaking his vows. I cooled off, watching the show.

"Please, baby, please, baby, please, baby, baby, baby, please."

"Again. Like in the movie."

"C'mon nigh, Ko-Mo."

"Take forty-seven. Action."

"I've been doing this for twenty minutes."

"Say it again but make me believe it."

I stood to the side of a column, a nice breeze coming from behind me. They were off by themselves in a rarely used, dusty part of the lot.

"I can't beg no mo'."

"Action, Or I send this to social. To Melissa. To UAN."

"Please, baby, please, baby, please, baby, baby, baby, please."

"Better."

"So we good?"

"Your boy is letting both of us down."

"What else you need from me?"

"Take forty-eight. Action."

"C'mon, nigh. Stop acting all Manassas."

"Oh, fuck you and Carver High."

"You'll get your A, I told you."

"I'm not letting it go because you suddenly remember you have a wife and two little babies depending on you, boo. You knew coming to the room for loving was wrong, now you wanna be right."

"Please, baby, please, baby, please, baby, baby, baby, please."

Four Ds knew better, yet the motherfucker was unable to do better. Married. Big house. Twins. Prized status and position at UAN. She had set Four Ds up and reeled him in for the okeydoke.

"Please, baby, please, baby, please, baby, baby, baby, please."

"Say it like you mean it."

"Please, baby, please, baby, please, baby, baby, baby, please, baby, please, baby, please."

"In Spanish."

"*Por favor*, baby, *por favor*, baby, *por favor*, baby, baby, baby, *por favor*."

Her cellular was in her hand. "Now in pig Latin. *Action*."

My cellular rang and they both jumped, saw me thirty feet away.

Brake lights on an old Honda parked ten feet from Four Ds came on and went back off. I headed toward Komorebi and Four Ds.

My phone rang again, and I stopped and answered.

Roger de Groot said, "Nia Simone Bijou is trying to get in contact with you regarding motion picture rights to the Forever series."

Fit to be tied, overwhelmed I said, "Let me call you back."

"You're too busy to take five to make at least two million?"

"Too busy and frustrated to say this motherfuckin sentence."

"Your check-engine light is on. You okay?"

"Right now, I'm busy being you, Roger de Groot. I'm in the middle of an existential crisis with my best friend, not unlike what you had with my old man. I'm pissed the fuck off, and I'm channeling you, pro bono."

"Your check-engine light is definitely back on."

"It's been on since I was born, will go off the day I die. Also, the judge just tried to run me over in his SUV. He tried to run me over, brandished his shotgun, and put threats on my life."

"What the fuck? Are you shitting me?"

"He tried to run me over, then made a death threat."

"No way. He's a judge. He's a public figure down there."

"A southern judge who thinks God should report to him."

"I can't believe the people back there. I can't get that mentality."

"I don't know how they roll in LA, but the upholders of the law ain't good at following the law out this way. Had his shotgun. In public."

"Just now?"

"Just now. He called me dead-nigger soup. He knew my fuckin address and told me what I had for breakfast. He knew what I had for lunch. He knew my route so he could run me down. I'm being followed."

"Suleman—"

"I can handle it, Roger de Groot. I'm a Motherfucker. You told me yourself, like it or not, I'm a motherfuckin Suleman. Nobody Hancock Parks a Suleman. About to step in a meeting. Will call you. Pi gone."

I hung up, check-engine light redder than blood, then feigned like I was passing by the Honda, cut left, ran screaming to the car, and slammed on the trunk with my fists. A girl yelled for her life and popped up from hiding in the footwell of the passenger seat. Busted like a motherfucker.

I went to the window, jaw tight, no fucks to give, and showed her my UAN identification like it was an MPD badge. "Get out the car. Now."

The passenger's-side door creaked open. A terrified teenager eased out, probably nineteen years old, already crying, shuddering, and apologizing. She had on booty shorts and a T-shirt representing Arkansas State University Mid-South, a community college about eighty miles away. Komorebi had imported an Asian face no one recognized.

In the most Arkansas accent I'd ever heard since my first born day, the Asian teen said, "She up and made me do this as a favor."

Not giving a damn I extended my hand. "Give me your gotdamn phone. And your identification, your license, *now*."

She did it with so much terror in her heart she was wheezing and palpitating. I used my phone, took photos of her, three of her ID, and the tags on her ride.

"Delete what you recorded. *Now*. Or I'll call MPD, and I don't think you want that. You're on UAN property participating in a crime."

Wheezing like she needed albuterol and Primatene Mist, she did.

"You recorded them at the Peabody. That's another crime."

"She asked me to."

"Get in your car. Drive home. Don't look back."

She dove in and drove away fast, so terrified she never looked toward Komorebi.

Komorebi watched me in silence; Four Ds was still on his knees.

I commanded, "Komorebi, I need to see your phone."

"Who you think you is?"

"*Now*."

"Who you think you is?"

"And, DaReus Danian D'Angelo Darellson, mane, unless you're asking her to marry you and replace Melissa, stand up and man up. You look stupid, Four Ds. It looks like she's pledging you and you know she won't let you cross the burning sands. Come over here and holla at your arbitrator for a second. Komorebi, I need to see your phone."

"Shit. Like hell you do."

"*Now*."

"Never."

"Give the fuckin phone to Four Ds or I'm walking back the way I came. Bring me her phone when you get up and come over here."

Komorebi shook her head. "Nope. Not giving you my phone."

Four Ds made a pained sound that echoed down here like it was a death knell for his marriage, job, and reputation. He shook his heavy head like he knew this was a no-way-out sitch and would end up above the fold in *The Commercial Appeal*, *The Bartlett Express*, and the *Memphis Flyer*.

"Mane. Knees gone numb."

"Mane, get your ass up."

He moaned, struggled to get on his feet, then was palmer housing like his corns were in so much pain he had to hobble like an old man.

When he was by me I told the shaking skyscraper, "Go home. Manassas wants me. Not you. She's been after me since that Cybill Shepherd thing. Time for me to set her Manassas ass straight."

My skin was so wet with sweat I felt my underwear sticking to my ass. Stress sweat had him looking like he had showered wearing his joggers and UAN polo. He was a man on the gallows, prepared to meet his maker rather than face his wife over what he had done.

He rubbed his aching knees. "Mane, the video of me and her—"

"Mane, she asked for money?"

"She wanted a better grade in thermal dynamics. I had to give her an A or lose everything."

"But no money?"

"Mane, you know she'll want me to drop money in her rainy-day fund."

"Mane, then have your checkbook on standby."

Four Ds palmer housed to his truck, moaned and groaned as he pulled himself in. He drove away in slow motion, eyes on his rearview until he disappeared. Standing three columns away from the nuisance of the year, I regarded Komorebi.

"All this to get my attention."

"Will you finally listen?"

"Your phone. Peabody recording. Show me. *Now.*"

"You ain't the boss of me."

"Now."

"Who the fuck you think you is?"

"Komorebi, I need to see what's on your phone."

"How come?"

"Bad experiences are good teachers. And don't record me."

"My phone is my personal life."

"Give me the fuckin phone."

"I'm not handing you my personal life."

"Just show me what you had your sidekick from Arkansas record at the Peabody."

"Nope."

"Please, baby, please, baby, please, baby, baby, baby, please."

A series of hair tosses showed her desperation.

She trembled. "Just the video."

I walked toward her; she walked toward me.

Leftover rage was still driving me, and it showed.

Her mouth was tight, scared like I might jump on her. Daisy Dukes and tennis shoes. Looked all of seventeen now. She pulled up the video, held it up to my face, didn't let me touch her phone. The recording showed Four Ds waiting at the bar inside the Peabody's lobby.

She had been conniving, asked him to watch the ducks, aroused and recorded them at the Peabody Hotel, the grandest, most historic hotel downtown, where the five mallard ducks that lived on the hotel rooftop marched onto the elevator. The Peabody Ducks then rode it to the lobby and duck-walked to the large fountain to crowds almost every day. Everybody loved to see the ducks. If a man's wife found out he had an affair at a spot on that level, if she saw them in a room on a bed making out, slow kissing and heavy petting, undressing nervously like a boy about to make love for the very first time, and not just him pulling panties to the side for a two-minute ass-slapping episode in the back seat of a hoopty tucked away between trees and bushes in Riverside Park, the betrayal would be magnified.

I said, "You're good at being bad."

"Manassas, baby."

"Professor Suleman. Not your baby."

"Professor Suleman, you look real mad right now."

"Respect my hard work like you want me to respect yours."

"All that mad for me?"

"Don't worry about it."

"You're madder now than that night at the Love Club."

I swallowed, dabbed sweat. "You're as patient as you are irritating."

"You couldn't be gone to LA forever."

"Today, I wish I had never booked a return flight to this hell."

"Professor, please, reread and reconsider the lower grade you've given me. We can talk it over in the setting of your choosing. Please allow me to explain my literature. It's important to me."

"Two minutes; then I have other more important things to handle."

"I can't in two—"

"Two minutes and we're done."

She took a breath, shifted. "From the first day of learning, Africans—and the children of—have been whip-fed the white man's culture, like it was the castor oil to erase all things African in our blood. Here at UAN, anything regarding Black culture or history is an elective. We study white all day and they never study Black. We were code-switching and bicultural as a tool of survival. White people ain't required to read about us, not about this part of America, but we were forced to read about their white and European history and lives and swim in their angsts, have to learn about their wars and battles from the moment they left England, while our kings and queens are erased; then we are forced to emulate the oppressor in language and dress and hairstyles, all as we are being rejected, lynched, and maimed either metaphorically or literally. Do the work? Harriet Tubman did the work, but she still needed the Underground Railroad. She still needed hella help. An extreme example, but still, we all need allies with rope to pull us over each wall. I did the work to the best of my ability, and I need a little more."

Komorebi was as right as she was wrong. I was as wrong as I was right. A Black man set aside what had happened on Pharaoh Road, took in the coolness while he listened to a Black woman and learned.

"That's my two minutes."

She was a hood girl struggling to assimilate, same as I'd been out of South Memphis. She had to do the work, but I had to remember that nobody wanted us. With whites we had the wrong skin and with monied Blacks we didn't have the right kin. We came from disposable zip codes.

"Professor? Well, are you going to say something back?"

Coolness and mustiness sat on me. I thought about my red Nova.

"Professor? Hello?"

The day I first drove it I was speeding up Kansas Street to get to UAN to take a final, a make-or-break moment. My GPA could've plummeted that day. An angel had seen me through that chapter. I had done the work the best I could and was still coming up short. I was back on that cold day, racing for the bus, watching it pull away, and I knew the driver saw me running my ass off, no gloves, books in my hands, in the melting snow, doing my best with what I had, feeling like a loser.

I told Komorebi, "You've missed the 31 Crosstown Kansas and need a ride to your next destination, so you can do your best to do the rest. You need help getting on the 31 Crosstown Kansas."

"Why would I be way over there by Carver waiting on a 31 so I can get jumped on by a jelly-ass Carver Cobra still mad because the Manassas whupped them in football in 1979?"

I corrected her, "Carver was undefeated in '79. Ain't you heard of legendary quarterback Winston Ford?"

"My buses are the 40, 52, 11, and the 4. Now, are you helping me boost my GPA or nah?"

"You did the work with the dull, hand-me-down tools you had at your disposal."

"Still confused. That sounded so wiggity, wiggity, wiggity wack."

"*Listen.*"

"Oh god. Not another lecture."

"Back in the day, Booker T. Washington way over on Lauderdale was pretty much the only high school the Blacks on the south side were allowed to go to. That before Carver was built in the fifties. When Carver was built, they didn't bother to build Black folks a cafeteria. Treated second-class from day one. Closed now. My skinfolk were educated in a second-class environment as they sat in secondhand desks, sweating or freezing, reading the torn pages of secondhand books that came from well-appointed white schools after the city had bought that side of town the best and brand-new books. They got everything first. If you raced and found a book with an undamaged cover and all the pages, you were lucky."

"So, I get a B or nah?"

"Nah."

"That mad face says it all. You're failing me?"

"Nah. You get an A."

"For real?"

"While other folks help each other fail upward to the White House, instead of helping you over the wall, I've kicked away your ladder. If you're not part of the solution, you're part of the problem."

Tears formed in her frustrated eyes. "Thank you. I mean that."

I had felt powerless, then came at her to prove to myself I wasn't powerless. I was taking it out on her. I put myself in check.

Almost apologetic, I asked, "What else do you need?"

"Mentor me."

"You're ordering me?"

"Asking."

"I didn't hear a question mark at the end of that sentence."

"I'm not good with punctuation."

"That's a big part of your problem."

"Well. I can hire somebody to tighten that up."

"The mechanics make it hard to read."

"I went to a public school and we did things our way."

"So did I. I understand the struggle. We don't talk how they write. Was a struggle for me too. Going across town was like going to a foreign country where you'd never be good enough."

"Carver and Manassas ain't so different."

"Now be a good student for once and correct your punctuation."

She looked confused, then understood. "Will you mentor me?"

"Miss Jackson. Give me some *respect*. We didn't grow up together."

"Professor Suleman, will you mentor me?"

I dialed it back. "Make it nicer."

"You okay?"

"*Make it nicer.* Show me some damn *respect* for once."

"Who spit in your Kool-Aid? Oh, *Right.* I did."

"Komorebi."

"Professor Suleman, will you please, pretty please with sugar on top, mentor me?"

"Too sweet."

"Professor Suleman, will you please mentor me?"

I let that rest, dead-nigger soup percolating.

I told her, "You got it."

"For real?"

I paused. "Ten two-hour sessions, twice a week."

"For real?"

"For real. Late or no-show, we're done."

"Now, see how easy that was? We could've resolved this a long time ago, but, nah, a brother was too scared to meet a sister for drinks so she could explain this from the get-go. We can do drinks now?"

"No drinks."

"I won't always be one of your students."

"Circle back when you're not. After you have a degree and are no longer a student at UAN."

"For real?"

"Anything else?"

"Follow me on IG."

"Don't push it."

"Twitter?"

"Stop it."

"Can I meet your sister?"

"No."

"Professor Suleman, are you really going to mentor me, or are you fucking with me?"

"Not fucking with you, Miss Jackson."

"Can I call you Pi, and you call me Koko or Kay or Kay Jaye?"

"Professor Suleman, Miss Jackson."

"This means so much to me."

As far as I was concerned, this was done. I walked away.

She did a hair toss and headed toward her Smart car.

I yelled, "Delete that video."

She yelled back, "It gets deleted at the end of our first session. Gotta make sure you ain't playing me, Carver. I know how y'all Cobras roll."

There was no sex on the video. Four Ds had come to his senses, pulled away from the heavy petting, stood up, adjusted his clothing as fast as he could, and, with an erection, apologized to Komorebi. He apologized, said how much he loved his wife, how much he loved his family, and ran out of the room. He remembered his wife, his obligations, and all he stood to lose. When he was gone, Komorebi had laughed her ass off. That was as far as she'd planned to go anyway. Manassas girls had morals too. The Asian girl from Arkansas had been hiding in the hotel closet, recording it all. She had recorded them in the lobby, had a key, then hurried up to the room ahead of them. All to get a better GPA.

Komorebi screamed and scared the shit out of me. She screamed like she was being attacked, let it loose like she was setting me up the same way she had Four Ds, only the charges would get me twenty years.

She stood at her car door, phone in hand. "*Dafuq.* This ish again?"

I yelled at her as I went back her way. "What happened?"

"The Black bat-signal just went up over the tristate area."

"What Black bat-signal?"

"Memphis Black Twitter on fire. That's our Black bat-signal."

"What just happened?"

"Sister and her family have been attacked for no reason by the police right across the bridge. Gotta go. Black Lives Matter on the move to make sure they don't Sandra Bland her and Tamir Rice those three kids."

"Drive easy. They'll team up and set up a speed trap on both the Memphis and Arkansas sides to put you in the same position. And the attitude you have with me, leave it parked on this side of the bridge."

"Oh shit, Professor Pi Maurice Suleman. It sounds like you actually care about something other than yourself for once."

"Be careful. White boys can walk around locked and loaded, but unarmed Black activists are treated like terrorists in their own country."

"And the ice cream truck tune is actually a racist song called 'Nigger Love a Watermelon.'"

"What?"

"Yeah, water is wet. Tell me something I don't already know."

Her phone buzzed again with updates.

She screamed again as she got in her ride and started it up. "The bastards just arrested a six-year-old little Black girl. What could she possibly have done to color outside their lines? This bullshit, this is why I write. This is why I need you. It's your obligation."

"I got you, Komorebi. My sister, I got you. Word is bond."

We were no longer teacher and student. No longer Carver and Manassas. A common enemy had bonded us for the moment.

"This is the part of my existence *wipipo* teachers here at UAN are too busy redlining because of a fucking run-on sentence or a damn split infinitive and deleting because reading Black pain bores them to tears . . . because they can't relate . . . a six-year-old. I just can't. I fucking can't."

"Komorebi, told you, I got you."

"Calling my girls now."

"Take a few brothers with y'all."

"We got this. We don't need male faces up front for our cause to be validated by Black or white America. Your help is appreciated but just do like the good white people who support our movement and help a sister's mission without hijacking us. Sisters started this; we still got this."

We didn't ask what they did because we knew being Black was enough to be traumatized for kicks, our PTSD the punch line for others.

She ranted, "Four white cops put a Black woman and three other girls, all minors, in handcuffs and made them lay out in the sun in one hundred degrees on burning-hot blacktop over a minor traffic stop. And they wonder why we grow up hating their asses until we fuckin die."

"Don't leave here and go there acting a fool."

She looked at her dashboard and yelled again. "Shit."

"What?"

"On E. Can I borrow some gas money until I get my income tax refund?"

I opened my wallet and gave her one hundred dollars.

She said, "You know this isn't a loan, right?"

"My contribution to the cause."

"I'll put half of it toward their bail, if we need to."

She screamed louder and it echoed in the parking chamber as she sped away in her trendy Smart car. She was me in Roger de Groot's office with my check-engine light on fire. Before the echoes of her outrage faded, my phone rang. It was Sis. In the coolness of the garage, all alone, I inhaled, answered. She was screaming her outrage too.

"Sweet Meat. It. Never. Ends."

"I didn't get the details. What you know about what happened?"

"Four of us practicing the ancient art of minding our own business were just pulled over and the police bum-rushed them with guns drawn. Didn't even say why they were pulled over. Just aimed guns at their heads and started yelling conflicting instructions. This some bullshit."

My phone beeped and it was Momma on the same hotline.

I let Sis go and clicked over.

Momma was furious too. "They are in a family van. A branded church van, at that. Church name all over it. It's streaming live. All brown-skinned girls. Three of the beautiful girls are minors. Guns were drawn on three Black children and a girl who barely look like an adult."

"Sis just told me."

"We group texting with my other Swimmers while I talk to you."

"Six years old. That's a first grader, a baby."

"This definitely changes how she sees the world growing up as a Black woman. The dehumanization of four of my young sisters in their formative years. I need to get over there on the other side of the bridge with everybody else and make sure they are going to be okay."

"Momma."

"It. Never. Ends."

"Momma. Take a breath."

"That's the problem."

"Breathe."

"They won't let us breathe."

"Momma. Breathe."

"I can't."

"Momma. Momma. Momma."

"They've been suffocating us since they stole us from Africa."

I held her on the phone for half a minute, heard her every exhale.

"Skipping chest day, not grading papers, not preparing tomorrow's lecture, not doing my photo shoot. Momma gone to Arkansas to protest."

Momma ended the call.

I needed to go over the bridge, needed to protect my sisters the way they cried for and protected the Black man no matter what, but I had to deal with being the recipe in my own ish right here, right now.

Sun high, I whispered, "Dead. Nigger. Soup."

Once a hashtag, I wondered who would march and scream for me.

WINDOWS DOWN, ANGER up, I called Four Ds as I drove down Union toward the river. I needed a punching bag. I wanted to unload all of my problems on him, but I didn't.

Relieved, Four Ds said, "Mane, I owe you big-time."

"Mane, my Black ass. Understand this. You're my boy. But I'm not going to be your Bill Barr or Rudy Giuliani. I'm not stepping in when you fuck up like this ever again. Next time you're gonna have to ride that train to its destination. Hug your wife and the kids for me. See y'all over the weekend."

CHAPTER 59

I PUT MORE security lights around my house, then installed the latest elite Ring doorbells on both front and back doors. The one in front hit me with an alert as soon as someone came off the sidewalk and entered my yard. I had ADT rush out and upgrade my burglar alarm. Went to the range by myself and tested both shotguns and my handgun. Could only use one at a time, but the next in line would stay loaded. I'd keep them at three areas. Front door. Back door. Bedroom. Didn't tell Momma or the Fastest Swimmers. Southern men handled southern men problems the way southern men did. This was between me and the Judge of all Judges. If he kept it that way, I'd do the same. I did everything I could think of to be safe and ready. I was tempted to ride out to North Memphis to the Dog Man who lived on Merton and buy two pit bulls and a rottweiler.

My life had become disrespectful to those who had been beaten on Bloody Sunday. I was better than this. Miss Virginia would be ashamed.

I was a professor at the prestigious UAN, but it might've been better if after Carver High I'd just skipped university and worked at Piggly Wiggly sacking groceries and restocking toilet paper until retirement.

I stood in my window, shotgun in hand.

The motherfucker knew what I had for breakfast.

CHAPTER 60

GEMMA BUCKINGHAM BUCKED, a woman gone mad, snarled, demanded, "Fuck me. Fuck me. Pull my hair; pull my hair. Harder. Harder."

I wore her down, gave her the ball of fire, anger, and indignation inside me, made her tap out. She snake-crawled away from me to catch her breath. I was worn down too. Wheezing. Dripped sweat like I was in the rain. When she was able to breathe, she laughed a soft laugh.

I asked, "What's funny?"

"Thirteen orgasms. *Thir-fuckin-teen.*"

"Thirteen is an unlucky number."

"Let's work on fourteen."

"After a short break."

"Let's shower and change the bedding."

Two hours later we were slow sexing on her big sofa chair.

Dressed like Batgirl with me in a Nightwing T, Gemma Buckingham glowed, fanned herself, still on cloud ninety-nine. "Wish I was an American or at least had some permanent status here."

I said, "Wish you were a citizen too."

"Wish all of my business dealings were on this side of the pond too."

"Me too."

"I've become neglectful of my duties abroad."

"I get it."

"Plus, it seems the current administration has recast the whole immigration system."

"We could get married. They do that for citizenship here all day every day."

"I've done it before. Over there. As I came, it was a thought."

"Or make an anchor baby and drop the anchor."

"Thought about that as you planted your seeds. A bridge too far, but not as far away as I would like to believe. It has crossed my mind."

"You want kids?"

"Not sure what kind of mum I'd be, to be honest."

"I wouldn't be an absentee dad. At times I think I could have a baby with someone and figure out how to just be a dad for a while."

"Good to know."

"Options?"

"I'm not world renowned in arts, science, sports, or entertainment."

"That the end of the road, then?"

"I would have to qualify for an entrepreneur license, which would not be a problem. But so far as financing, they demand that I invest a minimum five hundred thousand dollars to set up shop here in Memphis."

"Half a million."

"Or spend at least one million on a business venture I'm not sure would be viable."

"How would that go?"

"The million is dependent on location of said business. I'd have to spend enough to feed a small nation ten times over and have at least ten employees in order to set up shop in the USA."

In her eyes I saw her wondering if the ride would be worth the cost of the million-dollar ticket. Right now I needed to love abroad.

Soon but not too soon I asked, "Well, what can we do to fix it?"

"Well. I can't see what I would risk that much on in Memphis, not without an astute partner."

She pulled me on top of her, pulled me between her legs, put me back inside, sounded overaroused. She made me feel like I was an African king, a man destined to rule over Memphis.

It would cost a million dollars for her to stay here and be my queen. That was more money than people I knew would make in a lifetime.

She said, "The cost of love had never been cheap."

I agreed. "Not for the rich, not for the poor."

Later, in a gourmet kitchen the size of half my house, I cooked, made smoky chorizo tilapia with black olives, basil, and cherry tomatoes, with a splash of apple cider vinegar and a pinch of salt and pepper.

A black SUV was outside her window. It had been there since I had arrived. It followed me here. The unknown had never gotten out.

When I left the next day, the black SUV trailed me home, then parked on Blair Hunt and Kansas until sunrise. They sped away right after Widow Fatima left for her morning run. I waited an hour but had closed my eyes. I was exhausted because I stayed up all night, Lightning in my hands, waiting on a judge carrying Thunder to fuckin try me.

CHAPTER 61

I HAD SO much stuff coming in on behalf of Mr. Suleman and nowhere to store it, so I took up an office space at Union Centre with the nation's largest display of Blue Dog artwork. I signed a one-year lease for private office space to deal with all things the dead had left for the living to reckon with. From the fifteenth floor, I'd become Roger de Groot handling Suleman business. Like a good Motherfucker.

The top boss man at DC Comics hit me up while I was busy unpacking. Stood at my sky-high window and took in the view of Bluff City while we chatted. He loved my idea about using the Black Kryptonians.

I explained, "They wouldn't get straight to the yellow sun, but pass other suns, and each dose of radiation would impact them in ways unimaginable."

"X-Men or mutant style, so far as developing abilities?"

"As they pass from universe to universe. So, the potential for familiar Kryptonians as a new breed of unprecedented and unpredictable occupants in the DCU is unlimited. The new heroes and villains are possibly impacted by each sun's radiation in different ways."

"Pi, sounds awesome."

"Yeah?"

"Just what we need."

"Serious?"

"Serious. I can't wait to read what you have so far. Your writing is clever, yet user-friendly. The world you have created from scratch is unique without being esoteric or obscure. Love how it occurs across space and time. Well, I could sing your praises all day."

"You had me at hello. Thanks for everything that came after."

He sang, "Pi Maurice Suleman."

I clacked my tongue, "That's me all day long."

"Your father had a unique first name. Archimedes?"

"Yeah." His shadow covered me. "Archimedes Suleman."

"Yeah, if memory serves, Archimedes was the name of a scholar."

"Archimedes is the Greek mathematician who discovered the value of pi."

"Wow. Archimedes created the value of pi, and the author Archimedes created a son, named him Pi."

"Momma said my name was the only thing he gave me. But I lie and say it's connected to the day I was born to keep the conversation comfortable for me. Keep that between us."

"And Suleman?"

"Arabic version of Solomon. Means man of peace." Lightning stared at me from the corner. "How this Black man from Memphis has tried to live my life but have been denied that right since day one due to my epidermis."

He went on, "I was a big fan of your father's work. I met him at an event in Chicago."

I chuckled, imitated Roger de Groot's voice. "And it's deep too."

"Yes! It took me years to understand what the hell that even meant. Crazy day in Chi-town."

"Richard Pryor."

"Mudbone."

He fell into fanboy mode and told me the same tall tale Roger de Groot had told me, pretty much word for word.

He said, "Slapped it on the table over and over."

"I heard."

"I'm talking to the son of a legend. Talking to the son of Suleman."

"Son of Suleman. Guess that's who I am, always have been, and will always be."

"The son of Archimedes Suleman."

"Archimedes, the author of Pi."

"He was a good man. Sorry for your loss."

"I'm sorry I never met the man you met."

"What do you mean?"

"We never met. I only know of the devil, not the saint."

WITHIN AN HOUR I sent in the first twenty pages; the next hour they called my agent and offered me a twenty-four-issue deal to create Vathlo as I saw it, my imagination to be tied in with the current universe. I would be my own overseer. This son of Suleman would be able to destroy and rebuild a universe in the right kind of way, leaving nobody hurt when I was done. Any characters I created, I would own. The name I wore got me that part of the deal. I was as excited as I was scared, but I had worked hard all my life. Physical or mental labor never frightened me away from doing what I needed to do to get it done. For a lazy man, that could take two years, but I'd knock that out of the park in six months. I was changing highways and being able to merge unchallenged into my own lane now.

My publisher wanted another novel. Wanted to continue the Suleman brand with me at the helm. That would be another six months of work for each book. I told them I would think about it. I didn't have a view of a marina housing another man's yacht, but I was doing fine.

The man who had created the Motherfuckers and one of the Fastest Swimmers had come into my life with his last breath and refused to leave after the last shovel of dirt had been put on his coffin, refused to let me get on with my own story and leave his on the side of the road. He had gifted me with his lazy man's load. When the man who should have been named Roger de Groot the Fifth sent me the memoir my father had started, I assumed he was only a handful of chapters in, assumed he didn't get far before he was too sick to lift his favorite Montblanc pen or peck away on his six-year-old MacBook Pro. But he had written two hundred chapters, each chapter a confessional, each confessional at least twenty pages long. He didn't hold back; he told the truth and didn't try to wrap it in sugar. He didn't try to rewrite the things he had done and make himself look good. Every tall tale the man I would always call Roger de Groot told was in there, no matter how outrageous, damn near word for word the way Roger de Groot had told them to me. And he really had read my books, really admired my writing, so trusted me with the story of his life. He had never met me, knew I could toss it in a barrel and go *Fahrenheit 451* on his last book and nobody but Roger de Groot would be the wiser. He had made me the keeper of his deepest secrets. I hated him and he trusted me. Trust was the cousin to love. Now I was confused.

We could've been a good team.

We could've been a great team.

I started taking care of things with a fury, as if I wouldn't be alive to see tomorrow. Trouble was out there. Taunting. The same black SUV had followed me to my new office and parked across the lot facing my car. The judge had enough money to keep me under surveillance and had the power to make dead-nigger soup when his appetite was strong.

I walked with my handgun in my backpack, kept my rucksack at my side day and night, and when I was at home I kept Lightning loaded and on standby, ready for Thunder. I was a cook, could make soup too.

CHAPTER 62

MOMMA STOPPED BY to borrow my car again.

She never needed my car. It was her way of staying close to me. When she pulled up she wanted people to know she was driving her son's car to let them know she had children who took care of her and loved her.

I was at the kitchen table.

Pokey was in her backyard taking in laundry.

Mo Fo was washing his truck.

Their kids were helping with both chores.

Widow Fatima came out of her home looking toothsome.

The smiling widow eased on a wide-brimmed Banana Republic straw fedora and rose-colored cat-eye sunglasses. The sun hit her just right, revealed her body's outline, once again art in motion.

She was arousing. I was disarmed, distracted, aroused.

I'd have to go visit Gemma Buckingham to fix that problem.

WHEN MOMMA GOT back to my crib, she was dressed up in a smart pant-suit popping Carver colors and high heels that gave her a five-inch boost. Her makeup was on and she was all about the business.

"Momma." I laughed. "You've been drinking?"

"One vodka margarita with my sorority after the meeting."

"One?"

"Two."

"Get your story straight."

"And a half."

"And another half."

"Empty carbs while we talked about life." She giggled, playfully scrunched her nose. "Gave in to sororal peer pressure once again."

"You don't need to be drinking and driving."

"After raising five kids pretty much by myself and getting my degrees while changing diapers over beaucoup years, Momma entitled to eat or do whatever she wants to do with her life right now. If I ever decided I wanted to do crack, shut your mouth and hold the pipe."

I laughed. "Yeah, but you were driving my car."

"I'm not going to drink and drive my car. Don't be stupid."

Her delivery impeccable, I laughed harder. She did too.

Momma said, "I saw the Judge of all Judges over this way."

That ended my joy. "When?"

"Well, didn't see him. Passed by him on Kansas Street up by Regina Drake's store. He was coming this way, rolled south down Kansas."

"What time?"

"Late. After eleven. Might've been midnight. I was on the way to the gym. Recognize his big SUV anywhere."

"You sure?"

"We were the only two vehicles on Kansas. I was going north and he was driving fast, coming south doing at least fifty."

"This way. Toward Blair Hunt Drive."

"He must have himself a little trap on this side of town. Or a secret family. Wouldn't surprise me. Men like him will incarcerate a Black man for ten years, then visit that same man's grieving wife for ten minutes that very same night. White folks have Uncle Toms too."

I looked at my shotgun.

She said, "I'd like to be their kind of Confederate white for a week to understand how the delusional shape their own truth. I'd go into their Arkham unarmed just to find out the goings-on in their minds."

"We all would."

We let that settle. She wore a worried look.

She said, "Momma hungry."

"Yes, ma'am."

"Cheat day but make it as healthy as you can."

"Yes, ma'am."

"Alexa, play Momma Nike favorite music."

"Alexa, play Jhené Aiko."

"Alexa, play . . ."

We did that silliness until Momma told Alexa to play Whodini's "Five Minutes of Funk." Momma hit every lyric and broke out the old-school dances. I Cabbage Patched with her, lost the contest by a mile, then did the running man to the kitchen to hook my girl up.

Momma made Alexa throw down SugarHill Gang's fifteen-minute version of "Rapper's Delight" next, then had my Swiffer, was dressed like a boss in high heels doing the wop and rapping "Shoop" with Salt-N-Pepa. She was in a good mood, acting fifteen, cleaning my floors and wiping down my countertop. She did all that multitasking; she took out her phone and turned girly-cougar while she sweet-talked Black Kevin.

In between I looked outside. The black SUV was gone.

Momma stood by me. "You know Momma takes care of her Fastest Swimmers no matter what. Even when y'all don't know it. Baby Doll thinks that nasty lying-ass Dominican she was seeing went away because of that little kick upside the head done in self-defense. She rode on my side of town and waited for me to go to the gym before she acted crazy. Momma set her straight. Girl dropped charges and issued an apology all over social media, then closed all her accounts. Don't lie on or mess with my children for your midnight entertainment. That fecal-throwing heifer girl rather see one hundred agents from ICE than run across me by myself. I take care of my children no matter how grown y'all think y'all are. No matter how old you get, I'm still the same number of years older than you I was the night you were born."

I nodded.

A few minutes later we shut up Alexa and blessed the meal. Avocado toast on sourdough. Roasted tomatoes. Boiled egg whites. Radish. Cilantro. Light seasoning.

She said, "Momma loves when her Fastest Swimmers are all together, but I've always made a point to spend one-on-one time with each one of you. Today's your day with Momma Nike, Sweet Meat."

"Kinda figured."

Momma said, "Alexa, play Nancy Wilson, shuffle."

Momma sat down and looked over my statements. She knew how much I was worth and told me not to tell nobody I had more than two dimes because when people who don't have any money thought you had a quarter, they would ask to borrow a dollar and forget about the loan.

I nodded at my financial planner. "Momma make the rules."

"Until my last breath, what Momma say go. Anybody got a problem and think they need to borrow a thin dime from you, tell 'em to come see me, because I'm the bank holding your blessed purse strings."

I went back to my front window. The SUV was back.

She said, "You hear what I just said, Sweet Meat?"

I answered the queen of Kansas Street. "Yes, ma'am."

"'If we command our wealth, we shall be rich and free; if our wealth commands us, we are poor indeed.' Edmund Burke done said that, Sweet Meat. I teach that to my students every day. Since you been talking a little slow the last few days, Momma gonna explain it one time. That means wealth is more than money. It is a series of studied tactics and comportments. Now, act like you know how to behave and get to strategizing. Ain't nobody business if you got more money than Uncle Phil and move on up like George and Weezy, po' people find out my son rich, they think they rich by osmosis. All of a sudden, they go from asking for two dollars every time they see you to needing to borrow two thousand twice a month. Far as anybody business, Mr. Suleman left you nothing but that mountain of signed books his attorney sent you the other day. Nothing else. Momma right. Listen to Momma and you'll never go broke."

I went back to her. "I have to go over a list of assets, want to help?"

"Why would Momma give herself extra work?"

"See if you want something."

"That your boulder to turn over. Need nothing from him."

I sat down next to her at the kitchen table, two things on my mind. I looked at piles of my work, my projects, and Suleman business while rubbing my temples. Momma read my face and faced me, concerned.

She asked, "What's wrong, Sweet Meat?"

"Momma. He did his memoirs. Before he died."

"Your point?"

"He mentions you a lot."

"By my name?"

"By your first name only."

"Infinity."

"From when he met you until the end of his life."

"Said bad things?"

"Nothing bad about you. He followed you on social media."

She shifted like she was about to start cussin'. "Why on earth?"

"He followed me on social too. He read the two books I've written."

"Mr. Suleman ain't bother to see you one time and had the audacity to read your books and write about me in his little autobiography."

"He wrote about everybody. From his harsh perspective, of course. His family, his California children, his wives. And a lot about himself."

"So, Mr. Suleman went out of his way and wrote about me."

"And it wasn't ugly. He was hard on himself, so far. He was married with a child . . . a son . . . when y'all met. You were . . . a teen . . . young."

"And foolish. Young and foolish."

I nodded. "If you ever want to talk about it."

"If Mr. Suleman wrote about what happened way back then, if his mind was stuck on what I ain't ever cared to remember and would've forgotten not for you, and if he wrote it, scribbled the who, when, and how he saw things, be it a half-truth or full lie from my perspective, nothing for Momma to say. I'm neither debating nor reliving my past."

"Momma."

She hesitated for the first time, then slowly and softly said, "Momma gonna say this one time. Your daddy was stupid. S-T-U-P-I-D. Stooooooooopid. Don't care how much money he made or how many books he wrote or read. Smart people stupid too. But your daddy was straight-up stupider than most. Stupid people are happy with their foolishness, but the wise will do what is right. He never learned to do right until he was standing at death's gate about to ring the doorbell. That's as stupid as stupid can get. You ain't been stupid because Momma didn't raise you stupid."

"No. Momma didn't raise me stupid. I got there on my own."

I went back to the front window.

Momma was watching me.

I walked back to the table, sat down. "Momma."

"Yeah, Sweet Meat."

"Tough question."

"Tough life."

"You don't have to answer."

"Bring it."

"Serious, you can pass, especially if it's triggering."

"Nobody has ever presented Momma with a question she refused to respond to if Momma has an answer. If it's beyond my realm of knowledge, Momma not afraid to say so and won't feel stupid for not knowing, because you're the one who needed to know in the first place."

"You saw a Black woman get attacked. Might be a stupid question, but entertain my ignorance for half a second. Did you know Black women who were raped by white men? That happened a lot?"

"All the time. Almost every sister I met had a story. Especially if you were a domestic worker. Nobody talked about that. Women knew what women went through. We talked amongst each other. You were taught to move on, to cry, but not too long or loud, wash yourself off, be glad you survived, remember to watch your six, pray hard at church, then pray harder at home before you struggled to sleep. You prayed for a healing of mind, body, and soul. But most of all you carried a switchblade, wished Mr. Charlie dead every second, and kept it moving."

"A day in the life of a Black woman is nothing like that of a white woman. The book *Little Women* needs a laugh track when put up against *Twelve Years a Slave*. It can't touch the horrors in the novel *Mandingo*."

"*Mandingo* was the raw, sadistic abuse of slaves. That movie was lacking. The truly horrifying stuff from the book wasn't in the film."

"Shit too much for Hollywood happened to the Black men too."

"I'll bring you my copy of *The Delectable Negro: Human Consumption and Homoeroticism within U.S. Slave Culture.* Read it."

I went to the front window, looked out at the unknown.

Momma came up behind me, looked outside too.

Her check-engine light burned as bright as mine.

She said, "I wish I'd been wiser and had interviewed older Black folks before they passed. Most of the real old ones were born right after the 1900s, one generation after slavery ended. They were illiterate or only went to school a few years, maybe as far as fifth grade, because they had to work the fields day to night to make ends meet. Sharecroppers. Wish I'd gotten to know the lives of my godparents and grandparents when I was much younger. Wish I knew how everyone met, fell in love, fell out of love, and whatnot. A lot of them were first- and second-generation freemen and women with old habits. They still caught an old yellow school bus hours before sunrise to get carried off to Mississippi and pick cotton for ten dollars a day. Some remembered slavery and the days right after. Wish I'd learned oral history from them before they passed. Especially during my preteen years. Not much was ever said about their hard times as Negroes surviving in New Orleans, Mississippi, and Memphis. The girl beaten half to heaven in front of Lowenstein's, bet seeing things like that was common. I bet they all had been through the same just-because beating in some way. I should've had their histories from the cradle to the grave recorded in some way."

"Your point?"

"If Mr. Suleman wrote about me, he wasted his time and most of all his God-given talent."

"Welp."

"I would've done important work. Not stupid work. Those people who kept their heads low for Mr. Charlie and stepped off the sidewalks for Miss Ann, those stripped of dignity and survived so we could survive, they're gone now. Every truth, gone. Now it's all lost in the grave."

It wasn't the kind of warning dressed up as a conversation that white people in America ever had to have with their children. I let that caution-ary tale marinate, traded in Momma's memory. There was a lesson in her words, a lesson a stupid Motherfucker who was too busy with the worries in his head could easily miss.

"Yes, Lord. A crowd of amused white men smoked cigarettes and watched the girl be mistreated. Our pain, their entertainment on a sunny Saturday when Black folks went to town to shop where whites shopped and pay bills. Going to Sears and Goldsmith's was a field trip. We got dressed up. Then we were attacked. That girl. Can't ever forget her. We were called savages and hadn't touched anybody. We were kicked like dogs because we rejected Jim and the direction in which he crowed."

"Too bad there was no social media."

"We got on the line or went door-to-door and spread the word that Mr. Charlie and Miss Ann were upset. We'd all stay up at night holding vigil trying not to be caught off guard. Like you're doing now. Kept our shotguns by the door. Like you're doing now."

I didn't say anything. She didn't let it go.

"You have a Remington 870 at your front door and a Mossberg 500 at your back door. Both loaded to the teeth. Just like we used to do when Mr. Charlie's mood was foul, fickle, and deadly. We hunkered down, stayed shotgun-ready until he calmed down. Just like you're doing now, Sweet Meat."

Again I offered nothing because anything I said would be a protective lie. Didn't want to lie. She knew me. I'd shut down.

Momma nodded, a ton of worry lines under her eyes, and moved on the best she could.

"You have a student named Komorebi Jackson? Girl who went to Manassas and trying to write?"

"Yeah. What did she do?"

"Nothing. We met her at the protest in Arkansas. Smart girl."

"That's debatable."

"Did you know the ice cream truck tune is actually a racist song called 'Nigger Love a Watermelon'? She told me and Baby Doll that, and we didn't believe her and looked it up. We grew up running to give the ice cream man our money when we heard him playing 'Nigger Love a Watermelon'? How have I missed that one all my life?"

Momma looked out the window at what I was looking at.

She said, "Somebody has a real nice SUV."

"They do."

Momma paused, studied me, tendered her voice before she asked, "Something going on I need to know about? You are buying extra guns. Can't use but one at a time. I know you ain't sleeping much. Baby Doll can see your lights on all night from her kitchen. I see your lights on too. I see you out back restless. We came out in our backyards and watched you a few weeks ago. Thought you might be up waiting on a booty call with that London girl and we wanted to see what the yellow gal looked like. You've been acting odd. Something is up with you. We are quiet but we ain't stupid. We are waiting on you to say what's troubling you. And whatever it is started before Mr. Suleman passed. Momma listening."

"Nothing wrong on Blair Hunt Drive."

I went back to the kitchen table, sat down.

She followed me, did the same.

"You sure?"

"Yes, ma'am. Dealt with my father's funeral. Those siblings. He left me a load of work to take care of. Had a terrorist attack at UAN that is still resonating." My lie was already prepared. "Comic I'm working on, it's under my skin, that's all. I walk around acting out dialogue."

"This got to do with yellow gal?"

"Nothing to do with her."

"Why these particular questions about rape and whatnot?"

"I was thinking of my superheroes hitting a wormhole and landing in the Bible Belt. In that environment. Or at a lynching. Have them show up facing overseers yielding whips and the KKK and their ropes with abilities beyond those of mortal men, able to change the course of mighty rivers and bend steel in their bare hands. Or let them appear during civil rights, during assassination season and stop the MLK murder at the Lorraine, or again, land on Earth during the peak of America's slavery."

"A bunch of Black supermen. They cute?"

"Of course."

"What complexion?"

"White to a quarter past midnight."

"Like we are now."

"The Black Kryptonians will have more hues of Blackness than flavors at Baskin-Robbins."

"How they gonna wear their hair?"

"Natural, unique to them, each hairstyle the character's signature."

"And that would be the first America your Black superheroes see?"

"First thing. First impression. Right away they learn about skin color and race, two things they never had an issue with on Krypton."

"The Black supermen can do everything white Superman can do?"

"Maybe more. Maybe melanin enhances their powers."

"No sickle cell or lupus?"

"They can't get high blood pressure, diabetes, or prostate cancer."

Momma nodded, emotional. "Put some of them here, in downtown Memphis, the day that Black girl was beat for nothing. Undo what I saw. Make sure you spell Lowenstein's store name right. Have them save that sister from that Simon Legree. We couldn't help her, and I was too young to do anything, but with your words, you could undo that wrong."

Momma took a paper towel, dabbed the tears in her eyes.

I held her free hand with mine, and she squeezed it tight.

She said, "Have some of them fall in a different wormhole and land in Africa at Jamestown right before the first slave ship did. Meet the slavers at the port, show them Erik Killmonger was right, and then burn it like the *Hindenburg* before you make it sink like the *Titanic*. Revise our history the way the victors have done both ours and theirs. Let us win. The only place we ever win is in books and in movies. Let us win."

"I will."

"And Momma gonna say this one time. Because she is worried."

"Yes, ma'am."

"If something is wrong, if something is going on, talk to me, Sweet Meat. If you can't talk to me or the Swimmers, talk to somebody."

"Nothing is wrong, Momma. Nothing."

She nodded. "Momma know how it goes, and it's a shame. Black men will talk and confess and seek advice from their barber before they go to therapy. Hard to get a Black man to open up. Black man don't let nobody touch him in a particular but his woman and his barber. So far as loyalty, a Black man will keep the same barber longer than he will a Black woman.

If a Black woman moves to another apartment too far away and gas prices high, the brother gets a new woman near his zip code. Might get two. If the barber moves across town to a new shop, the same brother fills up his tank and uses GPS and follows that barber wherever he goes. I know brothers who will track the barber down before they switched up. A Black man will see six women, but no brother lets two barbers cut his hair. He's not letting no other man comb his hair, touch his face, stand that close to him for that long, fix his fade, then close his eyes and drift off while the barber hums and covers his face with a hot towel. Then the barber massages his freshly cut beard or clean face with natural oils. He ain't letting no one else touch him in such an intimate way while he tries to address mental health issues and spills his guts, but that one barber."

"Momma. Nothing. Is. Wrong."

"You need your hair shaped up. Your beard too. Baby Doll is your barber. She is free all day. You trust her. That's all I'm saying."

"Momma."

"Momma done."

CHAPTER 63

SKYPE RANG ALMOST a minute before she answered. Hoped this wasn't another bad idea. The video call revealed a jittery woman with whitish skin, light hair, pallid eyes, full lips. My oldest sister.

"I hope this isn't some enemy of my enemy is gonna suddenly be my friend bullshit."

She rocked back and forth like a child on a hobbyhorse, then winced with a shock of pain.

What I saw changed the conversation I had planned to have.

She couldn't hide it, so she didn't bother to try.

Her right jaw was swollen; she had a blackened left eye.

She didn't stop rocking on her invisible hobbyhorse. "Surprised?"

"What happened?"

"Someone intentionally used the wrong pronoun and I kindly corrected them. They kept calling us men, and when I'd had enough I asked them to leave us alone. We wanted to unwind and have a few drinks. They took it as a personal attack. And don't ask me why I chose this lifestyle. After going to four funerals for our friends in a month, we wanted to get together, have drinks, laugh, cry, and give toasts to their memories. Instead we almost became four more dead bodies thrown away like trash."

"This normal for you?"

She rocked, head down, and wiped her eyes, before she said, "Happens too much. We call ourselves the Beyoncés. Last month we were attacked by a straight couple who were very transphobic in a downtown Los Angeles bar-restaurant. They threatened to come back and kill us and leave our bodies off a roadside in a ditch somewhere between here and Vegas."

My throat tightened, hands became fists. West Coast or deep in the Bible belt, Hancock Parking Sulemans never ended. It was in our blood.

"They fucking threatened you in public?"

"They threatened us, and the bar's managers put us out."

"What the fuck?"

"They dragged us out."

"Dragged?"

"Dragged."

"They kick the people who fucked with you out too?"

"They treated the people who assaulted us like they were right for attacking us. They threatened to bury our bodies in the desert where we would never be found and were rewarded with shots at the bar."

I shook my gotdamn head. "I thought Los Angeles was liberal."

"Who told you that?"

"You know, West Hollywood."

She slowed down the hobbyhorse and shot me a side-eye look that screamed that with all that was going on in the world, her world, I must've been sleeping under a rock, or not listening to her pain.

"Your name is Pi?"

"Yeah."

"Professor Pi Maurice Suleman of Nashville?"

"Memphis."

"No different there than it is here."

"Why stay there?"

"Why do Black people stay in the South with that hate and racism?"

"Good point."

"So far as my situation, at least I can get a cake made out here."

Then I was on the hobbyhorse, problem solving, slowly rocking.

I asked, "Where would it be safe for you to go stay?"

"Safe? For us? Nowhere."

"San Francisco?"

"Even in San Francisco you end up in Colma."

"End up in a coma?"

"In Colma. The city of the dead."

"Damn. Okay."

She shook her head. "Can you answer a question? I've asked people for years, but no one seems to know the answer."

"If I can answer it, I will."

"Does the devil know it's the devil?"

"No idea, but I'll research that starting with the King James Version of the Bible."

Her screen shook like she had been slapped; she jumped like she was under attack.

I asked, "What happened?"

She took a deep breath. "Nothing. Was an earthquake."

"You need to go?"

"It was an earthquake. Those come and go faster than the expo line."

Frustrated, I dragged my hands down my face.

I asked, "Has anybody in your family offered to help?"

"I don't have any family."

"You have at least one sibling living ten minutes away."

"As far as I'm concerned, I'm an only child."

"They don't care?"

"You met them. Draw your own conclusion."

"I'm your brother."

"I don't know you."

"I'm your brother."

"But. I. Don't. Know. You."

"Know me or not, like me or not, I'm still your brother."

Her hobbyhorse picked up the pace. "What do you want?"

"Wanted to reach out and say hello. Now I want to help."

"I don't need your help."

"We are on the same family tree."

"A tree I wouldn't hesitate to cut down."

"Before you turn this tree into kindling, this tree that other people planted, let's try to be family for ten minutes and see what I can do to at least help you feel safe."

"You look so much like him and act unlike him at the same time that it's scary."

"I'm not him. Never met him. Had a chance to before he died but I turned it down."

"His eyes. I'm looking in his eyes. Only they're not angry and disappointed. He dressed me in a football uniform when I was six. The moment I looked in the mirror and saw someone that looked polarly different from me, when I saw what didn't match what I felt like on the inside, I literally had a panic attack. At six years old. He caught me dressed up the way I felt inside . . . and . . . and . . ."

"I'm not him."

"You don't know me, and I don't know you, so you could be him risen from the dead."

"I know you."

"Really? Who am I, Professor Pi Maurice Suleman of Nashville?"

"Memphis."

"Pardon my French. Professor Pi Maurice Suleman of Memphis, but same fucking difference. You know me so fucking well after being in my life for five minutes, tell me who the hell I am."

Pain owned her soul tonight. I couldn't imagine what life had been like for my sister.

"You're a lonely girl who yearned for a supportive father who would've taken care of you and no matter what made sure you were doing okay."

She stopped rocking and cried like a child who had never been loved a day in her life.

I'd grown up with something unfamiliar to her. Having a loving family was beyond anything she recognized. Stephanie born Steven. My sister who used to be my brother. Her story was my story.

We cried together.

We wore our hobbyhorses out as the teardrops fell.

Again I gently asked my older sister what I could do to help.

I said, "Pack up and move somewhere safer, if not totally safe."

"There is no safe city for trans women. We have no guaranteed city or state as a haven. Like there was a *Negro Motorist Green Book* for Blacks telling us where it was safe way back during Jim Crow, we need one for us so we can have dinner without our lives being on the line."

"If you could move, where would you go?"

"Right now, I'd go anywhere but Texas or Trayvon's Florida, but no matter where I *travel* as a transgender person, I'll need a transgender motorist green book."

"Let's start with Los Angeles." I looked at paperwork. "There is a Suleman rental property with a contract that can have it vacant in thirty days."

"One of the places he sat down to break wind? No, thank you."

"Hear me out. I don't know that part of the world, but it's off First Ave. and Leffingwell by a KFC, one mile from Beach Boulevard and Imperial Highway in a city called Whittier."

She laughed. "You're right. You don't have a clue about LA. I don't speak Spanish."

"What about Victorville or Simi Valley?"

She laughed. "Now he wants to send me to where the KKK attack people with machetes."

"Help your new brother out; I'm driving blind here. Take the wheel for a moment and let's figure out how to get you resettled where you feel safer and can get a cake made for your next birthday. Where would you feel safe?"

"Sweden, Norway, and Belgium are the safest countries in the world for us. But I'm not abandoning my friends. We are in this together. They are my real family."

"Where do you live right now?"

"Where opioid addicts get hugs and crack users get slugs."

"That could be anywhere."

"I live in a janky one-bedroom apartment with three friends. It's beautiful. If I'm lonely, I can step outside my door and engage with tweakers, the local opioid addicts, and the vets who are mentally ill. It's not so bad. I can jog a mile past a hundred homeless people and buy me a latte at Starbucks."

My gripe about being a Black man from Memphis was as second-class as the government's treatment. I'd been hit by a car every day, but my older sister had spent her life getting run over by a passenger train every hour on the hour. Men and women who look like my skinfolk have always had to find a place to feel safe as a community. We always had to huddle together and be leery of strangers who saw us as a bit too unique for their sensibilities. But my older sister's problem existed at a level of mine raised to some ridiculous factorial. She was an unwanted Suleman. I had been treated the same way. Our emotions bounced back and forth; we became drunks sharing the same bottle.

"I need you to move."

"Why do we always have to be the ones to move? We're tired of fighting the terrorists but they not tired of fighting us. We are being murdered faster than tourists dying in the Dominican Republic."

"Can you report it to the FBI?"

"The same FBI that said Kendrick Johnson rolled himself into a gym mat and died? That FBI? As far as the help we're getting from that FBI, it might as well be due to natural causes. Or worse. Because when that FBI find us beaten and shot twice in the back of the head, that FBI treats it like it was a suicide."

The rocking slowed down, then sped up again, doubled its pace.

"Why should I trust you when I've trusted the wrong people all of my life? You have no idea what it's like walking out of your apartment and scared you might be killed because you are alive."

"Look, I have a sister here in Memphis. She's bisexual."

"You have a problem with her lifestyle? If you do, then you have one with mine."

"I've never had any problems with her doing what she does the way she chooses it."

"Wow."

"She's my sister. You are my first sister. She defers to me because I'm older, and you have the same rights. You're older, so that means in the end, I'll do whatever you say."

"You have a bisexual sister and you have a good relationship with her."

"She's my best friend, even when we're cursing each other out."

"You actually talk to her like she's a human being?"

"We hang out at the clubs in Memphis almost every weekend."

"You're friends with your sister?"

"Best friends. I see her almost every day, and we do dinners pretty much every Sunday."

She wiped away her tears. "You were right. I grew up a lonely girl who wanted a father to have tea parties with, wanted a supportive father who would've let me do his hair for fun, tell me nothing was wrong with me, that being different was okay, and, yes, wanted to be taken care of no matter what. I dreamed of having a father who would say it was okay for Steven to feel like Stephanie and loved me enough to go out of his way to make me feel safe in this crazy-ass hateful world."

She cried a little while on her hobbyhorse, then nodded as her rocking came to slow, then stop, finally ready to let me be her brother and help her out in some way.

She said, "You're a writer. Like him."

"I'm a writer, but not like him."

"Me too. But not like him."

"Really?"

"I'm writing a book about my life, been writing it for years."

"Yeah? What's it called?"

"*The Girl Who Used to Be a Boy.*"

"I like that title. Love it, actually."

We connected there, talked about writing, then my helping.

As a Black man, it felt like almost every white man was my enemy. For my sister, until proven to be a trusted ally, every man alive was her foe, rewarded a round of shots for making her kind disappear.

CHAPTER 64

THAT BLACK SUV followed me until I crossed the state line, then left the highway. It had followed me when I was with Gemma Buckingham.

We caught a storm and high winds on I-20, drove through a downpour. The unstable weather didn't keep the parking lot from filling up four cars at a time. By eleven P.M., I had driven Gemma Buckingham seven hours away from her view of Memphis-Arkansas Bridge to ATL. We parked and sat in the parking lot of a place called Trapeze. I had on a pair of my old straight-leg Trues and a plain Black T that fit me like grandma's girdle. Cars and SUVs, mostly with tags from out of town, unloaded amorous couples. Classy people hurried to go have fun in a diverse crowd. Nobody I recognized, but it still left me feeling a little anxious.

She said, "You've been pretty quiet on our road trip."

"Thought you were listening to the Audible book."

"That's never stopped us from chatting destination to destination."

I needed to know if I was still being followed, if the people in the mysterious SUV had done a handoff and someone different had stalked me from where the SUV dropped off the highway to here. If the judge had his boys kill me in a different state, there wouldn't be any blowback.

She asked, "Things okay, love?"

I put one issue on hold and spoke my mind regarding another. "You've stood us up three Sundays in a row."

She sighed. "I told you the day before I needed to reschedule due to conference calls."

"Three weeks in a row."

"Work has become more demanding than I anticipated. When it's nine in the morning in London, it's three in the morning here, and I have to take conference calls or look proper for a Zoom video conference. The six-hour time difference between here and London has me dealing with things at the most unusual hours, and due to that, I sleep whenever I can. Sunday is the only day I can accomplish anything before the market opens Monday morning."

"But you have time for me to come over and chill by the river on Sundays."

"Only time you're not busy grading papers or cutting your grass, Professor."

"You pull me from my usher's post in church to see about you."

"While I'm working."

"Three Sundays in a row. Pretty much a month of Sundays."

"Enough."

"Not this time. We can drive five hours to hang out, but you can't find time to take a fifteen-minute easy ride up the highway to drop in long enough to say a quick hello to my family. Interesting."

"Once again, love, told you the day before I needed to reschedule."

"Sunday is a church day."

"Not for the agnostic."

"Whether you go or not, it's usually the day everybody in M-Town slows it down and takes time to go visit other people, see how people are doing face-to-face."

"I don't know anyone out here other than you, really, and that doesn't apply to me. Again, Sunday is the day I can accomplish as much as I need to before the market opens on Monday morning."

"But you have time for me to come over on Sundays and ride you until you tap out."

"It's not mandatory."

"Okay. Noted."

"We do that, then it's back to work for me. Back to writing or grading papers for you."

"Take a break. One Sunday off."

"This yellow gal has to work and keep her lights on at her home in London, my love."

My underlying conflict had me tense, quick to argue, made me need to argue to let off some steam. I didn't want to fight with her, ever.

A car whipped into the space next to us so close that I thought Speed Racer was going to sideswipe my Nova. An Afrocentric sister got out of her car in a rush. She straightened her tight dress. A white man came up behind her, hugged him like she loved him, kissed him like she missed him. They held hands and hurried for the building, her leading the way.

Gemma Buckingham said, "Bet they will make beautiful yellow babies tonight."

"We could do the same."

"Then I'd join your royal family and be subject to the rules of the queen."

"We're commoners. But our child could be treated like royalty."

"Not before I meet your mother. And of course, the sister that was incarcerated a night."

"Why the snark?"

"This isn't close to me being snarky."

"Hard to tell at times. Gets lost in translation."

"That was this yellow gal being sincere."

She wanted to fight. Her underlying issues unseen as well.

We watched other happy couples head inside; then I turned to Gemma Buckingham. She had on jeans, heels, and a Meghan Markle T-shirt. SPARKLE LIKE MARKLE. This could change things for us.

Gemma Buckingham asked, "Shall we go inside? Will Harry put a little sparkle in the Markle? Or shall we drive back to Memphis? Either way will be fine with me, honey. I leave the night up to you."

"I need you to be sure."

"This is something I'd never do in London."

"You need this."

"I need this."

CHAPTER 65

WE UNDRESSED, SHOWERED, wore towels, mixed with a professional crowd of diverse folks of varying religions who were hedonistic after dark.

We moved room to room, were voyeurs holding hands while strolling through someone else's wonderland. We watched two Black men take on a Black woman. After that we had a drink and watched a thin, short woman and a tall, full-bodied woman show out as their husbands watched. A woman stood next to us, measuring. Gemma Buckingham led me into a private room, and we kissed, eased down in the fresh-smelling white sheets and made out, took our time, giggled at our behavior, laughed, got aroused, went down on each other, teased each other with Christians and sinners outside our door. She stopped, gave me a look that said she needed more than this, then stood up, put her saintly towel on, and left the room. She came back with a beautiful dark-skinned woman, a sylphlike goddess with her golden hair in its natural state. She was from Papua New Guinea, a good-smelling girl barely five feet tall, but looked like strength, pride, and wealth, her body unbelievably toned. Gemma dropped her towel. The stunning woman checked me out, then raised a naughty smile as she dropped her towel in approval, dropped her towel in capitulation to her own lust, nipples erect like she was born ready. They caressed each other, adjusted to the newness, touched breasts, shared kisses, took to mission-ary with the stranger on top, made out, enjoyed each other, and when it was steamy, parboiling, Gemma Buckingham looked at me, and her unnamed lover did the same. They invited me to join the party and make it a threesome.

CHAPTER 66

BACK AT THE hotel room, rain fell hard enough to flood from here to Birmingham. No one had trailed me from the swinger's club. Gemma Buckingham had her back to me as I relaxed, spooned up against her.

She said, "You couldn't do it."

"Learned one delicious woman at a time is enough for me."

"You didn't stop me."

"No man can stop a woman from doing what she wants to do."

"You see me differently now."

"Not really. I'm still learning you."

"Why didn't you stop me if you were that uncomfortable?"

"I've never seen you in a bonnet."

She laughed, and so did I.

She stroked me, got me hard, mounted me. Gemma Buckingham was on a whole new level, bouncing up and down like Solange, working it out like Beyoncé, making me call out to God and feel reborn. She fucked me like she was afraid I'd leave her, then collapsed.

She panted, whispered, "Pisces are emotional."

I caught my breath, had come hard, room was spinning. "Taurus needs a physical connection."

"Memphis on the Mississippi."

"London on the Thames."

"Pi Suleman."

"Gemma Buckingham."

She moved her thighs like she wanted more, needed me inside her to be sure I still desired her.

I asked, "You done that before?"

"Never. Here in America doing many things I would never do back home in London."

"Nothing wrong with that."

She moved up against me closer, kissed me like she was glad I understood. What I understood was she was a grown-ass woman, and that pussy was her pussy. She fell asleep, no bonnet on her brand-new do. Got her hair did and slept on it raw so a Black man from Memphis wouldn't see her looking the way a secure Black woman should at bedtime.

I picked up my phone, went to the window, and counted raindrops as I sent a text.

Atlanta? I'm here to scope out a few spots.

Told you I hate Atlanta.

Happened to be here. Nowhere here is better than where you are?

Well, if I had to, I guess. Buckhead rocks. I like Lenox Square.

Buckhead is expensive. Maybe few miles up the road in Midtown?

Do what you think is best.

I need to do what's best for you.

Can we talk about this later?

You safe?

As long as I stay inside with the curtains closed.

The second I stopped texting, in a moderately jealous tone Gemma Buckingham asked, "Who are you messaging at this hour?"

"My sister."

"The one who was incarcerated for an act of unnecessary violence?"

"The one you met."

"I've never met anyone related to you."

"You told her you liked her shoes. We were in Los Angeles at the lift."

"Your sister who used to be your brother? You have so many bloody siblings in California."

"Since you've never asked, let me tell you anyway. My mother had four kids after me. Four amazing kids. Most of us are two years apart, more or less. Two of them were born the same year. What we call ghetto twins. They have the same dad. He was engaged to Momma; then she disengaged the affair. Other than that, we all have different dads. We don't look alike, not unless we're with Momma—her features connect us all."

"No need to have an attitude or be snarky, guv'nor. No need at all to be rude as your mum."

I let the *guv'nor* insult die, then asked, "How's your brother?"

She snapped, "What brother?"

Gemma Buckingham caught herself. I'd caught her too.

She had said *what* brother, not *which* brother.

I pressed on, "Gemma Buckingham. Nothing comes up when I google you."

"You googled me?"

"I googled you, nothing. Guv'nor, you don't exist online."

She moved to the other side of the room, stared at a wall. "Why are you doing this?"

"That's scary. Your mood turned like Memphis weather in wintertime."

"Answer me. Can't you enjoy things the way they are between us?"

"I want the bonnet."

"Please, Pi. Stop."

"So, is your father Nigerian or Gambian? You left me confused on that one."

"I don't want to have a row with you, Pi."

"Just answer the question. Like you said about religion, some of us just need simple answers to simple questions in order for us to believe. Nigerian or Gambian?"

She stormed into the bathroom, irritated.

I took a deep breath.

Love and the inevitable danced.

I whispered, "And Bob's your uncle."

I picked up my phone, sent Roger de Groot a text.

I told him I needed his services again.

Before I invested a million dollars in a woman, I needed his help.

CHAPTER 67

WHILE GEMMA BUCKINGHAM was over in Cobb County in Smyrna at Deeply Rooted Natural Hair Care Center getting her Afro hooked up and colored honey blond, I drove sixteen miles away and met with an agent named Maddox at 400 West Peachtree Street Northwest. I parked my classic red Nova with the Tennessee Shelby County tags by luxury cars at Twelve Centennial Park. Condos ran at 235,000 dollars. Each had a patio with a pool. Kitchens with granite countertops and stainless-steel appliances. From the private balconies, I saw Stone Mountain. Miss Maddox showed me four side-by-side units that were unoccupied. The Realtor jokingly asked the adjunct professor which two I wanted to buy. Rainy-day special price. In a hurry, skies getting darker, I told her to write up the paperwork for all four at the discount she had offered. Then, as the rumbles in the skies grew closer with the rising of the wind, I picked up Gemma Buckingham, told her how pretty she was, said she was as pretty as a Yoruba princess from the Egbado tribe. Her eyelash extensions made it look like two butterflies had landed on her pretty face to rest a spell. Under a sprinkling sky, we shared kisses and booty rubs, the kind that preheat an oven.

We left ATL right away, trying to get my Nova to outrun a new family of thunderstorms and tornadoes. The difference between thunderstorms and earthquakes was they told you a thunderstorm was coming, and you had time to get ready. My Nova didn't care for the weather and took off like it was tired of being wet and happy to be pointed back toward M-Town, damn near driving itself.

I was in Roger de Groot mode, mentally fixing the bullshit problems my daddy had left behind. Momma had raised us all to be problem solvers. If you're not part of the problem, then you're part of the solution. If I went from sibling to sibling, if this Motherfucker went from Motherfucker to Motherfucker, I'd be fixing and fixing and fixing a dead man's bullshit for as long as it took the State Department to go through Hillary Clinton's e-mails. Gemma Buckingham ended up on her phone again, and that gave me time to do some more thinking. While she talked business, I talked mine, called Maddox back and said to double the number of units, write an offer for eight and find the second four as close to the first four as possible. My West Coast sister could pack up her life and take a few friends, could get with the only family she had ever known, and feel safer. Atlanta had to be safer and less depressing than staying hidden in her cracker-box apartment out in West Hollywood.

In Atlanta she'd be closer to me.

I told myself that I could look out for her.

But right now I wasn't sure if I could look out for myself.

CHAPTER 68

WE WERE PASSING through Nashville, trying to talk it out, figure out this relationship.

"I'm so sorry for my behavior. I mean it, Pi. I love you. I guess I'm jealous of you and your mother. I've never had that type of relationship with my parents. I did it all by myself with no support system."

"You're divorced."

"My teen marriage wasn't about love. Never was. It was my chance at manumission and a massive business opportunity. I saw an opportunity, was emancipated, married at sixteen, divorced the next year, and profited. My parents had their own marital issues at that point and were reluctantly happy to give permission and sign me away."

"One less bell to answer. One less egg to fry."

"Had my own money to invest. Started my own company at seventeen. Might've still been sixteen. My first company. A small company. He offered me twenty thousand pounds to agree to be his wife and have no wifely obligations. I needed seed money to pursue my dream. That was my intent going in. That and freedom from my parents. The marital collaboration was never meant to last. He needed citizenship and was willing to pay me to sign legal documents stating I was his wife."

"Twenty thousand pounds. That was probably thirty thousand dollars in my money back then."

"I wanted an adventurous lifestyle. I admit I wanted a flashy lifestyle. I wanted first-class cabins and penthouse suites. I wanted swanky clothes. I wanted freedom. I wanted quality healthcare better than what NHS offered. None of those are free in this world."

"You were focused at sixteen."

"We kissed once, at the ceremony, then went our separate ways, never spent a night together."

"I wouldn't consider that a marriage."

"Neither do I."

"You were married and divorced."

"Divorce is common. We have an official Divorce Day in London at the start of January."

"Really? Why January?"

"Because after the holidays, when people who claim to love each other have actually spent time together, after the long holiday break, when they've had day after day of shopping and family and intense time with each other, people get irritated and start to wonder if they belong together."

"Obviously not."

"So they end it before Valentine's Day. No one wants to be tethered to someone they no longer love or can no longer tolerate being intimate with on a holiday for lovers. Makes the day stressful."

"Here and in London, why so many divorces across the board nowadays?"

"Because women have money. Women don't have to stay. We can change our minds and begin a new life. Staying in a loveless marriage two generations ago was an act of survival more than love. It might've started off as love, but without your own money, it gradually became a prison."

"Your parents."

"All I'm saying is a woman shouldn't have to stay where she is unhappy."

"Men have to pay alimony and child support; some don't leave because it's cheaper to keep her."

"And when he leaves, her livelihood is tied to his income, ability to remain employed, and willingness to pay. Financial dependence is not freedom. A woman nowadays can earn more than men. We're better educated. Shit has changed. We are on our road to freedom. We just have to stay smart."

"So, if you have your own skrilla men will become expendable."

"Scary, huh? The idea that women will have financial power and men will possibly one day be treated the way they've treated women for so long. We will all be Beyoncé upstaging Jay-Z."

"No more fairy-tale dreams."

"Fairy tales are false."

"We all grow up on them. They've influenced us all. Especially the endings."

"Did you know in the original fairy tales most of the women were raped? Sleeping Beauty woke up and saw the prince had not only had his way with her, but she had a bloody baby. Cinderella's sisters cut their feet to make the shoe fit. It wasn't always a glass slipper. The women in those tales of horror were locked in castles and abused simply because they were attractive women. Then the horrific abuse was rewritten, became an unasked-for kiss, or a different kind of assault, and romanticized."

I nodded, then asked what I really wanted to know. "Tell me more about your marriage."

"I prefer to not get into the details of that situation."

"Kind of figured you wouldn't."

"Please don't hate me for it. I love you."

"I love you too, Gemma Buckingham. I know I love you because I'm patient with you."

"You are the best man, best lover I ever had, and that is scary. You let me be me, this version of me. I don't feel like I'd ever have the issues I had with the others with you. I want to be with you."

"But?"

"I remember a line from a movie regarding love. 'The Chinese say it is difficult for love to last long. Therefore, one who loves passionately is cured of love in the end.' That resonates with me. So does when they say, 'Human nature is eternal. Therefore, one who follows his nature keeps his original nature, in the end.' We might change a while, but we all go back to being our true selves in the end."

"Sounds profound. Which movie?"

"An Orson Welles movie rooted in existential anxieties, fatalism, and cynicism."

"Which one?"

"*The Lady from Shanghai*. Welles brilliantly plays a man drifting aimlessly around a bewildering world that keeps trying to tie him down. Deals with social contracts between men and women."

"I kind of remember that one, but not like that. I remember he fought a lot."

"Rita Hayworth. My mum looks like her. She loves that movie."

"Yeah. It's a love story."

"It's not a love story. Just because people have sex doesn't make the encounter a love story. It can simply be a sex-until-we-stop-having-sex story. A fool who thinks sex equates to love is in a predivorce story. Never confuse orgasm with love. Will save you a lot of heartache. And legal fees."

I let that linger, my mind on the two quotes, on the message being delivered.

As Roger de Groot had posed the question to me, I asked her, "Tell me who you are."

There was a long, uncomfortable pause. "Pi, no pressure, please?"

"Tell me the source of your pain, what makes Gemma Buckingham who she is."

She looked away, fidgeted. "One day I will."

"Over Sunday dinner?"

She sighed. "Give me a little more time. Don't keep asking. Let me tell you when I'm ready."

"Okay, I'll tell my folks. They won't trip. They will see you whenever they see you."

She nodded. "Thanks for understanding."

"I'll tell you who I am. Part of the makings of me."

"Okay. If you must."

"When I was growing up almost every kid I knew lived with aunts and grandparents and single moms. Hardly a dad around. And it seemed normal. We were roses growing out of broken and cracked concrete.

Children who grew up with two parents, even if one was a stepparent, were the outliers. From where we were standing, when we looked east, it looked like all white kids were corny but had nice homes up and down Parkway with a momma and daddy. We were shut out of the *Leave It to Beaver* lifestyle. The system did that to us. Laws create culture and ours is one America molded to fit its needs. America could've done better but chose not to. They broke all legal and social contracts. The lack of money and opportunities for all Blacks. Depression. PTSD. So much alcoholism. The mass incarcerations brought on by a league of rich and powerful men like the Judge of all Judges."

She shifted, perturbed, her words bitter and sarcastic. "London is no better to her Blacks, West Indians, East Indians, or Africans. Funny how most Americans think there is absolutely no racism across the pond for some reason. Sunday roast with Yorkshire pudding or eating sticky toffee pudding doesn't make them treat Black Londoners any better than the Black Americans eating barbecue. Eating fish and chips at Old Compton Brasserie and taking afternoon tea at Prêt-à-Portea at the Berkeley hasn't made the European savages more civilized in their hearts. Statues of their slave traders are on display. They live First World lives but have Third World morals. They've corralled us same as you. You have your ghettos and we have our crowded council estates where we live stacked on top of each other. Our bigoted NHS are masters at discrimination."

"I have no idea what NHS is."

"Truly frustrating to constantly have to give a dissertation on being Black and perpetually maltreated in London."

"What's NHS? A Negro society?"

"Google and learn about my world as much as I know about yours, American. Make an effort, love. Maybe skip the comics this week and read a novel about being Afropean or research any novel by a Black British writer who speaks on racism in London."

"Afropean. Never heard that term."

"Put Superman and that white world on hold and get enlightened regarding mine. Make some sort of an effort. Google. If you love me as you say you do, if I interest you, you will study the nuances of my world as I've been forced to study yours as a part of my curriculum."

"You grew up in council estates?"

"Spot on."

"Estates sounds classy, but I take it that's the hood."

"Again, spot on."

"That was in Brixton?"

"We had a very rough spot in between. That era defined me."

"How so?"

"Pi, please. Stop."

I was starting to think the woman didn't want to talk because she lied on her lies. Her lies were becoming a Russian nesting doll.

"Can't imagine you living in a ghetto."

"We all start somewhere, love. But what's most important is how we end up, envious or envied. I refuse to live my life envious of others."

"Something happen to you?"

"Black man from Memphis, when you meet *folks*, tread lightly because you never know what they've been through. Everyone is a story. Everyone has a story. We all have secrets. Dark secrets. We smile, put on designer clothes, and do our best to look like sunshine in darkness, try not to look like the abuse and hell we've been through. We get real pretty to hide the pain. We laugh. We dance. We love. We live. But it's been hell."

Her mood was dark as the other side of the moon.

She put her hand on mine, tried to keep the bond from breaking.

Another long pause. "One day, if you still want me, I will be open and give you my biography, and then I'm going to be yours forever."

I echoed, "Forever."

She gave me silence, and I returned the favor two times over.

"I hate that I have to go back to London awhile." She chuckled, no eye contact. "I can only stay here a certain amount of time; then I have to leave before they send ICE knocking on my door. I'll do what is required so I'm not permanently banned from traveling here."

"I get it. It's a legal thing."

"A million-dollar problem, love. Not to be taken likely."

"You have to pay your way into the dice game and hope you don't roll snake eyes or boxcars right away."

"I considered the business aspect. The known carries the risk of no return on your investment. You open your business and feel it's set for success; then you have something happen, some factor beyond your control, and you lose it all. It's not a good financial plan, the unknown."

"But you'll be back."

"I promise. I'll get right back to my baby."

"What about your house on the river?"

"I've been the perfect tenant and my landlord wants me back soon. They are willing to use the home as an Airbnb for a short while, provided I sign a new lease within the next six months."

"Six months."

"Unfortunately. I have conferred with solicitors and attorneys, both here and at home, and all are of the same mind, that working it out from London would be the best route. Unless I do like the Canadians and other Londoners do and stay here illegally and take my chances."

"You could move in with me on Blair Hunt Drive."

"Oh, you know your mum wouldn't allow that."

I said, "Should I drop everything and pack up and come to London for a little bit? I could dip for a semester, find out who I am in London."

"You wouldn't recognize me in London. This isn't who I am in London. All the things I am doing, how I behave, it is because I am free of London. I'm not carefree there. This is me at a new pace, at the pace of Memphis, not at the bustling pace of Central London and Westminster. This is me not being irritable and quarrelsome. I get there, there will be no time for you. I will either be popping in and out of other countries on business or in my office in the Gherkin taking meetings."

"I could be there and wait for you to be available, like you do with me here. Actually, I could keep busy by teaching a few classes online."

"I have a family of both Africans and Europeans who miss me."

"You've hardly mentioned them."

"I'd have to split my time between friends and family in Clapham, Camden, Shoreditch, Brixton, Canary Wharf, and Richmond. Once I get back there, I already know it will be work, work, work, work, work. When you own a company, you work twenty-four hours a day."

"You had time for Lennie."

"Pi."

I backed off. "No problem."

In a *whatever* tone she whispered, "Thanks for understanding."

Fresh fractures grew across my heart, but I smiled under dark eyes. "I've been getting pretty busy myself unloading problems left and right."

"Work?"

"My dad."

"Mr. Suleman, my mum's favorite author in the whole wide world."

"I thought the funeral was the end of our relationship, thought all would be buried, but it's turned out to be the fucking opposite."

"Stressed?"

"Yeah."

"Pull over. Let me fix that. Do it how you did it back at the hotel."

"I'm good."

"Saying no to road head?"

"I'm good."

"Turning down a sloppy blow job?"

"I guess so."

"Wow. Just . . . wow."

CHAPTER 69

A COUPLE OF legal problems popped up because two of the Motherfuckers related to me by blood were butt hurt. I had to go back to Los Angeles to deal with a final lazy man's load of legalities my dead old man had left behind. This time it didn't bother me. Traffic didn't bother me.

Feeling three aftershocks didn't make me stop sipping my latte.

Gold diggers who had never learned to be goal diggers hit concrete again, and that time they broke their sharpest shovels. Motherfuckers went back home no better than they were when they had come. The man who had raised them had made sure it would be that way. Not one of them had stopped by or brought him a cup of soup or sent him a text message or drove ten minutes to do a wellness check as he lay dying in slow motion for at least five years. That was cold-blooded as cold-blooded can get. When I was there, they treated me the same way they had treated him. Gave that rudeness to me without offering a handshake or a hello before the courtroom shouting started. They made an earthquake inside that building, brought them thunderstorms and tornadoes.

Felt like I had been through more hurricanes than Texas, Louisiana, the two Carolinas, and Florida combined. Those were some motherfuckers. The motherfuckers of all motherfuckers.

I read Komorebi's work to keep my mind occupied.

We held a two-hour writing session over Zoom.

She said, "Be brutally honest, Carver."

"Respect."

"Dag. Can I at least call you Carver?"

"Miss Jackson. We can end this session early."

"*Professor.* May I have your honest opinion?"

"Mechanics aside, what you've submitted is pretty good."

"For real?"

"Brilliant in some parts actually."

She was excited. "I'm going to be the next Morrison or Angelou."

"Never. But you can be the first Komorebi Jackson."

"Professor."

"Yes, Miss Jackson."

"I met your sister, the one who DJs at Love Club. It was the day I went to Arkansas to protest with Black Lives. We ended up standing right by each other. I got a selfie with her. She's cool for a U of M grad."

"Okay."

"And I met your mother too. They were together. We selfied too."

I gave up a deep, deep sigh. "Do the work and we'll be cool."

"They're following me on IG. Will you follow me now?"

"No."

"You're actually in LA right now?"

"West Coast for a day or two. Seventy degrees. Cooler at night. Windows open, wearing a UAN hoodie. Chilling and representing."

"It's in the high nineties here. I'm so jelly right now."

I didn't tell her, but I sent her work to my literary agent in New York. He knew an African American in publishing named Jack Bouvier. That was like finding a unicorn. Black editors were as hard to find as Black justice. Wasn't a Black woman like Little Miss Manassas wanted, but it was a start. Could be the ladder she needed to get over that wall.

I ended the session, took in my space. I didn't stay at a hotel this time. I stayed in the three-level house in the Black Beverly Hills.

It was an area filled with six- and seven-figure-income brothers, sisters, and a couple of white folks. Miles of Black folks in hundreds of two- and three-level homes starting at about a million and a half for three bedrooms and no land to speak of. Nothing like that was in Memphis.

I stopped being a Swimmer, became a Motherfucker.

I put on a brand-new suit, held my arms out, and fell backward into the big swimming pool, did like Matthew McConaughey did in one of his Lincoln Navigator commercials, only I was cooler. Mine was sauced with M-Town's one-of-a-kind 38109 swag.

In the morning I walked the area, passed Black people jogging, walking dogs. Almost everybody waved at me. Most were African American. There were a lot of white people too. An Asian woman passed by pushing a baby stroller. Every other house was getting its lawn serviced by men who looked Latino. Crews of Latina women parked and went to clean Black folks' mini mansions. I was a stranger to their eyes, but no one called the police on a Black man from Memphis walking their streets admiring their big houses and cars with personalized plates. I apologized to the city for how I'd felt about her, for that misjudgment, but not for how I felt about my dead old man. That motherfucker woke up every day trying to figure out to make his life that much more complicated. Now the motherfucker had died and complicated mine.

When the golden hour arrived, I took a luxury ride and found PCH, rode with the top down and cool ocean air on my face. On the West Coast I was a different man. I was free of Memphis. I was a stranger everywhere I went. I stood out. A Motherfucker. I told Siri to direct me toward Malibu, where there were no drive-bys, unless it was the postman.

I called Four Ds and left a message. "Mane, you ain't gonna believe where I am."

WHILE I CRUISED the Fresh Prince's zip code, I called Gemma Buckingham to check in. She answered sounding like her life was in dire straits. She was in tears, watching a BBC news report about Duchess Meghan and all the racist tweets rained on her by sophisticated people across the pond.

Gemma Buckingham said, "She has endured so much. People don't understand. So many racist attacks. The British are horrible, unrepentant racists. I'm ashamed of my country. I don't blame these two for wanting to escape the incessant racism and judgment. I can't imagine why a beautiful, intelligent girl like Meghan would want to get involved with it in the first place. Ruthless savages."

"There are ten thousand ways to call a Black person a nigga without saying *nigga*."

"London has mastered them all. Most insults ring like compliments from your nana. Being Black in the UK is not an easy ride. White boys tied a Black boy to a lamppost and did a mock slave auction."

"America wasn't populated with your best. America was a dumping ground for criminals, rapists, and rejects. The racism that's killing us here was built there. Tell me who to send a thank-you card."

"Your president is dog-whistling there while our prime minister openly slanders women and does the same here. Brexit has them showing their true faces. Our true history has been erased here as well."

"You gonna be okay?"

Gemma Buckingham vented, "If they didn't know Meghan Markle was mixed race, half of London would probably want Kate's husband to give up his royal birthright so Meghan could be their next Queen. One drop of Black blood has made all the difference in the world."

She was back to her angst of all angsts. I said, "Yeah, well, imagine if she looked like Lupita, Yvonne Orji, or Naomi Campbell."

"*I bloody hate it when you do that.* Everything isn't a joke."

"I was serious. But okay."

"The knowledge that Meghan has one drop of Black blood should be celebrated as the country and the stiff upper lips finally becoming progressive, but instead has ruined it and in their bigoted eyes it has killed the value of her intellect and devalued the currency of her beauty."

I listened to her sob, didn't compare her anguish to anyone else's.

She said, "I'll ring you after I finish crying for her as if I am crying for myself."

CHAPTER 70

AS MY COACH flight made it back to the humid air I knew, my plane pitched and yawed and touched down hard in the land of the delta blues in the middle of the pouring rain. That night I found out Gemma Buckingham had done a Brexit. She notified me as she sat in first-class on a non-stop British Airways flight, right at takeoff, and the message was delivered by text. She did it like an earthquake, that event that came without a warning, and it wasn't until after it had shocked you that you realized what had happened. When I talked to her on Skype three days later, I barely recognized her voice. The London accent was stronger, deeper, unapologetic. The Afro was gone. She had colored and changed her hairstyle. Her naturally curly hair was brunette, straight and silky, rich, healthy, and reflective, super-glossy, in a half-up bun hairstyle. She wore plum lipstick, mascara, and a wash of bronzer. She looked very polished, was a brand-new kind of beautiful in clothes unfamiliar to my eyes; a style and creator more British. She was a new woman in London. Or her old self. In Memphis, she'd worn her hair in the style of Black freedom while she dressed for fun and adventure. Now her attire was smart, business, designer head to toe. I wondered which brand of perfume she wore. Wished I could smell her now.

Lips pushed up into a happy smile, she said, "Good to hear from you, Professor."

"Gemma Buckingham. You're back across the pond."

"Where everything is familiar. Where I understand what everyone says. Where I'm not the one considered to have an accent. The high streets, the bookshops, everything makes sense again."

I said, "A huge time difference is sitting between us."

"Six hours. Your day ends as mine starts."

"What does Memphis seem like to you from there?"

"A dream."

"Dreams are things that didn't happen."

"Some you wish could last forever. But we all have to wake up."

We sat on that a few seconds. Her phone was blowing up.

Gemma Buckingham said, "My day never ends. The self-employed are never off work."

"Is it raining where you are?"

"No." She laughed. "But give it ten minutes."

"The weather over there is fickle as a few people I know back here and other places."

"The weather over here has been known to change its mood at the drop of a hat, yes."

"Raining hard here."

"It's chucking it down there and we're having a rare spot of sunshine here."

"Been raining hard off and on since you left."

"Rain doesn't last forever. Storms always blow. Sun eventually comes back. Even here in London the sun shines bright every now and then. Over here when the sun is out, everyone is happier it seems."

I'd become that frustrated guy on the other end of the phone.

I'd become the next Lennie.

Her Pakistani assistant opened her office door and caught her off guard.

"Guv'nor, to welcome you home, your amazing assistant stood in the massive queue and managed to get you two tickets to your fav spoken-word artist, Princess Latifah at *Rebirth of the Griot*."

"Yaseera. On a call."

"Germany?"

"Memphis. Personal."

"Ooops. Sorry."

With the office door wide open, her remarkable door nameplate stood out.

It was bold, had Black letters on a beautiful exotic wooden plaque.

While Gemma Buckingham dismissed her assistant, I did a screen shot of her nameplate.

I paused. "Guv'nor, over here I'm Pi, Sweet Meat, Professor, nigga, depending on where I am and who is standing in my face. I could come over there and wear a new name. See who I am away from my family, my friends, America, and all I know. Become a Black man from Memphis in London. I'd be where nobody knew me and I could buy London clothes, reinvent myself, and be anybody I wanted to be."

"Pi."

"Yes, Gemma Buckingham?"

She detected a change in my attitude. Tight smiles were exchanged. Nothing was said.

I asked, "Gemma Buckingham, how long will you be in London?"

"I'm not sure."

"Indefinitely, Gemma Buckingham?"

"Pi."

"Gemma Buckingham."

Her phone rang. A business call from Belgium.

I said, "Gemma Buckingham. Talk soon?"

She nodded. "Cheers."

Instead of clicking the red icon and terminating Skype, I clicked the icon that turned off my video, then hit the mute button.

On her end the screen went dark and silent.

I made it appear that I had hung up.

She saw the dark screen then rubbed her temples and looked away.

Sighed.

So much frustration.

I loved her and watched her not love me.

While she chatted, I regarded my screenshot, used two fingers to enlarge the photo, zoomed in on her expensive office door, the door of a CEO with her name in stylish importance on a stunning plate.

The Belgium call lasted less than a minute.

She hung up, sat there in a trance, barely blinking.

Yaseera returned, opened the door, then took three steps inside.

Yaseera said, "Guv'nor, you seriously checked if you can become a citizen of the US?"

"I'd have to marry for love and after three years I'd be a citizen."

"Iiiiiissss iiiiitttt? That's excessive."

"Init? It's so jokes."

"After three years most couples can't stand each other. But at least you'd be a citizen."

Gemma Buckingham joked, "I could always join their military and fight their bloody wars."

Yaseera laughed. "You mentioned somethin' 'bout qualifyin' for an entrepreneur license."

"I could buy my way into the big poker game if I invested at least five hundred thousand on a business. And could cost as much as a million US. A million dollars. Is a lot to pay to keep a man or a woman."

"All that for some dick?"

"Blimey. Really? Stop being such a wind-up merchant and be serious for one second."

"And I can't stop you from being so tight and lend me five quid and I'm skint until payday."

They laughed the way women laugh in the absence of men.

Gemma Buckingham said, "Depending on location, as much as 774 *thousand* British pounds."

"Hope you don't mind. I did a bit of research on your behalf and found a study that said Memphis is ranked at number nine on the list of least educated large cities in the US. To risk and invest a million US there . . . and not invest that here in London where you know the terrain would not be wise."

"It's business. All relationships to some extent are business. Or become about business."

Yaseera said, "You've said a million times."

"And like businesses most intimate affairs fail within five years."

"You've said a million and one times."

"We have a bloody Divorce Day for a reason. Probably should have one for each season."

"No argument there."

She touched her brunette hair, hair now styled like the tresses of her idol. "It would cost me a bomb."

"It's a bit dear. He offer to go halfsies?"

"Not at all, Yaseera." Gemma Buckingham released a chuckle that sounded like irony. "I worked for my money. His father died and he was handed his. On one hand I was happy for the professor, and in the next breath I resented that as well. My dispassionate African father never gave a pence that he wasn't forced to give me and English mum for maintenance and I suffered for it for years. I made so many sacrifices to achieve my dreams and my lover inherited a bloody fortune overnight."

Her chuckle became a soft, seething laugh of hate and jealousy.

Yaseera laughed too, only hers was meant to diffuse, not cosign. "Usually a woman leaves a man because he's poorer, not richer."

"I've never been the usual woman. But that really wasn't an issue."

Gemma Buckingham looked at the computer as if she were looking at me, unknowingly gave me eye contact.

I jumped, then relaxed again.

She had no idea I was still watching this corner of her world on Skype. I saw a bookcase and zoomed in. Next to the two novels I'd written were *Cry, the Beloved Country, So Long a Letter, Aké, The Passport of Mallam Ilia*, and *Things Fall Apart*.

Gemma Buckingham said, "Pop over to Forbidden Comics and pick up my pull list tomorrow."

"I have the funny books you missed stored away in my office."

"And I have a novel on hold at Maxim Jakubowski's bookshop."

"Something erotic at the latter, I take it?"

They laughed.

I sipped infused water and watched the British women have girl talk. Really wanted to sip dark liquor while I watched what was said in the

424   ERIC JEROME DICKEY

absence of men. Even if I were drunk this would be sobering, hearing these excited utterances in the absence of a BMFM. I stood witness to the secret life of Gemma Buckingham, a woman with an amazing name-plate on the stunning door, a door that easily cost as much as a down payment on a five-bedroom home in the heart of Germantown.

Yaseera asked Gemma Buckingham how she was doing in a real and genuine way. She stopped laughing, her lips quivered, and she cried.

Gemma Buckingham told her assistant, "We'd popped back to the hotel for a bit of how's your father and afterward he was sleeping. The jet lag had him. I was exhausted too, my circadian rhythm disturbed as well, but my mind was on fire. It was one of the nights when we were in Los Angeles for his father's funeral. After I had met his rude mum over the phone. I stared at him. Upset. Tears in my eyes. This yellow gal was very perturbed. I put on a comfy hotel robe, poured myself a glass of wine, and stood on the balcony in the chill of the night. Needed my alcohol and my space. We never used a condom. My fault. I was not the woman I am here when I was there. Who I was there took more risks and was more daring than I am in London. I was in America playing with fire. Didn't want to put myself in a situation. But the possibility crossed my mind. He knew the risk as well. Babies came to mind. Marriage did too. I had to ask myself some hard questions. I knew he'd never leave America. Unlike mine, his family ties were strong. He'd barely been out of Memphis. He didn't have a bloody passport. Had to envision myself perma-nently living in his city. In that humidity. With those mosquitoes and tics. Had to ask myself if I had kids did I want them to have American values. Southern American values. London isn't perfect but across the pond they'd grow up in the presence of guns. The blatant racism would influence them as well. They have daily shootings. They have school shootings practically every day. That disturbed me. I had to ask myself if I would want them in that unconcealed southern racism and live in the presence of the wicked Confederate flag people. Had to ask myself if my children would be safe. And get the level of education I'd prefer. I pon-dered if that southern accent was the accent that I wanted my children to wear. I'd be the funny-talking mum, the odd one out in my household. Everyone in my home would be American but me. The biggest thing was contemplating family issues. Mine would be here in London, out of sight and out of mind. My mum and dad could visit the same way they have lived most of my life, separately. I wasn't convinced his family was the type of people I wanted my children to associate with, even if only on bank holidays. You marry a man, you marry his family. And to be honest neither his California nor his Memphis family left me with a favorable impression. It was a study in extremes. I know. I'm one to talk with the African and English families I've been gifted. You marry a woman and you marry her family as well. You marry her kinfolk, as they say over there. I'd rather mine remained single. Better for society. I wanted him. Only him. It was a sex thing at first. A fantasy. A woman taking care of her needs. He's a handsome man. We all want sex with good-looking men. We deserve sex with good-looking men. I read his books and was mentally aroused. His intelligence. His sense of humor. His kindness. He challenged me, made me reexamine how I viewed myself as a woman of color in some ways. It became more than shagging. But the shagging. He broke me good. He did things that had me tripping. One night with him and all I wanted was him. But I couldn't have only him. I'm too much a realist to be a true romantic. We all have to get out of bed at some point. We can have sex for twenty minutes, but there are over twenty-three more hours left in the day. Who are we when we're not shagging? Who are we when the orgasmic high dissipates? We have to let orgasms fade and face reality. Everyone is a package deal on some level. Their issues become your issues. Meghan Markle learnt that. Whoever you marry influences you. Their family becomes the family of your children. Your history becomes part of his life, and vice versa. It can be overwhelming. Meghan definitely learnt that. We are all package deals. We all show up carrying invisible baggage as well. I hid mine very well and he exposed me to his. All I said he took at face value. They all did. It was fun. He still has no idea what I've hidden. Almost told him the first time he spent the night. Wanted to clear things up. Glad I didn't. But I only wanted him. Not his baggage. Not his friends. Not his family. Just him. Just the fantasy. The wicked shagging. For myself. That was selfish of me."

Yaseera let her finish, then dabbed her eyes. "Guv'nor, I understand. When serious, all things must be considered. Like you repeat, in the end it does become a business, if not another job. Children take it to another level. For some, rushing to have children is rushing to unhappiness."

"Oh, stop being cynical."

"That's like asking me to stop being British."

"So true."

"Learned from the best. Primarily me own mum. She's almost as good as you."

"Am I overthinking this?"

"You're reacting to what you saw at home. To Lennie. That scarred you as well."

"Left me unhinged, dysfunctional, emotionally disabled."

"You left here in shambles."

"We were there for his famous father's outlandish set of funeral and memorial services and I allowed him to use me as his comforter, to take this body and do with it as he pleased to please him, was there to relieve him of all stress incurred by the occasion, tended to him as I used him to attend to my own needs. Sex, nap, sex, nap, repeat. It was an inner massage that induced multiple orgasms as therapy. I was stressed as well. Carrying my secrets was stressful. Being who I was there, who I needed to be there, that was at times nerve-wracking. At times I woke up confused, a stranger in a strange land, felt lost and it showed in my reaction, or nonreaction when addressed by my American name, and I didn't know who I was until I touched my hair, until I felt the power of my amazing Angela Davis Afro. I wore a bloody Afro there. I was Gemma Buckingham. I was pro-Black day and night. New attitude and wardrobe. You wouldn't have recognized me from a distance."

Yaseera swooned. "Guv'nor, I'm on a bit of a dry spell and need that in my life."

"It was stormy there. The storms in Memphis were terrifying and exciting at the same time. I love being frisky when it's tipping down. When it's nice weather for ducks I can have sex, nap, sex, nap, rinse, shower, snack, repeat. The thunder and hard winds added energy to each round of shagging."

"I would love to have a relaxing day in bed having sex and of course eating after being eaten."

"Indeed."

"Until drained. Then be creative in other ways. Explore, play, learn."

Gemma Buckingham nodded. "I love that. We were like that at the magnificent home I leased on the Mississippi River. We had fun all over the bloody house. I slept hard after good sex. Had me snoring."

"If you ain't snoring the sex was boring."

"All we did was shag and seemed like we couldn't do it enough."

"Dickmatized."

"Was seriously wankermatized."

Yaseera took a breath. "That changed for me after I had me baby. During pregnancy I was ravenous. After Zion was born it was as if my body changed and that switch was turned off for almost two years. Didn't care for sex, not at all. My husband suffered. Ruined my marriage. Then it gradually came back on. For a while just the idea of having a shag like I used to was . . . bodily fluids were disgusting."

"I can't imagine. The way I was with that Black man from Memphis, can't imagine."

Yaseera handed her a tissue, then asked, "Would it be different if this Black man from Memphis, as you call him, had arrived in your life before Lennie? Or perhaps long after?"

"Or instead of. Instead of. This Black woman from Brixton is ruined now. Absolutely ruined."

"Lennie devastated you. Crushed your heart. You left so abruptly."

"It's the best way to leave. If you stick around for a conversation, they will make it more difficult to go or convince you to stay in a burning building and inhale the toxic fumes. Sometimes you have to rip the plaster off and suffer the consequences of the pain. If you are unable to perform such a task, you wake up and realize you're unconsciously dating your dad and will eventually become your mum."

"Lennie went to Birmingham, and as soon as his train left, you packed and ran to an obscure part of America. Within minutes."

"Packed my favorite pants, landed in Memphis, Tennessee, saw Elvis's ghost, and began getting on with my life, got a new hairstyle and better attitude. You would not have recognized me across the pond. I wore higher heels, tighter dresses, and shorter skirts. Was no longer conservative. No longer cared. Relative to here, life was so inexpensive. Played games. Lived out a bucket list of fantasies. I woefully left here and quickly became someone else. No false hope, no redress, no looking back. I was free of Lennie and the humiliation and the heartbroken skin I wore in London. I became my alter ego."

"And now you're free of America."

"I can create an empire no problem. When it comes to men and love I am such a divvy."

"Aren't we all at some point? Especially after a pint."

"Never again."

Yaseera told her, "You are an ambitious woman of divine beauty and unconquerable intelligence, destined to have her name written in the fabric of the human narrative. You're my Cleopatra."

"She killed herself."

"Not until she was thirty-nine."

"As an act of devotion her servants killed themselves."

"Let's rethink this, shall we?"

They laughed. This was their self-deprecating British humor.

A storm raged outside my window as it did in my chest.

Numbness covered me as I listened, learned, and nodded.

Gemma Buckingham set free authentic feelings; my lover from London softly cried and blew her nose, vented what sounded like a long letter about love and her beloved country. The best things do fall apart. Her guarded words toward me and her teary-eyed confession to her assistant didn't match. I understood. People said things in the moment, released things to set free built-up pressure before they exploded. Folks said things in private, in anger, or when triggered, at times during or after orgasm, crowed things that they felt in the moment but might not feel forever.

Yaseera said, "Money aside. You'd have to give up all familiar. No friends there. No family. Everything you know would be thousands of kilometers away. Not everyone is built for that sort of change."

"Giving up her life and family for love hasn't done Meghan Markle any favors."

"Sometimes it's easier to keep it plainsies and just stay home."

"Keep it plainsies and stay home and live with the racism you know."

Yaseera asked, "How was it there? Just like on the telly?"

"I visited America, witnessed their unprovoked racism. They didn't do monkey chants and throw bananas, but I now understand how Black footballers feel when they play in Italy or Spain. And the Black Americans are no better with their colorism. This 'yella gal' . . . never mind. Can't begin to imagine what life was like for Meghan. She grew up in an African American area. Can't imagine what she endured."

"Was it that bad, really?"

"The professor was professional, albeit in an uneven and emotionally challenging mood due his father's death. He was an arsehole to all around him. We rode through the ghetto and he became ghetto. When we were in a very posh, upper-class borough called Hancock Park, for a moment I no longer recognized him. Frightened me."

"What happened there?"

"A white man bumped into him. Intentionally. He was ready for war. He saw it as defending himself and the culture. Compared to all I've endured, I saw it as a nothing burger. He didn't consider my life. I'm a woman. A Black woman from another country. There alone on a bloody passport. I was a bloody foreigner. I could've ended up treated like a bloody Mexican and incarcerated in the Los Angeles female version of Her Majesty's Prison. Brixton wearing red-bottom shoes and a new provocative dress that cost over five hundred US dollars over my Agent Provocateur."

"Jail at their version of Her Majesty's."

"Gave me bad memories from my incarceration here."

"Teen years. Flashbacks."

"Acted out because of my father's absence. Became a hooligan."

"You corrected your course."

"Maybe it was him lashing out at a stranger because of his relationship with his father."

"Your father?"

"The professor. Memphis."

"I can see that."

"I could relate to that, but I've never directed my anger due to my father at another wanker. Same for the anger I harbor for my mum."

"His relationship with his mum?"

"Pure love. It was pure love."

"Enviable. No room for you?"

"Enough."

"Sorry, love. Sorry."

She took a breath. "'Please, sir, I want some more.'"

"Enough."

Gemma Buckingham nodded, eyes blank, whispered like she was a child trapped in a Dickens novel. "'Please, sir, I want some more.'"

That phrase was on repeat.

Her assistant hugged her like a mother, rocked her and hummed as she gently finger combed the wealthy gov'nor's Meghan Markle mane, mothered her until the Dickensian murmurs faded, then ended, until her boss's nude lips stopped moving and eye blinking resumed, her eyelash extensions again two calm butterflies in a lazy flight.

Her assistant backed away, grinned. "You were saying?"

"If you visit a place for a short holiday, many things go unnoticed. Like a trip to the islands. You live in the luxury afforded to tourists but ignore and don't have to see the poverty. Their politics aren't yours. You don't see their truth. When you live there, you start to see the truth. It unravels right before your eyes. I lived in America. Ate their food. Saw their world beyond the myopic view tourism offers."

"How did you find it, overall?"

"Too many Black Americans are culturally trained, maybe massively brainwashed, and they have the remarkable ability to embrace Africa and shun Africans at the same time. They claim the motherland, fetishize the fatherland, but can have mental issues with Africans, especially if they are too African. Africa is a concept to them, a fantasy, not a reality. Their ignorance is a leftover present from white people, their disdain rooted in European standards, and the cultural confusion I witnessed the residual effects of colonialism, no doubt. I am African. They pretend to be African. I didn't find it amusing."

"You lived among the Americans."

"Black Americans might disagree, but I am on point based on my experiences and perspective. My conclusion is an accurate indictment and condemnation based on my personal knowledge and firsthand conversations as well as observations. This *yellow gal* experienced a new dimension."

"Yellow gal?"

"A pejorative that was thrown at me by someone I'd never met, and never will meet. Two words, how they were delivered, ruined me. I felt the way a Jewish person feels when they hear an antisemitic insult. I was back on the tube with my parents being laughed at. I was being called a mule again. Left me remembering all the insults Meghan has had to endure in pursuit of her fairy tale love. Felt like I'd been insulted by the queen of Memphis. I'm not one to grin and bear it, but I did that time. I think that watershed moment changed everything for me."

Yaseera scrunched her face. "Blimey."

"Said I looked so yellow I probably owned the color, insulted me, then invited me to dinner."

"Our racism is coy and coded."

"You have to read between the lines here."

"Americans aren't known for being subtle."

"It's as if they strive to be offensive at every turn. And I was tempted to move there."

Still fascinated, Yaseera asked, "How was everyone else there?"

The woman born in Brixton ranted on, told her assistant, "A few of the southern whites I encountered were equally obtuse and terrifying. I felt uneasy at times. You have a basic disagreement there and their solution is not to have a healthy debate, but to shoot you. Anything gun related happens, the first thing they do is rush to buy more guns. Makes no sense. I watched their news. And on a political level, any inconvenience imposed by their version of Parliament, even when temporary and good for others, is somehow a violation of their rights. Even when it's law and for the betterment of society. In some parts even little old women carry guns like they are bobbies. It felt like at any moment they would have part two of their bloody civil war."

"Their mentality escapes me."

"Cops aren't supposed to shoot an unarmed Black man. Doesn't matter if he's committed a crime. They aren't supposed to kill guilty people either. If they can keep bringing in El Chapo without a scratch, they can find a way to de-escalate and arrest Black people. Innocent until proven otherwise. Then everybody gets a trip to Burger King for a Whopper. I feared for my life day and night. And I still would've moved to that iron-hearted country and learned how to make grits and proper barbecue."

"What are grits?"

"Exactly."

"Can one try a grit?"

"Never asked."

"For American cock. Was the pleasure pump that good?"

"It was good kielbasa. The best I've had, to be honest. He was so bloody handsome and exotic. When it came to racism or being slighted, he had a bit of a temper, though. Almost put me in a bad situation in California. I could've become a hashtag. His southern accent melted me. Was hard to come to my senses and walk away."

"A Black man from Memphis."

"He put it *down*. Hung like a horse with a tongue like a giraffe."

"And he was a professor?"

"I learned that a hung professor from UAN will stimulate you in all ways, arouse you mentally, have you moaning all evening, half the night, then wake and run you like a river twice the next morning."

"Had to be hard to walk away from that."

"Was hard to walk after that. Could barely crawl."

"And his father was the famous writer who wrote the Forever series? That's one of my favs."

"He was the son of Mr. Suleman."

"You shagged someone famous."

"Once removed."

"The famous Mr. Suleman's son. Lucky you."

"You sound like my mum."

"All evening, half the night, run you like a river in the morning. I'd love to have that experience."

"So would my mum."

"I should book me a flight to America, get sexy, and walk their Beale Street, see who I meet."

"You should. You might not come back. I almost didn't. Not sure I should have."

"I don't have a million to spare, and I'm not as smart as you, and never will be one short of a sandwich for a picnic, but, love, but I know a bad deal when I see one. Walk away. Unless you can run."

"I did. Abruptly. And it has left me gutted. I can't remember how to do anything today. It's like I'm going mental or something. I'm a bit peckish as well. But I'm craving American food. It will pass."

"Do you fancy a builder's tea and a few biscuits to help you feel betta?"

"Sure. I'd love a cuppa, but no biscuits. On me diet. I must've gained a stone while I was there. They eat so bloody much. What they serve on one plate for each meal could feed a family of four people here."

"Builder's tea it is."

"Two sugars."

"I'm on it like a car bonnet. Might pop by Forbidden for your new funny books. Then to your favorite Russian's bookshop for your erotica."

"If you had a wanker like a Black man from Memphis, I'd marry you."

Yaseera laughed. "Cheers."

"Cheers."

The assistant left, opening and closing the expensive door with the impressive nameplate. Gemma Buckingham frowned at the darkness on the screen again, lips turned down, her mood revealed.

She was unhappy, angry, and frustrated, backed into a corner.

She mumbled, "Daft idiot. Over a bonnet. Over a bloody Sunday dinner."

I don't know if that insult wrapped in irritation was directed at me or at herself. For a moment it looked like she was about to burst into tears, but she shook it off. She sat a moment, annoyed, couldn't stop checking her phone, then pulled a stack of newspapers closer. British tabloids. *The Independent. The Daily Star.* The *Daily Mirror.* The *Daily Express. The Daily Telegraph. The Guardian. The Guardian Weekly. The Observer. The Sun.* The *Daily Mail.* All had Meghan Markle's face on the cover. The captions were as unflattering as they were bold and easy to read. Each paper in the land of the aristocrats was classless, tasteless, as harsh and skanky as the local *National Enquirer*. The tabloid press that killed Princess Diana called the mixed-race American-born duchess a palace wrecker, a Lady Macbeth poisoning the prince, and compared her son to a chimpanzee.

Gemma Buckingham's hair was just like Meghan Markle's. That harsh and racist tabloid scrutiny was the life she imagined if she had chosen to cuddle with me for what was left of eternity.

This was the movie *Notting Hill*, our version, the one with two broken hearts. She was Julia Roberts and I was Hugh Grant, the roles reversed. I was a boy eavesdropping on a girl, rocking, silently asking her to love him. It had to be her decision, had to come from her heart.

She had to want me.

She paced a while, arms folded, shaking her head, her hair moving side to side with her torment. Soon she pulled it together and sat back down. Gemma Buckingham was rapidly typing, then paused, stared at her screen, noticed something that made her do a double take, then jerked.

"Bloody hell."

She turned with a quickness, heels clicked as she raced toward her office door. Maybe it suddenly occurred to her that her assistant had come in and opened it wide. Again, she considered her computer. The way she glowered, I bet she was checking for the office door's clarity in her screen's reflection. Her eyes went from the screen to the entry of her office. Gemma Buckingham stood slowly, moved to the door, opened it wide, then sat in her chair again, stared into her screen again, then gazed back at her impressive nameplate from the vantage point of her computer.

Her magnificent door marker was CEO large.

She wanted everyone to know she was the boss.

Gemma Buckingham stood in front of her inscribed name, anxious, then returned to her high-back leather office chair and started typing a rapid message, never blinking, then stopped as fast as she started.

Her eyes widened.

I knew why.

She noticed the timer on Skype was still going, and that meant we were still connected. She shivered like the hairs on her neck stood up. Her expression changed, told me she no longer felt like she was alone.

Looking in the camera, she tilted her head, whispered, "Pi?"

My heartbeat quickened.

With a nervous smile, she asked, "Are you taking the piss?"

She felt my energy and I felt hers.

Gemma Buckingham's back stiffened. "Pi."

Her perplexed expression told me she wasn't one hundred percent sure if I was still there. A few uncomfortable seconds passed.

"Professor, are you there?"

She stared deep inside the camera, wavered between smiles and frowns. My distressed and complex expression mirrored hers.

She said "Hello" over and over more times and in more ways than the plea hello was spoken in an Adele and Lionel Richie song combined.

Nervous, she picked up her phone and dialed a number.

My phone rang.

She was calling me.

I didn't answer.

Again she forced a smile and singsong-whispered her message, "Professor Suleman, are you there? I'm not sure what is going on, but I think you may have walked away and left your computer on Skype."

Gemma Buckingham hung up. It looked like she was trying to remember all she'd said to her assistant as the Skype clock told a tale. She frowned back toward the high-ticket door that screamed her name in massive CEO-size lettering, swallowed, nodded, wiped away a tear, shook her head with her first thoughts, nodded with her second thoughts, cursed with her third. She gazed into the camera as if she could see me.

She listened, heard nothing.

Sophisticated, well-read, and aware of the world.

Soon she said, "Love is its own contranym; in my world, it's its own contranym. That which attracts us is also that which pushes us away. In my life, love has always been the ultimate contranym. It pulls or it pushes, creates or destroys, never at ease, always in action."

It was usually the woman pressing the man for more. It was usually the man being stubborn and following the rules laid down by society, guarding his true emotions, being evasive, while the woman was using snark as a defense mechanism and sheltering her soul from harm. Usually it was the woman who called the man out, and when the man was confronted, when he felt trapped, sometimes he fled, but he seldom capitulated to his heart. After all I'd gone through, at the end of the day, I just wanted to love her the best way I knew how. Even with her small lies, despite her little game being revealed, I told myself this relationship was corrigible. It was fixable. We could be more than sex. We could be more than lies. Gemma Buckingham could be who she was. I didn't mind. All Gemma Buckingham had to do was want to be in my world. Give my momma one Sunday dinner. Take a few jokes about being light-skinned and dish a few dark-skinned jokes out to folks who teased her with no malice in their hearts. And eventually, over time, be comfortable enough to let me see her in that overnight bonnet.

Two people meeting and falling in love was always about timing.

Her history was in our way.

This Black man from Memphis had come into London's Brixton-born life after a heart-crushing affair with an African named Lennie, if that was his name. He'd devastated her. I'd come after whoever was there before Lennie, and whoever was before him, and before him. I'd come long after her being married at sixteen. I'd come after whatever reason she needed to get away from her parents and get out into the world on her own. Be it by lovers or at the hands of her own family, damage to the heart had been done long before I had arrived in her world. She had told me she was damaged then.

I pushed too hard.

She ran back across the pond. Without a storm warning.

Love is a contranym.

The thing that attracts you.

The thing that pushes you away.

Gemma Buckingham wiped away more tears. "Loved you, love. Loved you."

She looked like she could push a clear history button on our affair.

With the soft click of her mouse she killed the transmission.

Our connection was severed.

We were more than forty-three hundred miles apart.

She didn't want me there.

She didn't say she was coming back here.

She said that she'd loved me.

Loved.

Her love for me was spoken in past tense.

It only existed on this side of the pond. When she wore her alter ego.

I stared at the darkness on my screen awhile. A tempest raged inside of me and made itself known in my eyes. The difference between thunderstorms and earthquakes was they told you a thunderstorm was coming, and you had time to get ready. Gemma Buckingham had come into my life as suddenly as an earthquake, and now I was riding the aftershocks, each farther apart from the one before, until nothing.

CHAPTER 71

THAT NIGHT I tried to dance my feelings for her out of my system. The Love Club was on and popping with booties dropping like there was no stopping. A Megan Thee Stallion number boomed and rattled the walls. No matter what race or religion, all the church, synagogue, and mosque girls had gone wild. Professional and blue-collar sistas were in a zone where they wouldn't be misjudged, drinks in hand, twerking as an act of femininity, Black power to the nth degree, an awareness of shared culture, and the ultimate self-confidence. Black women did the most, tore it up like they were home in Ghana, Nigeria, and Senegal. For many this was as close to the motherland as they'd ever get. This was their tribute to Africa. The same women would be in church come Sunday at noon catching the Holy Ghost and shouting for Jesus and the Lord.

Sis was DJing and showing out but had no time to sit in VIP and chat with her brother. She was glowing, laughing and drinking and dancing with the white boy who rocked his hair in the style of the Rastas.

When I passed Momma's house, Black Kevin's car was in her driveway. When I hit Blair Hunt Drive, I checked my rearview again. The black SUV had followed me all evening, to the club and back.

Both of my shotguns were riding shotgun, my handgun in my lap.

CHAPTER 72

MY HOUSE LIGHTS were off like I was six months delinquent on the bill with Memphis Light, Gas and Water. I stood in the darkness, a silhouette in Trues and a red Carver High School T-shirt, two shotguns at my side.

I said, "Alexa, play Peggy Scott-Adams on level two."

Standing in my front window, I cleaned my handgun.

The black SUV that had followed me was still there, now parked two houses closer to Kansas Street. They were situated with a good view of my front yard. Whenever they left, they were back on Kansas Street within thirty minutes, so I assumed they headed over to Southgate Shopping Center and did a bathroom break at Piggly Wiggly, the kind that couldn't be whizzed into a cup or bottle. It felt like I was on trial waiting on the Judge of all Judges to render a verdict regarding my life.

Widow Fatima left her home an hour and a half before sunrise. She had on running shorts over tights and a navy blue and burnt orange Auburn tank top that didn't hide her sports bra but was long enough to cover her butt.

She had a new hairstyle. It was in phenomenal locks that cascaded over her soft shoulders and went almost to her small waist. Silver with white highlights. It popped against her skin.

Her locks moved side to side as she took off jogging.

I'd been up pacing and writing, dealing with Suleman business, two shotguns and a well-oiled handgun at my side, London on my mind.

Widow Fatima made it back home an hour and some change later. Her Auburn University top was soaking wet, her skin glistening in the sunrise. She did her routine, went down to the end of her driveway, was by her Nissan and did some contortionist level stretches, did full splits before she did her gymnastic routine six times, then went inside.

That black SUV was still out there. My Blackness was right here, waiting as the sun made darkness surrender at the start of the new day.

Forty minutes later Widow Fatima came back outside looking brand-new, stood on her porch like she was posing, checking the fit of her clothing. Her halter-style maxi dress was form fitting from top to bottom, especially at her waist. Parts of that Caribbean-colored sundress hugged her like a jealous man. Like a lonely man who'd found the right woman and refused to let go. She opened her pink old-fashioned parasol, once again used her travel umbrella as a UV blocking canopy to stop the randy sun from manhandling her skin without pausing to breathe.

She sashayed toward her sorority sister Yemi Savage's house. The widow was carrying Tupperware. I guessed they were about to break bread with the sun and girl talk. Her new style had me. The widow's dreadlocks were incredible, and her melanin was undeniably marvelous.

After her parasol disappeared from my sight, I put a UAN bandanna on my head to keep my hair from catching dust and grass, then dressed in my designated work clothes and tended to my yard.

Nobody was going to keep me from putting fresh lines in my grass. I had my eye on the SUV and they had their eyes on me. If anyone got out of that ride, my guns were stationed right inside my front door.

Soon as the day started, Mo Fo opened their front curtains and Pokey's sewing machine started working overtime.

I smelled a few cakes being made in her kitchen. Their television was up loud and a couple of their five kids were up at sunrise arguing over a cake recipe. I laughed and inhaled the scent of sweetness. A minute passed and Mo Fo was on the other side of his house washing his truck.

We yelled our good mornings, then went back to our chores.

The unknown sat in that SUV, engine running, and watched it all.

An hour later the widow was coming back my way, no Tupperware in her hands, twirling her parasol as she did her West Indian switch.

She looked toward me and smiled. Her dimples came alive. Her jealous dress hugged her tighter. Sun was up on both sides of our street.

I stopped working, wiped away sweat, and waved at my across-the-street neighbor. She did a cute little sneeze into the bend of her elbow.

"You okay?"

"Allergies got me. Ragweed."

"Claritin time."

"Plus I stayed out too late and got up too early."

"Got your party on."

"Soca until midnight, then up at four to run. I just had a big breakfast with my soror and now I got the -itis real bad. I want to go back to bed, take a Rip Van Winkle nap, but need to finish grading assignments first."

"Same here so far as lack of sleep and grading assignments."

"How's it going over at UAN? Y'all have so much drama this year."

"Y'all got drama too."

"Our drama doesn't make the paper or trend on regular Twitter."

I laughed. "It would've if you'd made it to Smackover."

She came my way, gently smiling, parasol still twirling.

I lowered my voice like I'd joined the league of gossipers and asked, "You see that SUV that's been parked up the street at Kansas?"

"Uh-huh."

"What's going on?"

"Nothing that we can see. I was going to call MPD, but Pokey don't want nobody hurt or killed over nothing. Not in front of her kids."

"Windows tinted too dark to see inside."

"Memphis tags."

"Locals."

"Whoever it is ain't bothering nobody. It's America and they're parked legally on a city street in a vehicle with current tags."

I agreed. "They ain't blocking nobody's driveway."

"No need to go Barbecue Becky or get all Karen on them."

I needed them to make the first move, so no matter what happened I could get off on standing my ground, protecting my life and land.

Widow Fatima asked, "When are you going to build me a setup in my backyard like you did in yours? What you put together looks better than a brand-new teak patio set from Crate and Barrel. Say when, and I can get Mr. Moses to run me to Home Depot to get what you need."

"That's how you say hello? You passed by me yesterday and didn't say good morning. I guess none of your tires need changing."

She laughed and those dimples danced. "I waved at you. That was the same as saying hello. Not like you gave me a proper greeting today."

"You know, a neighbor working hard and sweating like a pig in the sun, and I heard from Pokey 'nem you make some good lemonade."

"You see me good enough to want some of my lemonade now? You ain't never offered me a cup of your good coffee the way you do Moses and Pokey 'nem. You got glaucoma when it comes to me."

I laughed. "What you talking about? I see you every day."

"I see you and you see me, but you don't see me like I see you."

"You got cataracts too."

"Perfect vision. That's the problem."

I said, "I've been seeing you for years, question is have you ever seen me? I know you don't mind being nosy about my backyard without knocking on my door and seeing if I mind. Mo Fo told me."

"Halfway speak for five years then expect my lemonade because you decide you want it."

"I don't never halfway speak to you. Didn't you ask me to build you a patio set for free?"

"Well, you ain't never come over on my side of Blair Hunt Drive and sat on my porch."

"Never been invited to come across to your side of the road."

"You want lemonade. Come to my front porch and get it. I don't run a delivery service. Bring your own mason jar."

We laughed.

She let her parasol down as she headed back inside her home, sundress flowing, flip-flops on her feet, no makeup on her face, no eyelashes that looked like butterflies had died on her face, long locks swaying.

I went back to tending to my yard, used yardwork mostly to spy on the trouble up the road, all while London lived rent-free in my head.

My neighbor peeped at me from her front-room window.

She smiled as she waved. I waved back, then watched her.

Then she came back on the porch. "You gonna be able to make that patio thing for me?"

"Next weekend, I can borrow Moses's truck and get the supplies."

"I'll pay you back."

"Okay, I'll keep the receipts."

Again she sweet-walked back inside and went back to standing in her window, peeping out her colorful curtains.

No new cars had been parked in her driveway overnight.

No man had been sitting on her porch.

No man was tending to her yard.

I pushed my trusty lawn mower across Blair Hunt Drive, cranked it up, and started cutting Widow Fatima's front yard. I saw her leave her window and head down her short hallway to her small kitchen. When she came to the front door, I was pulling out her weeds. She smiled and showed me a pitcher of lemonade, offered me a mason jar filled with ice made from the same batch.

I took the jar and she grinned, poured until some spilled over the rim. I licked it off my hand, then took a long sip. A FaceTime call came in. I answered to sixteen big and wide smiles, heard cheers and laughter as they all sang a thank-you song. It was my West Coast sister and the only decent people she had known before I came to town.

They were on the western coast of Sweden in Västra Götaland County. I had read up on the history of Stone Mountain, saw that was the place where they had the rebirth of the Ku Klux Klan and had the world's largest Confederate memorial etched into the rock's side. She would've had a daily view of the Confederate Memorial Carving, a reminder that went forty-two feet deep and stood four hundred feet aboveground. It was their racist Mount Rushmore and depicted slave-loving Civil War generals Stonewall Jackson and Robert E. Lee, plus President Jefferson Davis. Big Sis and her crew would have opened their windows and had a view of that intolerance engraved in quartz monzonite dome monadnock every day. They still did Civil War reenactments in that park. Couldn't imagine waking up and running across that bullshit. I contacted Maddox

right away and canceled that order in Atlanta for the eight condos so fast
it made the real estate agent's head spin. Now Big Sis was an expatriate
living abroad on Åsa Rundväg in a five-bedroom, four-thousand-square-
foot home with a two-car garage. She had a view of the sea. It had a two-
bedroom guesthouse too. High-quality home that cost two million and
came with a coffee maker. If she wanted to quit America and start a new
life in Sweden, then I was happy to help her. She and her crew were creating a safer space for themselves than they had had before.

They *squeed* in happiness, then sang "Single Ladies" together.

She was free of America. But that didn't mean she was free.

She was happy. That made me happy. I told Big Sis I'd get a passport one day; then I'd come to Sweden and meet her face-to-face. I'd try
to bring Sis with me. Might bring my momma and the Fastest Swimmers too.

Then she was gone, back to her friends, screaming with joy. She wasn't
on that hobbyhorse right now. I wished she'd never have to ride it again.
But I knew dogs didn't meow and cats didn't bark.

Widow Fatima pulled at her dreadlocks over and over, smiled at her
new do like she felt brand-new, then said, "Haven't seen you but once or
twice in passing since you made it back from LA."

I nodded. "Love your hair. Another Vegas trip?"

"Your Kansas Street sister did it for me while you were gone. I might
have to fire my regular beautician. I don't have a reason to back-and-
forth and get my hair done in Las Vegas, at least not right now. Needed
something different. These locks will hold me a few weeks."

"You look amazing. Traffic-stopping amazing."

"Boy, ain't no traffic on this street. Be different if I was on Poplar out
in Germantown and you said that."

"I bet the natural hair people notice you now."

"Big-time."

"When I let mine grow it was like being accepted into a brand-new
secret society while being kicked out of another one at the same time."

"Never been called a queen so much in my life. By white men too."

"Your beauty is universal."

"My booty is what?"

"Beauty. Not booty."

"I still remember you said I had a narrow ass."

"It's still narrow."

"Ain't nobody complained. Well, nobody I give a shit about."

We laughed again.

Sis sped by in her car, tooted her horn as she passed, a new man riding shotgun. It was the white boy from the Love Club who had driven hundreds of miles to meet her. We waved like we loved each other.

Momma came from around the corner and saw me chilling out.

She spoke to Widow Fatima, then rattled on, "Sweet Meat, where your car keys? Momma ain't got no gas in her car right now."

"Why don't you ever have gas?"

"Momma in a hurry. Sale at Piggly Wiggly on salmon, tilapia, and crab legs. I don't want my car smelling like fish. Get your grill ready."

I was hesitant, didn't want Momma followed by accident. But the stalkers saw me here, would know I wasn't behind the wheel. I softball tossed Momma the keys. She snatched them out of the air with one hand, then about-faced, took three fast steps, and hmphed, looked back at us.

"Miss Fatima. You're in the wrong sorority to be flirting with my son, but I'll try not to hold that against you too much."

"Nobody over here flirting."

"Heard y'all laughing all the way up to Kansas Street."

"Momma Nike, *you're* in the wrong sorority to accuse me of such a thing, and I'll remind you of that every chance I get."

"Miss Fatima, slow your roll. Remember those coral, rose, and blush colors you're always wearing is the mixture of blood and purity, and we'll get along just fine."

"We going there, Momma Nike? You started it. You just remember who came first and who's the hybrid and we'll get along just fine."

The SUV pulled away, made a left on Kansas.

Momma said, "Oh, it's on. Over here all cute, looking like Kelly Rowland, Lupita Nyong'o, and Naomi Campbell had a baby and named her Fatima."

"Momma Nike, you're prancing around my street looking all cute like Janelle Monáe, Liya Kebede, Lola Falana, Cynthia Erivo, Angela Bassett, Anok Yai, Yaya DaCosta, Tika Sumpter, DeWanda Wise, Maria Rambeau, and Kiki Layne did the do a time or two and spit out you."

Momma raised a brow and instead of a snappy comeback to crush that snap, she tilted her head, did a soft laugh, nodded, and started a slow clap. "Oh, that was a good one, considering your affiliation to an organization of lesser stature. Admit your jealousy and be redeemed."

"Yeah, I'm a little jelly of that tight belly of yours."

"I like your skin."

"My skin? You look younger than your children. You must have a picture up in your house somewhere hidden under a cover. I bet you do."

"If I had those long legs I'd be able to reach my top shelves."

"Just give me your abs."

"Go to the gym with me twice a week and you'll wake up with a set of your own by Christmas. Your stomach already flat. Give up the sugar and carbs and bam. I can't make you look young and pretty like me, but I can get your abs right if you give up bad food."

"Well, bam, that ain't gonna happen. I run between six and ten four times a week and do yoga so I can eat the bad food I love to eat."

"Sunday dinner, Fatima. Bring your best jokes and your full appetite."

"What are you bringing?"

"You sit any closer to my first-born son, I'll be bringing a broom to see how well you can jump."

"Nowadays ain't folks jumping a Swiffer? We're the Roomba generation, Momma Nike."

"Fatima, see you Sunday to continue this battle, if not before."

"Sunday?"

"Sunday dinner. I expect to see you there."

The SUV disappeared.

Widow Fatima smiled. "Yes, ma'am."

"Around two. We won't keep you long. Don't dress up."

"Yes, ma'am. I see how y'all do it."

"This week I'm wearing Wonder Woman pajamas."

"I have some new Wonder Woman pajamas too."

"Bring enough lemonade for twenty. Only gonna be ten of us with a few friends, but we guzzle lemonade."

"I can do that."

Momma took off speeding, seventies music blasting.

Across the road, Mo Fo sat on his porch, legs crossed, beer in hand, wearing an authentic LA Lakers T-shirt with Kareem's number.

I'd picked that swag up from the Staples Center.

Mo Fo called out a warning to Widow Fatima. "He puts honey on his corn bread."

I yelled back, "Sometimes."

"Should be no time."

Widow Fatima took my glass. "Honey on corn bread? Give me back my doggone lemonade."

"I guess we shouldn't talk about what I put in my grits, then."

"Lord, don't tell me you're one of them folks put sugar on their grits."

Pokey and their five kids came outside, all smiling like it was Christmas morning and Santa hadn't missed stopping by their door. Pokey rocked Magic's number and the kids were either Kobe or LeBron.

Pokey 'nem were all dressed head to toe in so much authentic Lakers swag, they looked like they were on the way to battle the Grizzlies at the FedEx Forum. Pokey lined them up like a choir and in unison they all yelled a well-practiced thank-you to me. I waved like it was no big deal. It was everything to them. They acted like it was their first time wearing something not made by their mother's sewing machine.

Pokey yelled she had made me a pineapple upside-down cake and was letting it cool off, told me the kids would bring it to me when I called her name from my yard, then said it was about time Fatima invited me over to sit on her porch, as long as she been liking me and burning her ear up asking all about me every chance she could get. Widow Fatima blushed and handed me back my lemonade.

"Why you smiling like that, Sweet Meat? Ain't that what your momma and all your siblings call you? That's an interesting nickname."

"What's your nickname? Nobody around here seems to know."

"Muff."

"Like Little Miss Muffet over here sitting on her tuffet?"

"Sweet Meat. Not even going to ask how or why on that one."

"Momma 'nem call me that because one time I barbecued and used too much brown sugar in the barbeque sauce, and the meat turned out sweeter than two Blow Pops and a Snickers bar."

We teased each other, then eventually changed subjects, looked for something to talk about, settled on the day I fixed her flat tire.

The day my father died. Not for his death that morning, I never would've ended up in front of Carver High screaming out pain.

The widow said, "I should've gone and smacked big-booty Smackover upside her fat head. Twice for making me burn up my gas to do it. Ringing my phone at that ungodly hour like I know her."

I was with her but bits of my mind were still across the pond.

Her born name wasn't Gemma Buckingham. On the leasing agreement at her mansion overseeing Old Man River, her first name was spelled A-K-U-A. I guess that was pronounced Ah-qui-ah, maybe Ah-kwee-ah. Her last name was St. John-Amaritiefio.

It was the same name that had been on her office door.

She was Ghanaian and Scottish.

I still had no idea who she was. Takes more than a postal code.

The SUV came back from the way it had left and parked again.

Mo Fo's front door opened and his kids stepped out one by one, then crossed the narrow street holding two of the biggest pieces of pineapple upside-down cake known to man.

Pokey yelled, "Fatima, y'all been out there flirting so long the cake done got cold now. You have to be hungry from all that talking and laughing."

"Girl, you are my new best friend, and ain't nobody flirting. Can't a man and woman sit down and have a civilized conversation?"

Pokey yelled, "Let me know when y'all set a date and I'll start working on a wedding dress and the menu so I can be your caterer."

"Had one of those before. Not in a rush to wear another one."

Mo Fo called out, "Last one home is a rotten egg."

Kids left in a race, made it to their porch. Mo Fo declared the winner. The kids had a good time pretending to shoot hoops in their front yard.

The SUV turned around, faced Kansas Street in a way that had my house in the rearview. The unknown would know when I went back home. They couldn't get in thorough my back door without climbing over Sis's fence, which we shared. Sis wasn't home. Five members of the KKK or one of its racist-adjacent groups could be breaking in my home from the back.

When I got up to leave, she asked, "Where you off to?"

"Have to go tutor a hardheaded student over Zoom for a couple hours. She's trying to make herself a better writer. Pro bono work."

"That's why you need to teach at an HBCU. We ain't perfect, not by a long shot, but we have some respect and fresh lemonade or sweet tea waiting on you at the front door when you're ready to come home."

I handed her back her mason jar.

She said, "I'm going out for soca with Yemi Savage and a few sorors later. Taking Pokey with me. She is a fun drunk. They all have kids and husbands, boyfriends, or whatever, so we're not staying out too late."

"Running tomorrow?"

"Tomorrow I rest. But I'll still be up at the same time."

I said, "I'll have Pokey's kids bring you a big cup of coffee in the morning, soon as I send some over to her and Mo Fo."

"Bring it yourself. I'll leave my front house blinds open, so you'll know I'm up and dressed and ready for some neighborly company."

"I'm up early like you."

"I run early because the air is clearer and the pavement's not hot."

"Before the rooster crows."

"Come on over when you ready."

"Before the sun comes up?"

"Right before. If you awake. Bring me that coffee."

The SUV that had followed me since my confrontation with the judge came back and parked up closer to where the south end of Blair Hunt Drive touched Kansas Street. I took a few steps in that direction. They eased away.

I walked down my driveway to my back door, made sure it was double locked, checked the security system, then looked for footprints.

I went in the back way. The shotgun I had left there was still there. I picked it up, racked it to scare anyone inside, then crept room to room, pulled the shower curtains back, checked inside my closets, peeped under my bed, checked the locks on the windows. Then I showered, shower curtain open, handgun on the counter, shotguns keeping it company.

CHAPTER 73

SIS STOPPED BY later. After she trimmed my hair and hooked my beard up, we sat on my sofa and sipped beer. We had the option of Blue Moons, Angry Orchards, Heinekens, and Coronas. I made mine an Angry Orchards night. Sis sipped Heineken. I was exhausted but did the cooking in my air fryer. We ate shrimp tacos, and binged-watched *Watchmen*.

Sis yawned. "Heard they fired Dr. Stone-Calhoun. Saw the video online. Wonder what she did. I mean, one week she's on the front page with the president of the USA, the envy of every Republican in the tri-state area, and damn near the next week UAN showed her the door."

Forcibly touched. Orally violated. Not put on her record. Wouldn't have to register as a sex offender. Not a day would be spent in prison. Early paid retirement from UAN. Sweetheart deal for someone who should've been locked up for at least three presidential election cycles. No front-page shame with *The Commercial Appeal*. The video of her on social being escorted from campus would be irrelevant in the long run.

That was the kind of justice a certain ilk was accustomed to.

Was hard to tell who won and who'd been shunned.

Sis said, "Slow down. You're outdrinking me tonight."

I laughed, but my eyes didn't smile.

Sis beamed. "Oh, I saw these cute phone holders for ten and got a gold one for you, too, since yours was raggedy."

Sis handed me a golden automatic wireless car charger.

She said, "Attaches to your vent. So your iPhone won't keep falling out and flying when you drive. Momma's phone fell out ten times."

I sat on anger, smiled at Sis, nodded as a thank-you.

Sis asked, "How you like your new shotgun?"

I lied, "Ain't had a chance to test it out yet. Eager to. Real eager to."

"We should go to Shoot Point Blank. We can have the rest of the Fastest Swimmers meet us and pop off some thirty-aught-six there."

"I think about popping off some thirty-aught-six every day."

"You okay?"

"'Sup?"

"You seem off since you went to LA."

"Had a few life-changing moments."

"You have a LA family."

"I told you about those folks."

She laughed. "Your daddy called them the Motherfuckers."

"With his dying breath."

"And they showed up with dogs, a horse, and a freaking ostrich?"

We laughed. That time my eyes did too.

THAT NIGHT, LIKE every night since LA, I kept Lightning at my side. My second shotgun was its sidekick, loaded and by the door. My Glock was in the small of my back, waiting for a vengeful judge to appear.

It would be the last night I'd have to worry.

It would be the last night that the unknown in a strange SUV hid behind tinted glass and parked close enough to my home to shoot me dead in the street. Thunder would sound and bodies would fall.

CHAPTER 74

AT FOUR THIRTY I walked through darkness to the bathroom.

After another two-minute shower with the music off, shower curtain pulled back, guns within reach, and bathroom door wide-open, I lotioned my body with my eyes on the monitor. The front of my house lit up when a car passed by. One of the Clarks from up the street. Recognized the Porsche Cayenne. An Echo was on the bathroom counter, the video showing my front door to the street. It was a backup for the Ring doorbell that sang every time someone's feet touched my sidewalk.

My big shade tree was now a liability.

I checked on the Mexican coffee I was making, then went to my front window and frowned toward my patient stalkers. The SUV waited in the dark. Hadn't moved for five hours. Gun bouncing against my leg, I sighed toward the widow's house. Her living room and kitchen lights were on. She was already in her front window, maybe looking this way. That was confirmed when her silhouette waved for me to come over.

I waved back. It was summertime warm and in mosquito land I had on minimum summertime clothing. That meant I couldn't sneak and carry my handgun in my waistband. A shotgun would be too obvious. Not wanting to deal with the widow, I filled my gotdamn thermos.

Before new shadows were made and while the beauty and calmness of the unknown felt like absolute terror, I carried the large UAN thermos filled with sweet Mexican coffee in my left hand, had my right hand free. I was doing my best to look normal, appear unbothered. I'd stuffed work, iPad, MacBook, Suleman business, and enough graphic novel notes to hide the loaded handgun inside. The loaded-down vintage leather backpack was all about sheltering the gun. I had to walk to Momma's house to get my car. She hadn't brought it back last night.

I shook off my insomnia and messaged Mo Fo, said I'd drop off his and Pokey's two cups of sweet coffee in about thirty minutes, after I popped across the street to make that same delivery to the widow for the first time. I kept my right hand open, made sure my gun hand was free and ready for a quick draw. I had practiced a hundred times at the range.

Dead-nigger soup.

The power of three words. Of all the options in my head, dead-nigger soup trended at number one. He'd had me followed. Knew what I had for breakfast. Knew what I'd had for my lunch. Knew my home address. Knew Momma and Sis lived near. The chef wanted dead-nigger soup.

CHAPTER 75

I RELUCTANTLY HEADED to the widow's house with the loaded handgun in my rucksack. The safety was on. The heat dictated what clothing wouldn't look suspicious before sunrise, so instead of dressing head to toe in all black or military camo, I wore joggers that stopped at my knees, a UAN T, and Old Navy flip-flops. When I was almost at Widow Fatima's front door, a second SUV turned off Kansas Street. It came fast and dramatically down Blair Hunt Drive, sped in from the south end, and passed by the first SUV. The new unknown paused in front of my house for a few threatening seconds before it continued on and parked curbside one house up from Mo Fo 'nem. They didn't turn their engine off. Kept their tinted windows up.

The brake lights flashed a moment, lit up the morning like a signal to their coworkers. The new unknown shifted to park and taillights went dark. All I could hear was the new morning yawning. Nobody got out. I would've turned around, but the widow had seen me and unlocked her door. Big thermos in hand, I smiled at my across-the-street neighbor.

I shifted my rucksack, said, "Mornin', Professor."

"Good morning, Professor. Hope this isn't too early."

"Perfect time."

"Before the devil gets to the boiler room and fires up the furnace."

She was barefoot in a skirt and Auburn T, legs shining up toward a brand-new heaven, the kind a man climbed step by step, no rush.

I had my UAN thermos in my hand. "I brought the *café de olla.*"

"Your backpack looking heavy. You running away from home?"

"Running from the devil."

"In that case I need to start distance training with you."

"Was going to drop some coffee off for you, then Mo Fo 'nem."

"You're traveling Santa Claus heavy to just be walking next door?"

I told her the part of my plans that was safe to tell. I was going to park on the river and watch a new sunrise, then go by Fannie Lou's Gourmet Chicken & Waffles for a quick breakfast before I drove east and copped a squat at a bistro table and worked awhile under the air-conditioning at the Starbucks on Highway 64, the one out by Wolfchase.

She said, "Glad you're hungry. I cooked. It's not chicken and waffles. Could've done that. What I made, I made enough for you."

"For me?"

"Who else at this hour?"

"Brad Pitt."

She laughed. "If I had known you were riding to watch the sun come up, and had invited me, I would've done breakfast an hour ago, packed it, and gone with you. I'd've driven my Z with the top off."

I checked behind me, frowned from one stalking SUV to the next, then headed inside. I paused in the doorway, then took a step backward, went back outside, eyed one, then the other, nodded.

Widow Fatima stood in the doorway and spied out with me.

My heart thumped. "Uber?"

"They'd be out by now if they called an Uber to get to the airport."

"All the lights are off in their house."

"Blair Hunt Drive is turning into the new Riverside Park."

She invited me deeper into her home. Her nest was a two-bedroom, nine-hundred-square-foot majestic crib. One wall in the living room was dominated by a Samsung eighty-two-inch smart TV.

She saw me checking it out, chuckled, then said, "I think I overdid it. Got the latest and greatest technology from Best Buy. It was on sale."

"You did good."

"Best Buy got all my money that week."

The Miseducation of Lauryn Hill was on low. She swayed and swam in her personal contranym as Lauryn Hill sang songs from the nineties. It was powerful and disarming; I was pulled into the sentiments, treaded in mine. That music was Momma's music for a long time. Her blues.

Without thinking, due to my upbringing, I slid my flip-flops off at her door, then refocused, evaluated her life. There was a Hamzer sixty-one-key portable electronic keyboard piano with a stand, small stool, head-phones, and a microphone. Then her art. In the dining room was a large triptych depicting dancing Caribbean women in long colorful skirts, head scarves, and tank tops. Stunning canvas photos of the widow deco-rated the Caribbean-hued wall near her organized-yet-overloaded wooden bookcase. My across-the-street neighbor had her wanderlust on display. She was a supermodel when dressed up. On stretched cotton and linen, she was effervescent in a little black dress, hair whipped, wide smile, dimples deep, dancing sexily in a crowded five-star club in Las Vegas. She owned the room, the world, and its attached universe. Reminded me of when I hit the doors at the Love Club. On another canvas that looked like it was made from hemp, she was covered head to sparkling sandals in an all-black abaya decorated with colored embroidery and sequins. She was in Abu Dhabi at the Sheikh Zayed Grand Mosque. Queenly images in Grenada, Trinidad, and Barbados were with photos in Tanzania. And on the largest canvas she was dressed smartly and laughing in a red phone booth in London. She'd been to London. She'd been to a place I'd never been yet was trying to escape.

The widow had a big smile, those dimples on fire, was as excited as a kid on Christmas, in a red London phone booth, but when I blinked I saw another woman's face, her faux name and amber complexion engraved in my mind.

The widow waved her right hand like she'd had enough. "Okay, I love you, Miss Hill, but enough of the blues is enough of the blues. I need to laugh. Alexa, play my favorite comedy."

By then the widow had two mimosas in her hands. One was almost empty. Heartbreak-numbing juice at sunrise. Chopped fresh fruit was in each champagne flute: strawberries, blueberries, and orange slices.

She handed me the fresh one, then took my thermos.

I took a sip. Could barely taste the orange juice.

"What you put in those mimosas?"

"Grand Marnier, tablespoon of Chambord, teaspoon of whiskey. I'm on my second. You told me you like mimosas. Made my specialty."

I nodded. "Mimosas for coffee."

"You're a drink behind. Catch up while I cook. Shoes off."

"Already did."

"Hope you like my salmon. New recipe."

"I hadn't expected a full breakfast."

"Me either. I had a restless night and woke up hungry."

"Restless?"

"Stuff on my mind that's hard to get off."

"What stuff?"

She dodged the issue by motioning at her full trash container. It was so full it refused to close. The smell from the fresh salmon croquettes and peeled onions was strong. Three more small Trader Joe's plastic bags of trash were by her back door. She hadn't taken out her trash in days.

"I opened the cans of salmon croquettes, then forgot to rinse out the cans before I put them in the trash. Professor, do you mind taking that out for me before the house starts to smell like a fish market in Seattle? You can look at my backyard while you're out there and see if I can make mine look as good as yours looks with benches and lights."

I grabbed her bags and went out her back door, still lugging my ruck-sack, the top open, the handle of my anxious gun winking at me.

The sweet smell of love wafted my way. A top-shelf heart-shaped box was crammed on the top of her big black trash can. The box was filled with at least thirty red roses. I read the business labels. The Million Eternity Roses. Expensive roses. Expensive as my monthly mortgage. A large I LOVE YOU FOR THE REST OF FOREVER style Hallmark card was ripped in half, then ripped in half twice again. With it was another handwritten note. I MISS YOU. I MISS YOU. I MISS YOU. Looked like it had been spat on a dozen times. Around five hundred dollars had been spent on a bouquet of the kind of top-shelf roses that lasted more than three years. Three years was long enough to date, marry, be changing the diapers on one rug rat while another was baking in the oven. I looked at the ground, saw what I'd missed in the darkness. Rose petals littered the grass from her back door to her nasty chins. Looked like she'd been driven to hysterics and haphazardly and emotionally smashed and crammed them into the trash as soon as the *please, baby, please* bouquet was delivered to her porch.

I dumped her new trash, stalled and looked over her backyard, tipped down the side of her house and saw both SUVs were still in place, then slipped back inside, eased in while she was on the phone, crept in without banging the door, stood at the entrance and ear hustled.

"Dat one big-mouth Selena called you talking my name? She so malicious. Me and the doctor, girl, we done. That situation-ship call for a bereavement card now. Truth is like the sun—ya can hide from it for a time but it ain't gine disappear. Ya can hide and buy land but ya can't hide and work it because the truth gotta come out. Good-for-nothing dog horn me fo' a country whore. Smackover. Arkansas, girl. Sky-blue hair in a marine cut. Wit chunky red legs got a boxy like a stripper hiding two deflated basketballs under her thong. Mek me look foolish. She creep me number from his phone and called me at two o'clock in the morning to wake me up out my good sleep, but she ain't know she was waking up the old, old me. How? Calling me an anorexic cunt. She look like she cunt been dug out so much a man get on top of her hole and feel like he falling in a six-foot grave. She call me an anorexic cunt. The new me wasn't gine bother wid she but the old me was in a very different mood."

She saw me behind her and was startled, if not embarrassed.

I raised my nasty hands and whispered, said, "Bathroom?"

She pointed. "You scared me to death."

I nodded. "You have plenty room. You could build a gazebo."

She went back to her call and I hit her bathroom, washed my hands, then used a sanitizer. When I came back, she was off the phone.

The widow sipped her mimosa. "Thanks for taking my trash out."

"No problem."

"I hate taking out trash."

"I think we all do."

"It is a necessary part of life."

She cooked and drank mimosas like they were infused water.

The five-hundred-dollar arrangement of sensual and clit-stimulating flowers was outside mixed with filthy trash bags and days of wet garbage and waste, all relegated to be made compost. The doctor from TSU's Hail Mary was destined to be ground up and converted into fertilizer, turned into shit for the soil, trashed for the greater good.

Trashed for the greater good.

Trashed.

Same as I had been trashed by a woman across the pond in London.

I said, "You were saying something about love a moment ago?"

"Was off in my feelings. Thinking. Being existential and getting my Lauryn Hill on. Trying to rationalize what can't be rationalized."

"What?"

"I don't think men are as concerned with love."

"That wretched four-letter word."

"We all catch it at some point."

"And try to get rid of it."

She turned her television on CNN. A commercial came on for a law firm, saying Boy Scouts who had being sexually abused by Scout leaders were entitled to financial compensation. Uninterested, she turned it right back off. It had flashed like a sign meant to redirect my thoughts.

She swayed, three sips from being tipsy, twitterpated before sunrise.

I studied other parts of her castle. Her wooden bookcases were a Black studies library. Among her hundreds of African, West Indian, and African American novels, positioned next to mine was the same novel Momma was throwing my way, *The Delectable Negro: Human Consumption and Homoeroticism within U.S. Slave Culture.*

I said, "You have books written by my father."

"He wrote so many books that after a while it was hard to keep up."

"He was a hard worker. Strangers loved him. Only strangers."

"Sorry for your loss, if I haven't told you."

"Thanks."

"Have your books too."

"You called me over for a refund?"

"I enjoyed them. Made the doctor from TSU mad."

"Why?"

"The doctor from TSU never liked you."

"Why?"

"He could tell I liked you."

"I couldn't."

"You weren't supposed to."

"Good job."

"You are excessively handsome and have eyes like a tiger. The first time I saw your eyes up close my legs trembled. I was afraid of you and attracted to you at the same time. Good thing we were neighbors."

"Yeah. You're intelligent, independent, no kids, have your own house, under thirty, sweet ride, and look like a model. A good thing."

"Anyway. I can do a lot, but writing a book, that is not my thing. How do you start a book?"

"I open a dictionary and hold it upside down, shake it until all the words fall out, do the same with a thesaurus, then put the mountain of scattered words together until they make sense."

"Smartass."

"Narrow ass."

She called out, chuckling, "Alexa, play my favorite music please."

Soca came on. We sipped mimosas. Strong mimosas. As outside began to glow, I inhaled her. She smelled Olay-with-shea-butter fresh. Colgate-white teeth highlighted her double-chocolate complexion.

Gemma Buckingham was in London and this Black man from Memphis hadn't heard from her, so I guessed we were no longer on the same sentence, in the same paragraph, in the same invisible book.

I was still holding on to that summer fling like it was the Bible. I needed to close the book and put it on the shelf with the rest of the tombstones.

Ghosted me, guess I needed to ghost her back.

Roger de Groot's way of looking at things told me to look at this a different way, his way. So I gave Roger de Groot the floor.

He told me that if my life was a book, then she had started reading the life of Pi, didn't like what happened in a short chapter, made her final judgment based on part, not the whole, then closed the book and put it down, eased it on a shelf with other tombstones she had started and wouldn't finish. Roger de Groot of European stock, a man who made no less than 650 an hour and paid 300 for a basic haircut, my scotch-drinking,

Ice Cube–loving friend and fixer, he hugged me, then patted my shoulder and reminded me that everybody doesn't like the same book, not even when it is a bestseller.

Maybe the straw that broke this green-eyed, brown-skinned camel's back was when I asked Gemma Buckingham about her brother, the one she said was sexually abused by a priest inside their church, and she'd snapped, "What brother?"

That excited utterance in a moment of anger was her truth.

She was a liar. Had lied from the moment she said her name.

I had done what my mother had done more than thirty years ago: fallen for someone because they were important, then talked so slow I ended up being as blinded as Stevie Wonder by her outer beauty.

My neighbor was in a zone of her own.

Her body language and deep frown said she imagined the doctor from TSU with a well-endowed woman who worked at Walmart.

My phone blew up.

The widow's phone blew up at the same time.

My across-the-street neighbor read her messages.

I read mine, began rocking like I was on a hobbyhorse.

She hand combed her dreadlocks and bounced her right foot.

Eyes wide, stiffened with the news, I shook my head in disbelief.

She stood up, paced. "Lord, Lord, Lord. That poor family must've tipped a saltshaker over and broke a mirror after they left shoes on the table. This type of bad luck is worse than saying both *good luck* and *Macbeth* in a theater."

She scrolled Memphis Twitter as fast as she could.

I said, "Fuck. Can't be. *Judge of all Judges* is trending."

"So is *Brownsville beauty queen. Dr. Stone-Calhoun.* And *UAN.*"

Rucksack heavy on my left arm, my right hand anxious to dig inside, I hurried to her front window, looked out at the two unknowns, scrolled Memphis Twitter again, read the rapidly scrolling updates in disbelief.

I said, "The Judge of all Judges and his beauty-queen trophy wife."

"All over Memphis social media it says they're dead."

"I won't believe that. Not until it's on the local news."

She jogged and turned her living room television on.

On the local news were pictures of the Judge of all Judges and his wife. Born dates and today's date were under each image. The newscaster was too shaken to speak without crying. Thunder was on the ground.

The tragedy in area code 731 was all over the local news, the lead story on every station. People from Jackson, Paris, Nutbush, Dyersburg, Union City, Savannah, Martin, Camden, and Lexington had Memphis's Twitter on fire. The scandal occurred sixty-four miles from Memphis, about fifty-four miles as the crow flies. It happened in the town named after General Jacob Jennings Brown, where yeomen farmers were hard-core Unionist during the Civil War. It was the city where an NAACP member was kidnapped and found dead in the Hatchie River, bullet holes in his chest, lynched for civil rights activities.

"Wait. Sweet Meat, Professor, there is a video."

"Of what?"

"It's trending under *Faces of Death*."

"No way."

"This is sick. Oh. My. Freakin. Frackin. God."

"What did you find?"

"The whole murder was recorded and put online."

CHAPTER 76

THERE WAS TOTAL darkness; then a video turned on, out of focus, and someone fumbled with a phone. A bedside lamp turned on. It was near sunrise in a room filled with fat-cheeked pasty dolls. The holder of the jittery phone made a noise that sounded like they were barely awake. They phone was out-of-focus recording, and the predawn videographer was breathing hard, very feminine, in a panic as an angry voice yelled. The angry voice was drunk and off-screen; the demands and slurs came from far away but were very close at the same time. A glimpse of blond hair came and went. Memphis knew that mane. It was Dr. Stone-Calhoun, the Bitch from Brownsville. This was the beauty queen's phone. She had been startled awake and began streaming before she could fix her breath. The angriness in the voice grew louder. There were frantic sounds, her pulling on a robe and house shoes; then the phone was aimed at her UAN slippers as she did a fast slip-slide across a cluttered and dusty room. Out of breath, she raised her phone to show what was outside her bedroom window lurking in the darkness.

His luxury SUV was visible on the side of the decrepit house, but he didn't need to be seen. The Judge of all Judges' outrage was as recognizable as Elvis Presley singing about a hound dog and a party at a county jail where wise men said fools rushed in with suspicious minds.

He yelled what sounded nonsensical: *"Bellicose niggers won't get the last laugh. Faux victim mentality. Nigger can't get mouth raped and not like it two times in a row. Nigger had no problem seeing the perversion to the end. You ain't bigger than him. Nigger just happened to record everything for his attorneys. You sat there laughing. Laughed after you had the nigger the way a woman should have her husband on his birthday. Set this up. Set me up. Colluding niggers. Tricksters. Tried to outwit me like y'all two Brer Rabbits. That's what you and that ugly nappy-headed bellicose nigger are. Two Brer Rabbits. And if you don't get to the front door right now, me and Thunder might decide to go rabbit hunting this morning."*

Her startled face appeared, then went away just as fast when she realized her wake-up face would be seen by the world.

Dr. Stone-Calhoun.

My rapist was unrecognizable first thing in the morning, hair undone. The judge yelling both her name and southern-fried insults went on as her cursing, fumbling, and grappling with the phone continued.

She woke up live-streaming like she knew he'd eventually come.

She yelled back, *"I don't appreciate jerking awake from my twelfth dream to lies and insults and my God-given name being called out before the rooster crows. Momma, I'm recording everything on my phone, so get off your bedpan and call the police to come get the judge right now."*

An old woman in the distance snapped for her to go back to bed.

The Bitch from Brownsville woke up in a nasty mood, like an evil queen. No humility for all she had caused. The ultimate hauteur. She woke up irritated and right out the bed showed her authentic self, broadcast an obnoxious display of overbearing pride and superiority toward others, demanded Memphis and the world stop living their lives and give an audience to hers, because she was white and privileged, the once-upon-a-time beauty queen, and because she fuckin said so.

The judge bellowed, *"Bellicose niggers won't get the last laugh."*

She snapped, *"Everybody, I just spotted the Judge of all Judges' SUV in the dirt driveway at my momma's home in Brownsville. Before I can get in a good yawn or smell my morning breath, I grabbed my iPhone, and I want all of Memphis to see the abuse I've endured with this man."*

Brimming with self-righteous indignation, she narrated her anger.

"Okay, I see hearts flying, so people are out there. Hey, Velma. Hey, Gwen. Do a watch party so I can let the world know about this man."

The judge yelled, *"Bellicose niggers colluded and expect me to pay for all of your wrongdoings? Will be a rainy day in hell before I—"*

She yelled as loud as she could toward the other bedroom in the back of the house. *"Momma, get to your darn phone. Call the police."*

She recorded as she cursed her way toward the persistent calling of her name, each harsh step showing she was in the home of a career hoarder. She yanked open the front door, then undid the screen door and stomped out on the wooden wraparound porch in the dimness of dawn to have it out with him. Judge Calhoun was in the front yard, drunk as a skunk, divorce papers he'd been served by a retinue of Memphis attorneys in his leathery hands. He spat like a rattlesnake as he marched to the bottom of the twelve wooden stairs, yelled at Dr. Stone-Calhoun.

The Bitch from Brownsville, the beauty queen who looked like anything but Miss Universe before sunrise, demanded that he get off her momma's goddamn property and act like he had some sense.

The judge took one wooden step at a time and closed the gap between them; each step creaked under his polar-bear weight. Again, she demanded for him to leave. He took five steps, was winded, then took five more. The Judge of all Judges sweated profusely, could barely breathe.

She bitch-laughed at him, lost her education, said disparaging things regarding his weight, and continued holding her new phone, then announced she was documenting the occasion for her divorce attorney.

She yelled, *"Facebook Live. I have four hundred witnesses so far. Memphis is watching you act a fool. Be careful what you do or say."*

"I don't care about no damn Facebook Live or dead."

"Police coming. Now, get off my momma's property."

He shook those divorce papers toward the two-faced woman who had betrayed and humiliated him, then raised them to the god that had always been on his side.

"Momma, call the police again. Dial 911 right now."

The Judge of all Judges screamed more vulgarities louder than a tabernacle choir. The Bitch from Brownsville's attitude remained a storm that moved from sensible to severe in the blink of an eye.

"Momma, tell them to get here immediately if not sooner."

Dr. Stone-Calhoun called the Judge of all Judges sweetie while she put on a hissy fit and told him to bless her little heart if he thought he could shut her off from his fortunes and have her back in Haywood County eating potted meat straight from the can when she deserved the freshest Almas caviar made, no matter what it cost, no matter what she had done.

She told him, *"Judge not, that ye be not judged."*

He snapped, *"Bellicose niggers everywhere I go, at every turn."*

She repeated for him to get off her momma's property.

His face reddened; his jowls shook as spittle flew with every word. *"Field of yellow cotton permed until I couldn't tell the difference. Without my money to support your daily charade, now I can see the cucabuds rising up along the edges and on the back of your neck."*

She cursed him.

He exploded, *"You sucked that nappy-headed bellicose nigga's ding-a-ling behind my back and damn near in my face, sucked him on the side of the road, begged to suck him in his car, and did it while I was in your car sleeping, laughed about it, and as a reward you expect me to pay you ten thousand dollars a month for the next twenty-five years, plus the cost of inflation and half my retirement and a third of the proceeds from the sale of the houses I bought before I met you, for doing it?"*

He threw the wrinkled divorce papers toward the camera like he was throwing bricks at his beauty queen's face.

He was a Christian stoning his adulterous wife.

He exploded, *"I'll tell everyone on that Facebook nonsense how you went out and got you a long, tall, dark-Black nappy-headed bellicose nigger for your personal use and had him in your mouth in his car on the side of the road and came back to me kissing on me and looking like you were a two-dollar whore from down at the bottom of Foote Homes."*

"Liar, liar, pants on fire."

She zoomed in on his rage. She laughed at him.

He cursed her to God for having the nerve to do what she had done.

She had sullied his reputation with a nappy-headed nigger.

He let the world know she had demanded a high-five-figure payment to hold her over until all was settled in court.

Judge scowled. *"Will be a rainy day in hell before you see one thin dime."*

"Get off my momma's property before I have you arrested for trespassing."

"Fooled by a colored passing for white. *Outwitted, I tell ya. Goddamn* Negra *outwitted me. I told her as long as she knew her place and echoed all I believed, our secret would be safe. Then she met . . ."*

"Don't you dare."

"Just another bellicose nigger."

"You want to come on my momma porch and spread lies?"

"Family secrets ain't lies."

"Keep lying on me and I'll tell everyone about all the Sudafed and Adderall you take to go with your morning whiskey."

"You cheated on me and now you expect to take my money too?"

"You're fat. You're old. And you're ugly. No woman in her right mind wants your smell on top of her. I slept in the same bed and put up with you for years and I'm taking what's rightfully mine as I go."

"Put that phone down. Know what's best for you, put it down."

"I'm letting everyone on Facebook Live know you're not in your right mind because once a month you sneak off to N'awlins and spend twelve thousand a session to get blood transfusions using teenager's blood because you think that will make you live forever."

"Shut your mouth and put the damn phone down."

"It's made you crazy."

"You and your lies and your ways have made me crazy, if anything. I'm the one who held on to your lies and put you in that beauty contest. I brought you and your cotton-picking family up from nothing. And you run off and betray me for an ugly nappy-headed nigger? Did you finally get homesick? Is that what happened on that goddamn video?"

"Careful what you say."

"Careful what lies you tell against my truth."

"After the divorce, I'll move up north with the Yankees and get me a young New York man when all is said and done. That's the truth."

"A Yankee? With my money?"

"*Judge of all Judges, I'll use part of your money to send you postcards of us at Christmastime from the beach in Cancún. I'll spend money from the first check you pay me and buy Almas caviar and have him feed it to me while I don't miss you a goddamn moment. That will be the last word in the matter. One more word and I tell more secrets.*"

"*You're not going to betray me and have me foot the bill. There will be no insult to injury. UAN can pay for your behavior, but I won't.*"

"*Judge Kline will decide. He will have the last say in the matter.*"

"*Oh, I done come here to take you to stand along with me before the ultimate judge. We gonna stand before him and hear his say.*"

As crickets and june bugs danced and chased blood-hungry mosquitoes, the Judge of all Judges performed a tricky display of cleverness and suddenly had his shotgun, Thunder, in his irate hands.

He told her he had planted his weapon, left his shotgun in arm's reach two hours ago so he would be seen without Thunder.

That was why he had crept up the creaking steps, to get to where he had stashed the shotgun among the southern clutter in front of the home.

He barked, "*Bellicose nigger, now who smarter than who?*"

The camera was on a man about to render his verdict, but I imagined she'd opened her mouth in horror but didn't have time to scream.

Birds squawked and scattered under the sudden echo of thunder.

The phone took flight, then had a rough landing. It hit the porch at an odd angle. It was still recording and had the judge center frame.

It was online for all to see.

Judge Calhoun pulled a bottle of Jack from his back pocket and sat down on the wraparound front porch. The wood creaked and strained and bent under his four-hundred-pound frame.

He downed a pint of his eighty-proof medicine in one long gulp.

Then he positioned himself.

He put the warm barrel of the shotgun in his old mouth.

A bloodied bonnet rolled by the camera.

The judge put his fat finger on Thunder's trigger.

Changed his mind.

Rattlesnake spat twice.

Pulled a second bottle of Jack from inside his seersucker suit coat.

Downed it faster than he had done the first.

He patted all of his pockets.

Coughed twice.

Cursed.

No more bottles of Jack.

He put the business end under his chubby neck.

Then moved the barrel to the side.

Sirens warbled in the distance.

Brownsville Police Department.

Haywood County Sheriffs.

"All over a nappy-headed bellicose nigga. I should've nevah kept your secret. You made me a cotton-picking colluder. Said that ugly nigga looked so much like the secret niggas in your family you had to help him with this, that, and the other. You helped all right. You helped him all right. And he snitched on you. He double-crossed you like you double-crossed me. So I helped you go see the only judge above me to get adjudicated on the matter. See you in the courtroom of all courtrooms soon."

The judge said he wasn't finished fighting with the conniving woman who had humiliated him.

"The nappy-headed nigger will get what he deserves. Sho will."

He scowled toward his estranged wife's unmoving body, then shot another insult regarding his wife's unruly hair, said it was now fully on display as her bloody bonnet rolled by like a tumbleweed in the breeze.

Sirens were getting closer.

The man who had sentenced many Black men said, *"You'll never put handcuffs on me. Never. You'll never take me to any jail anywhere."*

He prayed for God to send him to the same place his dead colored wife had gone. He saluted his general in the sky like a good soldier.

He chanted, rocked like he was saying a prayer. *"An Aryan brother is without a care. He walks where the weak and heartless won't dare. And if by chance he should stumble and lose control, his brothers will be there, to help reach his goal. For a worthy brother, no need is too great. He need not but ask, fulfillment's his fate. For an Aryan brother, death holds no fear. Vengeance will be his, through his brothers still here."*

The fast wail of sirens was damn near in the front yard.

"*She turned me into a race traitor. Brothers. All my brothers. Rise up and help me with my goal. But most of all, forgive me. Forgive me.*"

He closed his eyes. A man the size of a polar bear cried.

He bellowed, "*To God be the glory.*"

His last recorded words were his shaking voice to his shotgun.

Then he whispered, "*Thunder, take me home. Not halfway. All the way.*"

He put the barrel back under his chubby chin.

The Judge of all Judges eased his finger to the oiled trigger.

Thunder boomed.

Terrified birds shrieked from the two-hundred-year-old shade trees that had witnessed better wars.

More than four hundred pounds of deadweight fell out of frame, but the recording was crisp. There were a dozen uneven creaks and thumps, the sound of a giant toppling slowly down twelve wooden stairs.

The judge's tumbling had made the phone's camera fall.

It fell flat and pointed toward sunrise-tinted heaven.

Rain started to fall with the brand-new sun.

Rain falling under the sun was a sign the devil was beating his wife.

The devil had gone to Brownsville, done more than beat his wife.

A rooster crowed.

It was time for the Bitch from Brownsville to get her hair done.

CHAPTER 77

NEIGHBORS RUSHED TO the scene and became social media reporters. It was probably the most exciting thing many of them had seen. A dozen people posted the bloodied bodies being covered up. By then crime scene tape was up across the entrance to the walkway to the plantation-style house.

Professor Quarry and his wife, Sammie-Lynn, called first.

Sammie-Lynn was hysterical, in absolute shock, broken-down.

They had me on speaker as I stood in the living room.

The widow was in the kitchen, on her own call.

My eyes were on Blair Hunt Drive, phone up to my ear.

Sammie-Lynn blew her nose and rambled, "Somebody on Twitter said that iPhone had to be in a shockproof case. Every local news station is already out there interviewing the neighbors. The teary-eyed folks and shocked citizens in Brownsville said that happened and was recorded from beginning to end just like a movie because God wanted this madness seen by all of his faithful servants as a warning. Videos from BPD bodycams have already been leaked as well. This became a snuff video. Like the *Faces of Death* sick people used to watch back in the day when they had Blockbuster video stores and record shops everywhere."

I let her finish, then said good-bye, said we'd chat later.

As soon as she hung up, the widow's phone rang.

"Well, good morning, soror. Yeah, I just heard. They gave it a hashtag. *Faces of Death.* Before we get started, I'm a little busy this morning. Having a quick breakfast with a friend."

My phone rang. I answered, stressed.

Four Ds was in shock too. "Mane, you heard?"

"Mane, all Memphis done heard by now."

"That video. Mane, mane, mane."

"Mane, watching it now. Fucked-up. Imma have to hit you later."

I went to her window again, hunted for my hunters. Mimosa in hand, I went to her bookshelf and pulled down a novel by my father. One from the lauded Forever series. I stared at his face. It was my face aged.

I asked him, "What the fuck am I supposed to do, Suleman?"

Suddenly I was back in Los Angeles, meeting my father for the first time, angry, standing over his coffin, staring at my dead doppelganger. My father had been a sign. He'd shown me my fate. I'd seen myself expired. The unknowns in the black SUVs were my grim reapers, my black-hooded skeletons with scythes. They'd have to take me kicking and screaming. And they'd better be fuckin bulletproof as fuck too.

The widow was still on the phone, unaware of my angst.

My phone rang again. I jumped.

Anxious, I answered. "Yeah, Momma?"

"You done heard?"

"I done heard."

"Pearly white caskets dropping."

"His and hers."

"Gonna be a big funeral on that side of town."

"His and hers."

"Those rich people."

"Old-money Confederates crying this morning."

"Let's see what the NRA has to say on this one."

"Yeah."

"Momma gone."

I lowered my phone.

The widow was behind me laughing.

I turned to see if she was watching me. She was still on her phone, whispering, had her lips turned up and was making more mimosas.

She made a stank face. "I been done quit him. The doctor from TSU didn't act right and got left. Girl in Smackover. Two in the morning."

She laughed again, looked at me, and smiled.

"Selena, I'll call you back in an hour. Now, that's nunya business."

She brought me a fresh drink.

She asked, "What are you thinking about, Sweet Meat?"

I said, "The Calhouns . . . both of 'em . . . they are dead."

She had made biscuits, salmon croquettes, grits seasoned with light salt, pepper, vegan cheese, shrimp, tarragon, chives, and green onions.

She fixed my plate first, moaned and shook her head as she did. "That's horrible. Just plain horrible what that fool went off and did."

She sipped her mimosa, then chased it with coffee. "Someone just tweeted that the KKK-type websites are on fire too. Their racist hero is gone with the wind. His constituents and supporters will put swastikas on their KKK robes and fly Nazi flags at half-mast all next week."

She made the video broadcast from her phone to her big-screen television. She turned the volume up a little to hear the final argument better. We watched Dr. Stone-Calhoun's live broadcast, saw her death from her point of view, saw the judge's wrath during the predawn confrontation, saw it step by step from her waking in a rage to the direct and explosive gunshot from Thunder to her cold-blooded heart, sat with grits and salmon croquettes and witnessed the blood-splattering, horrific recording that was playing all over Memphis, saw what social media was eagerly spreading around the world as a new *Faces of Death* video.

On the video she was alive.

Thunder boomed.

Then Dr. Stone-Calhoun was dead.

Thunder boomed again.

Then the judge was dead.

The widow rewound the broadcast.

"Did you hear that, Sweet Meat?"

"Which part?"

"You hear what that drunk fool said?"

I was almost too jarred to talk. "Play it again. Let me listen."

"That drunk fool claimed Dr. Stone-Calhoun was a Black woman."

"I heard the drunk man rambling, but let me hear him again, the part at the end when he's talking about a nappy-headed nigger."

I closed my eyes to hear him better. I heard him call out to his league of brothers, brothers already embedded in law enforcement, politics, and every part of society, to forgive him and finish the work he had started.

She said, "He kept calling her and somebody bellicose niggers."

"Bellicose nappy-headed nigger."

"Ain't all niggers bellicose to white people?"

"Let them tell it."

She laughed like she was unsure. "Sweet Meat, would be something else if Little Miss Pinky pulled a Carol Channing and won the white folks' precious beauty pageant when she was a teenager. If Dr. Stone-Calhoun was imitating their lives all these years and fooled Memphis, UAN, the mayor, the senator, and the White House, this will never end. If that's true they'll probably turn this into a Tennessee Williams stage play."

"Nothing about her looks, smells, or sounds Black."

"I'm so confused."

"So was she, I guess."

She checked her phone. "*Nappy-headed nigger* is trending."

I asked, "Mind playing that video on your television again?"

The judge never spoke my name on the recording. He claimed his wife had cheated with a *bellicose nappy-headed nigger*. Every Black man the judge knew was considered a nappy-headed nigger, even if he was bald. Judge had said the bellicose nigger was ugly. No one would look in my green eyes and think he was talking about me. Not even gossip detectives Sammie-Lynn and Professor Quarry would consider me.

Like everything else lately, I could be wrong as a mofo.

News could have been leaked and news vans could be headed my way. So could those KKK loyalists eager to fulfill a dead man's wishes. The Judge knew my address and could've passed it on to a faithful servant.

The day of too many deaths was still as young as a newborn. Two SUVs of unknowns remained idling right outside this front door. And a loaded gun was anxious and on standby in my rucksack. I'd never hashtagged a man, had never been a hashtag, but there was a first time for everything.

CHAPTER 78

THE WIDOW SHOOK her head in utter disbelief, the same way the city had done when Elvis had croaked on the toilet back in the day. She went back to fixing breakfast and mimosas. It was impersonal to Widow Fatima, same as my father's death had been to Gemma Buckingham.

The widow said, "When a man loves you, he'll build you a new house; when he hates you, he'll dig you a fresh grave."

"A man like the judge will make you dig your own grave."

"He said that white woman was a Black woman."

I took my Chevy to the levy and gave what sounded stupid a thought. My mind was back on the night UAN had replayed the Cybill Shepherd movie. The Pink Palace. The Bitch from Brownsville had publicly attacked the Judge of all Judges when he had barely touched her perfect blond hair at the nape of her precious neck; then she had privately assaulted the drunken man again on the side of the road for the same crime a couple of hours later, after she had robbed me.

That same night while my iPhone recorded all her wrongs, she had attacked me, too, had raped me and had a category 5 conniption fit when my Black fingers grazed the blond hair curled in her high-class kitchen.

The widow sipped her mimosa. "Our father who art in Zion, forgive me for saying this, but if a man wants to commit a murder-suicide, please make his crazy butt do the suicide part first."

"Twice if needed."

She took a long sip. "You worked with Dr. Stone-Calhoun."

"Saw her almost every day I worked."

"So, you knew her, then."

"Do you ever really know white people? They smile in your face. Then come to hang you at midnight. They burned down Black Wall Street. What matters most is who they are when you leave the room. Fred Astaire danced in blackface. Shirley Temple did the same. Even the good ones ridiculed us to get a laugh from other white people."

"I sense some tension, and pretty much no empathy."

"They never sat at my dinner table and never invited me to theirs."

"Our interactions with certain colleagues rarely extend beyond the parking lot at work. They don't visit our front porches."

"They don't invite us to see their grass and we reciprocate."

"That murder spoke to me. Glad I didn't make it to Smackover."

I thought I heard someone outside, then put my hand in my rucksack, touched my gun. No one was there, just my imagination.

Widow Fatima went on, "Saddest display of misguided toxic masculinity I've ever seen. Well, they say the one you marry will more than likely be the one who kills you."

I went to the front window to double-check.

The original stalker was gone. The second unknown was there. Its driver's door was closing. Someone had gotten out and gotten back in.

Thirty seconds later the original unknown crept back up Blair Hunt Drive from the north end. The unknown paused by the unknown. The prowlers slowed in front of the widow's house, then took up their post again.

Soca music was on low. Music by Alison Hinds. A song the widow loved made her get up and make her body move. She paid death no never mind. She bent her knees a little, did a subtle little Caribbean dance, went down, came up, made it bounce, all waist and butt movements.

She distracted me. Effortlessly and with dexterity the HBCU professor made her left cheek wink, then made her right cheek wink. I went to her, to the tipsy dancing queen, touched her small waist, and she pulled her heavy dreadlocks back from her face and gazed back at my expression.

Grins were exchanged. I danced behind Widow Fatima, pulled up on her bumper as it went in perfect circles. Tipsy, alone, admiring each other, and in her Hotel California. Dancing soca to remember; dancing soca to forget. Barely after sunrise and we'd sipped mimosas like it was last call at the Love Club on a Friday night.

She amazed me, moved like a soca-wining specialist, her slow wine at first a zephyr, evolving into a West Indian tropical storm, then became a hurricane in the making. I held her sleek bumper, danced with her, did like the music said and tried to stick it, stick it, stick it, while she made it ticktock, ticktick, ticktock. She bent over, put one palm flat against the wall, looked back at me as she moved that Caribbean moneymaker deeper into my crotch. My neighbor was waking up the beast within. I got too excited, couldn't keep up with the category 5 storm, so I stood still and held on the best I could. Had to bend my knees to keep my balance when she pushed back hard and rolled it deep and slow. Real deep. Real slow. Her bones massaged my bone. I grabbed her waist, and she bent a little lower, put both palms on the wall, took it round and round, and did her rude dance. She was in a zone. She looked back, then turned around. I eased her closer to me. Her breath caught in her throat. I put my lips on hers. She moaned a bit, shuddered a lot. Then we kissed with no space between us, kissed until we heard Pokey's kids playing across the street. It hurt to pull away.

A tsunami of dopamine flooded my brain; serotonin filled the air.

The widow's pupils dilated. "Jesus. I wasn't ready for all that."

"Did I misread the moment?"

"We're across-the-street neighbors, Professor."

"We're neighbors and I crossed a line."

She whispered, "Can't unkiss a kiss."

"No, you can't."

"I've been eating salmon, sipping mimosas, and drinking sweet coffee. Would be nice if you'd warned me in advance so I could've flossed, gargled, and brushed my teeth and tongue before we had our first kiss."

"What now?"

"You tell me, Professor. You started it, so you tell me."

I moved her locks from her face, kissed her again.

We kissed until her nipples stood at attention and she pushed me away. Then she pulled me back. We started kissing and couldn't stop.

"Professor, Pi, Sweet Meat, neighbor, you done started something."

"Fine. I take it back."

"Just like a brother. All up on me like that and we haven't been on a proper date. Not one. I haven't been invited to your home or even asked to sit on your front porch not once in your evening shade. Not once in the years I've known you. Maybe you should go home before we start at the finish line, then end up struggling trying to find a beginning."

I backed away, but she pulled me back to her, put her hand up to my face, invited me back. Her body pressed against mine and moved with the beat to the music. We danced and kissed some more. Some more. Some more. Until the song ended as our cue to take a break or quit.

She swallowed, struggled to say, "Professor. We be neighbors."

"You're right, Professor. We be neighbors."

We backed away from the grinding. My erection was as obvious as the shade tree in my front yard, same for her hardened nipples.

She fanned herself to cool down. Did her no good.

"Behave yourself. Pokey saw you come over. I texted her and told her you were coming to look at my backyard so you can fix up my patio."

"Mo Fo was up too. I texted him and told him the same."

"Yemi Savage 'nem know you were invited by for a quick breakfast. Soror nosy and might've seen you cross from her house. You stay over here any longer, the whole neighborhood gonna start talking about us."

"Your front door is wide-open."

"They know ain't nothing going on here this early in the day."

"Ain't nothing going on. We're neighbors."

I backed away again. She pulled me back. We kissed some more.

Mo Fo's kids got lively outside.

We paused when we heard them, then went back to kissing.

She whisper-asked, "What are you thinking, Sweet Meat?"

My own death was waiting, chilling like a villain, outside in a pair of black SUVs. That plus this could bust open the abuse scandal and news vans could arrive looking for me at any moment. With the scent of another man's roses mildly perfuming the house, the more frustrating, heavier issue was Gemma Buckingham. I was with another woman, life on the line, and she was living rent-free in my motherfuckin head.

She repeated her question, then said, "Answer me, Professor."

"Never imagined you'd want to kiss me."

"You're a king. Everyone wants to kiss the king."

"African queens Amina, Kandake, Nefertiti, Yaa Asantewaa, Nandi, and Moremi should all return to life and bow at your feet, then gift you whatever is left of their armies and kingdoms. You're *the* queen."

"Bruh, you really . . . really . . . *really* want my sweet lemonade."

"Like you really want my sweet *café de olla*."

"Who said I want your coffee like that?"

"My bad."

The widow eased away, sipped her mimosa.

She hummed, maintained eye contact. "Question before you go?"

"Anything."

"I've kinda asked you once."

"Okay."

"But I need to be clear."

"Okay."

"You still seeing that girl?"

"What girl?"

"Whoever you were seeing that time you fixed my flat. And don't lie. You had on evening clothes in the morning. I noticed you hadn't been home all night. So I know you were creeping back from being mannish with her. I ain't forgot that time. You smelled like that morning's soap in yesterday's clothes blessed by some nice perfume that some woman wore the night before. You were in the middle of your walk of shame."

"Nah. That ended as fast as it started. I was her boy of summer."

"I don't need another Smackover situation, especially with a man who lives across the street from my house. Took us a long time to talk. Would hate to have a reason to stop speaking to you the rest of my life."

"No frama from me."

"She around? You know how I roll. I need to hear the honest truth and not an ugly lie. Tell me the real deal so I can decide if you're worth the bandwidth you're taking up in my life. No need to gaslight."

"Gaslighting ain't my style. Lying takes too much energy. She moved, left Memphis. Went overseas. Left without telling me good-bye."

"You need some more time?"

"I'm good. She moved. I've moved on."

"She moved. What about you? Did you love her? Do you?"

"It's hard to love someone determined to not love you."

She whispered, "What you're preaching makes me want to shout."

A serious moment sat between us, looked back and forth.

"Maybe you should go. Yemi Savage is coming over soon."

I turned to leave. She caught my hand.

We kissed like we were too afraid to rush to the next part.

Lips against mine, she whispered, "Seems like you like kissing me."

"Could do this all day until it got dark, then until light again."

"We should kiss the entire kissing song."

"What kissing song?"

"Beginning to end, nonstop."

"Okay."

"Alexa, play my favorite song."

"Playing 'Kissin' You' by Total."

When we were done, we held each other, eyes glazed over, bothered.

I whispered, "Can I please you?"

"What does that mean?"

"Means you don't have to do anything but let me please you."

"Exactly how does that work?"

I sat on her olive sofa, a showroom-pretty Pottery Barn sectional, then motioned for her to bring her mind, body, and soul and all else God blessed her with to me, to come chill and take a spell and refuge between my legs. My back was in the corner of the sectional farthest from her open front door, so anything we did would be unseen. She backed it up, eased down biting the corner of her lip, adjusted until she was comfortable, then rested her spine against my chest, her rooty-tooty booty against my erection. She felt hardness and her nostrils flared. She turned her body, moved her dreadlocks, and gave me her tongue for the kissing.

I sucked her neck and ear, massaged her breasts, pinched her nipples, then eased my hand down across her belly, went due south.

The widow whispered, "You are starting something."

"Sho nuff."

"In my front room with my windows and door open."

She reached for her remote, turned the television on, raised the volume. The news and the Calhouns appeared. I took the remote, changed to a movie. Cary Grant and Ingrid Bergman were making out.

CHAPTER 79

I RUBBED THE outside of her vagina, played with her while we kissed. With my fingers I moved her ladder-cut thong to the side and gave her the same passionate energy. My fingers worked that come-here motion, had her squirming and biting on my tongue and talking gibberish. I found the button. Massaged it in slow motion and kept on sucking her ear. She rocked against my hand like she was catching the spirit, squeezed her own breasts over and over, then opened wider, moved her limber legs as far apart as she could, mewled to Jesus, then pressed her hand on top of mine, showed me the fast and steady motion she liked and needed. She was intense, sounded like she was on LSD having a fever dream.

She reached back, touched my hard-on, measured it, moved her hand up and down until I joined her heated sounds and moaned.

She held me. "This is a religion changer."

Her phone rang. We jumped like we'd been busted.

The widow struggled. "Oh, Selena. Really?"

I finger-massaged her and whispered, "Take the call."

"No. It's my sorority sister in Texas."

"Yes. Answer her."

The widow bit her bottom lip, inhaled hard, and did what I said.

"Morning, soror. I'm sort of busy. Working out on my treadmill."

I whispered, "Talk to her."

She swallowed. "I have a minute. What's going on? Oh, you heard."

The widow did her best to sound normal.

I kissed her neck, pinched her nipples, and toyed with the sliver of pinkness on top of the most elegant darkness.

Two fingers stirred coffee and kept it hot.

"You know I'm up. I ain't never been a slugabed. So bigmouth Selena called you. Gossiping about me. She is so malicious. Nowadays? He don't mean dick to me. Girl, we been broke up. I quit him. Well, I changed my status on Facebook."

My fingers went deeper.

"Truth is like the sun—you can hide it for a time, but it is not going to disappear. The truth will come out. Some girl over in Smackover. Made a fool out of me. I was so bent out of shape the Face ID on my phone didn't recognize me for three days."

Fingers slid deep to my knuckles.

She pulled her lips in, nostrils flared, exhaled slowly, then said, "She called me at two in the morning and woke up the old me. Called me out of my name. 'Anorexic cunt.' I was angrier at myself than I was with him. Came home, burned so much sage, smoke detector went off, disinfected my space with bleach and Lysol, threw away old bedding, ordered new sheets on Amazon, made an appointment with my doctor to get tested, put on Mary J. and danced naked while I smoked some good Mary J."

I pulled out, eased back in.

"Then switched over to Amy Winehouse and finished my cry while I graded a few papers. Look, let me call you back. I have company and I'm up here running my mouth. Man company. Mind your business. That's right, *métete en tus asuntos, chica*. In an hour."

She ended the call, then was suddenly breathing hard, like she was coming from being trapped underwater, panting, squirming; only the way she worked against my fingers let me know she was about to come.

I sucked her ear. "You like this?"

"Oooooooo, shit." She moved against me as I kept on massaging her button. "You are so damn good with your fingers. Damn good."

"What if I want to kiss you another way?"

"Don't say that to me right now when I'm not in my right mind."

486   ERIC JEROME DICKEY

"Can I put on a kissing song and kiss you a special way?"

"Pi. Sweet Meat. Neighbor. You're bluffing."

"All out of wolf tickets."

She whispered, "My front curtains are open. So is my front door."

"This won't take but a couple of minutes; then I'm gone."

Like a man in prayer, I got down on my knees, a sinner humbling himself before a greater human being, to the essence of God.

She cooed. "UAN professor. You better be bluffing."

"HBCU professor. Last time. I'm fresh out of wolf tickets."

"You ain't trying to get nasty like that this morning."

I pushed her short skirt up.

She shuddered.

I slid her thong off.

Her eyes were closed tight.

I hummed. "You're tense. Got me locked out of heaven."

"Questions. I have questions."

"Okay."

"What does *pellucidity* mean? What does *infirmity* mean? What does *impenetrable* mean? What does *solipsistic* mean? What does *laconically* mean? What is a glib person? Miss one, we done, no come."

I answered them all.

"What does *equally yoked* mean?"

I answered that biblical inquiry with ease.

She tremble-whispered, "You have to . . ."

"Have to what?"

"Swipe up . . . swipe up . . . to unlock."

One long, lingering tongue swipe upward was the password, and the door to heaven opened wide. No facial recognition needed. She moaned. I kissed her dark skin upward to her bended knees. Her long legs were two roads leading to the same destination. Her skin was heated, glowing, soft, smooth, flawless, and her vagina was the same. It left me mesmerized. It was beautiful, a pulchritudinous slice of perfect pinkness rising from the mystery of absolute darkness. Pinkness bloomed from the color of power. That coral color surrounded by Blackness, that entrance to paradise, that opening to her heaven on earth, it was aroused, swollen. A sliver of cotton candy on double-dark chocolate. I stopped and looked at her like I'd never seen a vagina before in my life, amazed at the contrast. Her pussy was art fit for its own wing in a place that recognized artistic value, should have its own gallery for the perfect coochie aficionados in the British Museum.

CHAPTER 80

MY MOUTH COVERED her sex. Sensual notes rose from her O-shaped mouth. The widow was a mandolin, a musical instrument that caused relaxation and calm. I ate her out in the key of G and she liked it.

I showed her I was bilingual. I gave her French kisses. Slow, passionate kisses. Deep kisses. Lovers' kisses.

I had my hands under her tight little butt. She rested her right leg over my shoulder. Her face contorted into a sensual expression.

Somebody called her name through the screen door.

"Widow Fatima, you there?"

"Sister Cerritos Del Amo. Good morning. What's going on?"

Our elderly neighbor talked through the screen. "Our neighbor other side next to me had her catalytic converter stolen off her car sometime between eleven last night and five this morning."

"I'll tell everyone on this end to be on the lookout."

"How you this morning?"

"I'm well, and yourself?"

"I'm good."

"Long as you ain't evil."

They laughed.

She asked, "You know who this is parked in front of my house?"

"No, ma'am."

"I don't like people parking in front of my house. Makes me nervous."
Our neighbor left.

I said, "Alexa, play 'Tender Kisses' by Tracie Spencer."

Tracie sang and the widow tried to get away. I followed her. My French kissing was nonstop. The widow jerked and pulled a sofa pillow over her face to muffle uncontrollable moans. Her right leg tensed.

She came a long time. Came while Tracie Spencer hit high notes. I held her as she bucked my face, gave her kisses until she slowed down. It was a slow-dying fire with a few sudden hot spots. She panted a hundred times. I kissed her inner thighs. She clamped her hand over her heart.

She looked me deep in my eyes. "*Jesús. Me siento transformado, bendecido, y ya no inquieto. Me he convertido en un fénix que quema la angustia en una pira funeraria y resucita de las cenizas con renovada juventud. Mi alma fracturada finalmente sería libre, lista para seguir adelante y ser un mejor yo, listo para vivir otro ciclo de vida y todo lo que tiene que traer. Te amo, te amo desde el momemto nos conocimos para la primera vez. Te amo, maestro, maestro, maestro, te amo mucho.*"

"What was that?"

She struggled to form words. "I came so hard I think I just coded."

I eased away. She groaned and pulled me back. With her small hands and slender fingers in my bro 'fro, her nails on my scalp, she massaged my rows of dark cotton, opened her legs wider, put my lips, mouth, tongue, and teeth where she needed them the most. My tongue swam inside her heat, did a hundred and one lazy laps mixed with two hundred rapid tongue strokes. Her fingers danced feverishly in my hair. She made me purr, tamed me, pulled on my rows of black cotton, tugged with the pleasure she felt and made don't-stop whimpers. Each soft sound she made, each hum, pulled me into a zone, into the softness of her improvised song. She wiggled in circles, tensed, reversed her circles.

She nodded. "Come here and kiss me again."

She jerked with pain and pleasure as I did, her breathing ragged, desperate, famished. The widow held my ass, put her nails in my skin.

She struggled, on fire as she pulled at my joggers, yanked them down over my ass, made me take one leg out, then had me straddle her.

She inched me north, guided me toward her belly until I straddled her breastbone, had me be still until she was comfortable with me on her sternum. Eyes closed, biting the corner of her lip, she put my blessing between her beautiful breasts. She squeezed them against me, and I moved like I was inside a new orifice, rocked to and fro as she made the titty bun tight, enjoyed the way she did that. She set free a cavalcade of musical sounds, either ascending or descending, lived in the moment, was singing a song that told me she enjoyed it more than I did.

Her body remained restless, was wining like I was still dancing inside her, that land still smoldering and on fire. I reached back, fingered her as she feasted. Each time I pushed forward, when I neared her mouth, she smiled a wicked smile and opened her mouth, needed to be fed. I paused and she flicked her little tongue against the hat, tasted me as I seeped, teased me, then made me be still and sucked the head, tasted what we'd made, hummed like the spirit of lust was now her Black goddess. The widow put her nails in my ass again, gripped my ass, slapped my ass, then pulled me all the way to her face, and her lips spread as she set the pace to move. I was invited inside her erudite mouth for a new education, was escorted gently down her throat. She bobbed, sucked, hummed and hummed and hummed in call while I nodded my head, bit my lips, hummed and hummed and hummed in response.

She hummed to herself as she ran her tongue up and down the shaft, did the same at the hat, then playfully slapped my manhood against her soft lips. My body began to rumba, and I growled like a bear.

She got sloppy, with her hands moving in opposite directions, her sucking strong. My knees weakened. I used the back of the sectional to keep my balance as the world fell away. There was no gravity. My mouth was opened wide in astonishment. I was about to sing my own song of surrender. I didn't want to give in to nirvana. Where I was, I wanted to stay. It was a losing fight. I struggled. My back arched as my legs strained. She set the devil free and had me calling her name and yodeling like I was high on a mountain in the Swiss Alps. I exploded, emptied myself. She didn't back down. She was ravenous for what she'd earned and was there until the end, until nothing was left, until I fuckin went kaput.

CHAPTER 81

GRAVITY HUGGED ME, held me up, then dropped me like a rock. I fell from the sectional to the floor, eyes wide shut until I was able to control my breathing and look around the living room until I found the widow. She was on the sectional, covered in sweat like I was. Exhausted, drops of hot whiteness against humid darkness, she slid off the sectional and crawled to where I had collapsed and all but balled up into a knot.

In West Indian singsong she sang, "You. Started it. I. Finished it."

We heard a noise. She sat up, nervous, pulled her skirt back down, worried with her hair, then looked toward her front door again.

I tried to fix my clothing as I whispered, "Somebody there?"

She whispered back, "Heard something."

She found the remote, lowered the volume on her television.

We listened. Something dropped.

She sounded relieved. "Mailman. She came early today."

"So did you."

"A time or two."

Bills were put in her box; then the letter carrier moved on.

We were breathless. I picked up my rucksack to leave. She looked at me like I was nucking futs. I dropped my bag where I stood.

She struggled. "We're not done having fun."

"Don't want to overstay my welcome."

"If you're one and done, we done at the end of one."

"I can do two and through to please you."

She chuckled, kissed me. "Make me moan again."

The curtains were open. The front door was open.

Outside this front door the promise of hell waited for me.

In the widow's house was the promise of heaven.

Serious, she said, "Somebody came up to my porch. I sensed it. And it wasn't our mailman. Whoever it was didn't call my name."

"Would the doctor from TSU show up?"

"He came to my job. I called security. Sent him away."

"Would he pop up over here this early?"

"I wouldn't put it past him. Wouldn't be surprised if that Walmart girl from Smackover came this way and brought a storm either."

My eyes went to my rucksack as I inhaled the scent of roses.

Roses. One of the preferred flowers at a funeral.

Another sign.

She changed the channel on the television, went back to the local news. The Bitch from Brownsville stared at me, smiling over Russian Red lips. She was next to a large man who demanded dead-nigger soup.

CHAPTER 82

WIDOW FATIMA BIT her bottom lip as she spied outside. She checked to see who was watching, stood in her front window a minute before she closed her front door. I was near her, also checking to see who was observing. Grim and Reaper lurked. Like shadowy government agents.

The widow closed her curtains, then shut and locked her door.

She held my pinky finger and I followed her into her boudoir.

In her pristine bedroom, a room that smelled like lavender, the morning light made the light-red curtains glow and create a mood. The illumination fell across her queen bed in strong invitation. Donna Karan bedding. Hints of the day's early sun kept it so we could see each other as plain as a new sin. This wasn't being done in darkness.

I dropped my rucksack by her dresser.

We kissed until our rumpled clothes fell off, fell like leaves from a tree during a new season. She had on three pieces. I had on three pieces.

She whispered, "Oh, I'm definitely finna moan this morning."

The widow pulled away her top covers. She got comfortable on the edge of the bed and pulled her legs up, kept her knees together until they touched her dank face, her lower limbs as straight as she could keep them as she held her own calves. Her pinkness was on display. It was the view of all views, had to be better than being in Paris at the Louvre.

I played with her erect nipples, sucked her breasts.

She held on to my rows of black cotton.

She whispered, "Put it in."

I tapped her clit four times with my engorged blessing, drummed it.

"Put it in."

I gave her the tip, made her flower start to bloom, opened her a bit.

She moaned, "I'm going to need more than that to keep from fighting you this morning. Don't do me like this and smile about it."

She tugged at her dreadlocks, overaroused, pulled at me harder, demanded my girth and length rush inside her, wiggled and moaned like she needed to be filled, like that itch was so deep, her breathing pure fire.

She held on to me, whispered, "You have scratches on your back."

I whispered, "They're old."

"Must've been good to her."

"All that matters is if it's good to you."

"Put it in; put it in."

I took her back and forth, rocked in and out of her until she lowered her legs, moved her dreadlocks away, and she hooked my ankles with hers. Pulled me as deep as she could. She took the pain like it was the analgesic she needed to cure an unwanted heartbreak. I hit the spot of all spots and heard a vulgar hallelujah. She joggled, shimmied, danced, once again the wining specialist. My breathing was as measured as my strokes; with each hard exhale I fought to maintain control. Her choppy breathing was harsh, quick, in spurts, a runner suddenly doing sprints uphill.

Then someone banged on her door and rang her bell.

I rolled away so she could get up. She was off center, then rushed and pulled on fresh clothes, still barefoot as she went toward the front door. I went to my backpack, eased out my gun, stood by the doorframe.

It was UPS.

They brought her five dozen fresh roses, same as the ones I'd seen outside. She thanked the deliveryman, then carried her love offering straight out the back door to the trash. She washed her hands and came back to me. I was sitting on the edge of the bed, rucksack back at the foot of her dresser. She yanked her clothing off and hurried back to me.

"Sweet Meat."

"You okay?"

"Fuck no."

"What can I do?"

"Make me moan."

CHAPTER 83

WE FUCKED LIKE we understood each other on an unseen level, until she slowed down, her breathing like a woman beginning to drown.

I whisper-asked, "Neighbor. Professor. Fatima. You okay?"

"I'm coming hard, fuck I'm coming so hard, fuck I'm coming, fuck."

She jerked like people did on the first drop on a roller coaster, held me like I was her parachute, like she had become weightless, was parachute jumping from above the clouds and imagined she was an angel falling from heaven, this new sensation as arousing as it was terrifying.

She whispered, "Hold on a second."

Sounded like someone was on her porch. She looked that way. We stopped, listened. No one knocked. I continued stroking as she danced.

We rocked the boat, then switched it up again.

She positioned herself doggy style, but I surprised her, got behind her and took my second meal. I did that thing that had had Gemma Buckingham tripping. Her face flashed in my mind. All Meghan Markled from head to toe. I did that thing, did it better now than I had with a Black woman goddess from London. It had the widow tripping hard and falling fast. Then I was on my back, like a mechanic under a car. Was so good she twisted and turned to get away, felt so good it made her try to stand up to escape a swelling orgasm. She surrendered and it felt like she swooned. I moaned. I moaned a lot. It wasn't a quiet journey. Each sound

I set free was like that intoxicating burn a man felt when he took a hit of good Tennessee whiskey. She was medicine for my fractured soul. Good sex always sounded like someone was being tortured. I was killing it. Killing it every way but softly. A dozen positions along with a dozen brands and timbre of succulent moans, manly and babyish, uneven and overlapping, at times her soft squeals, most of the noise my heavy breathing.

Phones rang and went unanswered.

Sirens blared down Kansas Street, the Doppler effect ignored by her.

The sirens jarred me, ruined my rhythm.

That wretched *Faces of Death* video played in my head.

It wasn't my fault.

Like the president, this nappy-headed nigger took no blame.

The widow did a pelvic thrust, held it, tightened her abs, clenched and raised her sweet little butt, made her midsection rise like a mountain. I was on my knees, between her legs, and I held her thighs, kept her suspended. She closed her eyes and hummed as I went in and out.

She struggled to breathe. "That's my spot. You've learned my spot."

I double-stroked, then turned her over.

She reached back and put the palm of her hand against my stomach, made me chill. She crooned her anthem, "It hurts, you're too deep, but don't stop if I say stop, go harder and faster because I love it."

"You sure?"

"It's all in me. You done put it all in me. Feels so so so fucking good. Give it to me. Fuck me like you need to come. Don't hold back."

I repeated, "You sure?"

She laughed a little. "Shit, maybe I do have an anorexic cunt."

"It won't be when we're done."

"Come for me. Fuck me like you're desperate to come."

"Where?"

"Anywhere you want to. Any-fucking-where you want to."

Then we let loose, stopped being polite neighbors, lost control, went into a frenzy, growled and released uncontrollable grunts, moans, mewls, and muffled screams of passion. It was a battle where no one would lose. Skin slapped like an enthusiastic standing ovation. Our chests were rising and falling out of sync. I slowed and cursed to God. She pulled at me like she wanted all of my body inside her. I tried to comply, did my best to crawl inside. The bed shook, the headboard was tested, the room rumbled. I'd never met a woman who moved like that. We'd been thrown overboard in a hurricane and were drowning. Couldn't stop if we tried.

Nerves were on fire. The floor dropped from under our feet. We fell off the edge of the bed, tumbled into the weightlessness of orgasm.

CHAPTER 84

AS I LUGGED my backpack and hurried across Blair Hunt Drive to get back to my house, the doors to both Grim and Reaper opened, and six white men spilled out. Six armed white men in shopworn MAGA caps.

Reaper had my back and suddenly I was in that scene from *Boyz n the Hood*. I was Ricky running, his back to his enemy, gunned down in an alleyway. Only it happened on Blair Hunt Drive and I was Ricky.

One of the MAGA boys stood over me, "Dead-nigger soup."

I jerked awake, sat up fast on the widow's bed, tried to get my nappy head of cotton oriented. I hurried to my feet, went to the front window.

Widow Fatima was knocked out. Dead asleep.

Naked as Adam the day he was created, I went to her back door.

She had light woods and the old train tracks behind her crib. I could sneak out the back, creep up to Sis's small house, and climb over our shared fence and come in through my back door, come out locked and loaded, have the upper hand, not end up in a *Faces of Death* video.

It was time to man up. Was time for this southern gent to become as shred as a northerner. I reached for my T-shirt.

The widow opened her eyes, pulled it away from me.

She was woke. And grinning.

"Sweet Meat, we done run out of your sweet coffee, but I can offer you

some tea. Citrus ginger. Matcha. Sweet peppermint. Or rose Earl Grey.
I like to mix rose Earl Grey with Matcha and add agave."

"I'll try that."

She groaned as she got up, staggered as she went to the bathroom.

Restless, ready for target practice, I asked, "You good?"

She called out to me from the bathroom. "I guess I need to take mag-
nesium. After running ten miles and one more round of naughty with
you, if you go like that the next go-round, my legs will cramp up."

Psychological torture sent me to the front of her house, where for the
sake of my mental health I went to the main window and spied outside.

She said, "You keep looking out my curtains."

"Just being neighborhood watch."

"You're naked, and I like it, but don't traumatize the five children
across the street. Door still closed. Somebody knocked while we were
moaning. People already going to be talking about us this morning."

I turned on the television to see if I was part of the news.

She pondered, "If the judge knew she was a liar, why he just now calling her out? He died exposing her lies, one after another."

"Love." Again I was pulled across the pond. "When a man really loves
a woman, her secrets don't matter. He knows she's a liar and lives with it.
His choice. In his silence he was the protector of her secrets. He maintained her lie out of loyalty, did that to prove his love. Loved her."

"Until he felt he was betrayed by her and a nappy-headed nigger."

"He loved her, even if she didn't love him."

"Madness."

"Love makes everybody a little mad. And blind. Love distorts. You
see what you want to see, see it how you want to see it. You justify. They
lie to you and you lie to yourself on their behalf."

"It's not supposed to kill you."

"Neither will blowfish if you eat the right parts. All love ain't good."

"Guess I've been eating the bad parts. I reckon the judge did."

I went back to her.

"You are one nasty man. Would've been happy with a kiss."

"Now you tell me."

"I actually gave you some and we've never been on a date."

"Lord willing and the creek don't rise, Sunday dinner."

"Boy, that ain't no date. Gave you my lemonade. I'm up in here acting foolish, like I'm seventeen going on twelve. I don't want you thinking I'm just some kind of ho. Hope you don't think that."

"That's funny. Was hoping you didn't think that ish about me."

"This forenoon I needed something palliative if not curative. I needed an orgasm that wasn't done either by my own hand or by using technology from an adult store. And this feels more curative than palliative. Whatever was broken inside me, you're fixing it good."

"Same here."

"Never would've thought you'd be so selfless and passionate in bed. Imagined you being a handsome and selfish lover."

"Ouch."

"Thought you'd be boring and stingy, if not quick."

"You're pretty naughty yourself, Professor."

The widow purred like she was high on sativa. "Confession."

"Confess."

"I peep at you from my window. I used to ask God why he put a man so fine right across the street. And he was a professor. And he liked his momma and siblings. A family man. He was testing me. Just testing me. You never step out looking bad. Your hair. That beard. Never out of order. Not even when you're all sexy cutting your grass."

I scratched my itching left ear.

A sign.

She had made me come seeing shooting stars.

Another sign.

She called out, "Damn."

"What?"

She yelled, "It's confirmed. Dr. Stone-Calhoun's heritage and my natural hair have something in common. They both have Black roots."

The widow came back, dreadlocks hanging along her frame. She had hair-care products, got ready to oil her scalp.

I said, "Let me do that."

She sat between my legs while I went section by section and put tea tree oil on her scalp. Her smile was never ending.

Her phone rang. She answered. "Yes, I furloughed the cheating doctor from TSU. Smackover. Walmart. I'm busy. Yes, a man. Bye."

Soon we rested, television on, news about the Calhouns on blast.

Air conditioner hummed. Soca played.

Grim and Reaper stalked out on Blair Hunt Drive.

She checked mainstream Twitter. While we had fucked like rabbits, the bad news in Brownsville had made CNN, MSNBC, and Fox.

I got up to get dressed. Was time for my backdoor plan. She turned the news off, put her phone aside, pulled me back to the rumpled bed.

She said, "Alexa, play 'Kissing You.'"

CHAPTER 85

WE MADE IT do what it do until her phone rang.

She answered it in front of me.

"What you want? He still here. Well, I'm booed up right now. One thing led to none of your business happened next. Girl, bye. I'm with my man of the morning. Well, he is now. Go mind your biz. Girl, bye."

I asked, "Sorority sister up the street?"

"That was your Kansas Street sister being malicious. I called her last night to find out what you liked for breakfast. Now she's being as nosy as Pokey. She talked my ear off when she did my hair."

"You're friends with Sis now."

"I like your family. I never really had one. Y'all be over there all loud having fun Sunday dinners. Y'all a good crazy."

We heard the roar of a semitrailer truck.

It stopped right outside the widow's front door. That meant they'd stopped in front of my house. The truck downshifted and idled, sat rumbling like it was their destination. My iPhone was blowing up again.

She pulled on my T-shirt and went to peep out the front window.

"Sweet Meat, an eighteen-wheeler just parked on your side of Blair Hunt. Somebody hauling a ruby-red drop-top Chevelle and six more vehicles. Those cars are nice. One of them is a red-and-white Corvette. Carver High colors. These drivers must be lost. Everybody coming outside to look at those pretty cars before the driver takes off. Wait. Hold on. The driver got out and said something to Mo Fo and Pokey 'nem. Now he's walking toward your front door while he calls somebody."

That was who had been blowing my phone up.

I eased my joggers back on. She pulled my T off, stood naked as she handed it to me. I pulled it on, kissed her as I passed by, squeezed her narrow ass, then went outside, iPhone in hand, taking pictures of the cars from California. I had been tempted to have them bring the riding lawn mower, but my yard wasn't that big, not like Four Ds' property out east.

Those vehicles were from the Suleman estate.

To be disposed of as Pi Maurice Suleman saw fit.

I was a millionaire a few times over, still living on an adjunct's salary. That still felt surreal. So much bad luck had followed me for so long. Everything around me signaled that the season had changed.

The delivery had excited me, distracted me.

I had forgotten my backpack.

I had left my gun in the widow's bedroom.

Grim and Reaper hadn't forgotten about me.

CHAPTER 86

GRIM AND REAPER remained parked equidistant from my front door. Neither had moved to accommodate the auto lot on eighteen wheels.

I came jogging down the widow's driveway toward the two-lane street. Grim kicked in gear, made its engine roar, did the same as the Judge of all Judges had down at UAN when he'd tried to turn me into roadkill. I was in the middle of the road. An open target. An easy hit-and-run target. I was Ricky, a boy in the hood with no way out.

Not wearing running shoes this morning was a bad move.

Grim swerved and blocked me from going to my yard.

I stood looking at my reflection in the driver's dark window.

Grim stopped and the driver's-side window came down.

A well-endowed ginger was behind the wheel.

A heavyset Black man was at her side.

Both looked military.

Both had guns.

The looks in their eyes told me they knew how to use them.

These were the dead-nigger-soup-making motherfuckers put on me by the Judge of all Judges. I wanted to yank them out of that damn SUV.

She said, "Professor Pi Maurice Suleman. Blair Hunt Drive."

That put a chill down my spine, gave me goose bumps.

My shotguns were in my house, out of reach.

506 ERIC JEROME DICKEY

My widow-maker was resting at the foot of the widow's bed.

She said, "The Calhouns."

Her wingman said, "The Judge of all Judges."

She asked, "Did you hear about the Calhouns?"

I defiantly asked, "Who the fuck you?"

Redhead was offended. "Mr. Suleman, sir, we work for you."

"For me? What the fuck are you talking about?"

"You know Roger de Groot, right?"

I heard that name and surreality covered me.

I repeated, "Who the fuck are you?"

"He hired us to keep you safe from the Calhouns."

That stopped everything.

I gradually realized what Roger de Groot had done.

He'd sent an armed ebony-and-ivory team to watch over me. The brother's face looked professional enough so folks over here would be at ease and nonconfrontational. Her California-tanned white face being behind the wheel kept the police from harassing them if someone called it in. Still, both looked like they could be assassins if the price was right.

I took a hard breath. "He killed himself and his wife this morning. The coward took his own life. I guess I didn't need you after all."

"Oh, you needed us. You needed the fuck out of us."

Redhead told me they'd been parked in their usual spot last night when an SUV stopped on Kansas Street. It was the judge's two-hundred-thousand-dollar luxury gas-guzzler. It was around midnight. The judge sat parked about twenty minutes, then got out carrying a shotgun. He'd brought Thunder on a rainless night. She said they hit their high beams and startled the judge. He froze where he was. Redhead told me she hit the high beams again to be clear. She got out. Her partner got out. Guns unhidden. Redhead called his name. Judge Zachary Beauregard Calhoun. The brother asked him if he was lost on this side of Memphis. There was ten seconds of contemplation while hundreds of cicadas sang their nightly song. Thunder at his side, the judge walked backward a couple of steps, then turned and hurried back to his SUV. He left my zip code and drove the sixty-some-odd miles it took to get to Brownsville.

We let that marinate a moment.

Roger de Groot hadn't put me in contact with the team. If something had gone south, if the judge had been gunned down while on the wrong side of town, I'd have deniability. They could've popped him and driven away. The people who lived south in the apartments by the railroad tracks and the ditch right before Belz would be blamed before they came after an adjunct from UAN. The redhead would've never been a suspect, not delayed as she boarded a plane to her next assignment. Same for the brother. It wouldn't have been traceable to me and I never would've known Roger de Groot had saved me, not until it blew over and we once again sat in his sky-high office, sipping dark liquor and staring at yachts.

It was done.

They pulled away and passed the other SUV without slowing down. I expected the second SUV to follow the first. It stayed where it was.

Grim was gone; Reaper wasn't leaving.

Someone put their foot on the brakes and the light called for my attention. The engine was running. The windows were up. Air conditioner on. I hoped the first team hadn't left too soon. If that second SUV was trouble, they would have known.

They would have handled it while I handled the widow.

I looked for signs of bad luck as I crossed Blair Hunt Drive.

A 31 Crosstown Kansas rumbled by, going north toward Carver High. North was the direction of the Black man's freedom. North was where we went to taste as much jubilation as the white man would allow. While we were trapped on this Alcatraz, north was our luck.

Heat rising, skin turning dank, I looked around me.

The truck company's symbol was a horseshoe. Horseshoes symbolized good luck. A four-leaf clover blew by in the wind. Wind chimes sang from the Widow Fatima's back porch. A dream catcher hung over her bed. I scratched my itching left ear. Remembered how the widow's West Indian love had made me see shooting stars.

No black butterflies flew this way. The dogs were quiet.

The sun was out without being accompanied by rain.

I sent a group text message to the Fastest Swimmers to get rides to my house at sundown, and not a minute before. The eighteen-wheeler was loaded with new cars and trucks for the Fastest Swimmers. A car was

Momma's if she'd ever give in and take one. She'd have first and second choice. Momma had always wanted a Harley, so I'd had them ship that too. I wondered how Momma would feel when she saw that hog parked on the street and then saw a red-and-white 1960 Corvette, same as Momma's high school colors at Carver High, the same colors as her sorority. If she rejected both I'd have to make my driveway and the front of my house a new car lot for a while. The Fastest Swimmers could have any car or truck, and it all would go by our pecking order, so no one ended up butt hurt with their lips poked out. All I needed was my red car, the Nova sold to me by an angel who marched for equality and was beaten along with her husband when they dared to cross a white man's bridge in Alabama.

Obsessed like the rest, I returned to social media.

Nappy-headed nigger was still trending.

CHAPTER 87

MY ACROSS-THE-STREET LOVER came outside of her home.

Now she rocked a coral Kente dress that stopped above her knees. The covering over the top of her butt-length dreadlocks was the hue of a brand-new day. She pulled her dreadlocks back into a ponytail, her mane as wooly as my intimidating rows of black cotton. I'd left her bed and crossed the street without combing my hair or running inside to rinse off and freshen up.

Smelling like good sex, I watched her. She smiled at her Bermuda grass, then stood like a lioness in the Memphis sun.

With a wave I invited our Sarabi over to where bluegrass grew.

She called out, "Your momma raised you better."

"What I do wrong?"

"Sweet Meat, you better peregrinate those pretty green eyes back over to my side of Blair Hunt and get me. I could get hit by a car."

"Ain't no cars."

"That eighteen-wheeler blocking my view. I can't see both ways."

"Peregrinating."

"Come get me. It's the first time you've invited me over."

As my across-the-street lover sashayed down her driveway toward my side of Blair Hunt Drive, I grinned. She blushed. Anyone who saw us right now would know. I'd been over there and her front door had been closed, so folks on this end of the block had something to talk about.

California cars were being unloaded and she didn't question me.

She said, "Saw you talking to the people in the SUV."

"It was a couple. Brother with a white woman."

"Figures. I just knew it. They need to get a room or at least take that mess over to Riverside Park like everybody else does."

We looked at the second SUV, then shrugged.

I took her hand in mine.

We watched two Latin men handle a workingman's load of vehicles with Los Angeles tags, then walked from car to car, talking, laughing, flirting, and checking them all out. We went as far as the second SUV, stopped near its bumper, then looked back at the car lot I'd created.

We practiced minding our own business.

The red-and-white vehicles had me thinking. Suleman had bought several cars with the same Carver High colors my mother was wearing the day he met her. Those were her sorority colors too.

I'd take that to the levy and give it a good thinking some other time.

The widow said, "I'm bowlegged now. You made me bowlegged."

"Am I spending the night over there or you are coming over here?"

"We can break your bed. I think mine had a good stress test this morning. Tongue had me moaning, then that big dick had me shouting."

We laughed like teenagers, and I took her hand and led her toward my house. We chilled on the porch in the shade the way I imagined Miss Virginia and her husband, Herman, did on Kansas Street back in the day.

The widow asked, "What are you thinking about?"

"Barbecue sauce. Worcestershire sauce, smoked paprika, ketchup, brown sugar, apple cider vinegar, and Frank's RedHot sauce."

She said, "I use tomato sauce, apple cider vinegar, brown sugar, honey, Worcestershire sauce, onion powder, garlic powder, salt, pepper, and chopped peaches. The peaches make mine pop."

I chuckled. "Bet mine tastes better."

"Sounds like we're about to have a cook-off."

"You started it."

"You better get your own catchphrase and stop plagiarizing, Sweet

Meat. And just know when I call you Sweet Meat, Sweet Meat, it has nothing to do with barbecue sauce. Lord, Jesus. Nothing at all."

"Your narrow ass."

"Stop shaming and you ain't complaining."

After those thoughts I whispered, "Just thinking about barbecue. Enjoying the moment with you, watching that truck unload those pretty vehicles, and thinking about barbecue, that's all. And you?"

"Gonna be interesting. We live across the street from each other."

"Too much to handle?"

"I'm not trying to be nobody's part-time lover, full-time fool. Don't think because you got lucky once you can get lucky again. If you're mine, you can help yourself to me. You pick the wrong day, I'll still be creative and take care of you. I'll be getting what I want too."

"You're my girlfriend."

"Well, that answers that."

"You're taking me to soca and I'm taking you to the Love Club."

"So, we're exclusive."

"Yeah."

Again, sweet laughter. "Be careful what you ask for, Professor."

"You're my girlfriend. My first across-the-street girlfriend."

She grinned. "So, we're really exclusive? You can handle that?"

"Yeah."

"Well, okay. This will be different. For me at least."

I asked, "Professor, would you love to go on a date?"

"Boyfriend, I thought you'd never ask."

She took her key ring out of her dress pocket, took a key off, handed it to me. "Since I'm your girlfriend, you get boyfriend privileges. And if we're going to be across-the-street roommates, opens my front door."

A key was one of the oldest lucky charms.

A key that was gifted from one lover to another was considered to be a symbol of unlocking the door to the person's heart.

"Pi, I don't know if this is an extemporaneous action or me being emotional and impromptu. Or four or five years of wanting this. I could just be being silly. Feels like I just gave you a wedding ring."

I said, "I do."

"I don't. Not yet. Have to get my PhD before anything."

We laughed.

She grinned, proud, played in my hair. "It's dry."

"Had a good workout across the street."

"Get your head comb and your products."

She moisturized my rows of black cotton with shea butter, sweet almond oil, argon oil, coconut oil, then picked out my fluffy Afro-Mohawk, styled it to perfection.

"Love your hair. I remember when you started letting it get long. I was like, Lord Jesus, can he get any finer. In front of my face at that."

When she was happy with her work up top, she had me face her.

She motioned north. "Somebody's ears must be burning."

Yemi Savage pulled out of her driveway and cruised this way in her big-tire and swank-rimmed Jeep Wrangler.

Yemi Savage slowed down and took in the car lot I'd created on the street, probably noted the out-of-state tags, then stopped in front of the widow's house. We were blocked from Yemi Savage's sight by the eighteen-wheeler and the presents for the Fastest Swimmers. My lady called out her name and Yemi Savage saw her sorority sister at my house.

I waved at her.

Yemi Savage let her window down, a look of surprise owning her. She waved in slow motion with a brow raised. The attorney's hair was wrapped, and she wore a yellow-green and soft pink top. From where I sat, when she blinked, her eyelashes were two butterflies in flight.

Too much good luck was around me to give a fuck.

She called out, "Half the day gone and you ain't ready?"

My across-the-street girlfriend kissed me good-bye, then stood up and told me, "We're off to hunt and gather at Nordstrom."

"I'll be here car watching and waiting on my family."

"Let me get my purse and lock up my house. I need a long nap."

Smile bright as a diamond, she kissed me like I was her man. I held her by her blackberry jam. The Mack truck, all the cars, and my big tree teamed up and made it so no more than a couple people could see.

Again, we kissed, unable to let each other go.

Yemi Savage blew her horn two more times.

I grabbed my keys, gave her one to my front door.

She smiled like it was her birthday, Christmas, and Valentine's Day at the same time, then held it to her chest and got emotional.

She whispered, "You don't have to because I did."

"I've always been interested in you. Never acted on it. Never would have. Saw you when I moved in. Heart jumped. Wanted to know you."

"Why didn't you make a move?"

"Because if you rejected me and felt uncomfortable after that, I'd have to move."

She hummed with her own thoughts. "Took us long enough."

"We could've been divorced with two kids by now."

"Stop saying that before you jinx us."

My across-the-street lover kissed me three sweet times. Yemi Savage blew her horn three times, the code to get it moving. My lady hurried across Blair Hunt Drive toward her house. There was no curb parking for three houses, so Yemi Savage whipped her big truck up in the widow's driveway. Yemi Savage parked, didn't get out, windows up as she waited, foot on brakes. Her head was down, so she was probably on her phone, texting, but more than likely reading Black Twitter. This morning I was surrounded by death and rebirth, lived in a moment of juxtaposition.

As the widow went inside her home, my phone rang.

Number unknown.

I hoped it would be Roger de Groot, had a big bouquet of thanks in my heart I wanted to give him, but it wasn't a Beverly Hills number.

I didn't answer. No one left a message.

Right away it rang again. Still blocked.

Telemarketers didn't make two calls.

I had my finger over the button to reject it again, but I code-switched and answered the unknown. "Professor Suleman."

"Is this the handsome Black man from Memphis born on Pi Day?"

The phone number was unfamiliar, but the voice was unmistakable.

She said, "Mr. 3.14. Hello, Professor."

British accent.

Brixton.

It was a Black woman from London.

CHAPTER 88

HER BRITISH TONE had ambushed and infiltrated my ears. Memphis became a cityscape acid-washed in pastels. My tongue was as heavy as my heart. Nostrils flared. I shut down. Didn't know what to say. I sat up straight, looked toward where the widow had gone. I'd been dismantled, was living breathlessly underwater. The Black woman from London's face rose from memory. It was the memory of the first time I'd seen her at the UAN event, when she was the newest thing my green eyes had witnessed. I whispered the false name she'd given when we met.

"Gemma Buckingham."

"Hello from the other side."

It was a struggle, but I asked, "'Sup? How are you?"

"I heard about your coworker's murder. Condolences."

"Bad news travels fast. I've been watching it on social."

"Saw the bloody video."

"Yeah. We all have."

"I saw her once. Her husband too. Will never forget her unforgettable entrance. Like a queen before her servants. She was your superior."

A long, awkward, wordless pause passed.

I asked, "What's going on?"

She lost the smiling voice. "How are you?"

"I'm getting through."

"Los Angeles or Memphis?"

"Memphis. Hold on a second."

"Bad time?"

"Give me a few seconds."

"No worries."

My breathing shallowed.

A riot erupted inside me.

One of the men came to my porch, dripping wet with sweat.

"Señor Suleman. We are done."

I signed off on the fleet of cars. He handed me the tagged ring of keys to all the cars, then dabbed sweat with a blue Los Angeles Dodgers handkerchief and waved an exhausted good-bye.

At the same time my across-the-street lover came back out.

She waved like she was enamored, then blew me a playful kiss.

Her lioness locks, wild, free, touched her blackberry jam, bounced on her ass as she hurried into her sorority sister's Jeep. Yemi Savage backed out, then tooted the horn, pulled away. We blew kisses.

The eighteen-wheeler's horn sounded, and the big rig began negotiating the relative narrowness of Blair Hunt Drive.

"Hello, Professor. Still there?"

"Still here."

"You're busy."

"Was. Had a delivery. But that's done. I have a few minutes."

Closed my eyes and visualized amber skin and Megan Markle hair.

Awkward, I asked, "How's the weather in London?"

"Pleasure and pain."

"Pleasure and pain?"

"Pleasure and pain is Cockney slang for rain."

My voice tendered, smoothed out. "Pleasure and pain."

"Story of my life so far."

"We have a generous time difference."

"Eleven thirty A.M. in Memphis is five thirty P.M. in London."

"The sun is grabbing its coat and your day is ending there."

"My day is ending."

"With pleasure and pain, what we over here call rain."

516 ERIC JEROME DICKEY

"Feels darker than midnight now. Raining forks'tiyunsdown'ards, as my Scottish mum used to say. Bucketing, pissing down, as my African father would say. I'm a Londoner so I'll just say it's raining pitchforks in the heart of the Big Smoke. Cats and dogs as you always said in Memphis. Torrential here. Skies are dark as ink, no sign of changing."

"You know the bad news in Memphis. You okay over there?"

"How's the weather in the heart of Memphis? No thunderstorms?"

"Sunny and clear in South Memphis."

"Sun must be shining right on top of your house at this hour."

"Today it is; today it is."

"Last time we spoke over the phone things were the opposite."

"Was it?"

"Was storming there and sunny in the heart of London."

"A reversal of fortunes."

She hesitated. "Professor."

"Gemma Buckingham."

She paused. "Once upon a time you asked me to tell you who I am."

"I know who you are."

Her voice was vulnerable. "No, you don't."

"Who are you?"

There was a beat, a struggle to say what she wanted to say.

"After my African father went away and left my European mother all but penniless, we were forced to leave Brixton. I grew up in a council block, where my museum was the graffiti in darkened halls leading to nonworking lifts that always smelt of both fresh and stale urine."

"Why are you telling me this now?"

"Because I didn't tell you this then."

"Gemma Buckingham."

"Me, my white and colorless European mum, after my dark-skinned African father had entirely cut us off, we were soon evicted from our Brixton flat, humiliated in front of the world as we knew it, became class-less and were forced to live in disgusting hostels and unsafe squats. Hostels and squats. Two places the Queen would never speak of, let alone visit for a cuppa. We squatted in an abandoned building. We were trespassing with many more trespassers until the bobbies ushered us along with the threat of incarceration. We slept in front of a shop on a high street on the Brighton seafront a few nights, slept in the winter's cold and pretended we were camping in the rain under damp blankets at Cornwall. High streets were noisy and nasty but safer. My white mother asked strangers to feed her cold and shivering mixed-raced child, and under gray skies European people like her looked at my red-eyed and disheveled mum like she'd earned what she deserved for having a mixed-race child. But some had hearts and fed me, if not us."

"Never would have guessed. Sorry to hear."

"'Please, sir, I want some more.'"

"*Oliver Twist.*"

"A Scottish man saw me with my Scottish mom and asked me to say that for a biscuit. 'Please, sir, I want some more.' I had to behave like a well-trained monkey to entertain his wealth in front of my mum. He was Scottish, like her, and he was publicly punishing her for birthing me. For a biscuit. She allowed it. Encouraged it. She was desperate to nibble part of a biscuit. So was I. 'Please, sir, I want some more.'"

"Gemma Buckingham."

In a fractured tone she whispered, "'Please, sir, I want some more.'"

"Enough."

She marched on. "I lived where the rubbish bins were set ablaze at two in the morning because a Billy no mates was bored or stoned and needed a thrill. Where I lived you knew all the drug dealers who set up shop in the litter-filled courtyards beneath the blocks. You knew girls who were assaulted. One girl who was slightly older went to a guy's flat to have sex, and when he was done with his part a few of his mates who were hidden in a closet jumped out and picked up where he left off. They raped her in a flat two levels above where she lived. She really liked that boy. Poor girl killed herself. She jumped. She was dead, left a grieving mother, and for the rest of us the struggle continued. The drug dealers were always recruiting. I walked by a boy my age who had overdosed. Became common with the drug dealers waiting day and night. They seemed to have power. Girls would be their girlfriends to feel protected from other predators. The lesser of two evils. It was a risk. A dangerous risk. Pretty girls could get free drugs. Then learn nothing was free. You get high with them, then wake up bound and gagged in a van filled with young girls being trafficked to Russia, China, Venezuela, Belarus, Iran, or some unheard-of Muslim country. Girls disappeared off and on. I knew of three. Pretty girls. One was a mixed-race girl. It felt like my destiny. Had nightmares every night."

"So sorry you lived that life."

"I was a street urchin, more or less, like Storm in the comics, without the mutant powers. She is half-African. I related to her journey, minus the deceased parents, when I was a preteen. That's why I started reading more comic books, especially those featuring her. She was homeless and so was I. Five foot ten. Statuesque. A leader. I wanted to be her, until someone laughed and told me it was impossible because my skin was too . . . yellow. Storm's father was Black American, had dark skin. Her mother was from Africa, Kenya, had dark skin. Storm had dark skin. Therefore, I could never be Storm from the comics. That shattered me."

I let that rest. I felt the weight of her past. It was heavier than the Great Wall of China, the Three Gorges Dam, and the Great Pyramid of Khufu.

It was the weight she had carried hidden since I met her.

"But my African father came back for us. He was done teaching my white mum a hard lesson. By then the damage had been done. You don't live that life for two years, then are able to unlive it in your mind. I prayed to no avail. Seeing what I had seen caused me to become agnostic. My African father returned when I was thirteen. I prayed and felt abandoned twice over. Mostly by my African father. He was tangible. Despite my circumstances I resented my mother for needing him. I despised her for having to go back to a man, even if he was my father. I hated myself for having no options. I vowed to never rely on a man. Unlike my mum, a well-educated European woman who read your father's Black American books religiously, a brilliant woman who read the Forever series countless times and was so smitten she would have probably bedded Mr. Suleman if he'd ever come to London. She would've married your father if she could, as a cure to her loneliness at the start, and to feed her intellectual curiosities, but for security in the long run, just to be loved and have his money, as in the big picture many have thought they were in love but really married for money, to improve their station in life, that coupling being an act of survival on several levels, but never the purest form of love. I'd never set foot in council housing again. So, because of my mum I was determined to have my own flat at Knightsbridge or Kensington Palace Gardens. I was determined to make my own bloody money. I got away from my family for a spell. Too toxic. Didn't ring my mum for almost two years. I love my mum in my own way, but because of her I possess an adamantine, unshakable conviction that what I am doing is unequivocally right. Opportunity came at sixteen. Twenty thousand pounds. Didn't care if it was illegal. Some of the council-housing hustle was in my blood. I did not hesitate. It was business. Life is about business because the world is capitalistic. Every day it costs more pounds to get by, never a pence less. Not as easy for a woman to rise up from council housing and be able to afford a coveted flat in a preferred postal code like Chelsea or West Brompton unassisted, not as easy as it is for a European man, even when she's more educated, and especially if she is Black and not married to a European man. Takes brains, beauty, dedication, determination, good lawyers, and the proper amount of coins for a woman to properly survive in a world designed to make her fail. The life of most of the women I know, in some way, is a cautionary tale. I've learned. A woman has to be better than her useless mum, more ruthless than her father, and smarter than the softness in her own heart."

When she finished, her emotions had a storm brewing in my eyes, were bringing a soft rain to Blair Hunt Drive as I sat on her words.

I didn't run over her car with my train. I let her unload her lazy woman's load of angst uninterrupted. I was in my Chevy at the levy.

Angry.

I told her, "You're gonna miss Elvis week."

"I will only miss you. Only you."

"If only you'd stayed. Or promised to return."

"But it's not too late for us, Professor."

Angry to the point of being petty.

"I need to be clear on one thing that has irritated me since my father's funeral in Los Angeles. Since Crenshaw Boulevard, if it's cool by you."

"And Black man from Memphis, that is?"

"Meghan Markle."

"Your issue with her is?"

"All Meghans matter."

"All Meghans?"

"Meagan Good. Megan Fox. Meghan Trainor. Megan Thee Stallion. All Megs matter. They all live and breathe so they matter. Just like Meghan Markle over there, all the Megs matter just as much here."

"I disagree. And you know I do. It's triggering how Meghan Markle is being singled out due to her race. They are deliberately going out of their way and in a concerted effort mistreating her at every turn."

"So out of all the Meghans in the world, Meghan Markle's situation needs to be monitored and given special attention at the moment."

"Yes. Have you not seen the damage being done intentionally and without concern to the impact it will have on her family?"

"So at the moment, due to unfair treatment, Markle matters most."

"She's being attacked daily. Because she's mixed, half-Black."

"So she's being tracked and gunned down by the press every day. Only they can't shoot her in the back or choke her to death over a loosie. Meghan's life versus the life of all Meghans is the same as the injustice against Black lives versus all lives. They love the Black vote here but can't stand Black people. Blacks are the Meghans of America. All lives matter, like you said, but until they treat Black folks right, the way you focus on Meghan's plight over that, over here we gonna focus on Black lives mattering and give it special attention. Just like you want to give all your energy to Meghan Markle and have all the other Meghans take a chill pill, we need to give attention to Black lives, which is a part of all lives, same as Meghan Markle is a subset of the Meghans in the world."

"Well, it feels as if I exclude half of my soul. As if I am saying my Scottish mum and all the relatives from her side are insignificant."

"All lives matter, but we need the international spotlight on Black lives and how they're being Meghan Markled daily, with real bullets, not metaphorically assassinated, and killed in broad daylight due to race. For Meghan, maybe every day is a horrific Groundhog Day and a new insult is added to her lazy royalty's load of grievances, but she lives to tell the tale. Over here, we're getting hashtagged. One shot and a casket drops for Black folks. One shot, casket drops, a family destroyed."

Seconds passed before she whispered, "Touché."

"Not Touché. Truth touché. *Tru-ché*."

"This is why I need you."

"You left me."

"And this has bothered you without resolution in my absence."

"It's been heavy on my chest. My check-engine light won't go off. It was part of the reason you left me."

"Had no idea I was so irritating."

"I kept . . . explaining . . . things you should already know."

"We both did. Ignorance flows in the directions of both the Amazon and the Mississippi and shall remain that way without enlightenment."

"It was exhausting at times."

"You have made me love me more and see things from a different, better perspective. Maybe even from my father's harsh perspective."

"Well, I'll never know the advantages of having a white mother."

"The *advantages*. I thought I was clear on certain matters abroad."

We both stopped talking, and I focused on my breathing to calm.

I whispered, "I made a business trip, came back, you were gone."

Her inhales and exhales thickened with regret.

Hurt rose as it did when I went to confront a dead man who'd never visited me. Adults were survivors of all childhood traumas, traumas that caused arrested development in some way, even when unrecognized by the emotionality stunted adult. Suleman had never allowed me to be his son until dirt hit his pearly coffin. The song of abandonment and neglect had the bite of a bullet ant, and that bite was the sting of all stings, an agony that was pure, intense, magnificent pain akin to hiking up a mountain of blazing coal fresh from hell with a hundred three-inch nails being drilled in your heels, eyes, and heart.

It hurt. It fuckin hurt, with its epicenter being my heart.

She said, "Those cars along Blair Hunt Drive are from one of your father's grand and luxurious homes in California."

"What was that?"

"The cars in front of your home. I recognize most of them."

My rapid heartbeat quickened.

"You look good in your shorts. Your Trues. Was surprised to see you up so early. I was going to wait until the sun was up before knocking on your door. Then I saw you cross the street in a rush carrying something. Figured you'd only be gone a minute at that hour. The sun wasn't up. Came to surprise you and once again I've ended up surprising myself."

I studied the SUV parked on the other side of Mo Fo's home. The brake lights were going on and off. Someone was pressing and releasing, stressed, on their hobbyhorse.

In a soft voice laced with regret she said, "She's beautiful. The girl you were with, the one who stood on your porch and you kissed good-bye, the girl who just made your beautiful hair pop with style, she is beautiful."

"She is."

"She looked happy."

"Yeah. She did."

"Never saw a woman look so bloody happy."

"She is. Today she is happy."

"Her dreadlocks are amazing. Silver with white highlights. It pops against her skin. She looked like Storm. You spent the morning with her."

"I did."

"The night as well?"

"Where is this going?"

"The loving way she held your hand as you crossed the street with her, the way she just did your hair, all after you went into her home looking pristine and left much later in a state of disarray, I could tell she'd been pleased. Same for you. I recognize that satisfied look on your face."

"We had a good morning getting familiar on a different level."

"What does she do?"

"Professor. She's a professor. A very ambitious professor."

"UAN?"

"Our HBCU."

"The one the madman tried to attack, like they did yours."

"Yeah."

"Educator. Like you."

"Only smarter. World traveled, exotic to my eyes, like you."

"Yet we are day and night."

"Night and day."

"I saw her let you in her home. Saw her in the window. Saw her close her door and her blinds. I am ashamed of myself, but I couldn't bear it and knocked on her door. A few times. No one answered."

"We heard."

"I heard too."

"Well. Seek and ye shall find."

Gemma Buckingham chuckled painfully. "She's an ersatz for me?"

"She's the real McCoy. When I google her government name, a slice of her life so far comes up for the world to see. The parts she wants people to see. She's on LinkedIn so I see her work history and can verify her work ethic. I know exactly where she's worked. Her Twitter account has a blue check next to her name. She's Internet verified."

"No need to be so cheeky."

"Being honest. Anything else you want to know?"

"This been going on a while?"

"Our first time. This morning was the first time hooking up."

"If I'd arrived yesterday."

"Yeah. If. I might've even skipped cutting my grass."

"You carried your thermos. She was up waiting for you. I saw her close the front door and my heart jumped. She closed her blinds and I screamed. Came to the porch. Heard her. Heard you. She was indeed enjoying you, and you her. Was speechless. Hurt my daft heart a wee little bit. Just a wee bit. Took all I had to hurry away back to my bloody rental. Sat here in shock, barely able to breathe. Too numb to drive away."

I didn't say anything.

She said, "Your first time."

"Yeah, our Betty Wright moment. Today was the day."

"So, I could've possibly intervened."

Again, I offered nothing.

She said, "You're breviloquent. You're usually a man of many words, but now you're breviloquent. Ask me questions. Ask me anything. Please? I will answer honestly, as I should have done at the start."

"I no longer have any questions."

"Pi."

"Anything else, Gemma Buckingham?"

She asked, "Has she done Sunday dinner? Has it gotten that far?"

"She's excited about coming to Sunday dinner for the first time."

"Have you had meaningful, deep, metaphorically naked conversations with her, the kind that run from before sundown until after sunrise? I mean the kind of intimate parlay where you let down your walls, reveal all pains, cry together, and learn things you don't know? Have you had the type of conversation where everyone is willing to be completely vulnerable and tell all truths without judgment, and no one needs to apologize for who they are or things they've done?"

"That's not your business."

In a delicate tone she said, "Professor, I brought my bonnet."

"Gemma Buckingham."

"You've only been with her once. All isn't lost. Come to me, Pi."

"No."

"Come to me."

"Don't do this to me."

"Let's take a ride down by the river and over the bridge."

I swallowed, tempted to stand and run to that SUV.

"I brought my bonnet. Ready to love you forever."

Her brake lights flickered. I rocked like I was on a hobbyhorse.

I whispered the only words I could: "Gemma Buckingham."

She corrected me, said her true name. Her CEO-working-inside-the-Gherkin name. Her confession. Too much, too little, a few hours too late.

She'd been parked on my street, in the hot sun, humidity rising, windows up, air on, since before the Calhouns died, since before thunder roared and the rooster crowed under dark skies in Brownsville.

She'd pulled up as I made it to the widow's front door.

That was her. If I had looked back when I was crossing the street, it would have been a different day for three people. As bodies dropped in Brownsville, she'd been parked on Blair Hunt Drive, unaware of two deaths. Three deaths. Our relationship was born in lies, in secret lives, then died on a widow's bed. It would never be easy for damaged people.

Brake lights flickered rapidly but gradually slowed.

I couldn't take it. I stood up, was going to go to her.

A breeze came.

The winds changed.

A sign.

Something was about to happen.

Something not good.

Yemi Savage's Wrangler reappeared.

It sped down Kansas Street hard and fast, then made a hard slowdown where the main street gave a gentle kiss to Blair Hunt Drive.

The Jeep's hazard lights flashed strong.

The big-wheeled Jeep busted a squealing right from Kansas Street, moved like a Lamborghini sports car, curved left, and sped toward my home, a hurricane made by a Jeep sitting on monster wheels.

It passed my house on a mission. Then came to a hard stop when it was two car lengths in front of the SUV that housed London.

The passenger door on the Jeep flew open. The widow leaped down from the Jeep. She slammed the passenger door and West Indian anger appeared. The widow was a raging sun ready to consume the earth.

Gemma Buckingham asked, "What makes her better?"

"You had sex with me under false pretenses."

"I beg to differ."

"You gave me a fake name. She didn't."

"You pursued me."

"Oh wow. Didn't you pop up in LA uninvited?"

"She lives a stiff wanker's length from you, and you pursued me."

"Sure. Believe whatever you believe."

"It wasn't the other way around."

I chanted, "Nine-oh-one-eight-oh-three-oh. Nine-oh-one-eight-oh-three-oh."

"My initial Memphis digits when we met. Your point?"

"I dialed nonstop until I found you, like you wanted."

"No one forced you to make the effort and call a hundred numbers to find me. In record time. I mean, who actually does that?"

"No one forced you to give me half a number for kicks."

"You were persistent."

"That night I wanted you like no other. But the next day would've been just another day."

"You had sex with me and she was there all along."

"Stop talking out the side of your neck."

"Shag her as well?"

"Not until this morning."

"Only this morning?"

"Today was the first time. Wasn't even an option I considered."

"I am loving your fiction."

"No lies. I woke up grieving for you. Not as much as the days before, but I did. Before today we were just across-the-street neighbors. We rarely talked like that over five years. She was dating a doctor. Before that she saw men on the same level as far as I heard. Wasn't my business."

"You woke up grieving for me. Love, I felt the same way."

"It's called going through withdrawal in certain circles."

The Jeep headed south at a snail's pace, moved like a crawling baby.

It distanced itself from whatever storm was yet to come.

Gemma Buckingham asked, "What happened to make this morning's love affair with your toothsome neighbor possible?"

"You left me. Her guy cheated."

"The bloody universe conspired."

"No, you got on a plane when I was in Los Angeles. You left me like I was the latest Lennie in your queue. You made a choice."

"I did. It was the wrong choice."

The widow came back this way.

Her hard face looked for me, saw I was where she had left me, overseeing the temporary car lot of presents I had created because I could.

Eye contact was made. She didn't smile.

In the absence of a noticeable din I heard her rosy sandals touching blacktop, scraping the hot streets with each riled step. Rising heat and mild humidity watched, waited to find out what was going the fuck on.

Feet away from her housed a raging storm from London.

Gemma Buckingham and Widow Fatima.

"If I'd never left the way I did, when I did, how I did, that could've been us. The way I abandoned you, it wasn't very mature of me."

The widow sauntered straight ahead, moved steadily toward the SUV and the Brixton storm. She was one car length away, dreadlocks swaying with her incensed mood, unbothered by the dankness that put dewdrops on her midnight skin.

Gemma whispered, "That could've been us. If I'd come a day earlier, or knocked on your door an hour earlier, or just gone to one Sunday dinner and met your mum, or this morning called your name, then presented myself with a telling smile while you stood chatting at her front door in the dark, today, now, in this moment, that could've been us."

"I don't beg to differ."

The widow paused a foot from the SUV and checked her phone. It looked like the widow rejected a phone call, then raised her stern and unhappy face and set her glower into the front of the SUV.

"Come to me, Pi. Professor, come to me."

"You left us."

"Let me apologize. Allow me to put us back together in one piece."

The widow looked at Gemma Buckingham, directly at a solar eclipse, only the brake lights went dark as if Gemma Buckingham had gone blind.

"I don't know how it flies in London, but you don't treat people like that, you don't leave with no good-bye, have them track you down at work, then with British rudeness, blow them the fuck off on Skype like they never meant dick to you, not the ones you like and claim to love."

"Come back to me."

"Don't expect me to do someone else wrong because you're singing a new song. Regret may have given you the lyrics, taught you the words, but that's your tune to sing, hum, or hashtag ignore. I was your lead singer when needed, then put out with the choir. That's your song. All yours."

The widow stood in front of the leased SUV and pulled a couple of renegade dreadlocks from her face, then moved by my old lover.

Her attention shot back north, toward her sorority sister.

Yemi Savage was still creeping north up Blair Hunt Drive.

The widow walked by Gemma Buckingham's SUV and took to the buckled sidewalk. Brake lights flickered again as the widow passed by Mo Fo and Pokey's house and entered my yard.

The widow slowed more when she left the sun and took in the coolness of my shade. Right away she exhaled like she was worn-out. She grinned and slow switched, then sat on the porch next to me again.

I asked my across-the-street lover, "What just happened?"

"Had to suddenly postpone today's hunting and gathering."

"Why?"

"By the time we made it to Southgate Shopping Center, soror Yemi Savage realized it was the wrong day to wear white pants."

"Oh."

She asked, "Get it?"

"Got it."

"Good."

Eyes on the SUV, heart aching, I nodded. "That'll do it."

The widow chuckled. "Bad day to wear white pants."

"Something a man has never had to say."

"She had her accident before we got to Third, then did a U-turn by Piggly Wiggly and was driving back up Belz like a bat out of hell to get back home and change. Was blowing her horn. Ran folks off the road at Florida. She pissed me off, especially when she came down our street speeding like a fool. This is a residential district. Pokey's kids could've been out in the streets. I told her crazy butt to drop me at my house and she kept going until I snapped and called her out of her God-given government name. I went off on her for driving like that. Now she going to pretend to be mad at me at least until Monday at breakfast time."

"You mad at her?"

"Play mad. Sisterhood too strong to stay mad."

"Good to know."

"She's driving extra slow trying to be funny."

"I see."

"She was working my nerves asking about you as soon as we pulled off. Jealous. Claimed she didn't knock on my door this morning, but I know she was lying because it wasn't Pokey 'nem."

"Nah. Wasn't Mo Fo 'nem."

"Now I get to grade papers in peace and, yes, spend more time getting to know you better. We can do it again, if you want. After that sex session we had this morning, and this heat, let's just say I need another pitcher of lemonade to hydrate myself and I need a cuddle nap too."

"You're bringing a hella lot of lemonade for Sunday dinner."

"Hope your family likes my lemonade as much as I like them. Especially your crazy momma. She's an amazing woman. She's a phoenix, raised all y'all by herself, all of y'all have degrees, but don't tell her I said that. A rival sorority thing. If everyone had a momma like yours, the world would be a better place."

"You came out okay."

"But like I've told you, I've never had stability, not like your momma gave y'all. Never had good guidance like your momma give y'all. Had to figure everything out on my own. Did okay so far."

"Just be yourself around my folks on Sunday."

She laughed. "Who else am I going to be?"

Brake lights on the SUV told a tale. They flickered. Flickered. A candle struggling to stay alive in a soft southern breeze.

She sang, "Sweet Meat, my sweetheart, are we really exclusive?"

"Yes. Last time telling you that."

"I like hearing you say that. So it won't be my last asking."

"We're exclusive."

"No wife, wifey, fiancée, girlfriend, side ho, or fuck buddy?"

"No husband, fiancé, secret marriages, side dick, or fuck buddy?"

She shook her head. "Nope. Well, I am a widow, but everyone knows that. Been a widow so long, feels like I was never married."

"Then it's you and me. Starting today, it's you and me."

"This will be different."

"I hope so."

The widow said, "This was unplanned."

"What was unplanned? Breakfast?"

"Having sex with you during breakfast was not the plan."

"I'm dialing 1-800-BULLSHIT on that one."

"How come?"

"You shaved your coochie and legs."

She laughed. "You manscaped."

"You invited me over."

"You offered me sweet, sweet coffee."

"I offered to have the coffee delivered by Mo Fo 'nem."

"Okay, mostly unplanned. I'm a just-in-case kinda woman, and if things changed between us, I was going to leave its direction up to you."

"Yeah, this was unexpected."

"To be honest, I think I kept a certain distance from you so it wouldn't cross into that category of being friends, then becoming like brother and sister. I hoped that one day you'd be single, and I'd be single, and you'd know what equally yoked meant, and we'd take it from there."

"We're taking it from there. Equally yoked."

She said, "I done had sex with my across-the-street neighbor."

I asked, "Regrets?"

"Only one."

"Okay."

"Would've been nice if the first time we did this I had on stockings and stilettos."

"Stockings and stilettos."

"Midnight. Stockings and stilettos."

"At midnight."

"That was how I had imagined it with you in my mind."

"Really?"

"Fantasized about you so much. Wanted what I couldn't have."

"Really?"

"You have no idea. Once upon a time I almost talked myself into wearing that and a black trench coat and knocking on your door at midnight, when all the neighbors down this way were sleeping. Just come in, put you in a chair, ride you, do the do, and go back home and act like it never happened."

"Stockings and stilettos."

"At midnight."

"You should've come over that Halloween you dressed like Storm."

"Should've asked. What would you have done if I had shown up at your door at midnight in a corset, thong, and thigh-high boots?"

"Everything. Every fucking thing I could think of, and more."

"Nasty man. You are one nasty man."

"You need to hold up a mirror on that one."

"Professor, I was pleasantly pleased. I thought we were just going to be real basic in bed and get to know each other a couple of minutes, kiss good-bye, then get on with the rest of our mornings."

"We said an hour."

"Now you know good and well an hour in bed to a normal man is two minutes of fun and a fifty-eight-minute nap."

"My hour is thirty minutes."

"You done started this off real nasty, so next time I'm going to have to reevaluate my level of nasty for my ego and see if I should finish my nasty better than you can do the nasty and nasty you real good."

"The educator will have to give the educator a good education."

"You started it."

"It's all about who finishes it."

My phone was still on.

If she chose to listen, Gemma Buckingham heard every word.

The widow turned serious. "Sleeping with you this morning was a challenge. Professor. Pi Suleman. Sweet Meat with the sweetest meat. I ain't gonna lie. It was the panacea for my down-home blues today. You done reborned me in a way I needed to be reborned."

"It was curative."

"We should've done that yesterday and at least for four years before yesterday's yesterday. I think that maybe we got some catching up to do. Some serious catching up before I get into a doctoral program."

London ears heard the truth. I wanted her to have the truth.

When the widow and I had inspected the cars, we had stopped at the rear of the SUV. I had been four feet from Gemma Buckingham. *Unknowingly* I had been close enough for her to hear our conversation. She had been parked here since before the rooster crowed, had been treading in her angst awhile, her tears the storm over Brownsville.

The widow checked her phone. "Lord. Black Twitter is on fire and they ain't saying nothing nice. Their comments are vicious."

"People feel how they feel."

"The things he said. People don't get drunk and tell lies. People don't lie before dying either. He cried and said she came from a family of Black people. A family of nappy-headed niggers. Then lost his religion and shot her down in cold blood. In court those final actions, when emotions are that high, that would be considered a dying man's confession. Gonna be a lot more to this. A lot more."

"Until the truth comes out. For everybody, the truth comes out."

The SUV that was parked on the other side of Mo Fo's house pulled away. The driver in the SUV moved away slowly, wistfully, with downcast eyes, clenched fists, trembling lips, and tears. Not looking back.

Widow Fatima pointed. "Look. Our other visitor is leaving."

"Yeah. You just passed by whoever it is. What you see?"

"Light-skinned girl was inside. Cute face. Baldheaded."

"Baldheaded."

"She had her head down, was crying, so I didn't bother her."

"Crying."

"She needed a hug. A real big hug. But it wasn't my business."

The SUV went north, passed by Mo Fo and his happy family as they came back this way in his big truck. Gemma Buckingham disappeared as the street curved west, kept going toward where the street named after a civil rights soldier ended up at Vaal by the parking lot and other properties owned by Shady Grove Missionary Baptist Church.

Like the sensation from an orgasm, she faded. Orgasms faded. They all faded. The sensation faded quickly, as if you had never come. The problem was memories remained. I was in the company of a stunning Black queen who wanted to have me in her castle. She was an exotic West Indian southern girl. I knew her struggles, knew a lot of her personal history, she played no games, and we had the same Black American history. She knew my family. She was coming to Sunday dinner.

I didn't have to convince her to embrace her Blackness. She didn't jump aristocratic and ridicule my hometown. The widow loved me. The weight of love. For some a feather.

CHAPTER 89

THE WIDOW TOOK over my world, let my world know a queen had arrived, and commanded, "Alexa, play 'Slow Kisses' by Joe, on repeat."

She took my hand and led me into my house, into her second castle, closed my door, turned up my air conditioner, and took me to my bed.

When the ten-minute session was done, I gazed at my across-the-street lover like I was imagining myself in a charcoal suit and waiting for her at the front of a small South Memphis church as she came in, walking slowly, dressed in wedding-day white, a silk number with a brocade skirt, a V-neckline that made her sensuous, paired with a beaded bodice. My queen held flowers in one hand, brand-new PhD in the other. We had chemistry. We definitely had chemistry. The sun had made love to her skin a trillion times. Like the sun, I had touched her skin from crown to corns this morning. She'd touched and tasted mine from 'fro to toes. She grinned at me. From the heart I reciprocated.

She made it to her feet, did a mesmerizing sashay to my kitchen, locks swaying with her ticktocking, dancing to soca in her mind. She came back with two mason jars, both filled to the brim with sweet tea.

We sipped iced teas, cooled off, then kissed some more before we cuddled and closed our eyes, not sleeping, just talking and laughing as I traced my fingers over the shape of her body. Sunlight had definitely made love to her skin a trillion times. But the pinkness at the doors to her church showed me as far as the sun had gone, how far it had been invited. Today the sun envied me. She rested with her head on my belly, in silence, the sound of the seven wind chimes out back on my patio coming and going as I played in her heavy locks. I rubbed her breasts, those sweet peaches. Made her tingle and shake her tree.

She pulled her lioness dreadlocks back into a thick ponytail before she sat up on my rumpled sheets. I stayed next to her flat out on my back. Exhausted. Naked. Paul Gauguin's painting *Aha Oe Feii?* come to life.

I asked, "Is he gone for good?"

"What matters is I'm gone for good."

"He's sending flowers."

"Hand me my phone, please."

We were nude. I was in the middle of a Widow Fatima high, relaxed, on my back. Brown skin on stained, delicate, expensive chartreuse sheets on a soft pillow-top mattress sized for a queen. Hair and beard two weeks rugged and scruffy. Her softness was between my strong legs, on her back, breasts high, back of her head on my chest, left arm raised, her fingers massaging my facial hair. My left hand was under her left arm, palming, squeezing her left breast. Her dreadlocks fanned over our spent, dank bodies. Morning glow. Perfect shadowing. Her phone was in her right hand. In camera mode. Rapid shots. She took what seemed like more than two hundred selfies. Each shot aroused us. We kissed, deep kisses, ignored the camera. All shots were erotic; each rang as organic, unrushed, each the image of the perfect love.

She kept her lips on mine, whispered, "More?"

I sucked her bottom lip, whispered, "More. More. Then more."

"This doesn't scare you?"

"Scares and excites me."

"Me too."

She posted three of the sensual photos to IG and Twitter. Right away the likes started. She used a different photo as the header for each page. She made one her main-page photo on Facebook, then updated her status to being in a relationship. She was getting Beyoncé-level congratulations.

I asked her to send me the same photos and I did the same notification to the subsection of the cyberuniverse that knew my government name. Our phones started blowing up right away, hers ten times more than mine. Friends, family, colleagues, Greeks, and basic nosy motherfuckers. Big Sis was one of the first to post her seal of approval and congratulations, then messaged she hoped one day soon her brother in Memphis would be able to tell her and the rest of her crew overseas the same. We took more photos. The widow was feeling herself and it showed. We were retweeted and shared almost a few hundred times. So many positive comments about the strength of Black lives were posted. The comments on her page also spoke of female empowerment. The widow turned her phone off. I did the same. Phones off, we worked on minding our own business.

She whisper-asked, "Is she gone for good?"

"Doesn't matter. I'm here for good."

"Exclusive."

"Exclusive."

"Anything else, Professor?"

"What kind of sex do you like?"

She responded, "Avant-garde."

"Experimental, radical."

"At times unorthodox."

I'd create a character like Widow Fatima. Intelligent. Sensual. Confident in her own skin and never confused. Didn't take no mess, not even when she wore a sundress. Same dreadlocks, double-chocolate skin, and cavernous dimples. She was a queen's queen. I'd let her sip mimosas and rule my imagined version of Vathlo. Just like she looked out for her neighbors on Blair Hunt Drive, she'd be the one who ruled over the Black Kryptonians on their journey. She'd be a Black superwoman.

Momma would be in there too. Big Sis. Sis. Even Komorebi.

Gemma Buckingham. She'd be included as well.

The widow took my hand, led me to the bathroom. We showered together. Stood in my bedroom getting dressed.

We sat on my small porch like it was our private citadel.

Like king and queen.

Tomorrow I'd drive to Midtown Comics and buy a dozen T-shirts for her. I'd buy a dozen fresh ones for me. I'd buy her matching thongs, if she liked. A new start to mend a broken heart. And maybe one day we'd do a road trip to Atlanta, take in Trapeze. If that was what she needed, I'd give her all she needed. My mane Four Ds had said a man had to listen to what a woman needed, and then do his best to give her that.

If I'd fallen short the last time, I wouldn't fall short, not this time.

My across-the-street girlfriend went inside my place to use the bathroom. Soon as she did, I picked up my phone and went to photos. I had one photo of me and Gemma Buckingham. It was the one taken in Los Angeles, the one Momma had asked us to take during my father's homegoing. I deleted it. Yellow gal was no longer in my phone.

Right now, with Widow Fatima as my lover, I'd keep my mind on the professor at LeMoyne-Owen, would stay this side of the pond.

She turned on my living room television.

"Now they're showing photos of the Calhouns and the president."

She turned the news right back off. Checked out my space.

I whispered hidden emotions. "It wasn't my fault. Wasn't my fault."

She came back. "I *love* your shotguns. You should take me to the range with you next time you go. I'll take my .380. Haven't shot it in over a year. Had no idea you played the guitar. We can have a jam session."

"Just say when."

"Your house is nice. Messy, but nice. Looks intellectual."

"Most of my projects are on the kitchen table."

"I see you're a busy man. No wonder you're up late."

"I work part-time out of an office in the city, work for my father, handling a lot of his issues, but I do most of my work at home."

"So you and your daddy were close."

"Not at all. He's watching over me out of guilt. Maybe love. Not sure. Will never know."

"Are all those cars really yours?"

"All of them and at the same time none of them."

I told her it was my inheritance, and now my gifts to my siblings.

"Sweet Meat, I done lost my signal. Which Wi-Fi is yours?"

"Vathlo Island."

"Password?"

"Widow Fatima."

"What?"

"The password."

"Is what?"

"Is Widow Fatima. All caps."

"Serious?"

"You're my password."

"You're joking."

"Widow Fatima."

"Your password is my name?"

I nodded.

"Your password is my name."

"I just changed it."

She leaned in and kissed me. "Let's take the widow part off."

"What should I rename it?"

"Pi and Fatima Had Sex."

"I'll think of something."

Her sorority sister Yemi Savage left her Jeep parked in front of her house and came from up the street to be nosy. She was wearing black booty shorts. Mo Fo came over to investigate. Sis showed up holding hands with her white boy. His name was Malcolm Birdingground, but everyone called him Bird. Momma pulled up in my car, Black Kevin at her side.

Like they'd done when they were born, the rest of the Fastest Swimmers showed up one by one; then love and hilarity ensued.

Pokey brought a cake and I made enough coffee for everybody.

I stood in my backyard by the outdoor furniture I'd made with my own hands, Alexa playing Memphis music by Alberta Hunter, B.B. King, Isaac Hayes, and Al Green while I grilled steaks, pork chops, hot dogs, burgers, chicken sausages, octopus, shrimp, multicolored peppers, onions, asparagus, eggplant, and corn on the cob.

I was a millionaire squeezing a dollar until the eagle grinned.

Empathy for the cruel rose for a second, long enough for me to whisper, "Forgive us our trespasses, as we forgive those who trespass against us, and lead us not into temptation, but deliver us from evil."

Then all empathy was gone. New Testament became Old. In the land of CNN smiles over Fox News hearts, Martin became Malcolm.

"What have you gone and done did without asking my permission, Sweet Meat? Still as hardheaded as you were the day you were born."

I laughed. Momma shook her head then walked next to Black Kevin as they looked over the hoopties.

It was a good day in the life of Pi. It was a great day for the son of Archimedes Maurice Suleman. It was a phenomenal day for the son of the author who authored a hardworking son he never met.

I'd go back to working for and hating my old man tomorrow.

I'd forget about a woman from London with each exhale.

The same went for the Calhouns.

God bless 'em both to their just rewards.

No one was looking for this nappy-headed nigger.

Not yet.

Tomorrow would be whatever tomorrow would be.

But today was a good day for a Black man from Memphis.

ACKNOWLEDGMENTS

O ye faithful readers! Or as Rebel Glam in Barbados affectionately calls my loyal fans, hello, Dicksters!

It's great to see y'all again. If it's your first time to Dickeyville, welcome aboard. I hope you enjoyed the journey from the humidity in 901 to the smog in the 213 and back to Blair Hunt Drive.

The Son of Mr. Suleman (TSOMS) covers a lot of territory. Racism. Colorism. Self-love. Being of mixed race. One-drop rule. Sexual assault at the workplace. Micro aggressions. Mendacities as foundation for a relationship. Cultural differences. Politics. Being the son of a pedophile. Perceptions. The impact of enslavement and Jim Crow. Code-switching. The power of death. The weight of love.

The Son of Mr. Suleman started with a one-page passage I'd written for kicks a few years back. It was a scene where a nameless guy walked into his father's funeral. It was the first time the nameless character met his father. No one had known this love child existed. The nameless narrator looked so much like his old man the church rumbled and the widow fainted. Then the scene was put aside. I was already frying bigger fish. It stayed on my mind as I worked other projects. Two or three novels later, I still wanted to know who that guy was and why the first time he met his father the old man was in a coffin.

An article about an event in the 901 premiering a film by actress Cybill Shepherd popped up while I was online, and I decided to have this character's entry point be at that Southern event. I decided he'd be from Memphis. In my old neighborhood off Kansas Street. I created the university on the east side where he works as an adjunct. On page one, enter a mysterious mixed-race named Gemma Buckingham, a woman who was from London, and Meghan Markle–obsessed. Something clicked and I was excited with my new project. I began to populate and create more characters to add to this slice of the Dickeyverse.

While writing and improvising morning until night, I visualized TSOMS as a stage play like *Our Town* with Morgan Freeman as narrator, breaking the fourth wall and giving context and depth to moments past and those yet to come. Same as in the stage play *The Time of Your Life*, a plethora of unique characters enter Pi's world one by one, each appearance on the page their initial introduction and the strong first impression crafted for the reader or listener.

Reliable or not, each character is different and, in my imagination, has their own way of speaking, walking, and more. Character is about how someone reacts to animosity or blessings. I dropped in a ton of the former with sprinkles of the latter. All are wonderfully hypocritical at times, as people are in real life. I love the gray area. I aim at creating characters not caricatures, no matter how unconventional, and aim at having a dozen on the page in a rapid-fire conversation with each voice being so unique not many attributes are needed. Creating new and exciting characters has always been my goal since my first literary offering way back in '96.

For some this novel may feel different. Different is always good. Much better than doing the same novel over and over. Like acting. If I were a decent actor, I'd probably take on a role then move to something totally different, maybe a quality project in a different genre. Rom-com to drama to dramedy to mystery to suspense to sci-fi. For my own sanity. That was the best part of acting, not having to play the same role ad infinitum. When I was an engineer by day and doing stage plays in the evenings, I saw actors become disinterested; each night they basically dialed it in.

I feel that way about writing. It's better here. I get to tackle between one and two dozen characters both major and minor during each project. All ages, ethnicities, genders. On this playground I'm not limited by either the hue of my skin or my physical attributes.

That's freedom.

I don't have to do the same bit over and over.

I love sitting in the Dickey Cave and engineering new fictional characters, getting lost in the realm of fiction, then dropping characters into challenging storylines that reflect contemporary times.

Drumroll!

Time to give shout-outs to my amazing team.

Much love to Sara Camilli and the Sara Camilli Agency. Thanks for being my champion ever since. Hey, Ray! We have a few to go before I hit one hundred. I'm enjoying every page of the journey.

Best. Career. Ever.

I want to send big thanks and much love, peace, and blessings to the stellar crew back at Penguin Random House: Stephanie J. Kelly (editorial), Lexy Cassola (editorial), Katie Taylor (associate director of marketing), Becky Odell (publicist), Daniel Musselman (audio), and many other unsung heroes working to make each literary effort possible.

Now for a little code-switching.☺

Yo, homies!

To Karl Planer at the Planer Group, bruh, thanks for helping a bro when thangs were ruff!

To my bruv by another mother, Kayode Disu, chillin' across the pond in the UK. Thanks for the UK swag and helping a bro with all the Britishspeak as I worked the character Gemma Buckingham. I give you credit for all that's right; I'll take the blame for anything wrong. Thanks for bestowing on me my Nigerian name, Dele Lanrewaju Ojelade Dickey. I bet I'll be the only Dickey in Lagos. LOL.☺ I *finally* had Nigerian jollof rice and my life will never be the same.

Lillian Lyl de Buenos Aires, *un espíritu libre y gran amiga por* Facebook, *gracias por ayudarme traducir una parte del diálogo desde ingles hasta espanol, lo que necesite por la viuda* Fatima.

¡Al fin me ayudé mucho!

Anyway, time to get back to the cave while my thoughts are ablaze, and ideas are lining up like I'm a ride at Disneyland. If only I were four people. Time to go live up to my motto: Writers do.

Don't talk about it; be about it.

Dele Lanrewaju Ojelade Dickey out!

I have to learn how to pronounce that now. ☺

Black shorts, gray T, ugly socks

02-24-2020, 11:24 A.M.

33.9904° N, 118.3287° W

68 degrees, clear skies, and sun in the 90043

CNN on as I type, Remembering Kobe and Gianna Bryant

02-24 RIH Mamba and Mambacita

ERIC JEROME DICKEY (1961–2021) was the award-winning and *New York Times* bestselling author of twenty-nine novels, as well as a six-issue miniseries of graphic novels featuring Storm (*X-Men*) and the Black Panther. His novel *Sister, Sister* was honored as one of *Essence*'s "50 Most Impactful Black Books of the Last 50 Years," and *A Wanted Woman* won the NAACP Image Award in the category of Outstanding Literary Work in 2014. His most recent novels include *The Blackbirds*, *Finding Gideon*, *Bad Men and Wicked Women*, *Before We Were Wicked*, *The Business of Lovers*, and *The Son of Mr. Suleman*.